D0447222

ANDREW G.
NELSON

PERFECT PAWN

ANDREW G. NELSON

This is a work of fiction. Names, characters, places and incidents are either the products of the author's imagination or are used fictitiously and any resemblance to actual events, locales, businesses, products, establishments, or persons, living or dead, is entirely coincidental.

Published by

Fourth Edition: April 2018

ISBN-10: 0991129717
ISBN-13: 978-0-9911297-1-3

Printed in the United States of America
1 3 5 7 9 10 8 6 4 2

DEDICATION

To my wife Nancy, without your love, support and constant encouragement this book would never have been possible. Thank you for always believing in me.

And to God, through whom all things are possible

Other Titles by Andrew G. Nelson

JAMES MAGUIRE SERIES

PERFECT PAWN

QUEEN'S GAMBIT

BISHOP'S GATE

KNIGHT FALL

ALEX TAYLOR SERIES

SMALL TOWN SECRETS

LITTLE BOY LOST

BROOKLYN BOUNCE

NYPD COLD CASE SERIES

THE KATHERINE WHITE MURDER

THE ROASRY BEAD MURDERS

NON FICTION

UNCOMMON VALOR – Insignia of the NYPD ESU

UNCOMMON VALOR II – Challenge Coins of the NYPD ESU

ACKNOWLEDGMENTS

Writing a book is a personal journey, but it is not one that you accomplish alone. Life brings people and events that mold and shape you. It is through those experiences that you are blessed with the foundation to write.

In my twenty years with the NYPD I was honored to work alongside some truly great men and women and I consider myself blessed to have had the opportunity.

To my brothers and sisters lost in the attack on September 11th, 2001, and all those who lost their lives in the years before and after, you are never forgotten.

Fidelis Ad Mortem.

Les Pions. Il sont l'âme des Echecs.

(The Pawns: They are the very Life of this Game.)

- *Francois-Andre Danican Philidor (1726-1795)*

CHAPTER ONE

Keenseville, New York State
Saturday, April 28th, 2012 – 1:37 a.m.

Patricia Ann Browning didn't see the deer, standing in the middle of the road, until it was too late. Not that it would have mattered.

She was on her way home from the annual opening of her art gallery in Keenseville and she was in a great mood. It was a trip she had made a thousand times before, having spent her whole life in this area, and one which she was quite comfortable making, even at this late hour.

Browning had just hosted the first showing of the New Year and it had been a smashing success. It wasn't on the scale of a Manhattan opening, but everyone on the Adirondack art scene had been there including some well-known dealers and art aficionados from the Burlington area in Vermont. The months of working long hours, coupled with having to deal with the sensitive *feelings* of more than one artist, had finally paid off. She allowed herself the opportunity to bask in the glow of her triumph, a particular glow that was fueled just a little bit more by the wine she had enjoyed at the end of the evening.

The black sapphire, 2012 BMW M6 streaked along the misty thoroughfare like a spectral image highlighted by the moonlight filtering down through the trees. The vehicle's Bavarian roots made it well suited for its role in navigating the meandering mountainous back roads of upstate New York.

Browning had just turned forty-two back in September, but she neither felt nor acted her age. She took great pains in taking care of herself and the endless hours spent running around the gallery, staging new exhibits, served as her impromptu gym.

As she deftly maneuvered the car along the roadway one of her favorite songs from an 80's rock band came on the radio. She reached over and turned the volume up high. The sound system in the vehicle was impressive, even by an audiophile's standard, and it made the occupant feel as if they were actually in a concert hall. She leaned back comfortably in the leather driver's seat and joined in the chorus, singing out loud, as she gripped the steering wheel tightly.

"I would do anything for love, but I won't do that…."

As the BMW navigated a particularly sharp turn in the winding mountain road, the headlights illuminated the ill-fated animal standing in the middle of the roadway. It was the epitome of a *deer in the headlights* moment. Browning opened her mouth, as if to scream, but had no time to make an actual sound. At the same exact moment she instinctively slammed on the brakes and swerved to avoid hitting it.

While it was a valiant attempt, it fell just short of the mark. The car struck the animal, which appeared frozen in abject fear, catapulting it up into the air.

Had the vehicle had a slightly larger profile, the animal would have most likely been driven directly through the windshield and into the passenger compartment causing serious injury if not the death of the driver. However, the German engineers had succeeded in producing a crisp, aerodynamic design which effectively minimized the deer's impact. The low profile caused the animal to strike the hood at such an angle that its lifeless body was propelled into the upper most edge of the windshield and over the top of the vehicle where it crashed down on to the wet pavement directly behind the car.

In that same instant the windshield shattered at the point of impact in that familiar spider web pattern which further terrified the driver. As a result of this assault on her senses, she surrendered all control of the car as she desperately attempted to duck down and away from the perceived danger. Unfortunately, the BMW's seatbelt ensured that she didn't get very far.

The car, operating on its own at this point, careened wildly until it ran off the road and crashed headlong into a tree. At that exact moment, even as her body was pressing against the seat belt, one of the vehicle's crash sensors detected the pressure wave caused by the impact and sent a signal to the on-board computer. At about the same time other pressure sensors began to respond to the now crumbling engine compartment and sent their respective signals in as well. The vehicle's computer then began to calculate the severity of the impact. A millisecond later the computer determined that it was a catastrophic event and sent a fire signal to the vehicle's airbag system causing them to deploy at nearly 200mph.

The force of the airbag deployment propelled Patricia Browning back into the driver's seat, even while they were already deflating in front of her. While the airbags had done exactly what they were designed to do, the violence of the initial impact had rendered her unconscious.

From the moment of the impact with the tree exactly two-hundred and seventy-six milliseconds had passed, less time than it takes for the blink of an eye.

Steam rose from the shattered radiator where it was eerily lit up by the headlights. Somehow in the collision, the right blinker had also been activated, adding an amber and red flash to the mix. The car's radio continued to play the classic rock ballad; which only served to make the whole scene seem even that much more surreal.

If she had been conscious, she would have noticed the headlights come on from the pickup truck which was parked approximately fifty feet away, on the opposite side of the road.

A male figure, clad in dark clothing and wearing a baseball hat pulled low, exited the vehicle. He walked purposely around to the passenger side of the pickup truck and opened the door. From there he moved quickly in the direction of the hulking wreckage of the BMW. Under the circumstances it was completely unnecessary as it would be at least two more hours before another vehicle would venture down the deserted back road.

The man proceeded to walk past the crumpled remains of the BMW, back to where the lifeless body of the deer lay in the roadway. It was in fact a young three-point buck and weighed in at only one hundred and twenty pounds. The man lifted the remains up off the ground and carried it to the pickup truck where he unceremoniously dumped it into the back.

When he was done, he switched on the LED flashlight device that was attached to his baseball hat and moved to the tree line on the side of the road, just behind the BMW. He located the remnants of the cable wire that was looped around the large sugar maple tree trunk. The same wires which had, a few moments earlier, suspended the deer over the roadway. If anyone had been given the opportunity to examine the remains of the animal they would have discovered that this particular deer had, in fact, died *twice* tonight.

He withdrew a screwdriver and pliers from his jacket pocket and carefully removed the bolts that held the looped wires around the tree trunk. These he stuffed into his pockets before moving to gather up the remnants of the heavy gauge wire. When he was done he moved to the opposite side of the road and repeated the process.

In all, the planning had been quite meticulous. Everything had been factored in, from the particular curve of the road, to the probable speed the vehicle would be traveling at, to the time of night. Even the exact height that the deer had to be suspended at, to impact the vehicle properly, had been methodically considered.

All this was done specifically to ensure that it would both incur just the right amount of damage and at the same time allow for the *survivability* of the driver, at least in theory.

There was, after all, only so much a person could plan for. Fate ultimately controlled the rest.

The vehicle remained a particularly sore spot to the man, since the prissy little bitch had just recently had the nerve to buy herself a new car. Locating another M6 to measure accurately hadn't been the easiest thing for him. In fact it had required him to drive all the way down to Albany where he was able to successfully *appropriate* the car from one of the more trendy neighborhoods. The key to successfully stealing a car was that you had to take it from an area where law enforcement was already overburdened with other serious crimes and then get out quickly. The more time that passed the less likely it was that it would register on anyone's radar. Eventually it would just be chalked up to another unfortunate urban crime statistic.

When he was absolutely sure that he had recovered all the wiring, bolts and the ratchet tensioner, he deposited them into the back of the truck and moved toward the wreckage of the car. He was careful to avoid any of the liquids, which had spilled onto the roadway from the engine, lest he leave any incriminating footprints behind. The muffled music still reverberated through the closed windows of the car.

From his jacket pocket he removed an emergency extrication tool. It was a type routinely carried by first responders. One end held a shrouded curved blade to cut seatbelts with and the other a spring loaded window punch. He applied the latter to the still intact driver's side window. A split second later, the window collapsed in a spray of safety glass. The man put his hand inside the vehicle and located the lock release button and opened the driver's door.

He reached down and placed his fingers against her left wrist and felt the gentle pulse. He was relieved to find that all his intricate planning had been successful. Blood trickled down her face from a small laceration above her right eye, the result of being struck by the rearview mirror which had become dislodged from the windshield upon impact. Head wounds, even minor ones, were notoriously bad when it comes to bleeding.

Despite the exaggerated bleeding she had suffered no real serious injury. He gazed at her for a moment then reached down, running his fingers along the side of her face and gently brushing her brown hair to the side.

The man physically shuddered as his fingers touched her skin. He withdrew his hand quickly and pulled himself back to the task at hand. He reached down, depressing the release button on the seatbelt, and pulled the belt free from her body. He then grabbed her by her shoulders and dragged her from the car.

Once she was clear of the vehicle he hoisted her limp body over his shoulder, in a fireman's carry, and proceeded over to where the pickup truck waited. He dumped her into the passenger seat and closed the door, then headed back around to the driver's side.

If he had stopped to think about it, he might have bound her hands and feet, but it was not a significant matter to him. It wouldn't be a long ride and he doubted that she had any fight left in her at this point anyway.

As an afterthought, he leaned over and ran his fingers through the blood running down her face. He got out of the pickup and moved carefully back to the tree line next to the car. He smeared the blood visibly on the branches, closest to the roadway, then moved quickly across the road, to the opposite side, and repeated the act.

When he was done he made his way back to the pickup truck. He dropped the shifter into drive, made a U-turn, then slowly drove away from the scene with his victim, the tail lights fading as the truck passed around the bend.

All that remained was the wreckage and the fading sound of the song playing on the radio.

CHAPTER TWO

Ponquogue Beach, Suffolk County, N.Y.
Saturday, April 28th, 2012 – 5:20 a.m.

The problem with having an *internal clock* is that they rarely ever came equipped with a snooze button.

And so it was, with grudging acceptance, that James Patrick Maguire slowly opened his eyes and allowed them to adjust to the pre-dawn darkness of the bedroom. Sunrise was still well over a half an hour away, but the two plus decades of old habits died rather hard.

Maguire slid out of the bed slowly, but purposefully, so as not to disturb his sleeping companion.

Melanie? he thought, half groggily. *No, Melody,* he quickly corrected himself.

He walked quietly over to the dresser, opening one of the drawers and grabbed a pair of socks. Next he put on the long sleeve athletic compression shirt, which he used during the cold weather days, and the running shorts that had been lying neatly folded on top of the dresser. He then made his way toward the bedroom door and opened it slowly. He paused a moment in the doorway to look back at the long, lithe figure of the blonde haired woman that remained asleep in bed, her naked body only partially hidden under the sheet.

Who knew that venture capitalists could be so much fun, he thought, as the memories from the previous evening came flooding back.

The two of them had met the evening before at his friend, and sometimes client, Peter Bart's *Spring Fling* charity fundraiser, in the affluent Southampton area of Long Island, New York. It was an annual event which benefited a number of local charities throughout the tri-state area.

Maguire wasn't a big fan of these types of events, as he found most of the guests to be much too pretentious for his tastes. Bart on the other hand seemed to get quite a kick out of his discomfort and made sure that his was the first invite to go out for each of the events he held. It had been Maguire's intention from the beginning to make eye contact with Peter, proving to him that he had in fact attended the party, grab a drink and then promptly leave, but, as the 18th Century Scottish poet Robert Burns so eloquently wrote: 'The best laid plans of mice and men, often go awry.'

It had been just before 7:00 p.m. when Maguire had wheeled his red, 1969 Ford Mustang through the open wrought iron security gates. On a normal day the gates would have been locked down tightly, but today, with the volume of guests attending the evening's *gala*, they remained open. Still he knew enough to slow down and come to a stop as he pulled inside. He waved to Gregor Ritter who was standing off to the side of the road at a small podium.

"Evening, Gregor," he called out, as he put the car in park.

Gregor came around from his station and walked over to the car.

"Good evening, Mr. Maguire," the man said warmly.

Ritter stood at just over six feet tall and had close cropped blonde hair. His steely gaze, coupled with an athletic build, let you know immediately that he was not someone to be trifled with. If looks alone weren't impressive enough, his thick German accent made everything sound as if he was barking an order, something which was quite handy for a security professional.

When it came to his security detail, Bart took great pains in surrounding himself with the best of the best. Ritter had been a member of Germany's elite *Bundesgrenzschutz*, the federal border police. During his career with the *BGS* he had been a member of the *Grenzschutzgruppe-9,* the agencies elite federal anti-terrorism unit.

Maguire had long ago given up on trying to get Ritter to call him by his first name. The man was a true professional twenty-four / seven. From the moment the two men had first met there was a mutual respect given between equals. Something that is, more often than not, acknowledged with a discreet nod, as opposed to being openly spoken.

"I'm sure Mr. Bart will be very glad that you could make it," Gregor said.

"What choice did I have? He'd never forgive me if I didn't show up for one of his parties," Maguire said jokingly.

"He does start off every list with your name."

"Don't I feel special," Maguire replied.

"Well, try to enjoy yourself," the man said, a wry smile forming on his face, as he stepped back from the car. "There are even *more* guests here than last year for you to enjoy."

Maguire noted the hint of sarcasm, even under the thick accent.

Gregor knew just how much Maguire detested these gatherings.

"I hope it rains on you," Maguire said, as he put the car in gear and proceeded up the driveway.

Gregor burst out laughing, as he walked back to his position at the podium.

"*Rote Ford, ganz klar*," he said into his portable radio, giving the *all clear* for the vehicle to proceed up the driveway.

To the average guest arriving at the house the podium looked like your typical parking attendants station. Most assumed the man who greeted them was just calling ahead to alert the valets of an arrival. It wasn't and he didn't.

On the top of the podium, out of sight, was a control panel that featured several buttons. One of these would immediately engage a series of hydraulic driven, retractable, steel bollards in the driveway which would disable any vehicle that attempted to get past. Underneath, and discreetly out of view of the refined guests attending tonight's event, was a Heckler & Koch MP-5 submachine pistol, a weapon that Ritter was quite skilled in using.

While Gregor was the visible face of the security detail, he was certainly not the only one. Twenty-three other members patrolled the sprawling grounds this evening, as well as two snipers who discreetly watched the goings on from their roof top perch. Most of the others did not have Gregor Ritter's *sunny* disposition. If anyone had managed to get past Ritter without the *all clear* signal being transmitted, it would not end well.

Maguire made his way up the long and winding crushed stone driveway before veering off to the left at the last minute, heading toward the guest house where he pulled into a private parking area. He'd always had a hang-up about giving the Mustang's keys to any valet; preferring to park his own car. He killed the lights and turned off the engine. As he got out of the car he grabbed the suit coat from the back seat and began walking toward the main house.

The air was still relatively warm, but he could feel the cooler breeze coming in off the ocean. He knew the temperature would change dramatically before too long.

Maguire always loved this place in the evening.

The compound itself was just over ten acres and backed up to the Atlantic Ocean on its southern edge. It boasted a three story main house, guest house, two servant's quarters, a detached five car garage and an indoor sports complex. In addition, Peter had purchased the adjoining residence and converted it to housing accommodations for his security detail.

To call Peter's residence a house would be like calling the *Grand Canyon* a hole in the ground. It was both massive and yet quite elegant. The exterior was a tan colored, roughhewn stone which gave the impression of some medieval castle. Peter had it lit from the foundation up which, along with the full moon that hung in the sky above, only added to that dramatic feel. One could easily envision it being transplanted from atop some mountain fortress in old Europe.

As Maguire drew closer to the house, he could hear the sounds of the party carrying outside. He walked around the side, choosing to take the long way, rather than go through the front door.

Nights like this were too nice to waste.

He climbed the staircase that led to the rear deck and paused at the top to speak with the man standing post.

"*Guten abend,* Horst," he said to the security man. "Is the boss around?"

"*Ja*, he's in the library," replied Horst.

"Nice night for a party, everyone behaving?" he asked.

"*Ja, alles gute*," Horst said with a laugh. "But you know, some days it would be nice to have a little, how do you say, *action*?"

Maguire clasped the man's upper left arm. "Be careful what you wish for, buddy," he said with a laugh and moved to join the party.

He walked in through the opened back wall and surveyed the room.

If the rugged exterior was impressive, the interior of the main house was awe inspiring. The house measured nearly eighteen thousand square feet and boasted nine bedrooms.

With Peter's penchant for throwing parties, he had painstakingly designed the main living room on the first floor for that specific purpose. The room was nearly seventy-five feet wide and almost as deep. The entire back wall of the room featured floor to ceiling glass walls which provided a panoramic view of the Atlantic Ocean. These glass walls were actually doors that were constructed by a company that specialized in building airplane hangars. At the push of a button they would roll away, as they were tonight, and allow party goers to effortlessly move between the indoor space and the back deck.

As he glanced around the room, he *guesstimated* that there were around two hundred and fifty people in attendance at the party; more than enough to fill him with a sense of dread. He walked inside and peeked into the library where he saw Peter standing, engaged in an animated conversation with two other men. Bart spotted him and quickly waved him over.

Maguire sighed as he walked into the room. He hated the thought of being dragged into some boring business conversation, but as he drew closer the man broke away and came toward him.

"You made it," Peter said with a smile, as he hugged him.

"Don't I always?" Maguire asked, as he returned the hug.

"There's always a first time."

"Yeah, but then I would have to listen to you piss and moan for months."

"Don't be so melodramatic," Bart replied, "or I'll disinvite you from the U.S.S. Saratoga dive."

"Please, you'd never make it past the hanger deck without me."

Maguire and Bart had first met several years ago at a party in Manhattan. A mutual friend in the television industry had introduced the two men as they both shared a love of all things nautical; which included a passion for shipwreck diving.

Peter was in his late fifties and came from a very wealthy family, but unlike everyone else, who had begun their careers in upper management, at his own request Peter had started off in the working man's *world.* It was these humble roots that made him both very successful and extremely unpretentious when it came to dealing with people; which was precisely the reason why Maguire got along so well with him.

"You might have a point there," Peter conceded, as the two men walked toward the main room. "Do you plan on staying for more than fifteen minutes this time?"

"Depends on what kind of liquor you're serving."

The two men stopped at the doorway and Bart leaned in closer, whispering conspiratorially.

“I have to dislodge some rather hefty checks from these two,” he said, hooking a thumb back in the direction of the two men standing in the room, “but we need to talk later.”

Unlike many of his peers, who simply squandered away their wealth, Peter believed that happiness came from helping those who truly merited it. The *Spring Fling* was his way of shaming some of his other more fortunate friends into parting with some of their wealth for the benefit of others.

“No promises,” Maguire said. “The Met’s are playing tonight.”

“And you’ll be asking for tickets for the Yankee’s in October.”

“Dream on,” Maguire said with a laugh, as he walked out of the library.

“See me later,” Peter said.

Maguire proceeded further into the living room, making his way toward one of the bars set up around the room, and got a drink. He glanced down at his watch. If he played it right he would be sitting in front of his television by the fourth inning.

He eyed the room carefully, taking in those in attendance. It was filled with the same folks he habitually saw at events like this. People came to either see or be seen. It was an opportunity to move up a rung or two on the social ladder or to make some inroads in business. Maguire found it all mildly amusing, as he had no dog in the fight either way.

At this rate you might be able to catch the third inning, he thought, as he took a sip of his drink.

A second later, everything changed.

From across the room, Maguire saw her. She was a completely unfamiliar face and he couldn’t take his eyes off of her.

To say that she was stunning would have been a gross understatement. She had what could only be described as a timeless beauty, something both classic and graceful. What one generally imagined when they thought of Audrey Hepburn, Elizabeth Taylor or Grace Kelly.

She was tall, about 5'10", and had long, well-toned legs that gave the immediate impression of a woman who knew her way around the inside of a gym. He guessed that she was in her late twenties, but he was probably wrong. She had perfectly coiffed, shoulder length blonde hair that highlighted her high cheek bones and large warm brown eyes. The deep golden tan was the perfect contrast to the black shimmering evening dress she wore, which clung very nicely to the outline of her body and ended just around mid-thigh.

Despite being in a room full of people accustomed to standing out, she had a presence about her that made every other head turn as they walked by.

He watched as she twirled the stirrer in her drink; absentmindedly gazing around the room.

Most of the women present at this little soiree wore copious amounts of jewelry. Quantity was apparently the order of the day. The little amount of jewelry that she actually did wear only served to highlight her beauty. However, the most important piece to Maguire was the one piece she *wasn't* wearing on her left hand.

She looked terminally bored as some self-important stuffed suit, replete with a poor comb-over and pasty complexion, tried desperately to impress her with his bottom line. Nearby, a group of other *would be* suitors stood, talking amongst themselves while staring back occasionally, anticipating their chance to try and win her affections. An even greater number stood nearby with their wives, girlfriends, or significant others, and tried to stare discreetly, earning a look that would have frozen water when their attempts at discretion *failed.*

It had been his experience that there were generally two types of women that came to parties like this, the *haves* and the *have-nots.*

The have-nots were generally either on the arm of someone with money or looking for a vacant arm. The haves were those who had made their own way in the world. Successful women generally attended functions alone because men had a hard time playing the role of arm candy. Not only was this lady beautiful, she was clearly at the head of the line in the *have* department.

After a few moments of watching this painful drama play out he decided she desperately needed to be rescued.

Well, that was at least one of the reasons he told himself.

Maguire approached her from behind and gently tapped her on the shoulder.

"Hey, sweetheart," Maguire said, with a rakish grin, when she turned to face him.

Unbeknownst to him, a moment earlier she had decided to call an end to this evening. She had made her appearance, spoken to those people who needed to see her, and was now inclined to just go home and call it a night. Now she turned around sharply, with more than a slight bit of annoyance, to confront this newest *unwanted* attempt to gain her attention. When she had come face to face with him she was stopped dead in her tracks.

"I'm sorry for being so late," he said. "Traffic was even worse than it usually is."

She stared at him while she struggled to find the words to formulate a reply to his statement. Her eyes were locked on his and what stared back at her were the most amazing blue eyes she had ever seen.

When she was young, Melody Anderson and her girlfriends had often talked about boys. They spent countless hours talking about the latest heart throb and describing what attributes each of them thought was important. Invariably eyes would pop up and they would toss around such adjectives as *captivating, deep, soulful,* and *dreamy*. Yet as she stared into his eyes, she realized that all of them seemed so inadequate now. They were certainly powerful, yet comforting; piercing, yet inviting; cold, yet warm. In a word, they were a dichotomy and they were staring at her.

For a moment she had not only been at a loss for words, but realized that she had also been holding her breath. After what seemed like an eternity, she regained her composure and tried not to look too noticeable as she resumed her breathing.

"No need to apologize, darling," she said, playing along. "I'm just glad that you found me."

She realized that last part was true, she certainly was glad he found her. In the back of her mind she allowed herself to think that this night might actually be looking up for her now.

The two of them continued to make small talk, much to the growing consternation of her would-be suitor. Without a word he grabbed his drink and stormed off; not that either of them noticed or would have cared. Soon the others, who had been waiting for their moment to arrive, also faded away. What had originally started out as a wasted night for both of them had soon turned into the kind that only seemed to happen in the movies.

"Care to go for a walk?" he asked.

"Sure," she replied.

They made their way out onto the deck and he guided her to the steps, which led down to the long walkway in the back, that meandered down to the beach.

The relative warmth of the spring day had already surrendered itself to the chill of the late Southampton evening. The proximity to the ocean only served to heighten the sense that winter had not exactly given up its hold on the area just yet. Without a word he removed his jacket and held it up to allow her to slip into. It was a little large, but yet it felt so warm and comfortable on her.

"Thank you," Melody said.

She stared at him in his shirt sleeves and saw the way the material was stretched taut over his biceps. They continued to walk down the pathway until they reached the beach where she paused for a moment, to remove her heels, before they set out across the sand.

Soon, the sounds of the party were replaced by the sound of the waves crashing along the shoreline. The moon hung high in the sky casting its light down over the ocean like a field of sparking diamonds.

"You seem to know your way around here pretty good," she said. "I take it you've been here before."

"I've known Peter for a few years," he replied.

"I'm surprised our paths haven't crossed before."

"I usually made it a habit of coming and going rather quickly," Maguire said.

"That's too bad," Melody replied.

"I don't think I will ever make that mistake again."

She reached out and took his hand in hers, holding it tightly, as they continued walking along the shoreline.

By the time they returned to the house, the party was beginning to wind down. As they walked back up the path, neither seemed at all interested in heading back inside.

He took the lead and she followed him around the side of the house and back down the same path he had come through earlier in the evening. At the edge of the driveway she paused to slide her heels back on before they walked across the courtyard toward the front of the house.

"So, what's next?" she said, smiling coyly.

She felt more and more like a nervous teenager out on her first real date and not quite sure where things were heading.

"Well, I don't know about you, but I'm not a big fan of curfews," he replied.

"I was hoping you wouldn't be."

She reached into her purse and withdrew the small token and handed it to the valet. He rushed across the courtyard in the direction of the sports building where the majority of the vehicles for tonight's event were parked.

A moment later he pulled up in a metallic silver Mercedes Benz G63, an updated civilian version of the German military

SUV. He stood outside with the door open, until he saw Maguire motion to him that it was okay to leave. She was still holding his hand in hers and he was willing to let her lead him over to the open door of the car.

"That's a pretty car," Maguire said. "How are your driving skills, princess?"

She slowly let go of his hand, her fingers gliding teasingly against his. As her fingertips slipped past his, she turned and mischievously looked over her shoulder at him.

"Oh, don't worry about me, cowboy," Melody said with a smile. "I know my way around the block."

She removed the jacket and handed it back to Maguire and then slid into the driver's seat. Her dress hiked up just enough to give him a better view of her thighs and she made no attempt to adjust it. He flashed that devilish smile and closed the door behind her. The Mercedes roared to life and she lowered the window.

"Just try and follow the tail lights," he said to her, as he turned around and made his way across the courtyard.

Melody pulled out her cell phone and typed a quick text message.

"Don't wait up. See you in the morning."

She sat waiting and watching not sure if she had missed something. Suddenly she heard a low, throaty rumble of a car's engine and saw the reddish glow of tail lights appear against the wall of the guest house. The car backed out of the shadows and pulled out in front of her. She dropped the SUV into gear and followed him, as he led the way back down the long driveway.

As he reached the wrought iron gates he slowed a bit and tossed Gregor a quick wave before turning right onto Meadow Lane, the big Mercedes following close behind.

The physical distance between point 'A', where they currently were at, and point 'B', where they were going, was just a little under two miles. However, the reality was as different as the actual locations were. For starters, there was the slight problem of the Shinnecock Bay inlet that physically separated the two places.

So they took the long way around.

Driving east on Meadow Lane they passed a stream of multi-million dollar homes, with a heavy emphasis on *double digit* multi-million. Southampton had the distinction of being the oldest English settlement in New York State and was founded by the Puritans in 1640 with the help of the Shinnecock Indian tribe. It was ironic that what started from such humble roots would evolve to represent the upper echelon of wealth and affluence in America.

Many of the residents here didn't bother themselves with the mild irritation associated with Long Island traffic. For most it was as simple as driving west on Meadow Lane and heading to the Southampton Heliport. For an even more select few, such as the host of this evenings get together, they only had to walk down the driveway to their private helipad.

In all the drive was a little more than a dozen miles, but in the excited state they were both in it just served to heighten the intensity of the moment. The two cars continued their trek through the winding roads before reaching Montauk Highway where they turned left and proceeded west, toward New York City.

The Mercedes stayed close on his tail. He had driven slowly enough for her to keep up with him through the back roads, but in the open areas, where he knew she could see him clearly; he opened it up forcing her to keep the pace.

As they passed the Shinnecock Bay they turned left and headed back south toward the ocean. A few zigzags later they made their way onto County Road 32, past the Shinnecock Coast Guard station and then over the Ponquogue Bridge.

He smiled as he looked into the rearview mirror, the headlights from her car obscuring his view. Maguire had to admit, she was pretty good behind the wheel.

What he couldn't see was Melody Anderson biting her lip, as she gripped the steering wheel tightly and wondered when this ride would end and the other would begin. It was about this time that she became acutely aware of the physical ache that she was feeling deep inside of her. She squirmed in the leather seat.

Thirteen point eight miles later, the ride ended in the empty parking lot of a marina, the cars coming to a stop at the edge of one of the docks.

She grabbed her purse and exited the car with more than a slightly quizzical look.

"Please tell me we don't have to wait for a ferry?" she said, but only half-jokingly.

"No, actually I decided long ago that I wasn't a really big fan of foundations," he replied, taking her hand as he led her down the dock toward the lone houseboat moored at the far end.

"Plus, the neighbors are really quiet," he added.

Melody looked around the deserted marina; there wasn't another soul to be found.

"I see what you mean."

As houseboats go, this one was clearly not your average. It was just over eighty-five feet long and nearly twenty feet wide. Inside it featured a master bedroom and two guest bedrooms, one of which he had converted to an office. It also had two full baths, a kitchen, dining room and living room. The interior was completely done in oak and it had a central air and heating system. He wasn't a big fan of either and used them only sparingly, when the weather dictated, as he had grown accustomed to falling asleep to the sound of the water.

The boat could be operated from both inside as well as from the fly bridge on top. There were large seating areas on both the fore and aft decks which could also be completely enclosed if the weather was inclement. The fore deck also featured a full bar that had come in handy on a few occasion. The fly bridge featured a party deck that was nearly two-thirds the length of the boat.

As they approached the aft deck she noticed the name on the boats stern.

"*Mal Ad Osteo*?" she asked inquisitively.

"Inside joke," was his light-hearted response. "But you have to get the super-secret decoder ring first."

He stepped onto the deck and opened the small gate. Turning back he reached out and took her hand; helping her onto the boat. They walked to the cabin door and he opened it for her, allowing her to step inside, before walking in and closing it behind him.

Melody tossed her purse onto the floor and turned around quickly, grabbing him and pulling him close to her. She stared into those intense blue eyes for just a moment longer.

"The super-secret decoder ring isn't what I want first," she said, in a deep seductive voice, then kissed him.

•••

Maguire exhaled deeply, as he watched the woman's body turn slowly beneath the sheets.

He grudgingly pushed away the memories of the previous night, as he focused on the task at hand. He gently closed the bedroom door and walked back toward the cabin door, stopping to grab the running shoes he habitually tossed into the corner after every run, before stepping out onto the aft deck.

The cold blast of morning air that came off the ocean shocked away any last remnants of the previous night's escapades. He settled into one of the two deck chairs, putting on the shoes and tying up the laces before making his way up the dock.

At the top, he paused to stretch briefly before heading out toward the roadway. He smiled as he walked past the Mercedes Benz which, he noted, was parked at a very awkward angle next to the Mustang. It was lingering evidence of the sense of *urgency* at which they had arrived at the parking lot, just a few hours earlier.

Maguire looked down at his watch and noted the time, it was 5:33 a.m., and he started his run.

CHAPTER THREE

Upstate New York
Saturday, April 28th, 2012 – 5:35 a.m.

The man turned the nozzle off on the water hose before reeling it back up onto the caddy. When he was done, he turned off the garage light and opened the door, stepping out into the cool night air. He reached into his pocket, removing a pack of cigarettes and lit one up, as he listened to the sound of the water dripping off the tailgate.

After dropping the woman off, he had gone to great lengths in cleaning out the truck. First he had taken the deer carcass out to an area that was both far enough away from the crash site and one where he knew the deer would be quickly finished off by hungry predators. From there he headed over to the dump where he had discarded the broken cable and ratchets. Once that was done he had come back and began work on the truck.

First he had started with the interior, cleaning it with a bleach mix that would neutralize any residual DNA that might have been left behind. He didn't think it was necessary, but too much work had gone into the planning to be tripped up by something as careless as a blood stain. Next he used an industrial vacuum to remove any hair or other potential fiber remnants.

He didn't think it would withstand an in-depth forensic examination, but he wasn't worried about that. No, he was more concerned with making sure that the interior was clean enough to the casual observer.

When he was finished, he moved into the back, scrubbing out the bed of the truck and then hosing it down.

Off in the distance, he could see the night sky beginning to change colors. Soon the sun would be up and the real mystery would begin to unfold.

He took a drag on the cigarette and finally allowed himself to relax.

CHAPTER FOUR

Ponquogue Beach, Suffolk County, N.Y.
Saturday, April 28th, 2012 – 5:41 a.m.

There were few places as barren as the eastern end of Dune Road in Ponquogue, Long Island, but the solitude served a purpose for Maguire.

There were no distractions out here, no buildings, and certainly no other people. Anyone can run when you have things to visibly occupy your mind, but out here each sand dune looked the same, with a never ending supply of beach grass thrown in for fun. There were no land marks, and even if there were, they'd be lost in the darkness that seemed to envelope everything at this hour.

Dune Road ran east to west down the center of the narrow barrier island on Long Island's south shore. It began on its western edge at the Moriches Bay inlet then continued east, through the villages of Westhampton Dunes, Westhampton Beach and Quogue and finally ended in the barren beaches of Ponquogue, at the Shinnecock Inlet, where he called home.

The name Ponquogue came from the old Shinnecock Indians and is said to mean *pond in the place where the bay ends.* Throughout most of his winter runs Maguire was pretty convinced that it really just meant *God forsaken hell hole.*

The wind was now blowing fairly hard off the ocean and he could taste the saltiness on his lips.

He could have run anywhere, but the emptiness on this end of the island grounded him and reminded him from where he had come. There was nothing to interfere with the inner conversation he habitually had with himself. Most days, that conversation would revolve around his newest client or information surrounding the latest domestic or global threats, but today was different and he didn't know why. It was like an ephemeral specter was hanging over him, chasing away his thoughts and leaving him with a sense of dread. He plodded along hoping that the run would chase it away.

It didn't.

On most days he would make the fourteen mile round trip from Ponquogue to the edge of East Quogue and back without a second thought. If he was feeling particularly mean spirited he would move the route to the beach and run through the sand. But today, despite the sense of foreboding, he had some business matters to take care of and so he cut it down midway through. Even so, he upped the pace of the last two miles finishing at almost a dead run.

As he came to the end of the road he slowed his pace and made the turn back toward the dock. He glanced down at his watch and noted the time, 6:22 a.m., as he slowly brought his breathing back under control. He was more than a little disappointed when he noted that the Mercedes was gone, but he felt a sense of relief as well. As much as he would have preferred climbing back in bed with her this morning, and picking up where they had left off, he had a lot on his plate today. Besides, it was quite clear to him that, whatever this was, it was something much more different than he had ever experienced. He needed a bit more time to process everything that had happened over the last twelve hours.

He paused at the top of the dock and stretched out, before making his way back down to the boat's deck. He sat back in the chair he had left almost an hour earlier and reached into the cooler that sat immediately adjacent to it. He withdrew a bottle of water, as he leaned back in the chair, and took a long drink. The sun had just started to rise and he watched it break over the horizon. The world was just waking up and his day was already an hour old.

Maguire got up from the chair and made his way back through the cabin door where he kicked off his running shoes. As he walked down the hallway, past the open bedroom door, he paused for a moment as he caught the scent of her perfume, which still lingered in the air.

A moment later he proceeded down the hallway that led into the kitchen area. He switched on the coffee maker and grabbed an empty mug out of the cabinet above the sink, setting it down on the counter. He turned around and walked back down the hallway, through the bedroom and into the adjoining bathroom. He flipped the light switch on and out of the corner of his eye caught something that made him stop. He smiled as he reached up and pulled the taped letter, unmistakably written in lipstick, off the mirror.

Had to fly, cowboy, literally. I'll be back tonight. Call me.

Underneath she had written her cell phone number.

He had to hand it to her; she certainly had a flair for the dramatic.

Maguire laid the letter on the counter and reached over and turned on the shower. He stripped out of his running clothes and tossed them into the laundry bag before stepping under the steaming cascade of water.

He stood under the spray and allowed himself to relax, as he felt the hot water wash away the morning chill. He also felt a slight sting in certain places on his back, a lasting memory of some of the night's more intense moments.

Usually he would have rushed through this part of his morning, an old habit from an earlier time in his life. But today he allowed himself the luxury of a few extra moments to enjoy the soothing heat, as well as the recent memories, before turning the water off and reaching for his towel.

He stepped out of the shower and dried himself off. When he was done he wrapped the towel around his waist and stood in front of the vanity. He picked up the wash cloth and wiped away the fog that had engulfed the mirror.

Maguire stared at the image that stared back at him like a familiar stranger.

At forty-two years old he was not your typical middle-aged man. Standing two inches over six feet and weighing two hundred and ten pounds, he had a distinctive athlete's build, like that of an NFL Safety. The ones who appear deceptively small, as they cut across the field toward an unwitting receiver, before hitting them with enough explosive force to separate the receiver's helmet from his head and leaving said receiver grateful at least that his head was still actually attached to him.

His skin bore a deep tan that came from years of living and working in the outdoors and was pulled tightly over muscles that rippled just beneath the surface. As he stared at the image in the bathroom mirror, he ran his fingers through his wet hair. It was then that he first noticed the slight hint of gray appearing in the dark brown hair around his temples. He had guessed that it had been inevitable and was just happy that it had taken this long to finally appear. Morning stubble covered his chiseled jaw line, but this being the weekend he dismissed the thought of shaving.

Inevitably, his gaze came to rest on the two small, faded round scars located on his upper chest, just under his left shoulder. They were the only lingering physical signs of a night that had haunted him for the last two years. While the wounds themselves had completely healed the scars were a permanent visual reminder. With those reminders came the memories and they had not healed quite as nicely.

CHAPTER FIVE

Midtown Manhattan, New York City
Tuesday, February 23rd, 2010 – 8:15 p.m.

A steady stream of steam billowed from the manhole cover on the frozen city street outside the Sheraton Hotel in New York City.

The *Big Apple* is home to politicians, foreign dignitaries, as well as a countless number of celebrities and financial leaders. The eight million plus people who live and work here have long become immune to the dog and pony show that accompanies such luminaries whenever they are transported around the stone canyons of the city.

In fact, once a year the streets of Manhattan grind to a virtual halt as the United Nations, that fabled example of global political apathy that resides on the East River, hosts its annual General Assembly session. The U.N. General Assembly, or *UNGA* as it is referred to, is an opportunity for world leaders to gather together, wring their hands dramatically, verbally condemn the heinous acts of the rogue regime *du jour* and then pat each other on the back for another job well done.

When the pesky business of resolving the world's problems is postponed until another day, the delegates use their down time as an excuse to go shopping with their spouses on Fifth Avenue or attend extravagant banquets in each other's honor, all on the citizens of their countries collective dime, of course.

At the end of the day it was all just an act and not to be taken very seriously, or in the immortal words of William Shakespeare's *Macbeth:* "It is a tale. Told by an idiot, full of sound and fury, signifying nothing."

Then again, any organization that once counted Libya as a member of its Human Rights Council should not be taken very seriously.

So with everything that goes on in the city, there are very few spectacles that occur here that will break the purposeful stride of a native New Yorker.

A presidential motorcade however is one of them.

Maybe it is the sound that precedes the actual motorcade. The first thing you hear is the wail of distant sirens, followed shortly by the thunderous roar of the *outriders*, the motorcycles from the New York City Police Department's Highway Patrol, as they streak by.

As the first of them pass by it is like the opening act of a vintage heavy metal concert. Leather clad riders sit atop their Harley Davidson police motorcycles, engines gleaming with polished chrome, lights flashing and sirens blaring. A sight guaranteed to elicit a response even from the most jaded of Manhattan residents.

But what follows the motorcycles is the real show, cloaked in mystery and intrigue. As the deep rumble of the outriders pass then comes the procession of marked and unmarked cars. From within these vehicles, special agents of the United States Secret Service and detectives from the NYPD's elite Intelligence Division scan the crowds and windows overlooking the route, looking for any sign of trouble, the one person in this vast sea of humanity that doesn't quite fit.

The NYPD's Intelligence Division is unique when it comes to dignitary protection, especially presidential visits. During most visits throughout the United States, the Secret Service must call upon resources from its various field offices throughout the fifty states. In New York City they have the luxury of being able to rely heavily on the Intelligence Division to augment their own agents with a highly trained cadre of experienced detectives who have been conducting dignitary protection for decades. The result is a seamless joint protection detail.

Following close behind these lead vehicles is the presidential limousine, affectionately referred to as *The Beast*, which is also accompanied by an identical backup vehicle. The Beast, which made its debut in 2009, is, for all intents and purposes a Cadillac. However, it is in name only. While the outward appearance is that of a Cadillac, the chassis and driveline are from a Chevrolet truck. And that is precisely where the resemblance to any real world civilian market vehicle comes to an abrupt end.

In a secret facility, located inside Andrews Air Force Base in Maryland, the men and women of the US Secret Service, Special Services Division, merge real world with the shadowy world of *Top Secret*. The exact specifications of the presidential limousine will never be known, but what is known could easily have been ripped from the pages of any covert spy novel.

In addition to the body being comprised of thick military grade armor, the vehicle also comes equipped with a variety of other special modifications designed solely to keep the President safe. These range from an assortment of classified defensive countermeasures, *run flat* tires that are Kevlar reinforced, an armored gas tank which is equipped with a chemical agent designed to prevent explosion, a special night vision system, door handles that prevent unauthorized access to the interior of the vehicle, and a special communications system which allows the President to remain in secure contact while being transported.

The car is also sealed against biochemical attacks, features an independent oxygen system and also contains a reserve supply of the President's blood type. All of this for a paltry three hundred thousand dollars give or take. Taxes, tags and title not included.

Following the presidential limos are the war horses. These are the black Chevrolet Suburban's that carry the agents of the Presidential Protective Detail, Counter Assault Team, Intelligence Team, as well as a Hazardous Materials Response Team. Coming along for the ride are the President's military aide and his physician.

Thrown into this mix is the NYPD's Emergency Service Unit. This is the New York City Police Departments version of SWAT, but on steroids. The men and women of ESU are as equally at home performing their part of the counter assault role in dignitary protection details, as they are at doing high risk arrests, building collapses, train derailments or climbing the Brooklyn Bridge to talk down a would be *jumper*. It is jokingly said that if a nuclear bomb went off in New York City the only two things that would be left running around would be cockroaches and ESU trucks.

This comprises what is often referred to as the *secure package* of the presidential motorcade. The thirty or so remaining vehicles that accompany it transport assorted White House staff, communication specialists and the traveling press corps.

It is a performance played out each and every trip the President makes, whether it is a trip to speak at a thirty-thousand dollar a plate fund raising event or to spend an hour at the Lord's house on Sunday morning. For the men and women tasked with protecting the President, there is no routine trip and the threat level never goes away.

Tonight's visit involved a fund raising event at the Sheraton Hotel and Conference Center, which often plays host to a variety of events for New York's movers and shakers. The gathering this evening included a diverse group of individuals, from Hollywood hotshots to financial *wunderkinds*, all with the goal of getting a chance to stand next to the leader of the free world and, if everything went well, to perhaps get a photo to hang on their wall to mark the occasion.

The motorcade began its trek from the President's base of operations in NYC, the Waldorf Astoria. The Waldorf has long been the *home away from home* for the President of the United States or as the talking heads on the nightly news liked to refer to him: POTUS. While most visitors to New York City know the Waldorf Astoria to be a luxury hotel, what they don't know is that it is also a residence to a select few. Some of its past residents have included former President Herbert Hoover, General Douglas McArthur, inventor Nikola Tesla and even gangster Charles 'Lucky' Luciano.

In fact, as far as politics is concerned, the Waldorf Astoria is intertwined with the office of the president. The hotel has its own railway platform, known as Track 61, which is part of the Grand Central Terminal system. This platform was used by President Franklin D. Roosevelt back in the 1940's to allow him discreet access to the hotel and to keep his use of a wheelchair a secret. The train was large enough to house his armored Pierce Arrow motor car. Upon arriving the car would be driven off the train and into a private elevator that would carry him up to the hotel's garage.

Tonight, the motorcade easily snaked its way through the streets of the city. Much to the dismay of the average commuter in New York City, the President is never afflicted by Manhattan gridlock.

Dignitary protection can best be described as being inside the fish bowl and looking out. The average person stands on the outside perimeter straining for the opportunity to catch a quick glimpse of the person being protected, whether that person is a politician or a celebrity. Those on the protection detail spend their time looking outward hoping to catch a glimpse of the one person who might pose a threat to their *protectee*.

Tonight, Detective James Maguire stood at the arrival location with his Secret Service counterpart, Special Agent Richard Stargold. The two men had known each other for nearly a decade. Maguire had come to the Intelligence Division about the same time Stargold had been assigned to the New York Field Office. They had conducted dozens of presidential visits; along with an even greater number of vice presidential, foreign dignitary and UN General Assembly visits. Their professional life had also crossed over into their personal lives with Maguire being the godfather to Emily Stargold, Rich's youngest daughter. If Stargold was the typical suburban dad, commuting each day from the trendy Hoboken area of New Jersey to the New York Field Office in downtown Brooklyn, Maguire was his alter ego.

Stargold's law enforcement career had started right after college. He had attended Boston College where he graduated with a Bachelor's degree in Political Science. After college he joined the Secret Service, and attended the John J. Rowley Training Center in Beltsville, Maryland. From there he served in field offices in such postcard picturesque locales as Des Moines, Iowa and Portland, Maine; as well as a stint in Frankfurt, Germany. From there he completed a rotation with the Vice Presidential Protection Division where he had met his wife, Mary, who at the time was a D.C. lobbyist for a gun owner rights group. After a whirlwind romance the two married and a short time later their oldest daughter Sophie was born.

Being on VPPD had some perks and when his rotation was up he was able to secure a nice spot in the Financial Crimes Division at the New York Field Office, or NYFO as it was called. The former New York Field Office had been located in Seven World Trade Center, but was lost in the attacks of September 11th, 2001. As a result, the office was relocated to downtown Brooklyn, just on the other side of the East River.

Maguire, on the other hand, had taken a slightly more circuitous route to law enforcement. Immediately after he had graduated high school he promptly left home and enlisted in the United States Navy. At the time it seemed to be the easiest way for him to get away from his life in the sleepy little town of Perrysville, New York. After attending the Navy Recruit Training Command at Great Lakes, Illinois, he put in for and later graduated from the Basic Underwater Demolition/SEAL.

In laymen's terms, Basic Underwater Demolition/SEAL school, or BUD/S as it is called, is a grueling six month training course held at the Naval Special Warfare Training Center in Coronado, California. Those that make it through the ninety percent plus dropout rate go on to attend a seven month SEAL Qualification Training program. From there he was shipped off to Naval Special Warfare Group Two in Little Creek, Virginia and assigned to Seal Team Four.

If SEAL's carried passports, and collected stamps for all the places they *visited*, he would have gone through one and been working on his second, but they don't. Besides, wherever he went and whatever he did was classified anyway. The life of a SEAL is summed up in their motto: 'The Only Easy Day Was Yesterday.'

By the time he left the Navy in 1995, he had been awarded the Silver Star and the Purple Heart, which in the special warfare community is sometimes irreverently referred to as the *Enemy Marksmanship Award*. Maguire's Purple Heart was actually the result of a very well placed improvised explosive device, commonly known as an IED, that proceeded to shred the Humvee he and his fellows SEAL's had been riding in. The Silver Star was for what he did immediately afterward.

Seeing the extent of the initial damage the explosive had done to the vehicle the enemy decided to seize the moment. They began to move in on the wounded sailors who had since managed to extricate themselves from the vehicle. After making their way out of the mangled remains of the Humvee, Maguire and his wounded buddies began immediately assessing their situation. All of them had sustained injuries, but each man was singularly focused on what he could do to protect his teammates.

They took up a defensive perimeter and called for a medevac helicopter. It was then that the enemy made the fatal mistake of engaging them.

During the ensuing firefight, one of Maguire's teammates had lost consciousness from his wounds. The enemy fighters, envisioning a propaganda windfall, foolishly jumped at the opportunity to capture one of the *infidels*. Two of them had reached the limp figure and began to drag him away. They were caught up in the moment, relishing the potential media firestorm this would create for their cause. Unfortunately, for them at least, that revelry didn't last long.

Maguire had caught the movement out of his peripheral vision and turned to confront the threat. Realizing what was happening he gave chase taking out one of the bad guys with the last few remaining rounds in his M-4 rifle before transitioning over to his pistol and killing the second. He grabbed his buddy by the carry strap on his vest and dragged him back to the relative safety of the Humvee and began treating his wounds. The other two SEAL's closed in around them and provided close covering fire. Twenty minutes later a dozen enemy combatants lay dead or dying on the battlefield while all four SEAL's boarded the medevac chopper.

While convalescing from his injuries, Maguire had watched a news story about then New York City Police Commissioner William Bratton and the changes he was making to the NYPD. Maguire had matured in the Navy and was now starting to think about a career and a slightly more stable life. After deciding to retire from the Navy, he tested for and was accepted into the NYPD Academy.

To say that it was a culture shock was an understatement. The instructors at the Police Academy tried to make it hard, but after surviving *Hell Week* during his BUD/S training it all seemed so mundane to him. After graduating he found himself assigned to the 73rd Precinct in Brooklyn North or, as it is irreverently referred to by the cops who work there, Fort Zinderneuf of *Beau Geste* fame.

The Seven-Three is located in the Brownsville section of Brooklyn, with a little slice of Bedford – Stuyvesant thrown in for fun. Demographically, Brownsville is described as a residential neighborhood, but it is also dominated by eighteen public housing developments.

The list of Brownsville natives runs the gamut from boxing legends like Mike Tyson and Riddick Bowe, to entertainers like Larry King as well as any number of hip-hop artists and professional athletes. It is also an area wracked with poverty, drug addiction, violent crime and a murder rate that is one of the highest in the city. Tragedy and success were the opposing cornerstones of the community.

But for the cops that work in the Seven-Three it is what is colloquially referred to as a *shit hole*. The name routinely given to those commands where nothing good ever seems to happen. If a cop in a nice precinct screwed up, it was not uncommon for them to be told 'pick a command that starts with a seven and ends in an odd number.'

Life was different for the cops in Brooklyn North. When they were assigned to details outside their command, no one really screwed with them. For starters, they didn't play well with other officers whom they viewed as not having the same *experience* as them. Second, supervisors cut them a wide berth because they figured that they knew what the hell they were doing and even if they did screw up, there was no place worse to transfer them to.

The Seven-Three was a place where cops grew accustomed to gunfire. It became almost a normal part of the background noise. Inevitably, Central, as the police radio dispatchers were referred to, would put over a radio call for a signal "*10-10, shots fired. Male black, in his twenties, wearing all black with a doo rag, armed with a handgun, fled on foot.*"

In fact, the only part of the call that ever really changed was the location of occurrence and the direction they fled in. The reality was that this description matched just about every other person standing on a corner in Brownsville. So unless you happened to turn the corner and saw someone holding a smoking gun, or a body on the ground, chances are it was just going to be another "*10-90(Z), gone on arrival.*"

To most cops it was a dead end assignment, but for Maguire, it became so much more. The skills he had honed in the SEAL's had found a new purpose on the mean streets of Brooklyn North. He relished the chance to *toss a corner* and come up with a gun. In only a couple of years he racked up a name for himself with an impressive felony arrest record. In fact he became so good at it that he parlayed it into an assignment with the famed Street Crime Unit. The motto of the SCU was 'We Own the Night' and for Maguire, it was the time of day that he thrived in. His continued success was rewarded by a promotion to Detective 3rd grade.

Since its inception the SCU had enjoyed decades of success in arresting armed felons on the streets of New York City. This was even more significant considering the relatively small number of personnel assigned to it. Police brass figured that increasing the amount of officers would also increase its effectiveness, but that was not to be. In 2002 the Street Crime Unit was disbanded following a controversial shooting involving four members of the unit. For Maguire it was a tough blow. However his record had not gone unnoticed by those above him. The fall was relatively soft and he was transferred to the Intelligence Division which was undergoing a post 9/11 expansion. There he found his niche in conducting dignitary protection.

In short, James Maguire and Rich Stargold were polar opposites, which is most likely the reason the two men worked so well together.

On this particularly cold winter evening, the two men stood outside braving the bitter elements.

"You are still coming out to the house on Saturday?" Stargold asked.

"Absolutely," replied Maguire. "You seriously think I am going to miss my god-daughter's birthday?"

"No, not me. Mary on the other hand..." Stargold said, letting the last part trail off.

"Sheesh, you miss one party," Maguire replied.

"James, it was *your* birthday party," Stargold said.

"I'm sorry that I happened to be traveling," Maguire said, as he averted his eyes from his friend and began to scan the rooftops overlooking the arrival point.

"Um I hate to bring up actual facts, but you picked up a stewardess at a bar and dead-headed to Key West with her."

"Yeah, but you should have heard her sing *Happy Birthday*," Maguire replied, as he turned back and looked at his friend.

Both men began to laugh.

Just then their laughter was interrupted by a radio transmission.

"Rosewood Advance, Falcon Leader," came the radio traffic through the discreet ear bud in Maguire's left ear.

The Sheraton Hotel was given the radio call sign *Rosewood* and *Falcon* was the name given to the presidential detail. Falcon Leader was the call sign for the head of the NYPD protection detail.

Most people who have watched a Hollywood movie featuring a special agent in dark sunglasses speaking overtly into his shirt sleeve. In the real world they are actually speaking into a small radio transmitter that is cradled in their hand. The wire that it is connected to runs along the inside of the jacket sleeve to a portable radio. Another wire is connected to a coiled wire ear bud which allows them to discreetly monitor the radio transmissions.

Maguire raised his left hand and brought the transmitter up to his mouth.

"Falcon Leader, Rosewood Advance, you're clear for arrival."

At the same time a similar conversation was being repeated by Rich Stargold over the Secret Service secure communications frequency.

"Game time, brother," Maguire said to Stargold.

A minute later the motorcade carrying the President of the United States arrived at the hotel replete with all the pomp and circumstance normally associated with such an event. Despite the frigid temperatures that the recent snowstorm had dumped on the city, the two men were unaffected as they focused on the moment the presidential limo pulled up at curbside.

The most critical time for an advance team is this moment, when the protectee is most vulnerable. Leaving the relative security of the motorcade and stepping out into the fishbowl. Each member of the team's eyes dart from side to side and up and down. Their heads on swivels trying to identify any potential threats as the protectee moves indoors and to the holding room.

The advance team is the eyes of the protective detail at this point, they have poured over the site for countless hours and it is their responsibility to know every inch of the location. They are the ones that will lead the protectee from point ‘A’ to point ‘B.’ They must be intimately familiar with all aspects of the site, from the staging area, primary exits, secondary exits, emergency holds, and hardened locations where they can secure the protectee and fend off an attack.

“Rosewood one, Rosewood Advance, we have arrival,” Maguire said into the transmitter. “We’re preparing to move to your location.”

The advance team began to move through the side entrance of the hotel only to stop abruptly as POTUS decided to engage some of the staff who stood along a rope line.

“Falcon Leader, Renegade is stopping to press the flesh.”

Pressing the Flesh, as it is called, is the common act of handshaking and baby kissing, or in other words acting presidential. The trick to being successful is to be able to speak directly to your audience, in the briefest of moments, based on their station in life. To make them feel as if you are earnestly interested in them, personally, individually. Most have been successful; former President William Jefferson Clinton had turned it into an actual art form. While this moment lasts forever in the hearts and minds of the individual, it barely even registers in the mind of the President.

Renegade, which was the President’s radio call-sign, moved down the rope line. His engaging smile and easy tone made him extremely popular with the working class, especially those members who belonged to labor unions. On occasion he would pose with one, while another took a photograph on their camera phone. In most instances it was uploaded on a social media website before he had even moved on to the next person waiting in the line.

But it was the group upstairs, patiently awaiting his arrival, which he was actually interested in. The working class people voted, but it was those in the main hall tonight that controlled the money, money which helped fuel re-election campaigns. The first thing every politician wants to do when they get elected is to get re-elected. It's just the nature of the political animal.

The brief stop was all over in a few minutes and then the march toward the holding room continued.

"Falcon Actual, Renegade is moving."

The procession made its way through the kitchen area, winding its way past hotel staffers, who clamored for a glimpse of that famous smile, while Secret Service and NYPD post standers kept their watchful vigil.

A few moments later Renegade arrived at the holding room that was immediately adjacent to the main ballroom. He walked in and sat down in one of the chairs set up against the far wall. He grabbed a bottle of water and began going over the latest dispatches that an aide handed him.

"What's going on in Europe?" the President asked.

"It looks like they detonated a two hundred and fifty pound car bomb outside a court house in Northern Ireland, sir," was the aide's response. "PSNI was evacuating the area when it exploded. No initial reports of injuries and no claims of responsibility however even money is on dissident republicans unhappy with the way things have been unfolding politically in the north."

PSNI, or the Police Services of Northern Ireland, was the new name of the former Royal Ulster Constabulary. An agency which was both loved, and hated, by the citizens of Northern Ireland, depending on what political ideology you held. Nothing in Northern Ireland was ever easy.

POTUS continued to leaf through the papers.

"We also got word that Assad in Syria plans on hosting the leaders of Hezbollah and Iran in Damascus over the weekend where it is assumed that they will have less than complimentary words for you and rattle their sabers once again in the general direction of Israel," added the aide. "Oh and for good measure the Danish Prime Minister is doing a major cabinet reshuffle."

“OK, so basically everything’s normal in the world,” Renegade replied sarcastically.

“What fun would it be if everyone got along?” came the aides reply.

Somewhere in the background came the first strains of ‘Hail to the Chief” and then it was show time.

Presidential fund raisers generally lasted an hour or two, but the actual time the President was there might only be a few minutes. Time is money and in New York, one night of fund raising might mean making appearances at several different venues. Tonight was no different.

Renegade went out and made his speech, which was specifically tailored to bolster the support of those in attendance. Afterward, he posed with some of the big name contributors back in the holding room giving them a lasting memory of this night. At the pre-arranged urging of his staff, he said his goodbyes and made his way back down the labyrinth of corridors toward the waiting motorcade.

Once again Maguire and Stargold led the way, leaving the relative comfort of the interior hotel for the blast of frigid air that awaited them just outside the door. As they left the doorway each man stepped off to the side, Maguire going to the right and Stargold to the left, scanning the crowds in front of them. Ahead of them, an agent of the Presidential Protective Division held the limousine door open for President.

As soon as the President was in the limousine, the motorcade began to depart the location, proceeding down W 52nd Street.

“Falcon Leader, Trinity Advance, en route to your location,” Maguire heard in his ear bud.

At the same time that the President’s motorcade began to depart, the crowd had begun to disburse and Maguire caught sight of a figure a half dozen yards in front of him, frantically fumbling with something in his jacket pocket.

“Rich!” shouted Maguire, as he began moving in the direction of the man.

Maguire physically pressed through the lingering crowd, trying to close the gap between him and the mysterious figure. The man had turned suddenly and begun moving away at a quick pace. The crowd was breaking up and it was becoming harder for Maguire to keep track of the individual. He began to aggressively move people out of his way. Behind him, Rich was having the same problems.

The man turned the corner onto 7th Ave and headed north. He felt something odd and glanced over his shoulder. He saw a big man in a dark trench coat coming toward him. The rest of the crowd was moving out of the man's way and he was immediately overcome with a sense of dread. The man coming toward him moved with purpose and he correctly assumed that he was some type of law enforcement officer. At that moment he came to the realization that he had been discovered and took off at a full run toward W. 53rd Street.

Maguire watched as the man bolted and he gave chase. Behind him he heard Stargold yelling: "move, move," to the throng of pedestrians walking along 7th Avenue, as he joined the chase.

With all pretense of covert observation gone Maguire drew his Smith and Wesson 9mm service weapon and gave chase. The figure turned the corner of W. 53rd Street and disappeared. As Maguire rounded the corner he noticed people coming up out of the underground subway station who were staring back into the tunnel.

"Rosewood Advance, 10-85, Forthwith, W. 53rd and 7th, male white, dark jacket, possible weapon, ran into the train station," Maguire said into his radio transmitter, as he descended into the subway station.

There are two radio signal codes in New York City that are guaranteed to garner the immediate attention of any cop or dispatcher. Signal 10-13 is the most serious and means that an officer needs immediate help. A 10-13 is generally associated with gun fights, a physical assault, or some other major incident. Every cop who hears that call will drop what they are doing and respond.

A signal 10-85 is just below that and is the radio code most commonly used right before things escalate to a 10-13.

The radio transmission was picked up at the Intelligence Division base in Brooklyn, as well as by the communications dispatcher who was assigned to monitor the frequency during the visit. The dispatcher simultaneously transmitted it over the City-Wide Division frequency as well as Radio Zone 4 which covered that portion of Manhattan. It was all very quick, very fluid, and unfortunately too late.

Maguire had raced down into the entrance of the train station, taking several steps at once, his momentum slamming his body against the left side of stairwell wall. He felt himself slide along the slick tiled wall. As he hit the first landing he proceeded to turn to the right to take the next set of steps when he felt the sensation of being hit with a sledgehammer, not once, but twice.

Rich Stargold had turned the street corner seconds after Maguire did and begun to descend into the subway. As he navigated the steps he watched in silent horror as the body of his friend flew backward toward him. Unlike Maguire, Stargold had slowed his pace, as he made his way down the staircase, and was closer to the right side of the stairwell. As a result, when he turned onto the landing he had an unobstructed view of the gunmen and fired his Sig Sauer P229, striking him three times in the chest.

The gunman's body fell backward, his weapon clattering on the concrete floor. Subway riders, who just moments before had disembarked from the relative warmth of their train ride and who had been bracing themselves for the bitter cold of the city streets, screamed at the sound of gunfire. Figures ran away, back into the station to escape the carnage, as Stargold moved quickly toward the gunman. Reverting back to the training that had been drummed into him at the academy, he handcuffed the gunman and secured the man's weapon. He then returned back to Maguire who was struggling to pull himself up into a seated position.

"Where are you hit?" shouted Rich and he immediately transmitted a code that there had been a shooting and requested medical response over the Secret Service frequency.

"My chest," Maguire replied, as he leaned back against the stairwell wall.

Stargold ran his hands over his friend's body to assess his injuries. He pulled his jacket open and saw the blood discoloring the cloth shirt near his left shoulder.

"Hold on, James," Rich said. "The ambulance is on the way."

Maguire heard sirens wailing in the background which were followed by the sounds of brakes locking up tires on the city street above him.

Police Officers, including several heavily armed ESU cops from Truck One, descended down into the subway station with shouts.

"Shooters down," Rich yelled, holding his badge high above his head to avoid an instance of friendly fire.

The patrol cops immediately secured the area while the ESU cops began medical intervention on Maguire. They were joined seconds later by FDNY Emergency Medical Service personnel who worked to stabilize him. When they were satisfied, they loaded him onto a stretcher and carried him up to the waiting ambulance.

Stargold followed them up the staircase and watched as they loaded the stretcher into the back of the ambulance. An Emergency Medical Technician, assisted by an ESU Cop, continued to work on his friend. A sergeant from the Intelligence Division had arrived on the scene and approached Stargold.

"Rich, what happened?"

"I've got to go with him," Stargold began to say.

"No, we will take care of him," the sergeant said and turned to the detective that had accompanied him. "Go with Maguire. Call me as soon you have an update and let me know what's going on."

The detective nodded and climbed into the back of the ambulance.

“I need to know what happened, Rich.”

“James must have spotted him in the crowd and gave chase,” Stargold explained. “He called out to me and I followed after him. When I got into the train station, I heard the shots and saw Maguire go down. I returned fire and took out the shooter.”

“Did you see anyone else? Notice anything else?”

“No, nothing else,” Stargold said, as he gazed back at the ambulance.

In that moment he seemed to grasp the line of questioning and turned back toward the NYPD sergeant.

“No, I didn’t see anyone else,” Stargold confirmed. “There was just the one shooter that I saw.”

“Falcon Supervisor to Falcon Leader,” the sergeant said into his radio. “One perp down, unknown secondary.”

Somewhere in the city a decision was made and the presidential motorcade conducted an emergency redirect back to *Marine One* which was standing by at the South Street Heliport. From there it was a short trip to John F. Kennedy Airport where he boarded *Air Force One* and was in the air a few short minutes later, making his way back to Washington, D.C.

The official line given to the campaign donors at the next scheduled fund raiser was that the recent terrorist attack in Northern Ireland required the President to return to the White House in order to speak with his counterparts and to restore calm to the tenuous peace in this region of the world. The truth was that no one in the Presidential Protective Division was willing to take a risk that there was not a second shooter and no one in the President’s staff was going to argue against it.

As soon as they had stabilized Maguire the ambulance or ‘bus’, as it is known in police vernacular, began the cross town trip to Bellevue Hospital.

Just as the president's motorcade moves unrestricted, so does an ambulance carrying a shot cop. The bus departed the scene with a precinct patrol car leading the way and followed by an ESU truck. Every street, from the scene of the shooting to the hospital, was shut down either by a precinct car or a Highway Patrol unit. The Emergency Room staff was notified and waiting, as the bus pulled up to the E.R. entrance a few minutes later.

Maguire was wheeled immediately into the waiting operating room where a team of doctors and nurses worked feverishly to remove the two bullets that had lodged themselves in his chest. Outside the operating room cops began to gather. Their ranks swelled with each passing minute. Those keeping vigil would soon be joined by the Police Commissioner and Chief of Department and later still by the Mayor. The latter would seize the opportunity to use the tragedy to gratuitously call for additional gun control measures; all while being surrounded by members of his armed protection detail.

Seven hours later the doctors and nurses walked out of the operating room exhausted, but satisfied in the fact that they had once again cheated death. To the medical staff at Bellevue, the questions surrounding the other scars they had observed on the cops body would remain an unanswered mystery.

During the period of his recovery one thing had continually troubled Maguire. He had replayed the scene numerous times in his mind and each time he was troubled by the fact that he had never seen the actual gun or a muzzle flash. Investigators later explained to him the sequence of events that they had been able to reconstruct.

The lone gunman had made it to the second set of stairs where he stopped running and pressed himself against the wall, waiting to ambush his pursuer. In that moment the hunted had become the hunter. He instinctively aimed in the direction of the middle of the staircase, and waited. As Maguire ran into the subway station his momentum carried him into the stairwell on his left with such force that it had actually slowed down his forward progression. As a result he entered the landing at a point different from where the gunman had been aiming. The shooter was caught off guard and had to quickly readjust his aim, which he did, but he swung too far to the right. The result was that the guns barrel jammed into Maguire's upper left chest when it was fired.

The gunmen closed his eyes and managed to pull the trigger twice, as he fired blindly. When it was all said and done what separated life and death for Maguire was a mere two inches.

The nightly news carried a brief report of an emotionally disturbed gunman in the subway system that shot a New York City Police Officer. Despite the shooting being in the immediate vicinity, no connection was made with the President's visit. This was in part because none of the nightly news programs were willing to admit that the populist President could ever be the target of an assassination attempt.

The facts of the investigation determined that the gunman, identified as an unemployed factory worker from Jersey City, had simply grown tired of waiting for the hope and change he had been promised to materialize in his life. After his wife and kids had moved out, it started a downward spiral that he simply never recovered from. After months on the unemployment line he had made the decision that it was now time to force the change he had been patiently waiting for. He reached out to a few of his former co-workers and after some discreet exchanges was rewarded with a Charter Arms .38 caliber revolver. He went to great lengths to explain that he needed it for personal protection due to the neighborhood he lived in, but at the end of the day no one really cared about the reason, just the money.

On this particular night, he had stashed the gun in the pocket of his leather coat. As he tried to remove it, the hammer spur on the old revolver managed to get caught on the torn liner of his jacket. The pocket opening itself was too small to start with so his twisting and tugging just made it harder to pull the gun out. The ensuing struggle had prevented him from taking the shot before the President had entered the limo. The man had fled the scene out of frustration and his perceived failure at doing something as simple as removing a gun from his own pocket. It was not until he looked over his shoulder and realized that someone had seen him, that panic set in.

By the time he had gotten to the subway entrance he had managed to dislodge the weapon from his pocket. Ineptitude gave way to fury and he decided that if he couldn't take it out on his primary target, he would take it out on a surrogate. He thrust the gun forward in blind rage and waited for his prey to come into view. As the figure of the man came around the corner he realized that he had severely miscalculated his approach. In his final moments, and with the utmost clarity, he realized that he had managed to screw this up as well.

He succeeded in pulling the trigger twice before he felt a intense burning sensation in his own chest a moment later. The burning went away almost immediately and was replaced with a sense of, nothing. In fact, there was no pain at all, as he felt his body drop to the floor.

As the man lay on the floor, he stared up at the ceiling, watching as a yellowish light fixture flickered rhythmically.

That's strange, he thought, as he watched the light dim.

He was vaguely aware of activity around him and heard voices in the distance. A moment later he felt his body being handled roughly, as he was flipped over and his hands were pulled behind his back. He laid there enjoying the coolness of the damp floor against his cheek.

He began to wonder what was going to happen next. He reasoned that once he had a chance to explain his side of things that everything would be ok. Maybe he would even get a second chance. It was just then that he had the oddest sensation, as if the chaos of his life had been stripped away. In its place was a sense of peace and tranquility. He smiled, amazed at how good he was feeling.

It's all going to be alright, he thought.

Then, with a sudden rush, the life drained out of him.

For his actions that night, Special Agent Richard Stargold would be presented with the United States Secret Service, Director's Award for Valor, the highest honor that can be bestowed on an agent.

In June, Detective James Patrick Maguire would stand before the Mayor of the City of New York and the Police Commissioner during a private ceremony and be awarded the NYPD Medal of Valor. Four months later he would be retired on a medical disability.

CHAPTER SIX

Ponquoque Beach, Suffolk County, N.Y.
Saturday, April 28th, 2012 – 7:04 a.m.

Maguire took a deep breath and chased away the thoughts, pulling himself back to the present moment.

In spite of all the military action he had seen, the subway shooting still continued to haunt his thoughts after all this time.

In some strange way he argued to himself that the IED attack had been *normal* to him. Psychologically, he rationalized that it was him and his team, on foreign soil, actively engaged in warfare and it wasn't really personal. This had been an attack on domestic soil, it wasn't an armed conflict, and it was very personal. Rather than continue to run away the shooter had opted to stop and make his last stand against Maguire.

He questioned every aspect of that night a hundred times over. He wondered if he could have done anything different. Was there anything that he had done wrong, or had there been something he had missed?

His time spent in the teams had accustomed him to a different way of fighting. A small, special operations military unit operated much more differently than an inner-city police department. They had the capability of bringing the fight to their enemy on their terms. Even in the aftermath of the IED attack, his unit controlled their environment. The night of the thwarted assassination attempt he did not have the luxury of the enemy coming to him. He had to pursue the enemy and judge the extent of the threat, literally while on the run, despite the risk to himself, because he had been charged with protecting the public.

Deep down inside he knew the truth. Sometimes you just have to play the cards you're dealt. As a cop, you didn't have the choice of waiting for the odds to be in your favor before you went through the door.

In the end, he always came to the same conclusion; he would have done nothing different. It was the wrong place, at the wrong time, but ultimately the right outcome.

He walked through the bathroom doorway and back into the bedroom. He removed the towel and tossed it onto the bed. Then he opened the closet doors and began to get dressed. It was the weekend so he opted for a pair of khaki cargo pants and a blue polo shirt.

When he was finished dressing he sat down and put on a pair of hiking boots. He was just finishing lacing them up when he realized that something seemed out of place. Maguire glanced over his shoulder and spotted the black dress draped over the edge of the bed, positioned with precise intent. He laughed softly, as he leaned over and picked it up. He took a hanger from the closet and slid the dress onto it. As he was doing it he noticed that it had no tags inside and was clearly a custom made dress. Apparently Ms. Anderson had some friends in the fashion industry. He hung the dress up in the closet, smoothing out the fabric and stepped back looking at it.

Then a thought crossed his mind: *What exactly was she wearing when she left?*

He smiled at that mental image.

Maguire sat back on the edge of the bed and looked around the room. For a moment he wished that she hadn't left. As he sat there he moved his hand along the sheets. He imagined that he could still feel the heat left over from her body, could still smell her scent hanging in the air. He realized that he longed to feel her touch again. It was a feeling he hadn't felt in...? Well, not in a very long time.

But he was not the type to languish in a lost moment. Years of experience had taught him that the longer you lingered, the less you did, and the longer you had a target on your back. So he rose up from the bed, walked out of the room and headed back down the hallway to the kitchen where he poured himself a hot cup of coffee. As he walked the few steps to his office, near the bow of the boat, he still couldn't seem to shake the sense of dread that had been weighing on him since he started his run this morning.

Having his office here on the boat was a convenience he thoroughly enjoyed, especially during the winter months. Others needed a formal office in an actual building, but he was perfectly happy here. He grabbed the remote on the desk and turned on the flat screen TV that hung on the opposite wall.

He took a sip of coffee, as he powered up the laptop, and listened to the newscast play in the background. Every day it was the same monotony: Somewhere in the world, someone was doing something to someone much to the disdain of someone else. For all the lamenting by pundits and politicians, it seemed that the world was driven by chaos. More importantly, to him at least, that chaos fueled an entire global security industry, which in turn paid him quite well.

He began to sort through the papers on his desk, assigning them to piles in order of importance. When he was done he went through the previous day's mail. In addition to all the other stuff he needed to get done, he had at least a dozen calls to make. Along the way he thought about reaching out to Melody and see if she was free for dinner this evening.

Maguire looked at his watch, it was 7:26 a.m. and the news cycle was just about to repeat. He turned his attention back to the laptop and began going through the most recent emails. Most were security alerts from companies he subscribed to. It was always important to watch the global trends and check for any upticks in violence. Terrorism was like a car in the sense that there were almost always small signs before the big blowup.

The average person in the United States had no reason to worry about what *unrest* there was in Jakarta or Cairo, but his clients' interests were international and could be seriously affected by that unrest.

Two of the emails were from vice presidents of Fortune 500 companies asking about his services, another was from the head of a major European police agency wondering if he was still planning on vacationing in Europe this year and the final, and to him the most important one, was from Peter Bart asking if the rumors that he had been seen leaving with a certain venture capitalist last night were true.

That email elicited a laugh.

Society gossip traveled fast in Southampton. For a moment he allowed himself to think of the rare possibility of a normal relationship.

That moment didn't last long.

At the bottom of the hour, the news programming repeated its top stories.

"In regional news," said the perky twenty-something female reporter, "the New York State Police are reporting that they are investigating the disappearance of a Perrysville woman."

It wasn't the story that immediately registered with Maguire, it was the location that did. He looked up at the television screen.

"State police public information officer Andrea Dryer stated that the woman, forty-two year old Patricia Browning, was last seen leaving an art gallery opening in Keenseville."

The screen went from the newscaster to a somber looking Trooper standing outside the Troop B Station in Plattsburgh.

"At approximately 3:45 a.m. Saturday evening the New York State Police received a call of a one vehicle accident on County Highway 28," said Trooper Dryer. "Upon arriving at the scene, troopers found the vehicle, registered to Mrs. Patricia Browning, abandoned on the side of the road. The vehicle had sustained significant front end damage consistent with striking an animal. At this time, the whereabouts of Mrs. Browning are unknown. We are requesting that anyone with information please contact the New York State Police or their local law enforcement agency. Thank You."

Maguire inhaled sharply.

Suddenly, the specter that had haunted him this cold April morning now had a face and it was someone he had once known very well.

He grabbed the cell phone from his desk and thumbed through the contact listings until he found a particular phone number and selected it. The phone rang several times before he heard it connect.

"How much money do I owe you?" said the man who answered the phone.

"No, you owe me a favor, Bill," said Maguire. "I just caught the news and I need whatever information you have on the Tricia Browning disappearance."

Bill Malloy was the host of a major evening cable news show. He was one of those galvanizing folks who you either agreed with whole heartedly or loathed with a passion, but he was honest and that didn't always sit well with people. Maguire respected him which said a lot.

"Tricia Browning?"

"Yeah, there was a local correspondent on the air who reported that she went missing overnight in the Keenseville area," said Maguire.

He could hear the man writing on the other end.

"Sounds like something personal, James."

"This one is completely off the record, Bill," said Maguire, "and in return you get an *I owe you one* from me."

The two men had met a couple of years back at a function for wounded veterans. Malloy was drawn to the man's knowledge and insightfulness on past and present global events. It was ironic that he didn't know Maguire was himself wounded in action until after the men had parted ways. It was another Navy veteran who had seen the two talking and had asked if he was friends with Maguire. When Malloy said that they had just met, the Navy guy gave him the scoop. Malloy had made it a point to track him down and as a result the two men had become fast friends. After he left the NYPD Malloy even interviewed him on his evening television program and Maguire had appeared a few times as an expert commentator.

"Give me a half hour and I will get back to you."

"Thanks, Bill."

Maguire sat back in his office chair, his stare falling on the wall opposite his desk. It settled on one particular photograph.

All great men have what is generally considered their *look at me* wall. It is a place covered in the mementos of their career. It often contains a mix of photos, awards, documents and other ephemera which encapsulated the achievements and successes that they have enjoyed. Most of these walls are public; that is they allow visitors and potential business clients to see just how *connected* the person they are talking to was.

Maguire's wall was private.

No one came here and no one sat in this office. In fact, outside of a very small and select group of close friends, Melody Anderson had been the only real *visitor* to the boat for years.

This was his refuge from the world and he didn't want it spoiled.

On the wall were photos of Maguire with the current president, two former presidents, the Pope, foreign heads of state, U.S. politicians, along with a slew of celebrities and financial luminaries. All were personalized with well wishes. But in the center of this veritable collection of *who's who* photographs was a single black and white picture of a girl in profile. At first glance it appeared as if she was simply staring off into space, but upon closer examination her gaze was too intense, too somber. Anyone who would have had the chance to see it would describe the look as being hauntingly beautiful.

The reality of the photograph was that the young girl was staring off across Lake Champlain, toward the Vermont side, a heavy weight bearing down on her. What had started off as a romantic afternoon lunch had suddenly turned into something significantly more *complicated*.

Maguire allowed his thoughts to fade back to that sunny spring afternoon when he had pulled the car into the parking lot of Perrysville High School and up to the sidewalk where his girlfriend, Tricia Reagan, stood waiting for him.

It was one week before graduation and the Perrysville Class of '89 was enjoying the half days that were a senior class perk. In a few short months they would all go their own separate ways. For Maguire that meant a short drive north on the New York State Thruway to the campus of the State University of New York at Plattsburgh. He had been accepted into the fall semester class, majoring in Art History, the very same degree program Tricia was also enrolled in.

James felt like a million bucks. It was the first day that he had pulled the old Detroit behemoth into the high school parking lot. She was waiting there to see what the *surprise* was that he had teased her about. Judging by her initial response he had hit the mark.

"Wow!" Tricia screamed, as she opened the car door and climbed in. "This is so cool!"

They took a ride out to Corlaer Bay in his *new*, as in new to him, car. He had been working the last two years, saving up every dime he could, to buy a car. In addition to what he referred to as his day job, he had worked every free moment during the last year helping Susan McCarty around her farm. The McCarty's were one of those historical founding families that traced their roots back to the origins of Perrysville. Their 300 acre farm had been passed down from generation to generation. Her husband Thomas was the last of the McCarty's and he had passed away several years back. Susan McCarty had felt an obligation to keep the farm going in his memory, but she was all too aware that her own days were now numbered.

Several days earlier she had asked James to give her a hand with something in the garage. It was one of those old farm garages, painted in traditional red, which bore the scars of many years of being beaten by the weather. As they walked into the little used building, dust danced off the sunshine cascading down through the open door that was once used to bring in hay bales. She led him to the back of the garage where an old matted tarp was laid over the form of vehicle, wrapping it like a cocoon. She motioned for him to remove it. He gently withdrew the tarp, watching as the edges pulled away to reveal a mint, candy apple red, 1969 Ford Mustang Boss 429.

The car had belonged to the McCarty's only son, Robert, who had purchased it right before shipping off to Vietnam. Sergeant Robert McCarty, 101st Airborne, was killed in action during *Operation Lam Son 719* at the ripe old age of twenty-three.

The two of them stared at the gleaming machine from a forgotten era. Finally it was Susan McCarty who broke the silence.

"My son never lived his life, James," she said. "Never forget that. In his death, you've been given a gift. Honor him by never letting his memory be forgotten."

Maguire was in shock when she kissed him on the cheek and handed him the keys. After a few days of some TLC the car once again roared to life, ready to prowl the back roads of Perrysville.

Now as they drove through the country, he glanced over at Tricia. She sat back against the reclined seat with her bare feet up on the dashboard. The wind was blowing in through the open passenger window and it whipped her hair around playfully. She leaned over and turned on the radio, hearing a song by a brand new country artist that she loved. She raised the volume and began to sing along with the song. Tricia loved to sing and he thought she had the voice of an angel.

The two of them had first met when the Perrysville and Sharpsburg school districts had merged for financial reasons. The Sharpsburg district took over all elementary school classes, while the Perrysville district took over the junior high and high school classes. Perrysville was the larger of the two communities, with a population of about eleven hundred people, and was situated about a dozen miles south east of Keenseville.

He had seen her the very first day of classes, but it took a substantially longer time for her to actually notice him. A year to be exact; not that he had been counting. However, they wouldn't go out on an actual date until well into their junior year.

He and Tricia made an unlikely pair. She was popular; he was just another faceless student. She was the head of the cheerleading squad; he was a geek on the chess team. But they soon found that they shared a love of art, her on the appreciation side and him on the photography side. It was a common bond that they were both planning on pursuing beyond the academic world and into the real world.

On this particular day the future was a lifetime away and all he wanted to do was to spend the afternoon with her. He knew of a place out on Lake Champlain that was the perfect spot so they could be alone and just enjoy the afternoon together.

Lake Champlain runs down from Canada into the United States between the states of Vermont and New York. It has played an integral part in the history of the United States. During the Revolutionary War, it was the site of the Battle of Valcour Island which was a major strategic victory for the fledgling republic, under the leadership of the infamous Benedict Arnold. It also played a significant role during the War of 1812, which ended the final British invasion of the northern states.

In current times, it was generally considered a sportsman's paradise. The entire region was well known for its fishing, hunting, and an extensive array of leisure activities including climbing in the Adirondack Mountains.

In addition to the mountain ranges, the lush forests are dotted with large flat stone cliffs surrounding the lake area. It made for an exquisite setting to just sit back and take in the natural beauty of the lake.

They had just finished eating lunch and were sitting back on the bluffs overlooking Corlaer Bay, a tiny alcove that sat almost directly across from Burlington, Vermont. Their conversation jumped from topic to topic.

"My dad is taking me down to Manhattan in August for a seminar," he said. "He told me to ask if you wanted to go. He said we could visit some of the art museums while we were there. He also emphasized something about separate rooms."

"Parents are so lame," Tricia said with a laugh.

For a moment she thought back to the first time they had *done it*, which elicited a smile and a tingle inside her.

"Oh, I forgot to tell you that Lena and I are going into Plattsburgh tomorrow to pick up my prom dress," she said. "I didn't know if you wanted to tag along?"

"I'd love to, but I promised Mrs. McCarty I would run her into Keenseville before the weekend so she could do her shopping."

"That's okay; it'll give us some girl time. Besides, I know how much you love shopping."

Occasionally they would be forced to pause their conversation, as the roar of a huge KC-135 Stratotanker flew overhead, departing from nearby Plattsburgh Air Force Base. It was a fairly common occurrence, as it was a Strategic Air Command base and the 135's would conduct midair refueling of the FB-111 Bombers.

It was during one of these silent moments that he caught her staring out over the water. He pulled the camera, that he habitually carried with him, out of the bag and focused on her face. He loved her profile and, truth be told, the camera loved her as well. He waited for the roar of the massive plane to subside and chose that very moment to record her response to the statement he had waited all afternoon to say.

"I love you."

He had wanted to take a photo to capture her response. He did, it just wasn't the response he had anticipated.

The intense look the camera captured that afternoon was actually not so much intentional, but rather the muted response to his declaration of love. Three simple words which, in the blink of an eye, had irrevocably changed both of their lives forever.

The silence hung in the air between them. The moment caught forever on the thin film inside the camera that Maguire quietly put back in the padded bag.

It wasn't that Tricia didn't love him. She did actually. But something had happened, something she didn't have the words for. A week prior she would have leapt into his arms, now she was confused and the words to describe what she was feeling simply escaped her. What remained in its place was an awkwardness that effectively signaled the end of their romantic lunch.

A half hour later the picnic basket had been packed away, the blankets they had laid out on were rolled up, and they were on their way home. He turned on the radio, as they drove toward Perrysville, just to chase away the silence.

He pulled up in front of her house and put the car into park.

"Tricia," he said, halting for a moment searching for the right words. "I didn't mean to put you on the spot."

"No, James, it's not that," she said. "I just can't answer the way you want me too. I wish I could, but I just can't."

"I don't understand, Tricia; I thought you felt the same as I do."

"I did,... I do," she fumbled, trying unsuccessfully to find the right words.

"I mean I do care for you," she continued. "I just can't say the words you want me too, at least not now. I just don't know. I'm confused."

From the beginning of their relationship they had been very open with each other about how they felt. Too often people rushed into relationships and professed feelings they simply didn't understand.

Both of them had agreed they didn't want to do that. They promised that they would only say it when they actually felt it.

Maguire sighed.

He thought he had finally gotten it. He knew how he felt and, more importantly, he believed he knew how Tricia felt. He had been ready to validate those feelings, but instead he struggled to come to terms with how terribly wrong he had been. She was staring out the windshield, looking down the street.

He leaned over, kissing her on the cheek and wondering if this would be the last time.

She opened the door and quietly exited the car. He watched, waiting patiently. She never looked back.

Tricia Reagan hurried toward the house, feeling the hot stream of tears running down her face. The longer she remained outside, the more vulnerable she felt and she didn't want to feel that way, not about him.

Maguire waited till she opened the back door and entered the house before he dropped the car into gear and pulled away from the curb slowly.

Wow, he thought. *How had everything so right, gone so wrong, so quickly?*

He returned home and parked the car in the driveway. He got out of the car and removed the lunch basket and camera bag from the trunk before walking into the house through the back door.

Maggie Maguire stood in the kitchen preparing vegetables for the evening dinner.

"How was your lunch, dear?" his mother asked.

"Great, Mom," he answered. "Just great."

If she had noticed the sarcasm in his voice she didn't say anything.

He dropped the basket containing the remnants of their lunch on the kitchen counter and continued through into the dining room.

"I'm tired; I'm going to take a nap," he added and disappeared out of sight.

He continued through the dining room, into the living room, and climbed up the staircase that led to the second floor and went directly to his bedroom.

As he walked into the bedroom he closed the door behind him. He went over to the closet and opened the door, putting the camera bag onto a shelf before collapsing onto the bed. At the time he didn't realize that this moment had summarily ended his photography career.

He lay there for a while, staring out the window, not sure what he should do. He just felt numb.

There are few things in life that are as devastating to a young man. Being dumped by the love of your life, whether real or perceived, rests at the very pinnacle of the list.

That evening, he managed to suffer through dinner. If his parents had any inclination that something was wrong they didn't say anything. Both of his parents were educators and probably immune to the never ending *mood swings* inherent in adolescence.

Margaret "Maggie" Maguire was a 6th grade math teacher at the elementary school in Sharpsburg while his father, Shamus, was a sociology professor who taught at SUNY / Plattsburgh. Both were getting ready for the end of the school year and had a lot to discuss. James was just an innocent bystander to their conversation.

After dinner he returned back to his room and sat on the window ledge looking up at the stars. As night fell, and the room darkened, he succumbed to the emotions that were battering him on the inside and he cried.

A half mile away Tricia laid in her bed, struggling with the same emotions. Her mind raced as she tried to make sense of what had happened today.

She loved James. She felt it in her heart. So why couldn't she say it? After dating seriously for over a year now, what she knew, or thought she knew, had somehow changed.

That wasn't exactly true, she admitted. It wasn't something that had changed, it was *someone*.

As Tricia laid on her bed, looking out the window, she wondered what the future held for the two of them. How was she going to reconcile this? How was she going to come to terms with what she was feeling?

The Senior Prom was coming up and she knew she had to find the answer, and find it quick. It wasn't fair, to him, to her, to....

She chased the thoughts from her mind. She wasn't ready to face it.

Life was not only unfair; it was apparently extremely cruel at times as well.

In the end she surrendered herself to the same outcome as Maguire, tears streaming down her face.

The ringing of the phone brought Maguire back to the present.

He reached down and answered it. "Hello."

"Official word is that Patricia Browning got in a car accident with a deer and there was evidence that she likely suffered some type of injury," Bill replied on the other end. "However, despite the evidence of an injury, a search turned up nothing and no one has shown up at any of the area hospitals. It's as if she simply vanished. The state police are investigating and a search is being conducted throughout the area in the hopes that she simply walked away from the scene and has gotten lost in the woods."

"I appreciate the help, Bill," James said.

"You want the back story on it?" he asked

"Yeah, absolutely, Bill, whatever else you got on it."

"Ok, my local source at the affiliate said that she left an art gallery she owns in a place called Keenseville sometime around one a.m.," Malloy replied. "Apparently it was the inaugural showing of the year and so it was a pretty big event for the area. You know the type."

"Yeah, been there, done that and I think I still have the tux in the closet."

"Exactly, James," Malloy said. "Anyway, the show officially ended around eleven. That is at least when all the guests left according to the gallery manager. Browning stayed for a couple of hours to clean up."

"Thanks, Bill, I owe you," said Maguire. "If you hear anything more, get back to me."

"You got it," said Malloy. "I'll talk to you later."

Maguire let it all sink in. He knew the area intimately well, as did she. The road she had traveled on snaked its way through a dense, expansive, forest. If she had walked thirty feet off the road in any direction during the day she could have easily gotten disoriented and become lost. At night it was almost a guarantee. If she had sustained any type of head trauma or other serious injury she would be in a dire predicament by now.

Then there was the weather.

His lips tightened in a scowl as he looked out one of the boat's small windows at the harsh grey sky outside.

For all its picture perfect beauty, Perrysville still sat just a mere forty miles south of the Canadian Border. Cold temperatures were a part of life in the North Country.

Maguire had often heard the old-timers talk of winters so severe that you could drive across the lake from Ausable Point to Burlington. Not in one of today's fiberglass cars, but in honest-to-goodness old steel machines from the 40's and 50's. To him it was all nonsense, like the stories they used to tell him about *Champy*, Lake Champlain's very own version of the Loch Ness Monster. But then one day, as he and Tricia had been going through her grandmother's old photo albums, he saw old black and white photos of cars driving over the ice highway.

He checked his watch.

It was almost eight, which meant that if she had not been found yet, then she had been exposed to the elements for at least four hours.

He wondered about that for a moment. Technically it was spring, but that didn't matter. Temperatures at this time of the year would only be in the fifties or low sixties at the most. But at the time of night she would have been driving, those temperatures would have been hovering around the mid to lower thirties.

If Tricia had been dressed up for the opening, then she most likely would have been wearing a dress and heels. At the most she would have put on a fashionable jacket that would have offered little to no protection against the elements. The only thing she had going for her was that it appeared to have been a clear night without any rain, but hypothermia in her case was still a very real possibility and growing more serious with each passing hour since the accident.

Maguire sat there for a moment longer staring at the photo on the wall and took a final sip of the coffee that had grown cold. He had long ago given up on trying to exorcise the ghost that had haunted him for the last twenty-three years.

When the moment passed, he got up and began to focus on the task at hand in earnest.

CHAPTER SEVEN

Ponquoque Beach, Suffolk County, N.Y.
Saturday, April 28th, 2012 – 5:30 a.m.

Melody Anderson had awoken to the sound of the closing door. She laid there for a moment longer, allowing herself to become acclimated to her new surroundings this morning.

The bedroom had a musty scent to it. A wonderful reminder of the night they had just shared together. Outside, she could hear the sound of the water lapping rhythmically against the side of the boat.

Her left hand slid slowly across the sheet, feeling the heat from where his body had laid beside her just minutes before. She stretched out in the bed, feeling the material of the top sheet slowly sliding along her naked body, as she gazed up at the ceiling, wondering how she had come to be in this floating bedroom. It was so out of character for her, so beyond the norm. She was usually the one in complete control and, if truth be told, all of her prior romantic evenings had ended with barely a peck on the cheek.

Yet somehow, with a man she had known for less than twelve hours, she felt so absolutely comfortable. A feeling that was normally as foreign to her as the bedroom she now found herself in this morning.

She kicked off the rest of the sheet and laid there smiling to herself, as she began to recall all the intimate details of the previous night's activity. She became aware that she was absentmindedly running her fingers slowly along her skin. Her senses were so alive this morning, everything felt so erotic to her and she had the most wonderful ache..... right *there*.

Melody began playing the movie imbedded in her mind.

She had kissed him as soon as they had walked through the door, pressing herself hard against him. Melody had succumbed to some primal urge, needing to feel his body against hers. If she had caught him off guard with the kiss, he didn't show it. She could feel him kissing her back with the same raw intensity. He had kicked the door shut and grabbed her by her arms, pinning her body against the wall roughly and taking her breath away. Time stood still as they kissed, seconds seemed to turn into minutes, and she felt herself becoming lightheaded. She moaned loudly and she was acutely aware that she was being overwhelmed by a mixture of desire, passion and pure lust.

He had released her arms, one hand moving toward the back of her neck as the other began moving down her body exploring each sensuous curve. She felt his hot breath on her skin as his lips moved away from hers, down her jaw, along her neck to her shoulders, an erotic mix of kisses and playful biting. She squirmed under his touch and felt herself surrender to that inner animal that seemed to beckon to her from somewhere deep inside. She wanted him and she was willing to let herself go to a place she had never allowed herself to go before.

Her hands reached out to his shoulders and she pushed him back against the opposite wall suddenly and with a level of ferocity that he hadn't expected.

The light from the full moon filtered in through the window in the narrow hallway, casting an eerie pale glow that only served to punctuate the intensity of the moment. She knew that he could see the hunger in her eyes and he stood there, surrendering control to her, wondering where it would lead.

Melody began by working on the tie he wore. Slowly, methodically, she undid the knot and tugged it free, dropping it on to the floor. There was something different about her now, as if a switch had been flipped inside her. Any inhibitions she might have once had, had been chased away.

Her fingers moved to the buttons on his shirt. She got the top two undone before deciding it wasn't worth the wait and ripped it open. She'd buy him another. She then grabbed the edges of the shirt and pulled it down off his shoulders. He slid his arms free and let it fall to the floor with the tie.

She gasped audibly and bit her lip as she gazed upon his exposed muscular chest. Before she could do anything more, he had grabbed her and turned her around quickly, pressing her up against the wall. He was kissing the back of her neck and she felt him unzipping the back of her dress. Melody closed her eyes and shuddered as his hands moved across her shoulders and she felt him pull the dress free, letting it slide down her body to the floor.

She turned to face him wearing nothing, but her black lace bra, panties and heels. The moonlight highlighted every curve of her well-toned body and twinkled playfully off the diamond bellybutton ring she wore. As Melody stood there in the hallway she was struck by the dichotomy of the moment. She stood before him completely exposed and yet she had never felt so empowered

Melody realized that she was completely intoxicated by him.

He had reached out and pulled her toward him, lifting her up into his arms. She felt her own arms wrap around his shoulders as her legs wrapped around his hips. She buried her face in his neck, kissing him, as he carried her through the open doorway and into the bedroom.

As they approached the bed she let her legs drop, and he lowered her down slowly. She stood back and reached down to unbuckle his belt and then unzipped his pants. He kicked off his shoes and quickly removed his socks before stepping out of his pants.

"Someone's excited," she said playfully, as she reached down and removed his briefs.

Melody stood up and took him by the arms, pushing him back onto the bed in overly dramatic motion, her hands flicking upwards, as if to say 'I can handle you.'

She could feel the intense passion and desire inside her growing more insatiable by the moment. He laid there in front of her and she could see the same hunger mirrored in his eyes, those incredibly blue eyes. Melody decided to indulge her inner animal and she found herself rocking her hips back and forth playfully, as she reached back and unhooked her bra. She let it fall away from her shoulders slowly, allowing him to see her breasts.

She turned her back to him, grabbing the lace edge of her thong and began to slowly shimmy out of it. As she looked back over her shoulder she smiled mischievously at the man who had unlocked something deep inside of her; something she had never felt before. She leaned forward and reached down seductively and released each strap on her heels, stepping out of each of them in turn.

Melody turned back around and climbed onto the bed, straddling the object of her inner most desire. She wanted him, needed him, now. Melody moaned as she lowered herself down slowly; feeling him move deep inside. She reached up and she took his hands in hers, steadying herself as she rose up and down on him.

It was nothing she had ever felt before, a perfect union between the physical and the emotional. Her pace became faster, driven by lust and desire. Her moans filled the room as she gave herself to him completely. Yet deep inside she knew that it was she who was taking him.

Melody felt his hands slip from hers and move to her breasts, his fingers caressing her. She felt his pace keeping up with hers, the two lovers in sync with one another's bodies. It was almost as if she were fading off into some erotic dream. Time seemed to stand still even as it was racing ahead at a breakneck speed.

From an early age her life had been focused, driven. She had set goals and had a steel resolve in accomplishing them. She had come from the very bottom of the socio-economic ladder and had not let anything, or anyone, come in the way of her success. At thirty-six years old Melody Anderson had earned her spot on the list of the richest women in the United States the old way, by being better, smarter and more aggressive than her male counterparts, but that ambition had not allowed for anyone else. Even so, she had never felt that she had missed out on anything because of it. Success was her lover and she had always felt perfectly satisfied.

That was, until this evening.

Tonight she was drawn to him like the proverbial moth to the flame. They had just met, only just begun to get to know each other, and yet she had given herself to him utterly and completely. No one had ever made her feel this way before and her physical desire for him chased away everything else. The more he gave her, the more she wanted. It terrified and yet thrilled her at the same time.

"*Ahhh*....!!"

Melody arched her back and screamed, as she felt the orgasm grip her. It was as sudden as it was intense. Her body shuddered uncontrollably for what seemed like an eternity before she collapsed down hard against him; her face burying itself in the closest pillow. She could feel his firm hands grabbing her ass hard, continuing to thrust deep inside her. Their love making was at a frenzied pitch.

Her head was spinning. She reached out and grabbed wildly at the sheets as she fought for some semblance of control. Her body spasmed again and she surrendered herself to her own pleasure.

When the moment had subsided, she pushed herself up slightly, looking down into his eyes. She saw that look as a smug smile crept across his face.

"Oh my God," was all she managed to utter through her labored breathing.

He was still insider her and his hands continued to caress her.

"I'm glad you think so highly of me," Maguire said.

She laughed loudly before allowing her body to collapse back down on top of him.

"I'm not even going to argue that point with you," she said.

She was being honest.

Maguire ran his fingers playful down the center of her back, feeling her breath on his neck. Her long legs intertwined with his.

After a moment, he wrapped his arms around her and rolled her over and onto her back.

"What do you have up your sleeve now, cowboy?" she said half joking, wondering if she could survive anything more.

Her body ached in the most delightful way.

He was on top of her now, and she could feel him begin his rhythmic thrusts inside her again.

"Baby, I'm just getting started."

He lowered his lips to her chest and began teasing her playfully. She moaned loudly as his thrusts began to build in intensity, her hands violently gripping the sheets at her sides until her knuckles turned white

Melody's mind was racing wildly as she once again lost all control and submitted willingly to her desires. Something deep down inside of her wanted to protest, wanted him to stop. It wanted to convince him that she was not this kind of girl, but the truth was that she didn't even know who this girl was. In fact, she wasn't so sure that she was so much a girl as she was the incarnation of some inner animal that had suddenly become unleashed.

In the end her desires chased away any form of protest and she succumbed to her darkest desires. She reached up, digging her nails in his back, holding on to him tightly as she let him have his way with her.

Suddenly she felt him pull out of her. Her eyes opened wide as she was torn away from the fantasy that she was currently living in and she looked up at him. In that moment, it was readily apparent that whatever had previously been unlocked deep inside her had been awoken in him too.

She felt his hands on her hips as he physically rolled her over and then roughly grabbed her by her waist until she was up on all fours. He was incredibly strong and she moved effortless under his grip. He was behind her now, his hands gripping her hips tightly.

If it was not for the fact that she was so deeply aroused, she might have actually been afraid. Melody felt his hand slide along her back and a moment later felt her head pull backward as he gripped her by her hair.

This is insane, she thought.

Melody had long ago stopped worrying about whether she was being too loud or not. His rhythmic thrusting was turning her moans into deep primal screams as her body rocked back and forth. She physically ached and yet she was overwhelmed by an unquenchable desire for him. It wasn't as if she had lost all control as much as she had willingly surrendered it. He was taking her, but the reality was that she wanted to be taken by him.

He released her hair and gripped her hips firmly as he steadied himself. Melody buried her face into the pillows and held onto the bed tightly. She began to feel that growing sensation deep inside her and was shocked when she realized she was going to orgasm again.

Time stood still.

Melody's body was wracked by one erotic spasm after another. Her long blonde hair was matted and the sweat on her body glistened in the light of the moonlight streaming through the window. She felt physically spent and yet she craved more.

At the last moment he reached down, cupping her breasts roughly with both his hands and pulled her back hard against him. Her body lurched backward and she screamed wildly as he released himself inside her at the very moment her orgasm hit. She had lost track of them all by now.

Their bodies remained locked together in a moment of perfect sexual surrender, before they collapsed onto the bed.

They were covered in sweat and the small room was incredibly hot. The scent of their sex hung in the air. Neither moved, nor said a word, choosing to focus on catching their breath. The silence spoke volumes.

Melody felt his hand gently reach around her and pull her back against him. His lips were now on the back of her neck kissing her softly. She felt a chill down her body, like a bolt of electricity that both shocked her and left her feeling more alive than she had ever felt before in her life. She was exhausted, she was satisfied and, more importantly, she was sure that she felt something that she had never felt for another human being before.

Outside, the water continued to lap gently against the boat bringing her out of her reverie and back to the present moment. She felt a stinging sensation and realized that she had bitten her lip, as she relived the night's escapades.

Melody slid her body to the edge of the bed and sat up, resting there for a long moment. Her body physically ached. For a woman accustomed to working out hard, it was like nothing she had ever felt before.

She stood up and found her bra and panties and, with a little bit of effort, actually managed to put them on. She thought about the dress and shoes and gave up on that idea. She walked over to the closet and opened it.

The closet was divided into three parts. On the left side was an impressive array of suits. On the right were casual button down shirts along with a few polo's. In the center was a mirror that sat above a small chest of draws. Melody looked at her reflection and laughed out loud at the woman that looked back at her. At that moment she realized that she actually looked the way she felt.

As she searched through the shirts she found a faded long sleeve denim shirt. She took it down off the hanger and examined it closer. It had a strange looking design, a grey colored seal leaning against a globe, embroidered over the left pocket. That struck her as a bit odd. She hadn't taken him for an animal person. That being said, she was sure that she was going to learn a lot more about this man in time.

Melody slid the shirt on as she walked into the bathroom. She grabbed the lapels and brought the shirt up to her face and breathed in deeply to take in his scent.

After a somewhat failed attempt at fixing her hair, she gave up and made her way down the hallway to the kitchen where she rummaged around until she found a piece of paper and some tape.

She walked back down the hall where she picked up the dress and her purse. She looked through her purse until she found the lipstick container and wrote him a note. When she was done she taped it to the bathroom mirror. Afterward, she walked back into the bedroom and draped the dress casually across the bed.

It wasn't as if she felt he needed a reason to contact her, but maybe, in some subconscious way, she was marking her territory. It really wasn't her fault. She blamed it all on the *inner animal* that he had unleashed.

As much as she would have preferred to stay and have *him* for breakfast she had a flight to catch later for a pending business acquisition. Business never took a day off in her world; even when that day happened to fall on a weekend. Besides, at this rate, it would take her most of the morning to recover.

But, she thought, *if he played his cards right, she might be able to free up her evening for dinner and…….*

Melody let the thought trail off, grabbing her purse and heels, as she made her way out the back door and onto the deck. Her legs were wobbly and she was under no illusion as to the reason why. The water wasn't *that* rough today. She walked carefully up the dock and got into her car and started the engine. She sighed as she dropped it into reverse and backed up before turning the wheel over and driving out of the marina parking lot. She caught herself looking into the rearview mirror, watching as the boat fade from her sight.

CHAPTER EIGHT

Upstate New York
Saturday, April 28th, 2012 – 6:45 a.m.

Nearly four hundred miles away another woman awoke, but under much different circumstances.

Patricia Browning was lying on her back. She couldn't see; at least not clearly. As she struggled to come to terms with her present surroundings she began to feel a wave of panic begin to set in.

She could make out some type of diffused light through the edge of something, something that looked and felt like gauze.

That's right, gauze.... from a bandage, she thought. *My head must be wrapped up.*

Patricia slowly began to remember the details of the accident now. She'd been driving home from the gallery and had turned a bend in the road only to strike the deer that seemed trapped in the cars headlights.

Poor animal, she thought. She hoped it hadn't been hurt too badly.

In the background she could hear the low drone of medical equipment. The regular steady beat of a heart rate monitor, followed by another sound she tried to figure out, but couldn't. She was unable to talk; something was in her mouth obstructing her ability to speak. She assumed some type of tube. In the background she could hear the low muffled sound of voices, followed by the occasional ringing of a phone off in the distance.

Her mind was overcome with a mix of relief and confusion as she realized that she must be in the hospital. How bad were her injuries? She tried to move her hands, but realized that her arms were strapped down.

Her head hurt a bit as did her upper chest. Then she remembered seeing the deer hit the car's windshield, smashing it, followed by the air bag going off a moment later.

Patricia felt so groggy. Maybe they were just afraid she would wake up and try and remove the bandages.

She heard movement at the side of the bed.

"It's okay, Mrs. Browning," the man's voice said. "I'm Doctor Jones; I'm the head of Neurology. You were in a very serious car accident, but you are going to be just fine."

She felt a sense of relief wash over her and her body began to relax.

"I am going to give you something for the pain and something to help you sleep," he added. "Right now rest is the best thing you can do to help yourself."

She was tired. What had started out on such a wonderful high, with the gallery opening, had almost ended tragically. Patricia wondered if the wine would show up. She had been sure that she had not had much to drink, but what if she had?

It's a little too late to worry about that, she thought.

"I will send in a nurse with another blanket," she heard Dr. Jones say, "and I'll come by and check up on you in a little while."

After the man injected the propofol into the IV port in her left arm, he turned and walked out of the room, closing the door as he left.

They really ought to bottle this stuff for home use, she thought, as she listened to the melodic sounds of the medical equipment. She fought to try and figure out where she had heard the doctor's voice before. It sounded vaguely familiar and yet strange. Oh well, she'd speak to him when she was feeling better.

A moment later she began to feel very tired and she allowed herself to drift off to sleep, safe in the realization that she was being cared for by the attentive hospital staff.

It was of course all an elaborate illusion.

The bed had been purchased several months ago at an auction of old nursing home equipment. The man had considered it a bonus that it had an IV hanger already attached to it. He had paid for it in cash and hauled it off in his pickup.

Over the next few months he had gone to a variety of medical supply stores and pharmacies in three different states. There he had picked up all the medical items he would need to accomplish his goals.

The hardest part was gaining access to an adequate supply of the drugs he needed. He originally had planned on getting a job in a hospital as an orderly, but after conducting reconnaissance of a few hospitals, he decided that the amount of people that always seemed to be around would make it much too risky. He went and purchased an old laptop in a second hand store in Nashua, New Hampshire and spent a few days hanging out around upscale coffee shops plugging into their Wi-Fi service. Research was so much easier when no one knew you were doing it and, if they did find out, it was best that it wasn't your computer to begin with.

After a short period of time, he knew what he needed to do and he plotted out the exact route.

He headed back to New York, via Vermont, where he hit five veterinary clinics throughout the night. He spent only a few minutes in each, securing the propofol he needed. Before he left, he smashed most of the medication cabinets and in each of the waiting rooms he spray painted, in big neon orange lettering: *PUPPY KILLLERS*.

Local police would investigate for a few days, but as quick as it started it would end. With no new incidents and no leads, the case would eventually go cold. They chalked it up to some violent fraction of a liberal animal rights activist group.

It was after all Vermont.

The medical equipment, or at least the sounds, came courtesy of the internet. With a little ingenuity he was able to overlay bits and pieces of sound bites from which he made a track. From there he created a CD which he put in a player behind the bed and set it on repeat. If it wasn't exactly perfect, she would never know thanks to the medication. He made a second CD of voices and ringing phones that he played just outside the room.

The harder part was actually figuring out how to disguise his voice. Ultimately this was accomplished with the help of a reasonably inexpensive computer program. He knew that she wouldn't be able to talk back to him so he just recorded a series of statements. Once again even if it was imperfect, like the other sound tracks, it would still accomplish the task at hand.

The man sat down in the chair in the next room and rubbed his weary eyes. This was the hardest part for him, waiting for the next move in the game. Unfortunately, for him at least, the next move wasn't his to make. While it was hard for him to accept, it was a necessary evil. After months of grueling preparation he needed to rest, especially before things moved to the next level.

He reached over and grabbed the cigarettes off the table. He took one from the pack, lit it and took a long drag, as he stared back at the room. For now, he set his mind to babysitting the woman in the other room.

CHAPTER NINE

Southampton, Suffolk County, N.Y.
Saturday, April 28th, 2012 – 6:50 a.m.

The ride home took Melody back along the route they had navigated just a few short hours before; as she gave chase to the tail lights of the Mustang. As she continued her drive through Southampton, she passed Peter Bart's house and made a mental note to send a card to thank him for hosting such a *wonderful* party; along with a considerable check for his charity. It only seemed appropriate under the circumstances.

Her thoughts drifted back to the party and she couldn't help but recall how easy going their conversation had been. It was all so refreshing.

Her rise in the financial world had long ago introduced her to the quaint world of self-aggrandizing and pretentious communication. Everyone wanted you to know who they were and, even more importantly, who they knew. They spent half their time talking to one person, all while scanning the room to see if there was anyone else they *needed* to speak to as well. It was a game everyone knew how to play quite well and yet he seemingly played by a different set of rules.

Their conversation seemed to cover the whole gamut. They talked about traveling and compared notes on the places they had in common and shared their insight on places new to the other. For as well traveled as she was, he seemed to have gotten around quite a bit also. They touched on politics and she was surprised at how knowledgeable he was, not only on global events, but on the actual people behind the scenes. They even agreed to disagree on where to get the best pizza; with him promising to *broaden her horizons*.

He also introduced her to a *Kamikaze*, a mix of vodka, triple sec and lime juice. She found that she really liked it; probably a little too much. They talked about everything, everyone and nothing. He had a great sense of humor with just a *tinge* of sarcasm.

She was taken aback by the fact that he seemed very at ease with himself, as well as his surroundings. It was a trait she had often observed in men of power and position. Yet, unlike the vast majority of them, he was extremely down to earth.

Three hours later she knew that his name was James, although he said that most people that didn't know him called him Jim. She also learned that a much smaller group called him Paddy, which had less to do with his middle name and more to do with the fact that he was Irish. While the party around them had raged on, the two of them were completely lost in their own little world. More than a few people had probably thought about interjecting themselves into the conversation, but it only took a second to realize that they had hung up the proverbial *do not disturb* sign.

The one thing she still had no clue about was what he did for a living or if he did anything for that matter. She had probed, asking what had brought him to the party, but he only divulged that he and Peter were friends and that he had done some work for him in the past. However, what that work actually entailed she still did not know. In a way, it added to the *mystery* and made him even more attractive, if that was even possible.

And yet, what truly struck a chord deep down inside of her was the fact that, in a room full of people who were more than willing to tell you all about themselves, he was actually interested in just listening to her. Even more important, it had nothing to do with who she was professionally.

Just before the road ended, she turned off to the left and pressed a button on the touch screen navigation console in the center of the dashboard. In front of her the wrought iron gates opened wide and she pulled the car forward and up the long driveway. There actually were three entrances onto the property, but this was her private one.

As she made her way up the drive she passed the outdoor pool and tennis courts on the left hand side, slightly amused by the fact that she never actually used them. On her right was a perfectly manicured garden which featured a large pond in the center with a nearly one and a half story high statue of Neptune, the Roman god of water, in the middle of it. It would have been very easy to consider it an ostentatious display, even for Southampton, but the truth was that the piece held special meaning to her as she had always held a deep and abiding appreciation for the water.

The road she was on led to the main house, which you could only access by passing through a large stone structure called the gatehouse, named as such because it had a gated, arched opening in the center. This gate was synched to open with the one on the main road that she had just passed through.

The entire structure itself actually mimicked a medieval castle in construction. At the very center was a courtyard that was walled on three sides. They made for a formidable first impression to visitors. Melody pulled the car through the gatehouse and into the large square courtyard, turning toward the left where there was a series of wooden garage doors.

Each of her cars was equipped with individual transmitters that activated a specific door. This car, being her favorite, opened the one that was closest to the house.

The main house was situated on the back of the courtyard, the fourth wall as it was, and positioned exactly opposite from the gatehouse entrance. The house itself was three stories high and while the front had a traditional flat stone façade, the back was curved in the general shape of an amphitheater.

Visitors walking through the front door were met with a grand entryway with a staircase that looked as though it had been taken from the pages of a fairy tale. On either side of the staircase were entryways that led to the rear of the first floor, or the salon as they called it. This room featured floor to ceiling windows and, as a result of the curvature of the walls, provided an almost 180 degree panoramic view of not only the Atlantic Ocean, but of the Shinnecock Bay as well.

On the second floor, a gentle alarm sounded inside the office of Genevieve Gordon, alerting her to the fact that her boss had *finally* arrived home. She looked down at her watch and sighed. This was so completely unlike Melody that she had actually started to get concerned.

She got up from the desk and made her way from her office, down the long hallway and took the private elevator down to the first floor where it opened immediately adjacent to the garage door.

Genevieve stepped out of the elevator, just as the garage door opened, and let out an audible gasp.

"Oh stop it," Melody said, "I don't look that bad."

"I beg to differ, my love, have you even looked in a mirror?" Gen replied sarcastically.

The two women had known each other since their freshman days at the Wharton School of Business. From the very beginning they had become fast friends and had remained inseparable throughout school.

The two of them had made quite the impression in Philadelphia's social scene. Both women were attractive and enjoyed the attention they received whenever they went out. Where Melody Anderson was tall and blonde, Genevieve Gordon was about six inches shorter with shoulder length light auburn hair and bright green eyes.

Their friendship had resulted in the two women being interchangeably referred to as "GenMel" by their fellow classmates. Many of their peers were not quite sure as to just how close their friendship actually was. The truth was much more benign, they weren't *that* close. However, both women shared a mutually twisted sense of humor and enjoyed playing with the minds of their classmates. Besides, it was college they reasoned and it was supposed to be fun.

But as close as the two were on a personal level, they were polar opposites when it came to business. Where Genevieve was the consummate conservative business woman, Melody was the consummate risk taker. Genevieve succeeded by studious work and perseverance, Melody did so by sheer force of her will. That wasn't to say Melody didn't work hard, it's just that it seemed to come much easier to her. In many respects she was like a professional athlete who had a natural genetic predisposition. Where most people had to study laboriously to find the answers, for Melody Anderson those same answers jumped off the page at her.

The fact that she was wildly successful only served to irritate those who lacked her natural talents, but Genevieve Gordon had long ago decided that being attached to Melody Anderson's coattails was not necessarily a bad place to be and, as a result, she now earned half a million dollars a year doing it.

Gen followed Melody down the hallway and into the salon where she watched her collapse into one of the leather couches.

"First of all, where the hell have you been and what in God's name are you wearing?" Gen asked, in an almost horrified tone, as she took a seat on the couch opposite from Mel.

Melody sat there on the couch like a school girl, arms wrapped around her knees, pulling them close to her chest. If Genevieve didn't know better, she would have sworn she was drunk.

"Oh my God," blurted out Melody, almost breathlessly. "I met the most amazing man at Peter's party last night."

Gen had originally planned on going, but she had a migraine and bowed out at the last minute. Still, no one at Peter's parties was exactly what she would have called Melody's *type*. In fact, in the decade that the two women had known each other Genevieve couldn't actually say what that type was. It was as elusive as anything she knew. The last time Melody had gone out on an actual date, she had been home before the prime time shows had even started. She had grown accustomed to the fact that the only real relationship that Melody had was with her work.

To say that her curiosity was piqued would have been a gross understatement. She looked at her watch and realized that they had a little time before she needed to herd her friend off to the shower to prepare for this afternoons trip.

She reached over, picking up the house phone and pressed one of the buttons. She waited patiently until one of the kitchen staff answered.

"Can you please bring some coffee to the salon," Gen said and then hung up the phone.

"OK, Mel, dish."

A half hour later Gen sat there, her mouth open and, to be honest, more than a little bit aroused. As hard as the story was to believe, Melody was not the type of person to exaggerate about anything.

"So where does this *Prince Charming* live?" she asked.

Melody put her coffee cup down on the end table and got up She strutted over to the windows and pointed off in the distance.

"There!" she said declaratively. "He lives right over there."

Gen got up and walked over to where her boss stood, gazing out across Shinnecock Bay.

"The Coast Guard Station?" she said, even more confused.

"No," said Melody, grabbing her friends hand and moving it a few inches over to the left in the general direction of the Marina. "Over there!"

Genevieve looked out in the direction her friend held her hand and then looked back at Melody.

"Oh dear Lord, Mel," said Gen. "The man lives on a boat?"

"Uh huh," was all that she said, a mischievous smile on her face.

Gen looked at the shirt her friend was wearing, seeing the animal embroidered on it.

"Oh crap, please don't tell me he's one of those crazy animal lovers too," she managed to say in an exasperated tone.

Immediately she had visions of PETA picketing the front of the house.

"I don't know," Melody replied. "Guess I'll find out after the second date."

Gen groaned as she grabbed her friends hand, leading her out of the salon and back toward the elevator.

It was already late in the morning and someone had to take charge. They rode up in silence, Melody smirking as she imagined the thoughts going through her friends mind.

CHAPTER TEN

Ponquoque Beach, Suffolk County, N.Y.
Saturday, April 28th, 2012 – 8:39 a.m.

Maguire finished the last of his morning phone calls. He had managed to postpone the majority of the meetings that had been scheduled for this upcoming week until the following one. Most of the clients were accommodating, especially under the circumstances. The other factor was that Maguire always came highly recommended. A *consummate professional* was the general opinion and if it was one thing people in this industry appreciated, it was professionalism. In fact, they would pay extremely well for it and would certainly be accommodating when the circumstances necessitated.

When the business calls were finished he grabbed his cell phone and dialed the number written on the piece of paper. After a few rings it went to her voice mail.

"Mel, hi it's James. Listen I just wanted to call and say I really enjoyed our evening," he said. "I was going to ask if you were free for dinner tonight, but something has come up and I have to go out of town for a few days. I'll call as soon as I get a chance and hopefully we can get together for dinner or something when I return."

He pressed the end button, hoping that it didn't sound as lame to her as it did to him.

Maguire picked up the phone again and selected a number from the speed dial list. It only rang one time.

"So, is it true?" the voice on the other end asked immediately.

"Peter, why do you always ask a question for which you already know the answer?"

"So, it is true," Peter Bart replied, his voice feigning shock. "Do you have any idea how many men you have potentially pissed off? Now that I think of it, there are probably a number of women on that list as well."

"Are you done?"

"For now," Peter chuckled.

"OK, Listen, this is serious. Did you watch the news this morning?"

"Yes I did, why?"

"Did you hear the report about that missing woman from upstate?"

"Yeah, the one in the car accident, right?" Bart asked. "She hit an animal or something?"

"That's right. Well I know her or at least I did a million or so years ago," explained James. "I'm planning on going up and try to help look for her."

"Anything I can do to help?" Peter asked, his tone becoming serious.

"No. Yes, actually, I tried calling Melody to let her know I was going out of town for a few days. I didn't want her to think I was skipping out on her or anything, but I just got her voicemail and you know how shoddy reception is up in the mountains," he added.

He knew that last line would strike a chord with Peter. He had listened to him bitch for a month about getting hosed out of a million dollar stock deal because they couldn't reach him while he was on vacation in the Bavarian Alps.

"When I speak to her, I will let her know," said Peter accommodatingly. "Should I add how you professed to me your undying love for her and how every moment apart is like a knife in your heart?"

"Depends on how good you think Gregor really is," said James as he ended the call.

On the other end, Peter laughed hysterically as he laid the cell phone down on his desk.

It had been a long standing joke between the two of them. Peter had tried bribing, pleading and even cajoling Maguire into taking over as the head of his personal security. In the end, James Maguire was the first man Bart had found that he couldn't buy.

James got up and walked out of the office and headed back down to the bedroom; knowing what he needed to do next.

One of the main differences between the sexes can best be summed up in the amount of time it takes for each to pack a *weekend* getaway bag.

Women will generally spend an inordinate amount of time pulling out various outfits, ensuring that the tops and bottoms match perfectly. They will then, most likely, spend an equal amount of time making sure that they have enough outfits for both daytime and evening use without ever using the same item twice, if at all possible. After that they must decide on what shoes and accessories to match up with each outfit. Finally, bras and panties will be tossed into the mix. Even these will sometimes play an integral part of the selection process depending on whether it is a strapless top that is being taken along.

If they are going to a warm climate, with a beach or pool, they will also have to make sure that they have bathing suits. This is followed by a dilemma as to whether they should bring a one piece or a bikini, along with what kind of wrap they should select for when they are out of the water.

Once the clothing selection part of the packing process is completed, inevitably their attention turns to makeup, hair products, creams, lotions and other female necessities.

The entire process can seem like it takes hours, or even days, and in truth it often does.

Maguire walked over to the closet and grabbed the black over-night bag from the top shelf. He tossed it onto the bed and proceeded to put in four days' worth of underwear and socks, as well as an appropriate number of tee's and polo shirts along with an extra set of cargo pants. At the last minute he tossed in a casual button down shirt, along with a fleece pullover, just in case. He planned on being there no more than three days, so the fourth set was his emergency *back-up*. When he was done, he clipped a ball cap to one of the straps.

He then went into the bathroom and grabbed the small travel bag out of the vanity drawer that he habitually kept prepared. The last thing he wanted to do when he was running out the door was to have to search for stuff. The travel bag held all his toiletries, shaving cream, razor, deodorant, toothbrush, toothpaste, cologne, etc. Everything a busy professional could possibly require on a moment's notice.

Returning to the bedroom he put the travel bag into the larger one and zipped it up.

That completed the male routine of getting all of the *non-essentials* out of the way.

Returning to the closet he reached down and grabbed the *other* black bag from the back of the closet. For Maguire, and others in his trade, this was the real *essential* travel bag.

The bag was about three feet long and rectangular in shape. It was constructed of the same rip-stop material as the overnight bag and featured two carry handles on top. On the front were three large pouches that were attached to a *molle* webbing system. The interior featured two zippered compartments. The main compartment was the entire length of the bag and featured a padded divider, the other about two-thirds the length held several custom fit compartments.

He laid it on the bed and began to take an inventory. While this was completely unnecessary, it was more a force of habit.

The bag was always prepared. If anything had been used, he would have known and replaced it immediately upon his return, but old habits die hard. In truth, this bag could mean the difference between life and death, so due diligence was always taken to ensure that everything was as it should be.

Inside the main compartment was a military style Colt M-4. For the most part it was an exact mechanical copy of the weapon he had carried while in the Navy, just updated with some personal modifications and newer optics.

The traditional stock had been replaced with a Magpul UBR stock. The top rail was outfitted with a Trijicon ACOG 4x sight, along with a laser sight and an AN/PEQ2 infrared sight that worked with night vision systems. Additionally, it had a front grip with a Surefire lighting system. A silencer was strapped off to the side in the bag, should the need for such an item arise.

On the other side of the divider was a Heckler & Koch 53A3 that he kept as his backup rifle. It was a modified version of the original German G3 battle rifle. It featured an Aimpoint CompM2 sight along with a replacement front stock that featured an integral Surefire light system built into it.

What Maguire liked most was that both guns utilized the same .223 caliber round, so he didn't have to carry two different types of ammo. Beyond that, he reasoned, if he needed something bigger he was at the wrong party.

In the larger inner pocket were two hand guns. The first was a Sig Sauer P226, a holdover from his days in the teams. He just liked the feel of it and after all those years it just settled into his hand the right way, every time. In addition, he carried a Glock 17 as a backup. Again, both guns used the same .9mm cartridge so it kept the duplication down to a minimum. Both weapons had built-in rail systems which he used to mount lighting attachments. Secured in the inner pockets where three extra magazines for both weapons and a sheathed Mark 3, Mod 0 U.S. Navy diving knife.

Two of the three front assault pouches contained extra magazines for the rifles. A third contained a field expedient medical aid kit. Because sometimes things didn't always go exactly as you planned, especially when you found yourself at the aforementioned wrong party.

He removed each weapon from their enclosure and conducted a weapons function check. It was a drill he had practiced thousands of times before. After each check, he loaded a magazine, chambered a round, and top loaded the magazine. Afterward, he secured each weapon back in its spot with the Velcro straps. Once they were strapped back in, he mentally knew the weapons were hot.

After the weapons check was complete, he zipped up the bag and stared at the small subdued green patch on the front. In the center it featured the image of a *skeletonized* frog holding a spear. On the top were the initials ST on one side and the number 4 on the other. At the bottom, written in black, was the lettering *Mal Ad Osteo*. He smiled inwardly. Some things you couldn't get rid of.

To the casual observer it might have seemed unusual to bring along such items on what was seemingly a search and rescue scenario. However, to those in his line of work, more often than not, things generally didn't turn out to be what they seemed. Besides, it was better to have all the tools and not need them, then to need them and find that you were *shit out of luck*.

He took the bags and set them outside the bedroom door. He did a quick sweep of the boat, checking to make sure everything was turned off, secured and where it should be. He then grabbed the bags and walked out onto the back deck. He set them down and turned back toward the door. He reached down and grabbed a hold of a monofilament line that had a small pin attached to the end. It hung down from the door a few inches from the floor. As he closed the door he inserted the pin into the hidden latch, a spring attached to the line would pull the filament taut against the door. When he got back, he would immediately know if anyone had attempted to gain entry into the boat.

When he was finished locking the house boat up, he made his way up the dock and loaded the bags into the trunk of the Mustang. The he got in, started up the car, and sat there for a moment, thinking to himself. It had been over two decades since he had been in Perrysville. He wondered what he was going to find and whether he was doing the right thing. He pushed the thoughts away and dropped the car into drive.

CHAPTER ELEVEN

Southampton, Suffolk County, N.Y.
Saturday, April 28th, 2012 – 9:13 a.m.

The third floor of the house was Melody's private world. Technically it was only accessible via the elevator they had just ridden up in. The only people that had the access code for this floor, besides Melody, were Genevieve and Melody's personal housekeeper, Sandy.

The two women stepped off the elevator and proceeded down the long center hallway that ran the entire length of the third floor. On the right side was an ornate railing that provided views of both the heavy wooden beams of the vaulted ceiling above them as well as the majestic tile work of the first floor foyer below, which when viewed from this vantage point depicted an ornate Celtic knot design. Along the wall on the left side, midway down the hallway, was a single door that was accessed through a biometric lock

As they walked down the hallway Gen broke the silence.

"We're running out of time, Mel, and we still have a ton of stuff to go over," Gen said. "So please get your ass in the shower and do try to scrub him off of you while I find something for you to wear."

Melody noted the dripping sarcasm in her friend's voice and decided to have some fun with her. She quickened her pace so that she was several steps in front of her friend.

"Oh I will, dear," she replied. "And I'll be sure to start from the inside."

She reached the door and slid her finger onto the pad, hearing the click of the lock as the door opened. She looked back over her shoulder at her friend and smiled mischievously as she entered the room.

Walking into the third floor suite was like stepping into a different world. The first impression was its overall size. It encompassed the entire third floor and was the only area of the house that Melody had allowed herself to indulge her personal desires. The entire floor plan was one large open design and mimicked a chalet style that would have been quite at home in the Alps. In fact it was a visit to Switzerland that had left a lasting mark on her. When it came time to design her personal living space, she wanted to replicate a room that she could walk into and get lost.

As she stepped into the room, motion activated lights came on to their preset levels. The room was kept at a steady temperature. She enjoyed the sensation of being in the mountains, even when it was a hundred plus degrees outside. She walked down the short hallway, unbuttoning the shirt as she went along. As she entered into the main room she tossed the shirt in the direction of the bed and turned left, heading for the shower.

Gen let out an exasperated sigh, as she stopped and picked up the shirt which had missed its mark and landed on the floor. She turned right and headed toward the closet listening to her friend's amused chuckling fade behind her.

The walls of the suite were clad in split Norway pine logs meant to replicate the look of a log cabin. The ceiling peaked at fifteen feet and featured ten exposed log trusses. The flooring was constructed of clear pine, with large area rugs spread throughout.

While the room was an open design, it was subtly divided into three distinct areas with the help of two large, rough cut stone dividers that were spaced evenly in the room. Each divider featured a natural gas fireplace. On the left of one of the dividers was the *en suite* bathroom and to the right of the other divider was Melody's office.

In the center of the room was the bedroom area which featured a king size sleigh bed that was fashioned out of cherry wood and wrought iron detailing. The bed faced out toward the exterior wall. Immediately behind the bed was a twelve foot wide privacy wall constructed from pine logs. This prevented the actual bed from being seen by anyone who first walked into the suite.

Melody walked over to the shower and pressed a button on the central control panel and continued to get undressed. The shower itself was fifteen feet long and eight feet wide and the epitome of luxurious decadence. It featured three large overhead shower heads, which created a rain forest effect, and the walls were lined with adjustable pressurized jets that could be angled to hit the right muscle groups. Everything was controlled from the electronic panel that could be switched from constant on, to pulsating, to any of a hundred other different combinations.

In addition, the shower was also equipped with a sauna system. On the long interior wall was a granite topped bench that ran the entire length of the shower. The bench was wider on one end, and featured a curved seat carved into the stone that allowed her to lie down and enjoy the heat of the sauna. It was the perfect place to chase away the stress and strains of the daily grind.

After she had removed her bra and panties Melody stepped into the shower. She stood there, feeling the hot water cascading down over her body. She occasionally turned around to the various nozzles, feeling them kneading her aching muscles. Her mind was in over drive as she once again relived select moments of the last dozen or so hours. She wondered why this man was having such an effect on her.

She readily admitted that he was extremely handsome, but she had been around physically attractive men in the past and they had never affected her to this extent. There was something more to this man, something that she could not quantify. He exuded confidence and power, not based upon his station in life, but naturally so, as if he had born with it. Yet, at the same time, he was completely unpretentious. It was infuriating and she finally gave up trying to figure it out.

After a while she reluctantly called an end to the shower session. She turned off the water and reached out to grab a towel from the heated rack.

As she dried herself off, she was actually amazed at how sore she was. She made a mental note to get down to the gym and do some extra cardio. Melody wrapped the towel around her head and put on one of the oversized cotton robes before heading out of the bathroom.

She walked across the room, past the other room divider, and into her office. The area itself was sparsely furnished and matched the overall rustic feel of the rest of the room. She took a seat behind her desk, facing the ornate guest chairs that were rarely used by anyone other than Gen. Behind the desk was a pocket door, which provided access to a walk in closet and on the other side, was a concealed door within the wall which led to a private staircase. The staircase had originally been installed to provide an emergency exit in the event the elevator could not be used. It allowed egress via another, equally concealed, door inside Genevieve's 2nd floor office. However, at the last moment, a modification was made and the stairs were continued down to a safe room in the basement.

Gen walked out of the closest carrying two outfits with her and walked toward the desk. She held them up for her friend's approval.

"I don't want to go," Melody said melodramatically, turning slowly in her chair.

"Seriously?" Genevieve asked. "Are we actually going to have this conversation?"

"Ugh," she said, as she hung her head down and spun around in the chair.

Genevieve sat down in one of the chairs.

"What the hell?" said Gen. "This is so unlike you. I have never known you to put anyone or anything above business. "

Mel leaned back in the chair and stared up at the ceiling.

"I know, I know," she replied. "I wish I could explain it, but I can't."

Gen looked at her and was both sad for her and yet, at the same time, quite jealous. She wondered what kind of person could have had the capacity to affect her friend this way.

"Listen, chicky, you need to get your head out of his bed and back into the game here," she said. "We're not talking about a bullshit deal here; this is a major acquisition. If not for your bottom line, then think of all those poor working class bastards that are counting on you to make sure they have presents under the tree this Christmas."

"OK, OK, I get it, Gen," Mel replied. "Sheesh, you missed your calling. You should have been a motivational speaker."

Melody got up and walked into the closet, selecting a matching white lace bra and panty set. She put them on and walked back out into the office.

Gen stood up and grabbed her friend by the shoulders, looking her in the eyes.

"I love you, Mel, and that means making sure that whatever stupid thoughts you have rolling around in that head right now doesn't interfere with your judgment."

Mel kissed her friend on the cheek. "I know and you're right; now isn't the time."

She looked down at the two outfits and grabbed the blue pinstriped business suit.

"This is perfect. Just grab me a white blouse and the blue Ferragamo's."

She reached down and hit a button on the desk.

Both ends of the exterior wall were constructed of wood logs, but the center portion was constructed of floor to ceiling, electro-chromic glass panels. The panels themselves were translucent right now, a result of an electric charge that altered their level of opacity. When switched off the glass became transparent and offered the most amazing view of the oceans.

The button she had depressed caused the glass panels to be opened electronically. As she watched, they slid on rails until they disappeared into the wood encased walls on either side.

Melody stepped out onto the curved balcony, which ran the entire length of the back of the house, and took a deep breath of fresh air as she tried to clear her mind. It was cool outside and she felt her skin tingle. As much as she loved the interior, there was a part of her that lived for the ocean.

She would often find herself sitting out here alone, looking out as the waves crashed onto the shoreline below. She marveled at the power and majesty. It made her feel small, like a child, and she found some strange level of comfort in that.

Despite her current position, her life had not always been an easy one. She had grown up in the Richmond Hill section of Queens in an otherwise unremarkable middle class neighborhood. It was a place where people were born and raised and then, ultimately, worked and died. Even so, there were very distinct differences in the *middle income* spectrum and, if truth be told, she had grown up on the losing end.

Melody was the oldest of three children, born to an alcoholic father and a disconnected mother. She had spent the formative years of her life struggling to come to terms with who she was. Despite her grim prospects Melody had decided that she was going to be different; that she was going to change the course of her life. In her freshman year of high school something had clicked inside her and she closed the door of the past and set out to reinvent herself. She was determined to leave the hardscrabble existence she was born into and make her own way in the world and, if necessary, she would do it by sheer will alone.

She became a voracious reader of any economic and business book she could get her hands on. While her friends were going out on dates to concerts or the movies, Melody was spending her nights at the local library devouring everything she could read on the subject. By her junior year she was arguing economic theories with her teachers. Even more importantly she was winning the majority of them.

It was also during her junior year that she had gotten her first job and her first taste of financial freedom. It was the late nineties and she caught the tail end of the tech bubble. With the help of a relative she had begun investing and found that she had an inherent knack for it. She embraced it with the same zeal that others reserved for fantasy baseball. What had started off as a part time hobby soon turned into a full time passion.

By her senior year she had distinguished herself as an economic powerhouse. Her GPA, coupled with stellar recommendations from some of her high school teachers, aided her greatly in obtaining significant scholarship offers.

It was, however, during this period of time that she had managed to clash with one particular faculty member, Professor William Oswald Thomas, whom she earnestly believed would stop at nothing to sabotage her academic future. It was this belief that had caused her to stand her ground against him at all cost. If she was going to fail she would do it in battle and not in submission.

Professor Thomas was a miserable wretch of a man and she had loathed his class from almost the very first day. He was condescending, arrogant and worst of all, in her eyes at least, simply wrong. The two bickered incessantly; at times to the complete exclusion of the rest of the class which sat in silence watching the two of them square off like some modern-age economic gladiators. It was not uncommon for the bell to ring and the class to depart, leaving just the two of them arguing about some theoretical model.

Every day of her senior year was a horror for her as the time drew closer for his class. Her grades were outstanding, but every paper it seemed was sent back to her with some type of disparaging comments; comments which only served to further fuel the fire that already burned deep inside her.

Early one March morning she had been sitting in her home room class when a secretary's assistant came in and handed her a note. She opened it and read the words:

To: Melody Anderson

From: Professor Thomas

Meeting in my office at 3:30 p.m. Do not be late.

The fire inside her smoldered and she fumed as the day progressed. She had, in effect, had enough. If Professor Thomas thought she was an easy target then he was sadly mistaken and she was prepared to give him both barrels.

At three o'clock she walked out of the school and sat on the back steps.

What an insolent little prick, she thought.

It was a typical Thomas' move, making her wait a half hour of her time, just to find out what the little megalomaniac wanted to argue about this time.

By three twenty-five she had just about worked herself up into a veritable frenzy. She stormed back into the school and headed straight to his office. She paused for a moment in an effort to gain her composure and knocked on his door with purpose.

"Enter," she heard from the other side.

She opened the door and stepped in, biting her lip to contain her anger.

"Sit down, Ms. Anderson," he said, pointing at a chair in front of the desk. He never even bothered to look up from the papers that held his attention.

Long before William Oswald Thomas had made his mark in the academic world he had made his name in another one. He had come to academia from the business world where he had earned the moniker 'Wild Bill' from friend and foe alike. He was a brilliant economist who had been sought out by President Ronald Reagan early in his presidency to help get the country back on track.

Back in those days, he was considered to be a rock star in the business world. A word from him, either way, could mean the difference between a company's success or its dismal failure. Political and business leaders alike sought out his counsel and such counsel came at a steep price.

And then one day, without any warning, he simply walked away and faded into academic obscurity. Rumors swirled about, but every one of them was simply an uneducated guess. Despite his well-documented professional career, he was always something of an enigma when it came to his personal life. William Thomas didn't make it any easier as he made a habit of never responding to any personal questions.

The truth was not quite so cryptic. In the end, he had simply grown tired and had lost the fire. That was, until now.

He looked up at the young woman who sat opposite him and stared at her for a moment, their eyes locking onto each other like two legendary foes that, while physically weary from battle, refused to mentally give up an inch of ground.

To Thomas the young woman was insolent, brash, and arrogant. For her part, Melody eyed him with utter disdain.

She sat waiting for the opportunity to unleash her fury.

To hell with the future, she thought. She was not going to lose this battle.

As she stared at this pompous jackass Melody saw something she would never have thought possible. He actually smiled at her.

Oh my God, she thought. It was worse than she had even imagined.

For a moment she felt her heart sink. There was only one reason for that kind of response; he knew something that was going to effectively end her future. Despair gripped her mind. It wasn't because of the possibility that she could lose, that she could accept, but what truly frightened her was the possibility that she could lose without a fight.

What was it that he knew? She wondered.

"Ms. Anderson," he began. "I have spent the better part of forty-five years of my life pursuing economics. I have come full circle, at first in the academic world being instructed by professors who influenced my life; then into the business world, and finally back in academia. I had hoped that by coming back to the academic world I would be able to influence other young lives. It has been my passion, my very life."

"When the school year started I imagined, as I have done every year that I have been teaching, that I could impact the young men and women in my course. Throughout my career I have always felt that the majority of the students who have passed through my class have left better then when they arrived. However, from almost the very first day of this school year, I was faced with one particular student that has been the bane of my academic existence."

His lips pressed tightly against one another, his jaw clenching tightly, as if to drive home the point.

He paused a moment longer before continuing.

"You have been argumentative from the very beginning, choosing to believe your wildly speculative opinions over the tried and true theories of world class economists, myself included," he sneered. "In truth I cannot ever remember meeting someone who held themselves in such high esteem, who placed so much into their own opinions, even at the lowliest rungs of the corporate ladder. And yet here you are, daring to match wits with someone who is clearly not your equal young lady."

The last part stung her heart like salt in a gaping wound.

Melody started to respond, but he commanded her silence with a single upright finger. Immediately she felt her face flush as anger welled up deep inside her.

"I have devoted my entire life to the pursuit of economics. I have done so at the peril of my personal life, preferring to pursue the professional one to the fullest extent possible," he continued.

"To those of us who understand it, the financial realm is a religion unto itself. Despite all the personal sacrifices I have made, I remain its devout acolyte."

And then something changed.

William Thomas removed his glasses and set them down in front of him. As he stared across the desk at her, Melody watched as his entire demeanor changed.

"Ten years ago I walked away from it all. I had made my way, often by sheer force of will, and I had succeeded in changing the very nature of the way the game was played. At the pinnacle, at the very height of my success, I decided to walk away and teach. Perhaps it was a poor choice, but it was the one I chose."

He stood up and walked over to the window and stared down at the kids, playing in the street below, who were oblivious to the life altering conversation that was occurring just two stories above them.

"At the beginning of the school year I sat, as I have done every year before, and played mindless head games with you students. And just like every other year I have been met with the same doe-eyed stares that have made me truly question whether or not my choice to go into academia was the prudent one."

He turned around to face her again.

"And then came you, Ms. Anderson."

Melody sat there completely confused. Her arch nemesis had somehow transformed himself into something resembling a human being. Worse yet, she could feel the fight slipping from her body, betraying her at the point she needed it most and it confused her. At that very moment, she didn't know what she was supposed to be feeling.

Professor Thomas walked back to his desk and sat down in the chair. He saw the quizzical look in her eyes.

"Confusing isn't it?" he said.

"Uhm, yeah, just a bit," she replied.

"Don't be," he replied. "I promise that it will all make sense soon enough. You see, I have been waiting for you."

"I don't understand," she blurted out and she really didn't.

"You don't play by the rules Ms. Anderson," he responded. "In a world that sees its students driven by theories, graphs, charts, models, and laws; you push back. More simply put, you are the one student I have been waiting for all my life."

"Now I really don't understand," she replied. "You hate me."

"Hate you?" Thomas laughed, "Oh, my dear Ms. Anderson, that couldn't be further from the truth."

"Yes, I have been hard on you for the simple fact that I had to verify, for myself, that what I saw in you was actually real," he said. "I was concerned that after all this time that I had spent searching, that I was *settling* rather than finding the true student of economics. So I pushed you, and when I thought I had pushed you as far as I could I pushed even harder. Each time, I saw you respond to every single argument. You never let up, even when confronted by an authoritative figure, by someone who had literally written the book. It was then that I knew that I had found the one student in a million."

"Ok," she asked. "So why exactly am I here?"

"I'm glad you asked, Ms. Anderson," Thomas said. "For the past few months I have been talking with a former colleague in the business world and sharing with him my observations of your capabilities. That colleague is also a senior faculty member at Wharton. Based upon my recommendations they are prepared to give you a full scholarship, Ms. Anderson."

Melody gasped.

The full weight of what he was saying hitting her like the proverbial ton of bricks. Till this point she was just happy that she would be able to attend a community college. What she was being offered right now was the chance of a lifetime and she was completely at a loss of words.

Professor Thomas laughed a warm, hearty laugh.

"Shall I take that as a yes?" he asked.

"I really don't know what to say," she replied. "I came in here hating you and now you're offering me the opportunity of a lifetime."

"Don't lose that edge, Ms. Anderson. You will find in the business world that most people who evoke that feeling deserve it. Most will use you until there is nothing left and then discard you like yesterday's trash," said Thomas. "However, if you say yes to my offer, there is still a lot of work to do."

"Yes," she blurted out without any hesitation.

In that very moment Melody Anderson's world had changed forever.

For the next three months she spent every day after school learning from her former nemesis. Their relationship was still stubborn, but each day revealed more common ground and an ever deepening respect for one another.

In June of that year, she graduated *Sum Cum Laude*. Neither her father, nor her mother, was in attendance. When her name was called Professor William Oswald Thomas stood up on the dais and clapped.

As the graduating class broke up, each student leaving the school for the last time, he sought her out.

The former student and professor hugged each other and they were both aware that each other was crying.

William Thomas had no children; Melody Anderson had no relationship with her parents.

Thomas pulled back, holding her by the shoulders and stared approvingly at Melody.

"Ms. Anderson," he said. "I have never had a student who simultaneously brought me so much consternation and yet so much joy, as you have. If I ever had a child, I could only hope that they would live up to the standard you have set."

"Professor Thomas. You're stubborn, opinionated and on occasion quite simply wrong," Melody said, as a smile slowly crept across her face. "That being said, over the last several months you have been more of a father to me than the person who has held that spot in my life for the last seventeen years."

A classmate of Melody's stopped for a moment and took a picture of the two of them.

And then it was over.

In September Melody started her academic career at Wharton and William Thomas continued his with the latest senior class.

They emailed each other daily, Melody coming to rely on him to reassure her that she had truly earned her place at the school. No holiday or birthday passed without a card. The previous Thanksgiving he had made the trip out to the school and she had treated him to a traditional KFC Chicken dinner.

In the end, Melody had truly become the child he never had.

On a warm spring day, in her junior year, she was unexpectedly summoned from her classroom to the Dean of Admissions office.

"Ms. Anderson, please sit down," Dean Miller said. "I know you and Professor Thomas were quite close, as were he and I. I wanted to be the one to tell you. Sadly, he passed away last night from a heart attack in his sleep. I'm so sorry."

Melody Anderson remained stoic. After a moment she acknowledged what he said with a silent nod and stood up.

"Thank you, Dean Miller," she said, then she turned and walked out of the room.

Melody made her way back to her room, locked the door, and laid down on her bed, sobbing uncontrollably. She allowed herself to grieve. Day turned to night and back again into morning. When she had finally gained her composure she got up, packed a bag and headed home.

Professor William 'Wild Bill' Thomas was laid to rest on a dreary, overcast day. His funeral was attended by some of his fellow high school faculty members, a handful of business people and politicians, as well as a few others who had known him throughout the years.

After the church service Melody accompanied the casket to the grave site. She stood there alone and watched as the workers lowered it slowly into the ground. One of the men handed her a shovel.

"Goodbye, *Pops*," she said quietly, as she turned the first shovel of dirt onto the casket. She then turned and walked away, heading to her car which was parked on the cemetery roadway.

"Ms. Anderson?"

Melody turned around to look in the direction of the man who now approached her. He was dressed in a dark suit and she assumed he was from the funeral home.

She actually hadn't given it much thought, but now guessed that there might be some balance due on the funeral cost. She hoped that it wouldn't be too much; she was already living pretty much hand to mouth.

"Yes?" she replied.

"Ms. Anderson, my name is Michael Collins," he said by way of introduction. "I was hoping that I might meet you here, Prof. Thomas had given me a photo to identify you by when the time came."

He handed her the photo. It was the one taken of the two of them at her graduation. His arm was wrapped around her shoulder and they were both smiling.

She looked back at the man.

"Do you mind if I keep this?" she asked.

"Oh, absolutely," he replied. "But that's not why I'm here. I would like to discuss with you Prof. Thomas' final arrangements."

"OK, I understand, but I'm still just a student," she said. "If the costs exceed what I have in my savings, I'll be glad to setup some type of payment plan."

The man stared at her quizzically.

"Excuse me?" he said.

"The funeral costs, I'll be happy to pay them I just might need a little time," she explained.

"No, Ms. Anderson, it's okay. The funeral has already been paid for."

"I don't understand then, what do you want from me?" she asked.

"I'm sorry, please let me start over," said Collins. "Ms. Anderson, I am the executor of Professor Thomas' will. You see, he had no family. More importantly he specifically directed that you were to be the sole recipient of his entire estate."

He handed her an envelope. She opened it, removing the letter from inside and began to read it.

"*My Dearest Melody.*

The fact that you are reading this means that I am no longer with you. Please do not mourn my passing, celebrate the life I have lived. I have enjoyed my life to the fullest and I wish the same for you. Over the last few years you have brought more joy and happiness to my life than I could have ever possibly imagined. In watching you grow, I feel as if the transgressions of my life have been redeemed.

At one time I had wished that I had a child like you. Now I know that God blessed me by bringing you into my life. You may not have been my biological daughter, but you were my spiritual one and I could not have been more proud of you.

Your life is about to change, please live that life to the fullest. Do not make the same mistake as I did. When the opportunity presents itself, allow yourself to live, love and laugh.

Goodbye my dear Melody, till we meet again. William"

Melody Anderson looked up at Michael Collins, tears streaming down her face.

"Ms. Anderson, you have just become an extremely wealthy woman," he said.

At twenty one years of age, Melody Anderson had become a millionaire, nearly one hundred times over.

"Melody?" repeated Gen. "Are you okay?"

Melody turned to look at her friend and realized she was crying and shivering uncontrollably. Gen grabbed her friend and brought her back into the bedroom, wrapping her up with the blanket. She hit the button on the desk to close the windows.

"Seriously, are you okay," her friend asked, more than a little bit concerned.

Melody looked over at the night table and the framed photo that sat on it.

"Yeah, hon," she said, as she wiped the tears from her eyes. "I'm fine. Honest. Let's go and close this deal."

Melody got up from the bed and took the clothes with her to the bathroom. She pulled her hair back into a ponytail and applied a minimal amount of makeup before putting on the business suit. When she stepped out of the bathroom she had transformed herself from emotional basket case to hardened businesswoman.

Genevieve smiled.

Melody was one of those rare individuals that literally could put zero effort into getting dressed and still looked as if she had just stepped out of a fashion magazine.

"Time to kick some corporate ass," Gen said.

Melody headed out the door and down the hallway toward the elevator with Gen in tow.

They had a flight to catch.

CHAPTER TWELVE

Ponquoque Beach, Suffolk County, N.Y.
Saturday, April 28th, 2012 – 9:32 a.m.

Maguire navigated the Mustang through the winding side streets of the village of Hampton Bays; making his way up to Route 27 or Sunrise Highway as it is more commonly known to the majority of the residents of Long Island. From there he proceeded west, toward the Nassau County border, until he got to the Route 111 exit where he headed north. A short ride later he pulled onto the Long Island Expressway and made his way west toward Manhattan.

The Long Island Expressway, or Interstate 495, was one of those necessary highways that everyone on Long Island dreaded to navigate. The fact that it had the word 'Expressway' in its name was actually insulting to most motorists; who often found themselves stuck in bumper to bumper traffic. In most other places you had rush *hour* traffic; on the L.I.E. you had rush *hours* traffic. Being a commercial traffic route, and subject to massive random construction projects, it was not uncommon to find yourself sitting in traffic either at two o'clock in the afternoon or two o'clock in the morning. With Long Island traffic, you just never knew.

Maguire continued to make his way through Nassau County, Queens, and finally through the Bronx before he *officially* made his way into what was considered to be New York *State*.

To the residents of New York, the state has always seemed to be divided into two very distinct places, that being Upstate New York and Downstate New York. At one time, Upstate New York was everything north and west of the Bronx, and downstate was considered New York City, and by extension the counties of Nassau and Suffolk on Long Island. However with the population explosion in New York City over the last few decades, many former residents sought refuge in the surrounding northern counties. As a result the counties of Putnam, Rockland and Westchester were now included in the downstate category.

For those who live and work in Downstate New York, the rural countryside seemed a lifetime away, but within a short drive Maguire had left the concrete jungle in his rear view mirror. He swapped it out for lush green forests; which gradually began to incorporate mountains in their landscape as he made his way further north.

The drive up the New York State Thruway was very scenic. It was especially impressive during the early fall months, when the change in season brought out a panoply of colors in the leaves just before they fell. Many flocked to the area to photograph these vibrant scenes.

Maguire was fine at the beginning of the trip, but now, as the car made its way north, he began to feel that sense of dread he thought he had left behind more than two decades earlier.

He leaned over and turned off the radio. He had too much on his mind right now and still had another six hours before he arrived up in Perrysville. His thoughts wandered from what had originally happened to Tricia to whether he could get back there in time to figure it all out, before it turned tragic. Maguire also wondered what he would find when he got back to Perrysville. As he drove, his mind began to replay the movie of his childhood.

It had been nearly twenty-three years ago, but it seemed like only yesterday. He and Tricia hadn't really talked much since that awkward lunch. When they did, each seemed cautious. Their words were guarded, unsure. Still he had believed that, whatever the issue was, they would be able to work through it. He had still been looking forward to going to the prom with her. He felt that they needed a chance to just relax and unwind. He had hoped that a night of fun would cut through the tension and give them an escape from the uneasy feelings they were clearly both struggling with. It would be an opportunity for both of them to hit the *reset button*, so to speak.

They had decided to meet separately at Perrysville High School for the prom. Tricia's girlfriend Lena had spent the night at her house so that they could get ready together the next day. Since Lena had her own car, Tricia decided that she would just ride over with her and meet him there.

Maguire pulled the Mustang into the parking lot which was already nearly at capacity. Guys in tuxedoes and girls in fashionable gowns made their way toward the gymnasium doors.

He was running late because he had stopped in town to get her a corsage. As a result he had to park the car at the far edge of the lot. He leaned over, grabbing the clear plastic box, and then got out of the car.

As he made his way through the parked cars, his meandering path took him in the direction of the open promenade between the high school building itself and the detached gym. In the distance he could make out Tricia standing there in her shimmering blue dress. Even at this distance she looked absolutely stunning and he couldn't wait to reconnect with her. As he drew closer he could see that she was engaged in a conversation with someone just out of view. His curiosity got the better of him and he slowed his pace down, coming to a stop next to a parked van. The van obscured things just enough that he would remain out of sight, in the event that she should look over in this direction.

Maguire was still too far away to actually make out the conversation clearly, but it appeared that it was very *animated*. Whoever she was speaking with continued to remain just outside his field of view. He desperately wanted to know who she was talking to, but he also didn't want to risk being seen. Finally, Tricia turned around, arms crossed in front of her and her back toward her antagonist. Time paused for what seemed like an eternity. A moment later a figure appeared and moved into view, it was Paul Browning.

Maguire's mind was racing.

What is Tricia doing talking to him? he wondered.

More importantly why was she talking to him now on prom night? As if on cue to answer this question, he watched in horror as Browning grabbed Tricia by her shoulders, spun her around, pulled her close to him, and kissed her.

Maguire felt his body go limp and he physically slumped against the van.

Paul Browning was his arch nemesis. The fact that Browning was the arch nemesis of just about every other male student at Perrysville High was of little consolation at this particular moment. Browning, it seemed, bullied just about everyone who was not on the football team.

He got away with his proclivity for terrorizing the students of Perrysville by the fact that he came from a wealthy family. His father owned four car dealerships throughout the surrounding area and was very big in local charitable causes; including the high school sports program. The fact that his donations were more out of interest to his annual tax burden, than his desire in helping others, did not bother Donald 'Big Daddy' Browning one bit.

His magnanimity often resulted in junior getting a free pass for his youthful *indiscretions*, much to the chagrin of his victims. Not that it would have mattered. In this case, the apple did not fall far from the tree. Big Daddy Browning had himself been a bully when he was in high school. He considered it to be a rite of passage and of course those weaker kids just needed to *toughen-up* a bit. In Big Daddy Browning's world those kids were being taught a valuable lesson. The world's a cruel place and worse if you happen to be one of the wimpy kids.

When Maguire looked up again, they were gone. He scanned the surrounding area, but saw no sign of them. He felt as if he had been sucker punched in the gut. He struggled desperately to get his bearings.

He turned and headed unsteadily back toward the car, dropping the box containing the corsage somewhere along the way. He was having difficulty breathing and felt the nausea welling up inside him. As he reached the car he couldn't contain it any longer and dropped to his knees vomiting uncontrollably.

James pulled his thoughts back from the past. There was too much that had to be done and being caught up in an old childhood trauma, that had occurred over two decades ago, was not going to help him in the slightest. He reached over and opened the glove compartment and retrieved a protein bar from inside.

In his line of business eating was often a luxury so he kept a supply of protein bars at hand at all times. While they would never be confused with gourmet food, they fulfilled their intended purpose. If he actually had the luxury of time, he might have even pulled over and broken out one of the MRE's, a military acronym for *Meal, Ready to Eat*, from the trunk and had himself a proper meal. He laughed when he remembered that his old Senior Chief in the teams fondly referred to them as *Meals, Rejected by Ethiopians*.

As he snacked on the protein bar he refocused his mind back on the facts at hand. What he knew was that sometime within the last twelve hours Tricia had been in a car accident and was now missing. Since there were apparently no calls, prior to the initial one, it was unlikely that someone had picked her up, right? He admitted to himself that it was unlikely, but not entirely implausible. This was after all the *country* and, even in this modern age, there were some older locals that still didn't have cell phones.

The question then became, *was she ok*? Unfortunately, the odds were that she most likely was not. Had she been ok, she would have insisted on calling her family or friends which would have rendered everything on the TV moot. If she was hurt and picked up they would have taken her to the hospital. Champlain Valley Hospital was, at the most, only a half hour drive up Route 9 to Plattsburgh. In that case, hospital emergency room staff would have notified the state police.

Unfortunately, at this stage, everything pointed to Tricia most likely being hurt and on her own in the woods.

He felt the urgency growing more tangible with each passing minute and realized the dread of the past had been replaced with something new. He stared out the windshield, lost in thought, wondering whether he would actually make it there in time to be of any good. If he had taken the time to look down he would have seen that the speedometer had passed ninety miles an hour.

By the time he had passed through the outskirts of Albany, the state capitol of New York, two-thirds of the seven hour trip was over. He watched as the highway signs ticked off the progress of his journey; from Saratoga Springs, to Lake George and finally to Exit 33. It actually was the exit before Keenseville, but it was closer to the scene where the accident had occurred. As he pulled off the highway, he felt odd; as if he was crossing back over into a life he had purposefully left behind.

Maguire drove through the winding back roads. They were treacherous enough during the daytime, let alone late at night. He pulled up to the intersection of County Highway 28 and turned left, keeping an eye out as he navigated the twisting and turning road. As he pulled around one particular bend he saw the remnants of crime scene tape hanging like bizarre streamers from a few trees. As he came to a stop it struck him as really odd that there was no one else around. He shut off the engine and turned on his hazard lights.

He reached underneath the seat and removed the holstered Sig Sauer P226. It was an exact match to the one in the gun bag in the trunk. He made it a habit of keeping some form of protection at hand, no matter where he was, when at all possible. He didn't expect any problems, but it was the back woods and it was always better to be prepared. Stepping out of the car he clipped the holster into the small of his back. He walked back to the rear of the car, opening the trunk and removed the fleece jacket from his bag and put it on.

Maguire walked back to where the remnants of the crime scene tape were fluttering in the wind and stopped, taking in the entire scene. Tricia had been traveling in the same direction that he had just come from. As he walked along the road slowly, he scanned it from side to side.

Remnants of shattered glass twinkled in the sunlight and other debris from the car still peppered the edge of the roadway. There was a section of pavement which was also discolored by fluid that had drained from the engine.

He walked slowly along the roadway, first on the east bound side, and then on the west bound. As he examined the edges he looked to his left and noticed some gouge marks on one of the trees that appeared to be new.

As he made his way back along the other side, he noticed that there appeared to be similar marks on one of the trees on this side as well. It struck him as odd and he wondered if they had strung something across the roadway to keep people from entering the scene.

He returned back to the area where the car had come to a rest and examined it more intently. As he looked around the peripheral edges he spotted it, small droplets of dark stain on the green leaves.

Blood.

This is where Tricia entered the forest, he thought.

Maguire also noticed that the ground extending out from this spot also showed heavy signs of foot traffic. It didn't take an expert to see that the searchers had clearly plodded through it, but something else felt wrong to him, nagging at him. He walked back east along the road, about a quarter mile, and then cut back into the woods.

He began to make his way through the unmolested brush. This was spring in the Adirondacks and everything was green and fresh and *wet*. It had that new, crisp scent in the air. Not like the middle of summer when everything in the woods seemed heavy and musty. While the initial scene was heavily trampled the ground out here was generally pristine; with only the occasional animal tracks cutting through.

Spotting animal tracks was quite easy. Animals do not conceal their movement and have set characteristics. Tracking a human being is quite different. When you track humans you spend more time looking for the things that shouldn't be there. You learn to look for bent blades of grass which point the direction in which someone has fled. In the case of overturned rocks, the darker and wetter the rock, the closer the quarry is. To the trained eye, spider webs can be like nature's little trip wires.

Maguire worked his way back toward the accident scene in a modified concentric, inward-spiral search pattern. The woods in this area were particularly dense and it made the search a bit slow. As he drew within seventy-five yards of the accident scene the wet ground became littered with heavy boot prints.

After he had completed the search on that side, Maguire went and replicated it on the other side of the roadway with the same results. It was slow and tedious work, but something he had been trained in and had a good eye for.

When Maguire was done he was certain of two things. First, the search was conducted by well intentioned, yet completely inexperienced, individuals. Second, and more importantly, he was absolutely certain that Tricia had never stepped foot into these woods.

He made his way back toward the car and sat there, taking it all in. It still puzzled him as to why there was no activity at the location. Had they also come to the same conclusion? He doubted that. There didn't seem to be any disciplined pattern to their search method, other than walking around aimlessly. He also wondered why the search had been limited to such a confined area.

He grabbed his cell phone and scrolled through the numbers till he located Bill Malloy's.

"Two calls in one day, I think that's a record?" Malloy laughed.

"Hey, I need you to discreetly reach out to the locals up here and see if they have any updates on this missing person case,"

Maguire said. "If they ask, tell them you're doing a human interest piece"

"Ok," Malloy said. "How's the weather up there?"

"Miserable," Maguire replied. "It's always cold and wet up here in the spring. Get back to me as soon as you know something."

"Will do."

Maguire started the car and turned the heat up. He dropped it into drive and made his way toward Perrysville. It was already late and it was beginning to get dark. As he came toward the edge of town he spotted an old familiar haunt and decided to pull into the parking lot. As the car came to a stop, the cell phone rang.

"What did you find out?"

"No change. Browning's still missing. Search earlier in the day met with negative results."

"Are they still listing the State Police as the point of contact?" Maguire asked.

"No, it's all been turned over to the local sheriff's office," Bill replied.

"Ok, thanks, Bill," Maguire said. "If you hear anything else let me know."

"I will," Malloy replied. "Watch your back."

Maguire disconnected the call and put the phone into the inner pocket of his jacket. He then turned the car off, got out and headed for the door of the diner.

CHAPTER THIRTEEN

Southampton, Suffolk County, N.Y.
Saturday, April 28th, 2012 – 10:35 a.m.

The two women walked out the front door of the house and down the steps to the waiting car where the driver held the passenger door open for Melody. Genevieve walked around to the other side and got in. It was a short drive down to the western edge of the property where the helipad was located. A gleaming Sikorsky S92 helicopter sat awaiting their arrival.

Melody began to mentally focus on the day that lay ahead of her. This was actually a very big moment for her and she was about to sign a contract that would give her the controlling interest in an advanced weapons manufacturing firm. The very same firm that was soon going to be awarded a U.S. government defense services contract that would be worth billions.

She reached into her bag and removed her phone. The screen indicated that she had a missed call and that there was a voicemail message. She felt her heart race as she selected the icon for the voicemail.

"*Mel, hi it's James. Listen I just wanted to call and say I really enjoyed our evening. I was going to ask if you were free for dinner tonight, but something has come up and I have to go out of town for a few days. I'll call as soon as I get a chance and hopefully we can get together for dinner or something.*"

Melody was simultaneously excited and disappointed. She had been hoping that she would hear back from him. It was a brazen act leaving her number there and she had wondered if it might be too forward. She was anticipating getting back from her trip early enough that maybe they could get together. Now she knew that was off the table; at least for the moment.

She leaned back against the leather seat and allowed herself a moment to bask in the fact that he was actually interested in getting together with her again. She wondered what the future would bring. Unfortunately the thoughts only lasted a moment longer until Genevieve brought her attention back to the present moment.

“Let me guess,” Gen said. “That was Gilligan calling from his floating house looking for a piece of ass tonight?”

“Oh my God would you stop already,” Melody said. “If I didn’t know you better I would say you were jealous!”

Genevieve stared out her window and shook her head dismissively.

“I’m just saying you don’t even know him, Mel. I mean for crying out loud, the man lives on a boat and has freaky animals embroidered on his shirts,” Gen said by way of argument.

The car pulled up to the helipad and they both got out, making their way toward the waiting helicopter.

“Ok, enough,” exclaimed an exasperated Melody. “If it will make you happy I will invite him over and you can grill him.”

“Fine,” said Gen. “I’ll make a point to sharpen my claws.”

“Sheesh, I didn’t get raked over the coals this bad when I was in high school.”

“Well, fortunately for you, you didn’t date in high school,” Gen said sarcastically, as the two women climbed up into the helicopter.

The S92 was particularly adept at providing VIP’s with the luxury they had come to expect. The spacious interior cabin of the helicopter allowed passengers the ability to stand up and move around comfortably. The main seating area in this helicopter was comprised of four tan leather swivel chairs with tables and was used primarily for business purposes. The rear seating area had two matching leather couches and was divided off by a polished oak partition wall that could be closed for privacy. Mounted on either side of the wall were flat screen TV's. The helicopter also featured a private bathroom in the back.

In addition to the visible interior amenities, the S92 also utilized an active vibration control system which incorporated sensors and structurally mounted force generators. The result was that it provided not only a more comfortable flight, but cabin acoustic levels that allowed its occupants to carry on normal conversation, something that was extremely difficult in other helicopters without the aid of headphones.

Each of the women took their usual seats. While Gen immediately went to work on her iPad, Melody gazed out the window.

Up in the cockpit, her personal pilot, Major Robert Miller, United States Marine Corps, *Retired*, began his preflight check. Bob Miller was a combat veteran who had served tours in both Iraq and Afghanistan. After those rotations were up he had flown countless hours in another Sikorsky helicopter, the VH-60N, but back then it carried the call sign: Marine One.

This job, however, paid a lot better.

Miller and his copilot did a visual check of the immediate area outside to ensure that no one was near the helicopter. When they both confirmed it was clear the engines came to life and the rotor blades began their slow, steady buildup until they became nothing but a blur. He rose up on the collective and the helicopter began a smooth, steady ascent from the helipad. With an experienced hand he worked the cyclic, dipping the helicopter's nose slightly and they began their trip.

As they passed over the Shinnecock bay, Melody looked down toward the marina. His car was gone she noted sadly.

"Back to work, Missy," said Gen. "It's refresher time."

Melody sighed and opened the leather portfolio that Genevieve had prepared for her on Global Defense Logistics; a Leader in World Wide Weapons Systems.

She rolled her eyes as she read the introduction.

"Doesn't anyone put any thought into corporate names anymore?" Melody asked.

"Actually, GDL was around long before advertising was a big concern," Gen replied. "Besides, they didn't need to make a splash since they already owned the whole damn pool."

The report went on to explain that GDL's corporate headquarters was situated just north of Washington, D.C. in the bucolic hills just outside of Annapolis, Maryland. While the corporate H.Q. was on the east coast, the firms technical operations were all conducted at their research and development facility which was situated just northwest of Billings, Montana on a thousand acres of land. It employed almost two thousand people, the vast majority of whom where software programmers. The report also listed each of the current board of directors, along with their biographies, as well as the last decade of financials along with recent major contracts and acquisitions.

On paper it looked like a solid enough company, but there was growing dissension within the corporate offices. The companies' founder, Charles Wainright, who had been the President and CEO of the firm since its beginning, had passed away a little over a year ago. He had left his controlling stake in the company to his two sons Richard and Charles III, whom Genevieve had taken to affectionately referring to as Dip and Shit, after discussions with her counterpart on the GDL board. In truth, most of the GDL board members had a few other *colorful* names they used for the two men. Unfortunately, they were on the short end of the stick, so to speak, in terms of control of the company.

At the time of his death, Wainright's company was working on an advanced weapons acquisition and targeting computer program system, code name: *Dragons Breath*. While the system was initially being aimed specifically at the US Navy, its application could be tailored to suit the needs of the other military branches as well.

In essence the system took all the guess work out of naval weapons target acquisitioning. The system integrated everything into one seamless computer program. If you could see it, you could shoot it and shoot it with exact precision. More importantly, it didn't matter where it was that you were *seeing* it from.

For example, if an F/A-18 Hornet fighter jet was flying a combat mission over the Hindu Kush in Afghanistan and got an audible missile-lock tone, from a mobile surface-to-air missile site below, even before the pilot could physically begin to respond, data was already being sent from the jet's computer system back to the aircraft carrier it had launched from in the Arabian Sea. That signal was translated by an adaptive computer program that factored in everything from weather at the missile launch site to the pitch and roll the carrier was currently experiencing. Prior to the counter-measures being deployed on the F/A-18, the weapons system on the carrier, or any other ship that was integrated into the carrier group, could fire off a salvo of deadly ordnance to rain down upon the target.

To put it simply, it was going to be a really bad day for any foreign military or terrorist organization that wanted to fuck with the United States.

Testing was currently underway to adapt the system to work on land based vehicles, as well as helicopters and other aircraft, hence the interest by the other branches. A unique code key in the software allowed only the designated equipment in that particular group to be linked. This meant that there was no fear that a naval vessel in the Sea of Japan would accidentally fire off a salvo of rockets over China which, for obvious reasons, could have major international consequences.

Quite frankly, the only problem facing Global Defense Logistics was the aforementioned Dip and Shit.

The officers of Global Defense Logistics were what you would call 'old money' people. In that way they were not unlike members of *La Cosa Nostra*. They did not want the family business splashed all over the front page of the papers. Richard and Charles III didn't seem capable of understanding this concept or even caring about it for that matter. To the two brothers, money was everything and life was simply about having fun.

In a world that was growing increasingly more narcissistic and wholly dependent on social media to establish who was *in* or not, these two were more than willing to squander their inheritance on making a media splash wherever they went. And they did so at any given opportunity, which did not sit particularly well with the board. More importantly, it did not sit well with those in power in D.C. who directed financial favor down GDL's path.

In truth, Wainright's two heirs were as dumb as a box of rocks. Richard and Charles III were both in their mid-twenties and had never worked a day in their life. Nor, they were quick to point out, did they have the inclination to do so now. Both had gone to Ivy League colleges where they had been brainwashed into believing that anything to do with the American *war machine*, including Global Defense Logistics, was inherently evil and they wanted absolutely nothing to do with it.

Well, that wasn't all together true. Both men, it seemed, were eager to accept a handsome compensation package which would ensure that neither would ever have to work again in their lifetime. After all, at the end of the day, money trumped ethics.

Most of the board members were more than happy to endure a *takeover* as long as it would rid them, once and for all, of those two idiots. Melody Anderson's reputation as a highly successful businesswoman, with a knack for turning everything she touched into gold, was all the convincing the board members needed to go along.

At the conclusion of Genevieve's report was a leaked intelligence brief that was rubber stamped on each page with the words *Top Secret*. The briefing papers explained details of both past, current and future projects. Beyond the Naval testing being conducted, the project was also being green-lighted to expand outward, not only for overt military usage, but some potentially *covert* use as well. The company was poised to have amazing good fortune poured down upon it. They just didn't know it yet.

Melody stared back out the window and smiled inwardly.

She reveled in the art of the deal. Where others were satisfied with simply focusing on one issue at a time, she focused on the overall big picture. Like a spider spinning a web, each individual line interconnected with another to form a trap for the unsuspecting who lacked a clarity of vision.

Yes, that was what Melody Anderson had always lived for, but even as she thought it, the words were chased away by something else.

"Mel?"

Melody swiveled in her chair and looked over at Genevieve quizzically. Like a student caught by the teacher daydreaming in class.

"I know your mind isn't here right now, but it really needs to be," Gen lamented.

"I'm fine, Gen," replied Melody, as she arranged some of the papers on the small desk in front of her. "Where do we stand with the board members?"

"Overall we are good," Gen answered. "Originally there were a total of ten officers when Wainwright first started the company. He held the controlling shares at fifty-two percent. The remaining nine held the minority. Three will be stepping down after the acquisition is complete. They've decided that they are going to spend their time and money in relative obscurity. Combined they represented only about a ten percent stake. Those shares are being bought out by the remaining minority so that's a non-issue for us."

"How are the ones that remain going to handle a woman having a controlling stake in their baby?" Melody asked.

"I haven't had any pushback on that issue at all. I think they had all heard about your reputation for making money and there may have been one or two calls made from up on the *Hill*," replied Gen. "That settled them down a lot. Only one was making a bit of a fuss early on, but it doesn't matter as he is one of those who are going to be stepping down."

"What about Dip and Shit?"

"No problems there either," she said. "All indications are that they are going to take the money and run as fast, and as far away, as they can. They never did like daddy's business and they are chomping at the bit to get out from underneath it, especially before *Dragons Breath* gets announced."

"I'm shocked," said Mel.

"Actually, it gets even better," Gen replied. "Word is that they are already working on the spin so that when the news does hit they are going to claim that's why they left. They figure it will play well with their *tree hugger* friends and garner them major babe points."

Mel nearly choked on her drink at that last part. "Are you serious?"

"Absolutely, even I couldn't make up something that absurd."

"What else do we have?" said Melody.

Gen pulled out a USB flash drive and plugged it into the port. She turned on the nearest TV screen and began the power point presentation.

Over all it mirrored the report Mel had just read, but it put faces to the names of the board members and key personnel. In addition, it provided a visual overview of both the corporate H.Q. in Maryland as well as the facility in Montana. The Montana facility was actually quite deceiving. While its outward appearance was physically imposing, the hidden truth was that the structure was almost three times as large underground. It also featured a private runway for easy access, as well as a fully functioning air operations facility to maintain the companies various corporate jets.

GDL also had an extensive research and development section that dealt in a wide variety of projects that were not wholly limited to computer programs. They were also a pioneer in defense hardware, including advanced light weapons design and next generation armored battle vehicles. There was even a section that dealt with reactive personal body armor that was poised to revolutionize the industry.

At that moment an audible ping came over the aircraft's internal communication system followed by the pilot's voice.

"Ms. Anderson, we're getting ready for our approach. Should have wheel's down in about ten minutes."

Melody pressed the button on the communication console. "Thanks, Bob."

She stood up and stretched out her arms before heading back to the bathroom.

When she returned Genevieve was just finishing putting the papers into her leather portfolio briefcase.

"Are we all set?" asked Melody, as she sat back in her chair.

"Yes we are," Genevieve answered. "We should be back by dinner time."

Melody looked out the window and watched as the helicopter began its descent. She caught a glimpse of the helipad and within moments felt the wheels touch down effortlessly. As soon as the helicopter was on the ground, the pilot cut the engines.

Melody and Gen got up and walked toward the front door which was just being opened by the ship's co-pilot, Tom Reynolds.

"Thanks, Tom," Melody said and threw him an off-handed salute.

"Happy hunting, ma'am," he replied.

Upon exiting the helicopter, they were met by two burly plainclothes security officers who escorted them toward a glass atrium adjacent to the helipad. At the same time members of the GDL ground crew began the task of refueling the helicopter for its return trip.

They walked through the glass door and stepped into a large lobby where they were approached by an impeccably dressed older gentleman who extended his hand toward Melody.

"Ms. Anderson," he said shaking her hand. He was about to introduce himself when she interrupted him.

"Mr. Pope, I am so glad to finally have the chance to meet you," Melody said. "I believe you already know Ms. Gordon."

Melody turned and surrendered Wilson Pope's hand, watching as he shook hands with Genevieve.

"Ms. Gordon, a pleasure as always."

Melody smiled at Genevieve. She had often wondered what she would do without her. It was not only the big things that Gen did, but the minor ones that made such a difference. Like the photos and biographies of each board member that helped her to immediately establish a personal connection. Taking the time to learn as much as she could about them was a tool she had often used, either to disarm or to use as leverage against a potential business partner. In this case, it was the former.

The board members of GDL were happy with her acquisition of the company; anything to rid themselves of the troublesome Wainright heirs. But in creating a connection, it made the whole affair much more palatable.

"Everyone is waiting for you, Ms. Anderson," Pope said. "If you would follow me, we can head on up to the board room."

"Please, lead the way, Mr. Pope."

Wilson Pope directed the two women toward the private elevator with the security detail in tow. There were no buttons in the elevator. One of the officers spoke discreetly into the concealed transmitter in his hand and the elevator began its assent.

The elevator itself was constructed of bullet resistant glass and rode up on the exterior of the building. As it climbed higher it afforded impressive views of the well-manicured grounds of GDL.

It was a short ride to the tenth floor which housed the executive offices, including those of the chief executive officer and the board room. The elevator came to a stop and the doors opened on the reception area. The room was tastefully decorated with a polished black granite tiled floor and mahogany walls that featured a coffered ceiling. It was a theme that was continued throughout the entire floor. Like most things in the corporate world it was designed to impress and it achieved its goal.

There were two large receptionist style desks in the middle of the room. They sat on opposite sides of the room from each other and both faced the direction of the elevator. Each was constructed of the same mahogany wood and topped with granite counters.

The desk on the right belonged to the executive receptionist, Pamela Hayes, who found herself working on her much needed day off. Hayes was a twenty-something go-getter who had first made a name for herself as a part-time employee working in the mailroom. Her enthusiasm and willingness to take on any task offered her had led to a full time job followed by a succession of positions which culminated in her current assignment. The fact that she was also young and attractive did not hurt.

As she sat there today she couldn't help wonder to herself how attractive she looked right now. The upheaval, which had ensued since Charles Wainwright's death and was about to end today, had caused her to put in more hours of overtime then she could even count. It seemed that as long as someone was inside, she had to be sitting here. She felt tired and worn out.

The desk on the left was manned by a security officer who controlled both the elevator as well as access through the doors behind him; which led to the interior offices. While the executive receptionist's desk top was covered with papers, blotters, and phones; the security officer's desk contained a series of a half dozen monitors, discreetly hidden behind the high counter. From here he could scan any of the interior or exterior cameras in the GDL complex. Directly under the desk was a custom designed rack that contained a Heckler & Koch MP-5 machine gun.

As the group walked toward the large double doors, Pamela Hayes stood up. "Good afternoon, Ms. Anderson."

"Good afternoon," Melody replied, as she stopped to face the woman. "And you are?"

"Pamela Hayes, ma'am," she replied. "I'm the executive receptionist."

"I'm sorry for ruining your weekend," Melody said.

"No trouble at all," Hayes said.

The security officer had already entered the code which operated the security doors. The doors were armored and could only be opened by the security officer's terminal or through the main security office located four floors below the complex.

Wilson Pope ushered the women through the doors and into the executive suite.

As they walked inside, Melody was immediately struck by the sheer opulence of the interior lobby. The room was massive and the cathedral ceiling rose up to what would have easily been the 11th floor. Mahogany panels covered the lower portion of the room, but above them were beige walls that gave it all a more open and airy feeling. Polished, fluted granite columns lined the walls like silent sentries. In the center of the ceiling was a large domed skylight that allowed the sun's rays to cascade down and fill the room with brilliant light. On the floor, directly under the skylight, was a large rotating brushed aluminum globe.

It was all quite dramatic. Clearly global defense was a very lucrative business.

They continued through the lobby, walking toward the far end where there was a glass wall with a pair of double doors, behind which was the GDL board room. Melody could see the members sitting inside. Along the way they passed half a dozen offices on either side of the hallway. As they approached the board room the doors opened, as if on cue. Closer inspection would have revealed discreetly hidden sensors in the wall panels immediately outside the room which activated them. The board members stood respectfully as Melody entered the room; that was all of them except for Richard and Charles III. Both men sat at the far end of the table looking rather bored.

Pope motioned for Melody to take a chair at the other end of the conference table and Genevieve took the seat to her immediate right. The rest of the men sat down and, as if on cue, everyone began opening the leather portfolios in front of each of them.

"Gentlemen," Melody began. "First let me say that it is a pleasure to finally meet all of you. I appreciate you all coming out today for what is a largely symbolic act. However, given the long and storied history of Global Defense Logistics I felt that it was only fitting that we mark this occasion together."

"You, gentleman, along with the late Charles Wainright, had a vision for this company. I believe that you have been good stewards in ensuring that it always went down the right path. I am pleased at the opportunity to become part of the GDL family and continue that direction."

Gen sat listening to Melody while simultaneously watching each of the board members. She tried to gauge the impact that Mel's speech was having. It was clear that her opening statements had gotten their attention. All of these men had a vested interest in this company and Melody's words were taking some of the sting out of this acquisition.

"I'm sorry," said a voice from the far end of the room. "But really is this going to take much longer?"

Everyone turned to look at Richard Wainright who sat looking back with utter disdain written all over his face.

"I mean I know you all think this is vaguely important, but I for one would prefer to dispense with all of this and get on with my life, once and for all."

"Hear, hear," cried Charles III, in a completely mocking tone, as he looked up from the text message he had been reading on his phone.

In that moment, the members of the board received all the proof they needed that they had reached the proper decision.

Melody caught Richard Wainright's stare and held it purposefully until the man blinked and sheepishly turned away. When she was satisfied that he had been put in his place she continued.

"I am sure each of you has had an opportunity to look through the paperwork that my legal department has put together for you," Melody continued. "So, if there are no questions, then I propose that we sign the agreement."

And with that closing remark, each one got up and signed on the proverbially dotted line. As Richard Wainwright signed, he turned toward Genevieve and said, rather smugly, "I assume you know exactly where to wire my money, sweetheart."

Genevieve turned and locked eyes with him. If looks could kill, the wire transfer would have been rendered moot.

A curt "Yes," was the only reply he received.

Richard Wainwright got the message immediately and hurried for the door, his brother in tow. As they walked out of the room they were immediately met by the two security officers who had the thoroughly enjoyable task of escorting the men out of the building for the final time.

After the formality of signing, the room broke up in a lively form of corporate celebration. While they saluted the new direction of the company, lunch was brought in. Over the next two hours each man took their turn to get to know the new chief executive officer of GDL. If they had any lingering concerns about Melody Anderson, they were dispelled almost immediately as they talked with her. In the end they all felt as if the corporate reigns had been passed to a worthy successor to Charles Wainwright.

As the afternoon's event was coming to a close, Melody turned to ask Pope a question.

"Wilson, what's the story with the receptionist outside?"

"Ms. Hayes?" he asked. "Well she's been here for about ten years. She's been the executive receptionist for almost three years. In fact, lately it seems as if she lives here."

"Go ahead and have human resources find a replacement for her."

"Of course, Ms. Anderson," he replied. "Is there a problem?"

"No, I just believe that sometimes change can be an important motivator."

"Yes, ma'am," he replied. He was unsure if he had missed something in the earlier exchange. "Would you like to see your office now?"

"That would be great."

She looked over at Genevieve who was talking to two men, one of whom appeared to be very animated in a *techie* sort of way. Gen caught her eye and excused herself, following after Melody as her and Pope walked backed down the hall they had come through earlier.

Half way down he turned to the left and opened a door which led into a large anteroom. A secretary's desk sat in the middle of the room, facing the door they had just walked through. Off to one side was a leather couch and coffee table for waiting visitors. There were two doors, one to the left and one to the right. Pope led Melody to the one on the right and they entered the CEO's office.

It was sparsely furnished, but the room itself was elegant. The back wall was made entirely of glass and gave the occupant a panoramic view of the property. On the right was a large desk and chair. Immediately in front of the desk were two leather high backed wing chairs. On the left was a small conference table.

"This was Charles' office," said Pope. "In the last few months of his life he did most of his work from home so this office was just closed up."

Melody walked around the room taking it in. She paused in front of the window and looked out over the rolling hills. In the distance she could see the Chesapeake Bay.

"There is another office across the hall which was intended for an executive assistant, but Charles didn't have much need for that," Pope continued. "I assume you will have use for that now?"

"Yes, we will," Melody replied.

"I've left a binder on your desk; it contains the names and bios of those in our secretarial pool. The prior secretary was with Charles from the beginning. When he passed away she decided to retire," Pope explained. "However, should you choose to bring someone else in that is certainly your prerogative."

"Thank you," Melody said. "I'm sure there are many qualified people here at GDL from which we can find to fill that position."

"Well, I am sure that you have a lot to do. If there is anything I can do to help with the transition, please do not hesitate to call me."

"Thank you very much, Wilson. In the coming weeks most likely either Genevieve or myself will be flying back and forth between here and Montana. If you wouldn't mind, can you please let the staff and security people know?"

"I will do that," Pope replied. He shook hands with Melody and Genevieve before leaving the office.

Melody pushed one of the leather chairs to the side and sat down as Gen joined her.

"Well, chicky, you did it," Gen said. "Shouldn't we be drinking?"

"We're almost there. There are just a couple of things that I wanted to talk to you about."

Genevieve looked at Melody quizzically. "Is there a problem?"

"No, quite the opposite," replied Melody, as she gazed out the window. After a moment she looked away, turning her gaze back to her friend.

"You know I couldn't have done this without you, Gen. So often people see my name associated with a venture and they think how amazing I am. We both know my successes have been facilitated to a great extent by all the work you do behind the scenes."

"You don't have to say that, Mel, you know I would do anything for you," Gen replied.

"I know I don't, Gen, but you deserve to hear it. You also deserve this," Melody said, as she reached down and pulled a folder out of her portfolio. "I had legal draw it up."

She handed the folder to Genevieve who opened it up and looked through the paperwork. After a moment she dropped the papers into her lap and looked over at Melody, shock spreading across her face.

"Mel, this is a stock transfer for twenty percent of GDL. Are you nuts?"

Melody laughed loudly. "I do recall you making the case for that argument earlier today."

"This is serious. Do you have any idea how much money we are talking about?"

"Yes, I do."

"I can't accept this," Gen said.

"You can and you will. This is now *our* baby, Gen. A chance for us to move into much more diverse waters. I wanted you to be fully invested in it."

"I don't know what to say, Melody."

"There's nothing to say," Melody replied. "But, for the record, you're buying the drinks for the next twenty years."

"Deal," Gen said laughing.

"Feel like making some other changes on our first day?"

"Sure. What?"

"Not what, who," Melody replied. "Pamela Hayes"

"Who?"

"The executive receptionist"

"Oh, ok, what did I miss?" Gen asked.

"Nothing, just a feeling I have. Most of the time we walk right past receptionists and we never know they are even there. Quite honestly most of them are more than happy to be obscure. Not this time. I don't know, call it a hunch."

"You've always been a good judge," said Gen. "I say go for it."

Melody got up and walked over to the desk and sat down. Underneath the glass top, was a directory that listed all the department heads along with the main phone numbers. She located the number she wanted and dialed it.

"Yes, Ms. Anderson," came Pamela Hayes reply.

"Ms. Hayes, can you please come to my office."

"Yes, Ms. Anderson," she said, then hung up the phone.

Pamela Hayes stood up and walked toward the door.

"Buzz me back, Tony," she said to the security officer. "I have to go see the new boss."

"Good luck"

Pamela Hayes was on the verge of tears. Wilson Pope had already called her and said that she was being replaced. She didn't know what she had done wrong, other than to say hello. She had given so much to this company and now she wondered if she was being kicked out.

She walked up to the office, took a deep breath, and knocked on the door.

"Come in."

Pamela opened the door and stepped into the room.

Melody Anderson was sitting behind the desk, the other woman who she had come in with, was sitting in the chair adjacent to the desk.

"Please sit down," Melody said, motioning toward the free chair.

Hayes sat down feeling more than a bit uneasy.

"Ms. Hayes," Melody began "How long have you been working for GDL?"

"About ten years, ma'am," she replied.

"Have you ever thought about a change?"

"No, ma'am," Pamela replied, trying hard not to let her voice crack. "I enjoy working here,"

"Well, I appreciate your dedicated service," Melody said. "But I came in to improve things and part of that means making changes."

Here it comes, Pamela thought. "Yes ma'am, I understand."

"So effective immediately I am placing you on a mandatory two week vacation," Melody replied. "Have you ever been to St. Thomas, Ms. Hayes?"

"Yes, ma'am," Pamela replied before the words caught up with her brain. "Wait. What? No. I mean....You're not firing me?"

"Fired?" Melody said. "No, Ms. Hayes, you're being promoted. Starting in two weeks you are my new executive secretary. That's your new office outside."

Pamela Hayes sat there in stunned silence. After a moment she regained her composure enough to speak. "I'm not sure what to say, Ms. Anderson. Thank you seems so inadequate."

"It's more than adequate, Ms. Hayes," Melody replied. "By the way, was that a yes or no to St. Thomas?"

"No, ma'am. I've never been out of Maryland."

"Well, go home and pack," she said. "I'll have the tickets sent to your home by courier."

Melody stood up and extended her hand across the desk. "Congratulations and enjoy your vacation. I'll see you back here on the 14th."

"Thank you so much, Ms. Anderson."

Gen shook her hand next and the two women watched her leave the office.

Gen looked over at Melody. “That never gets old does it?”

“Never” said Mel. “Now it’s time. Let’s go celebrate.”

“I’ll take care of the travel arrangements on the flight back.”

CHAPTER FOURTEEN

Perrysville, New York State
Saturday, April 28th, 2012 – 9:15 p.m.

Deputy Sheriff Keith Banning thought he had seen a ghost.

He was on the downhill side of his twelve hour shift and was driving his patrol car along route 21. As he passed Margie's Country Kitchen he instinctively scanned the parking lot and felt a lump in his throat when he saw the old red Mustang parked near the front door to the restaurant.

He wheeled the patrol car around and headed back toward the restaurant. He pulled into the parking lot, taking the empty spot adjacent to the car, and gave it a closer once over.

It certainly looked like the right car, but surely it couldn't be, he thought. *Could it?*

Banning exited the patrol car, unconsciously adjusting his gun belt as he walked toward the front door, and entered the restaurant.

Margie's was one of those places that seemed like it had been around forever. Certainly it had opened long before he had been born and decades later it continued to operate, although the ownership had changed a number of times during that same period. The original owner, Margie Steiner, was a local resident who had opened the restaurant in the late 1940's to serve the summer crowds that habitually flocked to the Lake Champlain area.

In the 1950's the entire area began to see a population boom when the United States Air Force took over the old Army barracks in Plattsburgh. The increase led to Margie deciding to make the restaurant a full time business. She retired in 1969 and sold it; along with the name. Every half dozen years or so another owner would come into the picture, make what money they could, and then sell it again.

Unfortunately, *Margie's* had long ago seen its heyday. The interior was just as dated as the outside. To the casual person passing through, it would have looked atrocious, but to those who called Perrysville home, the interior was just as comforting as the food. The current ownership kept the place going, but deep down inside they were just waiting for the first opportunity to off load the business to the next person willing to take a gamble.

Banning made his way inside and scanned the seating areas.

The dinner crowd had finished for the day and had long since departed. All that remained now were a few truck drivers making a final pit stop before heading north into Canada. Banning continued to look around and was about to chalk it up to an overactive imagination when he spotted him sitting at a corner table, at the far end of the restaurant. He approached him cautiously, still not 100% sure his eyes weren't lying to him. By the time he drew within a dozen feet he was certain that he knew this ghost by name.

"Well they might as well just close the doors to the city, now that they already let in the riff-raff," said Banning.

Maguire looked up slowly from his plate and took in the cop standing in front of him. Banning stared back at him and then watched as the man made the mental connection and smiled.

Maguire stood up and greeted the man with a handshake.

"Geez, Keith how the hell are you?" he said. "Grab a chair. Sit down."

Banning took the seat across from Maguire and sat down.

"I saw the Mustang in the parking lot and almost ran off the road."

"Yeah, I guess it still stands out after all these years."

"Any other time I'd ask what brought you back, but I have to assume it's about Tricia."

Maguire nodded. "I saw the coverage on television and thought I would come up and see if there was anything I could do."

"Yeah, it's been a pretty bad time over at the station," replied Banning. "Sheriff Browning has been even more of a prick than usual, but we figure that at least this time he has a good reason."

"Sheriff Browning? Are you serious?"

"I'm as serious as a heart attack. There have been a lot of changes since you left, Jim," Banning replied. "About two years ago his old man had managed to bribe, or plant, enough people in key positions that when the old sheriff stepped down he was able to buy junior his dream job. Unfortunately, that dream quickly turned into a friggin' nightmare for the rest of us."

"I guess not much has changed after all has it?" Maguire said sarcastically.

Banning thought about that for a moment. "I guess you're right, Jim. Small towns, they're all the same."

"I hear you," said Maguire. "I just thought something would have gotten better, but it seems as if I took a step back in time."

"Nothing changes here, Jim, you should know that," said Banning. "Like this place. New owners come in with the best of intentions, but the place and its occupants never seem to notice. Eventually they give up and just submit to the status quo. They just stick around long enough to make their money and then get out."

The two men's revelry was interrupted by the arrival of the waitress.

"Hey, hon," she said, directing her comment to Banning. "You want your usual?"

"Nah, Julie, just give me a cup of coffee."

"Sure thing," she said before looking over at Maguire. "You need anything else, sugar?"

"No, thanks, I'm good."

The waitress returned a moment later with Banning's coffee and instinctively refilled Maguire's. The two men waited for her to leave before they continued their conversation.

"I'm still shocked that Browning was elected sheriff. Even with his daddy's money he still wasn't exactly on a lot of people's Christmas card list."

"You're shocked," laughed Banning sarcastically. "Imagine how we all felt. They passed over senior officers in the department to literally elect a used car salesman."

Maguire noted the last part of that statement was dripping in venom.

"Is he really that bad?"

"Well, let's see. Last month he was coming down County 16 from Keenseville when he clocked one of the patrol guys doing eighty-five in a fifty-five zone going to meet up with the State Police on a prisoner exchange," said Banning, as he took a drink from the coffee cup. "He called the guy in later on and wrote him a summons."

"Are you kidding me?" Maguire said. "What an ass."

"That's one of the names he's earned," said Banning with a laugh. "The guys in the office have quite a few others that are a little more *colorful*. Truth is no one trusts him. If they didn't like him before, that little gem just cemented the deal. It's hard to imagine having a boss you don't trust if you might have to go through a door with them."

"Well it sounds as if Browning hasn't changed."

"Nope," replied Banning, as he raised his coffee cup in a mock toast. "Just like old times."

"That being said, is there anything new on Tricia?" asked Maguire.

"Nada," said Banning, as he took another drink of his coffee. "It's like she disappeared off the face of the earth. It's kind of freaky if you ask me, Jim,"

"What makes you say that?"

"Well, it's like after the accident she was just *gone*," explained Banning. "We all just kind of figured she was picked up and taken to the hospital, but nothing. We were out dicking around at the crash scene, trying to see if we could pick up a trail or something, but then here comes the Sheriff and he just started having guys resume patrol."

Maguire didn't mention that he had already been out at the scene. He was more interested in getting Banning's take on things. In fact this whole conversation was a ruse. Maguire had known it was Banning well before he had even approached him. He had spotted the marked car as it was passing the restaurant and then watched as it looped back around. He had identified Banning as soon as the man had stepped out of the patrol car.

There was no point in letting Banning know that. He'd been gone away from here for a long time, better to play it close to the vest until he had a chance to figure out who the players were, at least for now. Besides, he needed some intel and Banning seemed more than willing to talk, so he let him.

"Wow," Maguire said, feigning shock. "That is weird."

"Yeah, at this point no one's holding out much hope."

"Either way, it has got to be tough on Paul," said Maguire, gauging the reaction to using Browning's first name.

"Eh, fuck him," was Banning's response. "I mean I feel bad for Tricia, but I felt bad for her the day they got married."

The two men's eyes met.

"Ah fuck, Jim, I'm sorry. I didn't..."

"No sweat, Keith, I already knew," said Maguire. "Besides, that's ancient history."

"Yeah, sure," replied Banning with more than a twinge of embarrassment. He quickly diverted the topic. "So, speaking of which, where the hell have you been hiding all these years?"

"Me? Nah, not hiding," Maguire answered. "I just needed a change of scenery so I left here and headed west. I ended up getting a photography gig out in Seattle."

"Seattle? What the hell was in Seattle?"

"Rain mostly," said Maguire with a laugh. "Lots of friggin' rain and trees. Actually, I just got back east about a year or so ago. I work in Manhattan now."

"Geez, and here we all assumed you were living the high life all these years," Banning said with a laugh.

"High life huh? Well there was that time I was photographing bald eagles on Mt. Rainier. That was pretty high up there."

"A word to the wise here, Jim. I'd work on making that story a bit more interesting," said Banning. "A lot of people have been counting on you to be the success story for all those poor bastards still trapped here. You talk about taking pictures of birds and they'll be leaping to their death in the Ausable Chasm for Christ's sake."

The two men shared a spontaneous laugh.

Maguire was happy to see Keith Banning again after all these years, but he was still hesitant. Banning had always been an affable person, and the two men had gotten along well in high school, but that had been a long time ago and people tended to change over time. He just wanted to make sure he hadn't changed too much before he showed any of his cards.

"Far be it from me to burst anyone's bubble, but the truth is a little more prosaic. I just needed a change of scenery. Unfortunately, it seems as if all I changed were mountain ranges and gave up a lake for an ocean. That being said, the job was decent and it paid the bills."

"I hear you, Jim," said Banning. "It's just that when you upped and left the stories grew more interesting with every passing day. I swear after a few years they had you living in some tent in the Middle East shepherding goats around."

Maguire laughed. "You know, there were more than a few days where that would have actually sounded good to me."

"So what are you, some kind of starving artist?" Banning asked.

"So to speak," Maguire replied. "I do a lot of freelance photography stuff for papers and magazines. It's cheaper for them to pay me to take pictures locally then to ship their own people across the country. I offset it with some portrait studio stuff. Not a whole lot of money in it, but I like being my own boss."

"I guess," said a clearly disappointed Banning.

"But enough about me, how the hell did you become a cop anyway?" Maguire replied, shifting the conversation.

"Well after high school I didn't know what I wanted to do so I hung around here and got a maintenance job at the Air Force base," Banning said. "That lasted a few years till they shut us down in 1995, part of the whole 'Base Realignment and Closure Act' bullshit. They might as well just have said what they were really doing to us in simple terms, which was fucking us without the kiss. It was like they rolled up the town overnight and then took the welcome mat with them when they left."

Maguire saw that the level of anger in Banning's voice matched the look on his face.

Banning took a sip from his coffee cup, as he regained his composure. "Anyway, about that time they held a test for the sheriff's department and I did well enough to get hired. I figure there were worse ways of making a living and you couldn't beat the benefits. The rest, as they say, is history."

"Wow," said Maguire. "Good for you. Wish I had planned ahead and gotten myself a career."

"Well, it sure does beat pushing paper behind a desk from nine to five."

"Or taking pictures of animals in the pouring rain," Maguire said with a laugh.

Banning looked down at his watch.

"Hey, Jim, I hate to cut this short, but I have to get back out there before that thorn in my ass starts looking for me," Banning said. "You gonna be back here for a while? Maybe we can get together for a beer."

"Yeah, I'd like that, I'll be around for a bit," Maguire said, standing up and shaking hands with Banning.

"Ok, are you staying here in town?"

"I'll be at my folk's place" Maguire replied.

"Ok. Hey I was really sorry to hear about them" Banning said.

"Thanks, Keith, I appreciate that."

"Man, the sheriff hears that you're back in town he just might have a coronary."

"Well, let's try to keep it quiet then," Maguire asked. "I don't need him pissing in my coffee for the time that I'm back here. Especially, now that he's armed with a gun and a badge."

"Sure thing, Jim," replied Banning. "I'll see you soon for that beer."

Banning turned around and walked out the door. Maguire sat back down, watching as the patrol car backed out and headed out toward the road.

Julie the waitress came back over to the table.

"More coffee, hon?" she asked.

"No thanks," he said.

"Are you and Keith friends?"

He paused for a moment as he searched for the right words.

"We were," he replied, "a lifetime ago."

The waitress nodded and laid the check on the table.

Maguire sat at the table a few minutes longer, finishing the remaining coffee. He looked down at the check, it was $12.37. *I guess you stayed in business up here by charging a fair price*, he thought. He got up from the table and reached into his pocket and tossed a twenty dollar bill onto the table. He always did have a soft spot for waitresses.

He walked out of the restaurant and headed toward the car. The temperature outside had dropped considerably, which was not uncommon in the Adirondacks. He turned up the collar on his fleece jacket and zipped it up. Again his thoughts were drawn back to Tricia and he wondered where she was. He got in the car and turned the key, hearing the engine roar to life. He backed out of the parking lot and headed out on the road, toward the house he had left more than two decades earlier.

It was a fairly short drive and before he had a chance to digest it all he found himself pulling up to the house. He noted that the lights were on in the living room as he pulled into the driveway. He thought about pulling the car into the garage to hide it, but decided against it. It really wouldn't matter he reasoned to himself, Perrysville was a small enough town and by the morning half of it would already know he was back. He stopped the car near the back door and leaned over, opening the glove compartment, and removed a set of keys for the house. He exited the car and and opened the trunk, pulling out the two bags.

Maguire walked up to the back door, pausing as he reached it and set the two bags down on the small deck. He took a deep breath before sliding the key inside the lock and turning the door knob.

Walking through the back door was like stepping back in time. Nothing had changed and something deep inside him half expected to hear his mother call out his name. However, the reality was that he knew it would never come.

It had been almost eight years already and he remembered it like it was only yesterday. He had been on a protection detail with the Deputy Prime Minister of Israel when he was advised to contact the Operations Unit *forthwith*. He knew something was wrong, forthwith was an adverb that was not used lightly in the NYPD. In fact it was only used two ways. Either someone was in trouble or you were in trouble.

The detective that answered advised him that he needed to contact an investigator from the New York State Police, Troop B, and gave him the number. Maguire knew something bad had happened and steeled himself for the worse.

The investigator shared more with him than he normally would have out of professional courtesy. The man had previously served on the New York State Governor's security detail and had a good working relationship with the detectives from the Intelligence Division.

It was late October and he told Maguire that his parents had been driving north on the thruway to attend a faculty dinner dance at SUNY Plattsburgh. They were still trying to piece things together, but it appeared that they were involved in a hit and run accident with what they believed to be an apparent drunk driver.

Prior to the accident the local 911 dispatcher was notified of a late model red pickup truck swerving in and out of the northbound lanes just south of Plattsburgh. A short time later multiple calls came in for an accident in the same area. When troopers arrived the local fire department was on the scene attempting to extricate the occupants of the vehicle. The troopers determined that his parent's car had gone off the road at a particularly steep embankment, flipping over numerous times before coming to a rest against a large tree. The force of hitting the tree had caved in the vehicles roof trapping his parents inside. Despite the monumental efforts of the fire department and emergency medical personnel they both passed away at the scene.

The preliminary investigation uncovered evidence that they had been struck on the front driver's quarter panel. There was a red paint transfer that was readily visible. The vehicle had been towed from the scene as evidence and they would be lifting samples from the panel and attempting to identify the exact vehicle. The investigator took down Maguire's cell phone number and promised to get in touch with him as soon as they knew more.

By the time Maguire had gotten off the phone, a second Intel detail had shown up and relieved them from their assignment. Maguire's partner drove him back to their office in Brooklyn and his sergeant told him to take as many days off as he needed, but as Maguire drove away he realized he didn't know where to go.

There was no point in going up there; there was certainly nothing he could do. He had seen too much death in his life to have any illusions. He realized from the beginning that there was nothing that would bring them back. He felt a sense of incredible emptiness inside him. So much time had passed between them that he didn't know how he was going to reconcile it all.

In the end he just went home and opened a bottle of Jameson Irish Whiskey and drank till he passed out.

When he had recovered, he prepared himself for the ordeal that he believed would follow. However, sorting out their personal affairs turned out to be a very uncomplicated.

Maguire reached out to the one person whom he knew would have all the answers. A close family friend who was their attorney and had all the paperwork already prepared. The funeral arrangements had all been made years earlier, from casket selections to cemetery plots.

Shamus Maguire was, if nothing else, a meticulous planner.

James was their only child and the sole heir of their estate. Neither Shamus nor Maggie had any living siblings so there were no long lost relatives who might surface feigning shock at the loss of their dearly departed family member. Their entire estate was remarkably easy to handle, but that wasn't to say that their estate was in anyway small.

While the Maguire's had lived a very unpretentious lifestyle, Shamus Maguire was actually a very astute stock trader and had enjoyed great success during the early days of the computer and internet industry. He was also smart enough to read the proverbial tea leaves and left the market in the waning days of 1999, before the collapse of the dot.com bubble.

Their financial plan was to ensure that, when the time came for them to retire, they would be able to pursue their other passion and travel around the world. In addition both carried million dollar life insurance policies to ensure that the other would be well taken care of for the rest of their lives. That plan however did not factor them leaving this life together.

In the end, when it was all said and done, Maguire inherited the house and just over three and a half million dollars.

Maguire never could find it in him to return back to the house or to Perrysville for that matter. Even though he couldn't go back, he wanted to make sure that the house was tended to. It had played such an important part in his life and he didn't want to make any decisions based solely on his emotions at the time. As a result he had arranged for a trusted local handyman to maintain the general upkeep of the house, both inside and out.

Timers had been placed on the interior lights and there were a number of motion sensor activated lights throughout the exterior to chase away anything more than a curious raccoon. He even had it decorated during the holidays, all to maintain the illusion of a lived in residence.

As for the inheritance, he had no use for it, but he was also not naïve either. He sat down with a financial adviser and the funds were placed in a highly diversified portfolio. He figured he owed it to his parents to at least be a good fiscal steward for their money.

Maguire made his way through the kitchen, taking in everything from the scent to the dated décor. It was like a sensory overload. Everything was the same as when he left and yet, at the same time, it all appeared foreign. He continued through the kitchen and dining room then entered the living room where he set his bags down on the floor.

The house felt chilly, as the thermostat had intentionally been set low. After all, there was no need to tend to the daily comfort of any guests. He thought about turning the thermostat up, but opted instead for something a little more familiar. He went over to the wood rack and selected several of the logs from the wrought iron holder. With just a little bit of effort he had a nice fire burning within a few minutes. He stood up and went over to the bar and found an unopened bottle of his father's favorite whiskey. He opened it and poured himself a drink before taking a seat in his father's chair.

He stared at the adjacent chair where his mother would have sat. How many days had he come home to see the two of them here reading together.

Maguire gazed at the fire and took a sip of the whiskey. He felt the warm burn as the liquid went down his throat.

It had been nearly twenty-three years since he had last been in this house. In fact, he had been away from it more years than he had actually lived in it. The house was silent except for the crackling of the burning wood. He leaned back in the chair and rubbed his weary eyes. He hadn't known what he had expected to find.

It all seemed so surreal to him, sitting here. He contrasted where he had been all those years before and where he was now.

Maguire looked over at the staircase that led to the upstairs bedrooms and took another drink. He decided that he wasn't prepared to move beyond the living room at this point. Exorcising those ghosts would have to wait until tomorrow. He reached around and removed the Sig Sauer from the small of his back and laid it on the wooden end table next to the chair.

He spent the remainder of the night in the living room finishing off a significant amount of the whiskey before fading off to sleep in front of the fire. A half hour later the automatic timers cycled off and the house went dark.

CHAPTER FIFTEEN

Southampton, Suffolk County, N.Y.
Saturday, April 28th, 2012 – 10:55 p.m.

"*We're sorry; the person you are trying to reach is unavailable at this time. Please try your call again later.*"

Melody groaned as she hit the button to end the call. She had been trying to reach James for the last hour, but wherever he was there was no service. She laid the phone on her night table and resigned herself to the fact that she was not going to hear from him tonight.

She got up and walked out onto the deck. There was a light breeze coming off the water. Melody leaned on the railing and stared out across the bay to where the houseboat sat moored to the dock. There were no lights on. She let her mind wander back to where she had been just twenty-four short hours ago.

"Penny for your thoughts."

She turned and saw Genevieve walking toward her. In her hands she held a tray which had two large drinks and a pitcher that contained a creamy, beige colored liquid.

Melody reached out and took one of the glasses.

"Thanks, hon, I needed this," she said.

"I kind of figured you would," Gen said. as she set the tray down onto the patio table. She picked up her drink and joined Melody in leaning on the railing looking out over the water. "I thought we would be celebrating tonight, but I guess your mind is somewhere else."

"So did I, I'm just having a tough time with it all," Melody said and took a sip of the piña colada. "Mmmm, that is really good. Damn you missed your calling."

"I concocted a new recipe," Gen said. "I'm getting ready for my retirement gig as a bartender in Cabo. I've got a whole other pitcher chilling in the fridge."

"Hey, after today, you might just be able to buy your own resort," Melody said, as she gazed back out toward the marina.

Genevieve stared over at her friend, "He really did get under your skin, didn't he?"

"Big time," said Melody with a sigh.

Genevieve took a sip from her drink. "He'll call you, don't worry"

"You really think so?"

"He'd have to be crazy if he didn't," Gen said. "And if he doesn't, I'll go over there and personally kick his ass and sink his little dingy."

That made Melody laugh.

"I don't ever remember feeling this way about anyone," she replied. "Part of it scares the crap out of me and yet I feel more alive than I have ever felt before."

Genevieve took Melody's hand and looked into her eyes. "Hon, you know I want only the best for you, but I'm also going to be your voice of reason. Go slowly."

Melody smiled. "Yes, ma'am, I promise. I will use my head."

"Know what I think?" Genevieve said with a mischievous grin.

"No, what are you thinking?"

"It's hot tub time, girlie."

Genevieve turned around, grabbing the pitcher from the table, and headed back toward the opposite end of the deck to where the sunken hot tub was. She set the pitcher down on the deck, stripped out of her clothes, and slowly stepped down into the hot soothing water. A minute later, Melody followed suit.

It was a calculated move. She knew that if she didn't do something, Melody would be staring across the bay till the sun came up. She had never seen her friend act like this before, at least not over a man. She decided that she would do everything she could to divert her attention away from this mystery man, at least for tonight.

"We did good today, didn't we?" Gen asked.

"Yes we did," Melody replied, as she felt the soothing hot water engulfing her body, "but the real work begins Monday. I know everyone was in that euphoric stage today, mostly because they rid themselves of those two thorns in their collective sides, but I'm not counting on that to last very long."

"Agreed," said Gen, as she took a sip from the glass. "We have the test trials coming up this summer for *Dragon's Breath*. That's going to preoccupy everyone for the next few months. Even though that will be the proverbial bread winner for a long time to come, we still need to focus on diversification."

"That's exactly what I was thinking. Their current projects list is pretty heavy, but there's one or two that I would really like to nudge to the top," Melody explained.

"I know what you mean. I know the military ones are where the big money is at, but I had my eyes on several which seemed very marketable to both the military as well as the private sector. Which ones piqued your curiosity?" Gen asked.

"The reactive armor one was at the top of my list," Melody answered. "I guess that's my inner sci-fi nerd poking out. I see the potential for crossing over into the civilian law enforcement market on that one as well."

"I like that one too. I'd also like to take a closer look at some of the light weapon systems coming out of R&D. There are a couple of *black projects* that we were denied access to prior to the acquisition."

A black project was a highly classified military or defense project, unacknowledged publicly by the government, military personnel or defense contractors. These projects are routinely denied to exist. Examples of such projects would include the SR-71 Blackbird and B-2 Spirit stealth bomber.

"Like what?" Melody asked, as she leaned back in the tub and closed her eyes. The hot water and the piña colada were having the most amazing effect on her. She could feel the stress draining away from her with every passing moment.

"Pope gave me a flash drive before we left. It outlines all the current projects as well as those still in R&D," she explained. "One is for a man portable weapons system that has its foundation in the Dragon's Breath technology."

"Ooh, now you're really appealing to my inner nerd" Melody laughed.

"Basically it is part of an integrated system that allows complete connectivity between the soldier and weapon via an integrated computer. The soldier has a completely enclosed helmet that features a full screen heads up display. The display shows positioning on the field of all friendly and enemy combatants. If a previously unseen enemy fires a weapon, the system *hears* the shot, so to speak, and puts a target on the display."

"That's pretty impressive," Melody said.

"Ya think?" asked Gen rhetorically. "The real magic comes from the programming. Once the shooter targets an enemy the computer takes over and does all the work. It feeds the weapon all the pertinent information regarding distance, wind, etc. Imagine a sniper that doesn't need to make any adjustments. Just *Focus, Fire and Forget.*"

"You're talking about reinventing warfare," Melody said.

"The potential is staggering," Genevieve replied.

Melody let the full weight of what Gen had just said sink in. Prior to today all of her fights were limited to the financial battlefield. Now something that she controlled was going to have real world ramifications and, more importantly, affect the lives of America's soldiers.

She glanced over at the fire pit that sat in the middle of the deck. She watched as the blue flames flickered and danced at the whim of the breezes coming off the ocean. There was something mesmerizing about fire. It was inherently beautiful and yet at the same time its beauty was equally matched by its danger. She took another sip of her drink.

"I'm planning on flying out Monday morning to take a look at everything, or at least as much as I can," Genevieve said. "I'm also stopping at the corporate office first before heading out to Montana. I want to get the lay of the land and see how things go on a regular work day. Want to come?"

"I would, but I have that board meeting in Manhattan to go to."

"Want me to postpone my trip till later in the day or maybe even Tuesday?" asked Gen.

"No, I think it's best that we show we are going to be involved right from the very beginning," Melody said. "I'd rather hit the ground running on this one. Besides, I'm interested to see what you're going to find when you get there. How long do you plan on being gone?"

"I was thinking I'd be back late Wednesday evening. That should give me ample time to figure out where we stand with not only *Dragon's Breath,* but also some of the other projects."

"That's fine. We'll do dinner when you get back and go over all the sordid details."

In the back of her mind Melody was thinking about Maguire and when she would see him again. What seemed like an eternity had only been a mere few hours earlier. Right or wrong, she yearned for his touch. It would be nice to get out from under Genevieve's voice of reason for a while.

She took another drink and finished it off.

"Time for refills," Gen said, as she leaned over and grabbed the pitcher to refill the glasses.

When she was done she handed one to Melody and raised her own in a toast. "To us."

"Onward and upward," Melody replied, as she tapped her glass against Gen's.

CHAPTER SIXTEEN

Perrysville, New York State
Sunday, April 29th, 2012 – 12:13 a.m.

The man sat behind the steering wheel of the pickup truck and peered intently at the house he had driven past thousands of times before. He took a long slow drag of the cigarette and exhaled deeply. It was simultaneously eerie and yet exhilarating. As he watched, the interior lights went out. For a moment he allowed himself to speculate what would happen if he just snuck into the house and..........

He chased those thoughts away.

He had to caution himself not to lose his focus. He had gone to great lengths to plan everything and he was not going to fail because he had deviated from the precise script he had written for himself.

He thought back on all the planning he had undertaken and was actually surprised that a large part had now been rendered completely unnecessary. During the initial stages he had continually erred on the side of caution because he simply had been unable to accurately gauge the potential response.

In the case of the propofol he was unsure as to what her reaction was going to be; so he held back on the dosage until he could measure her response. The hospital environment was simply a ruse that he had put into place to keep her quiet. The reality was that there was no place for her to go. The wrist and ankle straps would keep her in place, but it was better to have her be a compliant *patient* than a person being held forcibly against her will.

In fact the drug had worked perfectly, much better than he had ever imagined, and so he continued to keep her under. If he had to bring her out for any reason the hospital scenario would continue to work because she would have no concept of time.

Another issue he was unable to prepare for was how long it would take Maguire to actually get here. He had originally guessed that it would take about a week, but there had been no guarantee. He had planned for things before and been proven wrong.

That part actually still bothered him. At the time he was almost afraid that something had already happened to him. He was greatly relieved to see that the funeral announcement indicated that they were survived by their only son.

Really, he thought, *who doesn't attend their own parent's funeral*?

Now he realized that he was actually going to have to proceed with the next part of his plan. He was still a bit less comfortable with that, but he would get past it. You couldn't achieve success without risk or the willingness to do the less than pleasant tasks.

He continued to watch the house for a little while longer.

A short time later he started the pickup and pulled away from the curb. He did a U-turn and headed away from the house before he turned his headlights back on.

CHAPTER SEVENTEEN

Perrysville, New York State
Friday June 23rd, 1989 – 12:23 p.m.

Principal Michael Waters stood in front of the graduating class of 1989. He gripped the edges of the podium tightly as he spoke to the students and guests who were assembled in the high school gymnasium.

He looked out at the sea of gold and black and paused for a moment as he prepared his closing remarks. It would mark his eighteenth and final year as the principal of the Perrysville High School. Tomorrow would begin his first official day of retirement.

Waters had begun preparing for this moment almost a year ago. Somehow, the fact that it was his last commencement speech gave him a profound sense of freedom. The pressure of doing the *touchy, feely* politically correct speeches all these years had emotionally drained him.

How many of his prior students had gone out into the world envisioning that it would be filled with rainbows and unicorns only to find their dreams battered and broken on the rocky shoals of reality? he wondered.

He would not have that on his conscience for his final speech.

There were two hundred and fifty-three seniors graduating today. At the moment two hundred and fifty-two were seated in the auditorium, a mix of horror, fear and amazement in their eyes.

"Today is a turning point in the lives of many of you," he continued. "Most people will tell you that this is one of the most important days of your life. They are lying. It is a lie that is told from generation to generation and just because it is repeated so often gives it no more credibility. The truth is you will only vaguely remember this day twenty years from now."

"Those well-meaning folks will also tell you that these are the best years of your life. I am happy to inform you that, except for a select few among you, this is a lie as well."

He allowed his gaze to linger a moment longer on Paul Browning before continuing.

"For the rest of you gathered here today this marks the beginning of a new chapter in your life. One that I honestly hope will be filled with many events that will bring you happiness and joy."

"Over the course of the last four years I have had the pleasure of watching you change, from wide-eyed freshmen, filled with wonder, to seniors with your dreams of the future. I am profoundly sad to say that most of them will not be realized. You are not stepping out into a world of endless possibility; you are in fact going forth into a world that is cold and ruthless. You will be required to prove yourselves time and again before you are offered the chief executive officer's job. You will face challenges in your life that you cannot possibly fathom now."

"Today, the sun will set on my time as an educator. It will be the culmination of a career that has spanned some forty years. When the sun rises tomorrow you will all have to face your own future. The only advice I can give you is this," He paused for a moment, letting the last words hang in the air for effect.

The gymnasium was absolutely silent, save for the sound of the overhead fans doing their best to beat back the heat on this late June day.

"Have the courage to let go of your past and embrace whatever the future has in store for you. Be willing to suffer; be willing to dare; be willing to risk it all in chasing a dream that seems stupid to everyone else. The world does not owe you anything, nor do you have the right to ask the world to give you anything. Remember that life is hard; it is harder when you try to please everyone else around you."

"When you come to the difficult choices in life, don't choose the easy way. Choose the ones that you believe in and by doing so you will remove all of the 'what ifs' that will haunt you in twenty or thirty years. In doing so you might very well find yourself living in a cardboard box under a bridge, or surviving on spaghetti-o's and cigarettes. That is the price we must sometimes pay for our folly."

He paused again staring out into the sea of students enrapt in his *swan song* speech.

Maguire stood outside the high school building, his gold gown draped over his left arm the black graduation cap held tightly in his hand. Somewhere inside his parents sat, believing that he was sitting somewhere among the graduating class.

He leaned back against the wall and listened to the principal's speech as it carried through the windows.

"In twenty years you might find that those who sit here with you today are remarkably different. The mighty may fall, the meek may rise. Dreams of making a million dollars and living the lifestyle of the rich and famous may actually manifest themselves in the reality of a spouse, two kids and living paycheck to paycheck. Life does not favor anyone, but it generally rewards those who find a way to overcome the obstacles, to find a way to persevere even when you are battered and bruised."

"In closing I would like to read you a motto which comes from a rather obscure United States Navy unit. As you go forward with your lives, I hope that you keep these words at the forefront of your thoughts. *The only easy day was yesterday.*"

"Thank you and God bless each and every one of you."

With that statement, Michael Waters and the Perrysville Graduating Class of 1989 closed the final chapter on their respective high school careers.

As the students and guests erupted into raucous cheering, one individual sat seething in anger, as he gazed upon the nearby folding chair that remained empty.

Maguire woke up with a start, his hand instinctively reaching out for the handgun on the end table as he attempted to acclimate himself to his present surroundings. There was no threat, just the ghosts of his past haunting him in his dreams again.

He stood up and stretched and checked his watch. It was 5:52 a.m. He made his way into the kitchen and looked out the window over the sink. He could make out the first light of the sun coming up over the horizon. It was like the shimmering rays of a red beacon.

He thought back for a moment, what was it the old sailors used to say? *Red sky at night, sailor's delight. Red sky at morn, sailor's take warn.*

Was it a sign of things to come, he wondered?

He reached up and opened a cabinet door. It was more out of habit than anything; the cabinets were devoid of any food items. He groaned and closed the door. He would have to go out for his coffee this morning. He made a mental note to stop by the store and pick up some essentials at some point during the day.

Maguire returned back to the living room and gathered up his stuff and walked toward the staircase. Now was as good a time as any to make the dreaded trip up to the second floor.

As he walked by he looked into the little sitting alcove that sat near the base of the stairs. There were two chairs and a small table in the middle with a chessboard that sat on top of it. The game was still in play some twenty-three years later. His father had taught him the game at a very early age and some of his fondest memories were of the two of them sitting there for countless hours locked in some epic battle.

Shamus Maguire was a master of the game of chess and he had taught James that in order to be at one with the game you needed to understand it intimately. To respect each and every piece as well as their capabilities. To this point the board and all of its pieces had been hand carved by his father. His initials, SM, were etched into the bottom of each. He said it was a rite of passage. That when you labored over creating something you were less inclined to lose a piece without giving every consideration to the move.

"Many people get too caught up in what an individual piece can do," his father had told him. "They place too much importance on whether it is a major piece like a rook or minor one like a bishop or a knight. In their hubris they might very well find themselves checkmated by a perfect pawn."

"A perfect pawn?" James asked.

"Yes, a perfect pawn," his father replied. "Because they are so numerous, pawns are often relegated to a supporting role. They are maneuvered around and sacrificed to advance a particular strategy, but, in rare cases, the pawn can be played in such a way that it can checkmate the king, if it has the right support."

He smiled as he recalled the conversation; as if it had happened only yesterday. He reached down and moved his bishop to f4 and took the pawn, placing it off to the side

As Maguire headed up the staircase he stopped for a moment and looked over the framed photos that adorned the wall. His mother had started at the lower end and, through the years, worked her way up toward the top of the staircase, marking milestones and special events in the life of the family. There were pictures of him as a child, a few with Lake Champlain as a backdrop. A group shot when he had graduated from elementary school. Another was from a rare family vacation trip to Disney complete with Mickey. At the end was a photo of him in his Navy dress blue uniform from when he had graduated the U.S. Navy Recruit Training Center in Great Lakes, Illinois. He had sent it to his mother simply because he had no one else to send it to. He had never dreamed that she would have actually displayed it. It was like walking through a time line of his life.

He navigated the last few steps to the second floor landing and walked to his bedroom. He opened the door and paused. If the stairwell was a timeline of his life, the room was a time portal. He stepped through the doorway feeling more than a little bit apprehensive. The walls were still adorned with posters of faded rock music legends. Over by the window was an antique desk, which was complimented nicely by an equally antique IBM 386 computer. He laughed at the sight, thinking he felt as old as that computer sometimes. Against one wall was a book case with two ugly orange chairs and a wooden coffee table.

He laid the bags on the bed and he reached into the pocket of his jacket and withdrew his cell phone. He saw that there was a missed call from Melody. He would have to call her later, at a more decent time and after he had some coffee. He took off his jacket and laid it on the bed along with the pistol. He then grabbed a change of clothes, and the shaving kit from the bag, and headed down the hallway toward the bathroom. Any further trip down memory lane would have to wait until later.

If his bedroom was an *homage* to the 80's, the bathroom harkened back at least another decade. The avocado green porcelain toilet, tub and sink competed for attention against the Mylar accented pink floral themed wallpaper. For reasons still unknown to him Maggie Maguire had actually loved the look. James, on the other hand, had always thought it looked rather garish and not even nostalgia could change his opinion.

He turned the shower on and listened to it sputter to life as the trapped air cleared the pipes. He let it run for a few minutes to clean out the line and to get it hot. He set the kit and clothes on the edge of the vanity and got undressed. He stepped into the shower and felt the blast of hot water on his skin. That was one thing he had sorely missed about the bathroom, the water pressure. He lingered longer than he normally would and the heat felt good on his aching muscles. He reminded himself that sleeping in the old chair was certainly not the worst place he had ever slept in. Grudgingly he turned off the water, grabbed a towel and dried himself off.

He shaved and got dressed before picking up his laundry and heading back to his room. Maguire tossed the clothes against the wall by the closet door. Some old habits would never change. He sat down in the chair by the desk and put his shoes on. When he was done he walked over and picked up the bags. He opened the closet door and stepped inside.

It was an old large walk-in closet that was lined with cedar. He laid the clothes bag on the floor, just inside the doorway, and walked toward the back wall that contained a series of shelves. Most were filled with old cameras, lenses, other accessories and a few books. He knelt down and depressed the wooden slat, just under the second shelf, and heard the click. The wall popped out slightly allowing him to pull it open.

Behind the wall was an additional four feet of storage space. He had found it one day as he was putting some books on the lower shelf. At the time he thought it was really cool and had let his imagination run wild as he speculated as to the reason why it was there. In the end he never did figure it out and lost interest in it about the same time that he found an interest in girls. Maguire pulled the door open and laid the gun bag inside. He then closed the wall until he heard it lock back in place and stepped out of the closet, closing the door behind him.

He grabbed the pistol from the bed and clipped it onto his belt before putting on his jacket. He walked out of the bedroom and headed back down the stairs. As he made his way out the back door of the house he walked over to the garage, entering it through the side door. Maguire turned on the lights and looked over his father's work bench. He selected a small roll of monofilament fishing line and a pair of scissors. Maguire cut off two, three inch pieces and returned the items back to the bench before heading back inside the house.

First he opened the front door and placed one of the pieces of fishing line against the jamb and closed it. Even though the front door faced the street, and made an unappealing target, he still wanted to make sure he would know if anyone had come calling while he was gone. He repeated this at the back door as he left. After securing the doors he got into the Mustang and backed out of the driveway.

Maguire drove through the back roads of Perrysville and headed north till he reached County Highway 16 and turned toward Keenseville. Just as he pulled into town he stopped at a small diner that catered predominantly to the breakfast and lunch crowd. He parked the car out front and walked inside.

Stepping inside he was hit by sensory overload. He could smell the heavy, greasy aroma of food being prepared in the back and the sound of dishes clinking as they hit the metal counter to be served up. The crowd in the diner was small, but vocal, and consisted of mostly older men. They were the typical early morning coffee group that one usually finds in small towns. Each day they gather together around small tables to talk about everything and everyone. Some days the topics revolved around the latest local politics while other days it might center on fishing. More often than not they just liked to complain and if they didn't have a topic at hand then they would talk about anyone in the group that was absent that particular day.

Most of the diners looked up inquisitively as he walked in and then went right back to their conversation. Maguire walked over to the counter and ordered a large black coffee along with a bacon and egg sandwich from the waitress behind the counter. As she turned to put the order in Maguire asked her a question.

"Excuse me, would you happen to have a phone book handy?" he asked the woman.

"Sure, hon, in the back by the phone booth," she said, pointing. Then she turned around and called out his order to the cook behind the counter.

Maguire turned around and headed in the direction she had indicated. He walked down a long, wood paneled, hallway which led to the back of the diner. He laughed when he located the phone booth sandwiched between the restrooms. It was an old throwback from the fifties. One of those massive wooden booths that at one time would have featured an antique rotary phone mounted on the wall with a seat and folding glass doors for privacy. At some time in the past the rotary phone had been replaced with a more modern version, but it still possessed its charm. Affixed to the top of the booth was an old porcelain sign that proudly proclaimed that it was a Bell System public telephone.

He peered inside and located the local phone book on the shelf underneath the phone. Maguire sat down and began thumbing through the pages. It was not a difficult search; there was only one art gallery in Keenseville. He took out a pen and a piece of paper from his inner jacket pocket, than wrote down the address. When he was done he walked back out to the counter.

"Find what you were looking for, hon?" asked the waitress, as she placed the coffee container and bag on the counter.

"I did. Thank you," Maguire replied and handed her a ten dollar bill. "Keep the change."

"Thanks, sugar, you have a great day and don't forget to come back."

"I'll do that," he said with a smile. He picked up the coffee and the brown paper bag and made his way toward the door. The waitress stared just a moment longer before returning back to work.

Maguire got back in the car and set the bag on the seat next to him. He propped the coffee cup up on the dash, leaning it against the windshield, and drove the few blocks over to the address that he had written down on the paper.

Keenseville was a town lost in time. Stores came and went, but the buildings themselves never seemed to change. In fact, all that ever seemed to change was the name on the sign that hung above the plate glass windows. In a way it was what helped to maintain its quaintness.

In that way, the art gallery was no different. It was an old, two story red brick commercial building that sat on the corner. At one time it had been part of a row of storefront buildings that lined the street. Over the years, several of those adjoining buildings had lost their battle with time and the elements. After they were torn down the owners never rebuilt, hoping that in time a strip mall developer might come in and offer them money for the land. The developers and the money never did come and the lots became little more than large, unused parking lots.

The front of the art gallery was your typical large pane glass window storefront that had its wood trim painted over in a high gloss black. Just behind the windows were several pieces of artwork to lure in prospective customers. A black sign hung above the entrance with the letters *L'amour Brisé* in gold lettering.

Maguire pulled the car just past the location and made a U-turn so that he could face the front of the building.

He reached up and grabbed the coffee container from the dash. He pulled the plastic tab back on the lid and took a drink. When he was done he placed the cup back up on its perch, watching as the hot steam began to fog the corner of the windshield. Maguire reached over and grabbed the brown bag and removed the sandwich from it. It was comfort food and that was what he needed right now.

When he was done he crumbled up the paper wrapper and put it back in the bag. He checked his watch and took another drink. It was just before eight o'clock. He reached into his jacket pocket and removed the cell phone.

The phone rang a few times before he heard it connect and a voice, that was not quite yet awake, said "hello?"

"Morning, sleepy head, have a rough night?"

"Huh?" came the startled reply, as Melody struggled to wake up. "James? Is that you?"

"Yes it is," he said. "Sorry I missed your call last night."

"That's ok," she said, as she sat up in bed. Her head still ached from the night before. "What time is it? Where are you?"

"It's almost eight and I'm in a little town in upstate New York, which you've never heard of before, thinking about you."

That perked her up.

"What's so important upstate that it is keeping you away from me?"

He thought about that for a moment and took another drink.

"It's personal," he replied.

"Oh, ok. I didn't mean to pry," she said apologetically.

"No, I didn't mean it that way," he explained. "I meant that I wasn't up here on business."

"Gotcha," she said. "I hope everything is ok."

He heard the concern in her voice.

"Actually, no, it's not. Someone I went to high school with got into an accident up here and went missing," he explained. "I thought I'd come up here to see if I could help."

"I'm so sorry, James," she said. "Is there anything I can do to help?"

"Thanks, but I can't think of anything," he said. "Actually, I'm coming up empty myself."

"That sucks."

"Pretty much," he said. "I was hoping that we would be able to go out to dinner, but now I'm not sure how long I am going to be up here."

Melody thought about that for a moment, she had wanted to get together with him as well.

"Well I might have a solution to that problem if you're game?"

"Oh I'm game. What do you have in mind?"

"Is there an airport up there?" she asked.

"Matter of fact there is. What are you suggesting?"

"If you're free, I'll fly up to you tonight, we can have dinner and you can stay there and take care of whatever it is you need to do," she explained. "All you have to do is find the restaurant and pick me up."

"Plattsburgh International Airport," he said. "How does seafood sound?"

"Sounds perfect to me," Melody replied.

"Let's plan for around 5 o'clock?" he said.

"That works for me," said Melody.

"Well then what are you doing lying in bed, gorgeous?" Maguire said with a laugh. "Go make your travel arrangements and text me with the flight information when you get it."

At that moment he saw a side door open and a woman with short blonde haired step outside. What immediately caught his attention was that she didn't appear to be dressed for the outdoors. She wore a white blouse with a short black skirt and heels, even though the temperature outside was still fairly cool. He watched as the women walked around to the front entrance and unlocked the door to the gallery and stepped inside.

"I will," she replied. "If anything changes I'll let you know, otherwise I will see you later."

"Looking forward to it, Melody," he said and ended the call.

He continued to watch the front of the gallery. There were lights on now in the interior. Maguire took another drink from the cup which he noted was already beginning to get cold. He grabbed the bag and the cup with him, as he got out of the car, tossing them into one of the sidewalk garbage cans as he made his way over to the gallery.

He tried the door, but found that it was still locked. He knocked on the door frame.

The woman he'd seen earlier approached the door and peered out. Even through the glass, Maguire could make out the weariness in the woman's face; the redness in her eyes served as proof of an evening spent crying.

"Sorry, we're closed," she said through the closed door.

"I'm not here to shop. I'm a friend of Tricia's," he said.

The woman stood for a moment staring at him. He didn't look threatening and there was something vaguely familiar about him. She unlocked the door and opened it hesitantly.

"What can I do for you?" she said.

"I was hoping you might be able to give me some information about Tricia," he said.

"I'm sorry, you'll have to speak to her husband, Sheriff Browning," she replied and began to close the door.

He put his hand on the door to hold it open. "I don't think her husband is going to really want to speak with me. My name is James Maguire; I'm an old friend of Tricia's."

In that instant the woman realized why he had looked so familiar. He'd certainly changed in the last twenty years, but in truth they all had changed. He just seemed to have aged better than most.

"I'm so sorry, James," she said, opening the door back up. "Please come in."

Maguire stepped inside, scanning the interior of the gallery. If the exterior of the building was small town, the interior was big city. Polished chrome, brushed aluminum and bright lights accented exposed steel beams and aged brick walls. The gallery featured an eclectic assortment of pieces ranging from abstract paintings and pop art, to statues and hand crafted metal work. Leave it to Tricia to bring together so many diverse pieces into this setting and still manage to make it work.

"Would you like some coffee?" she asked. "I just made a fresh pot."

"That would be great," he replied.

Maguire followed, as she made her way toward the back of the gallery.

"Please, have a seat," she said, pointing toward the brown leather couch. She took the carafe and poured two cups.

"You don't remember me do you?" she asked. She turned around and handed him one of the cups before sitting down in the chair opposite him.

"Thank you," he said. "No actually, I don't"

"That's okay, you were pretty distracted back then," she laughed. "I was only in school for senior year."

She saw his face frown a bit as he thought intently and just as quickly she saw the recognition. Maguire looked at her closer now, she had certainly grown-up.

"Lena, wow," he said. "I'm so sorry I didn't recognize you sooner."

"Don't be silly, James," she said with a laugh. "We all have a few years down the road. I consider it a compliment that I don't look like I did back then."

"Well that's true, but you look fantastic. Although I seem to recall you having darker hair."

"Yeah, you know what they say, *blondes have more fun.* It's just too bad we can't stay young."

"Unfortunately no one warns you just how tough getting old can be," he added.

"I don't know about that. The years certainly seem to have been kind to you," Lena replied, as she took a sip of coffee. "Under normal circumstances I'd ask what brought you back to town, but I think I already know the answer. What can I help you with?"

"I heard the news reports and thought I might come up and lend a hand," Maguire replied. "Unfortunately when I got here I found that no one seemed to need it."

"Not surprising to be honest," Lena replied. "There was no love lost between Tricia and that asshole she was married to. I'm sure he made an attempt for P.R. purposes, but that's about all I would expect from him."

"Seriously?" Maguire asked.

"Seriously," she replied matter-of-factly. "Paul Browning is, and has always been, a USDA Certified Grade 'A' asshole. In fact, he pretty much bullied Tricia all her life. It has only been in the last half dozen years or so that Tricia found the strength to begin to push back."

Maguire felt a wave of anger begin to rise up inside him. He had tried to hide it, took a sip of coffee, but she had seen it flash across his eyes.

She leaned over the coffee table and took his hand in hers; the two stared at each other, as if connecting on a different level. There was a sense of empathy in her eyes toward him, as if they shared a common bond, a common emotion.

"James, there is a lot that you think you know, but there is a whole lot more that you don't."

"Educate me then," Maguire replied.

"Where do I begin?" she said out loud, not sure if it was directed to him or herself.

She got up and walked back over to the coffee pot and topped off her coffee cup. She turned around, raising the carafe up in his direction. "Want a top-off?"

"Sure, I'll take some more," he said. "From the sound of that last statement I might be here awhile."

Lena refilled his cup, sat the carafe back down and returned to her seat.

She reached over and picked up the pack of cigarettes off the coffee table.

"You mind?" she asked.

"Doesn't bother me, Lena," he said.

"You know, I quit for five years," she said, as she lit the cigarette up and inhaled deeply. "It's amazing how quickly you fall back to the old habits when something goes wrong."

"If you only knew," he laughed.

"This is so complicated, James, I'm not even sure where to start."

"The beginning?" he said sincerely.

"Everything begins back in our senior year," Lena answered. "What do you remember, James?"

"Well, for me it is pretty straightforward," Maguire said. "In senior year Tricia and I were dating and making plans to attend college the following school year. Then, out of the blue, it was over."

"But it was you that left, wasn't it?" Lena said.

"At the time it just didn't seem like there was much left for me here."

"What about Tricia?"

"It looked to me like she had made other choices that didn't seem to fit the plans we had made together."

"Did you ever talk to her about it?" Lena asked.

"Lena, if this is your way of explaining things to me you missed your calling," James said to her. "People in Manhattan pay therapists five hundred dollars an hour for this type of *explaining.*"

Lena laughed. "I was getting there, just in a sort of circuitous route"

"Circuitous?" Maguire said with a smile. "I think it's more like heading to Canada via Mexico."

"Ok, well just bear with me. I'm trying to compare what you know with what I know," she explained. "So why did you leave?"

"Honestly, things seemed a little strained to me in those last few weeks before school ended," he said. "I knew something was wrong, I just wasn't exactly sure what it was. Then I saw her and Browning kissing at the prom and I figured it out. After that the plans we had made didn't seem like they were worth pursuing."

Lena stared at him. She could see the pain in his eyes and didn't know how to proceed.

"So that's why you left?"

"Yeah, you know what they say, 'two's company and three's a crowd,'" Maguire replied.

"And four's a mess," Lena blurted out.

"Huh? Four? I don't understand."

"What you think you saw was not really what you thought it was."

“Lena, I’m pretty sure you lost me. What the hell are you getting at?”

“It wasn’t Browning that Tricia was attracted to, it was me,” Lena said.

Somewhere in the back of the studio a clock ticked, marking off each second that passed in silence.

It was Maguire that first broke the silence “You?”

“Me,” replied Lena, taking a long drag of the cigarette.

Now it was Maguire’s turn to stand up, as the weight of what Lena had just told him sank in. He walked over to a wall where a large oak secretary desk sat. The wall above the desk held a bunch of framed photographs; most of them featured Tricia in them along with a host of artists and members of the art industry.

Maguire stared at them.

She hadn’t really changed; she was just a little older, but still just as beautiful. It was the same vibrant eyes and smile that was simultaneously both sensual and disarming. As he began to look beyond the images of Tricia he started to notice Lena taking on a prominent place in many of them. He struggled with all of it, as if everything he believed to be true was suddenly, and violently, ripped apart and tossed into the wind.

He turned back toward Lena who stared back at him. He could see a mixture of fear and apprehension on her face. As if she was waiting for the verdict to be returned.

Maguire had lived his life angry at what he felt Paul Browning had stolen from him, and yet now he was standing across from a woman who was telling him that she was the thief.

As he continued to stare at her, he found that he had no anger left inside him.

“Ok, I get it. I think. But where does Browning fit in? I mean I saw them kiss and they got married,” he said, as he sat back down on the couch. “I feel like I have the borders up, I just need you to fill me in on the rest of the puzzle now.”

Lena felt a wave of relief pass over her body. She shuddered, as if to make that mental feeling more tangible. She hadn't been sure what to expect. In a way she had anticipated a more angry response, but she didn't sense anything along those lines from him.

"Like I said, it started in our senior year," she began, crushing the cigarette out in the ashtray. "When I first moved here to Perrysville, it was Tricia that helped me to get acclimated. She and I spent a lot of time together getting me up to speed with where I needed to be with classes. It was one of those things that just sort of happened unexpectedly. We were both confused about it and there really was no one else to talk to. Tricia was really torn apart about her feelings for you and what we were feeling. It really was a bad time."

Lena paused a moment to let what she had said sink in. When she felt he had processed it all she continued.

"The night of the prom Tricia went out to look for you. When she came back I could see there was something really bothering her. I assumed you guys had gotten into a fight. We went into the bathroom and that's when she told me that Paul had confronted her outside and told her that he knew about her and me. To this day we still have no clue as to how he found out, but he threatened to drag us and our families through the mud. He said he would laugh as our reputations and our futures were destroyed. He really is a very sick and twisted individual James."

Maguire listened intently and yet at the same time he replayed that part of his life in his mind. Filling in pieces of a puzzle that now made things seem so crystal clear. He remembered how Tricia was always meeting up with the *new girl*. He had never been jealous and he was happy that she had someone to spend time with when he had to work.

"Paul spun a horrific tale," Lena continued. "He told Tricia that if she didn't drop you and go out with him, that he would spread all sorts of stories about us. He said that he would say that you knew all about us and encouraged it. He promised that he would go out of his way to ruin our families and that no college was going to let us in. She wanted to talk to you about it, but then you just disappeared. I know she went over to your house several times, but your mother finally told her that it was pointless because they didn't know where you were either."

Maguire's thoughts came back around to that night. It was true that he had disappeared after the prom. He didn't remember where he had gone just that he had done a lot of driving. The next morning he had gotten up early and headed into Plattsburgh. As chance would have it he parked near the military recruiting station. He got out of his car and walked up to the sailor who was standing outside having a smoke and asked the fateful question: '*How do I get as far away from here as humanly possible*?'

Plattsburgh had always been an Air Force town, so getting a local to consider any branch other than the Air Force was a victory that the Navy recruiter was not going to pass up. The whole process was actually quite easy. He tested extremely well, both on the written and physical aptitude tests, and took his oath of enlistment a short time later.

Joining the Navy had been the easy part. The hard part had actually been explaining to his parents that he had joined the Navy after his high school graduation. It was not that they disliked the United States military, but they had grown up in a different time and place. In addition, both were deeply rooted in academics and earnestly believed that there was always another path to world peace besides military action. James had not intentionally set out to draw the proverbial line in the sand, but as the two sides hunkered down in their philosophical fox-holes, it was clear that a line had in fact been drawn.

The last image Maguire had was his father sitting at the dining room table wringing his hands while his mother sat in her chair in the living room crying. He had gone to his room, packed what he had needed, and walked out the door.

The sound of Lena's voice drew him back to the conversation.

"You have to understand, James, we were both kids. We believed his threats. Besides, we didn't have an answer for what we were feeling for each other and coming out of the closet wasn't actually *en vogue* back then, certainly not in Perrysville."

He let those words sit for a minute, putting himself in their place.

"I don't think it goes over well here today either." He replied.

Small towns were the antithesis of big cities, not only in looks, but in their outlooks as well.

Everything he previously believed in had been suddenly, and irrevocably, thrown to the ground and shattered. Maguire had changed over the last two decades and, as a result, his opinions and thoughts on things had as well. He looked across at Lena and found that he had no enmity toward her or Tricia for that matter. Paul Browning however remained an entirely different story.

There was only one piece of the puzzle that seemed to be missing.

"Ok, so answer me this, Lena," he said. "Why did they get married and how are the two of you still connected?"

"That part is a bit tricky," she said. "Please understand I am not blaming any of this on you, but you have to realize that when you left there really was no one else for us to turn to. What would probably be classified today as adolescent sexual experimentation became a source of comfort for us. Basically, it became her and I against Browning. He just wanted the arm candy girlfriend for the attention and he kept her on his arm by threats and intimidation. I look back on it now and it was just another form of his bullying, except this was on a psychological level."

"Leopards don't change their spots," muttered Maguire.

"No, and as Tricia became more successful in her career, he became more abusive. It was as if he couldn't bear to see anyone else but him succeed. Eventually he bullied her into marriage. That came about the time she had first opened the gallery. He cornered both of us and said if we didn't go along with what he said he would have the bank's funding for the gallery removed. Browning said he knew enough *decent* people to affect our client list as well as our artists. He said he could destroy our reputations in a heartbeat and then laugh while we spent the rest of our lives trying to rebuild it."

"What could we do, James? We were between a rock and a hard place, so Tricia agreed. All it did was re-enforce the physical and emotional bond between us. We realized we were all each other had. The marriage itself was a sham; they just occupied different rooms in the same house. For the most part they weren't even there at the same time."

Lena paused and drank her coffee.

Maguire watched her as she glanced around the gallery at what the two of them had built. He wondered what she was thinking.

In her mind, Lena wondered if it had all been worth it.

She reached down and grabbed the cigarettes. Maguire reached over and lit it for her. He could tell that releasing all of this was taking a mental toll on her.

"Thanks," she said, taking a drag. "Browning always considered himself to be a ladies man and they all knew he was stepping out on Tricia, so everyone was sympathetic to her when she dedicated all her time to work. In fact, under the circumstances, it actually worked out pretty well for us. No one questioned all the time she put in here at the gallery. They just assumed she was burying her pain in her work. So we just built our world here. We had the second floor converted to an apartment and I moved in up there. It was like our own little sanctuary from the world."

"That lasted for a while, but then when her client base expanded outside the state and she started to get a lot of exposure something changed. It was like he needed to exercise his dominance over her again. She was at the house during one of the regular appearances she made and he came home after a night of partying. He had always been aggressive with her, but in the past it had only been kissing and what you guys call *grab-assing*. This night however he decided that he wanted a little more and forced himself on her, she fought back as best she could, but he raped her."

The words hung in the air, as Maguire could see Lena physically cringe at the words she had just spoken. He struggled to suppress his own anger that raged just below the surface. She took a long drag on the cigarette and regained her composure.

"Tricia told him she was going to file charges against him, but she said he just laughed at her and told her to go ahead. She said it was like he was gloating in the fact that he had defiled her and had no fear. Tricia said that he had gone over to the wall safe and took out a thick folder and handed her a very intimate photo of the two of us together. He told her that she could keep that one because he had a lot of others. He then told her that no jury in the world would convict a scorned husband who had just learned the awful truth about his *Lesbo* wife."

"She backed down from pressing charges, but Tricia did tell him that if he ever tried that again a jury would be the least of his worries. Something must have scared him though, because it was shortly after that he decided to have daddy buy him the sheriff's race. After he was elected he became even more filled with himself, but the two of them reached an uneasy agreement. He lived his life, she lived hers. In fact, I think the last time they were ever together in one place again was the day he got elected. After that it was all about him playing cop. It got him the exposure that he so desperately craved and he actually left us alone."

"Well, I guess that explains why the search was ended as abruptly as it was," Maguire said.

"I'm surprised he actually did that much," Lena scoffed. "But I guess it was the bare minimum he had to do. I spent the whole morning yesterday making phone calls to hospitals, friends who live out where the wreck happened, anyone I could think of. I finally went out there and there was no one around. I called that *sonofabitch* and asked why no one was searching for Tricia. You know what his answer was? He said he had a whole county to serve and protect, not go and waste the resources of his entire department looking for someone who had probably just found a new *kitten* to play with. Then he hung up on me."

"Charming as always," replied Maguire, as he set his now empty coffee cup on the table.

"Let's just say that Paul has a twisted sense of humor. It was never about him wanting Tricia, he honestly never cared. I think in some way having her just satisfied his ego. He simply wanted what he couldn't have. Getting it satisfied the need, but he never really even wanted it. Tricia being *gone* would be one helluva gift for him. The problem would be over forever and he would even get sympathy for being the widower."

"So what are you going to do now?" he asked her.

"Sit here and wait I guess," she said. "I almost didn't come down to the shop today, but I felt something compelling me. I guess I know why now. What are you going to do?"

"Try to get some answers," he said. "If I do I'll let you know."

Lena got up and walked over to the desk and grabbed a business card. On the back she wrote down a number. "This is my cell number, James, please let me know if you hear anything."

Maguire stood up and took the card, putting it in his jacket pocket. He took Lena's hands in his and he kissed her forehead.

"I promise. As soon as I know something I will let you know."

"Thank you," she said, as she walked him to the front door. "Please be careful, James. I don't know what's going on, but I have a really bad feeling. Browning runs everyone and everything in this county, don't underestimate him."

"I'll be careful," he said and walked out the door. He heard the audible click of the door lock being engaged behind him. Maguire got back in the car and headed out of town.

CHAPTER EIGHTEEN

Upstate New York
Sunday, April 29th, 2012 – 7:53 a.m.

The man sat in the chair and took a drag on his cigarette, as he watched her chest slowly rise and drop in a rhythmic manner. The hospital gown clung tightly to her body and only served to highlight her ample breasts.

It all seems like such a waste, he thought.

Everything had been planned in a methodical manner, controlling that which was actually within his ability to control. But now, as the plan began to unfold, he was left with the realization that, as much as he didn't want to, the next move was his to make.

He wondered whether he had felt that he would need her for a longer period of time or was the truth that he simply wanted it to be longer. Deep down inside it made him sad to think that this was the end.

As he crushed the cigarette out in the ashtray he stood up. He walked over and checked the IV bag.

He looked down at her face and gently moved her hair to the side. He let his fingers slide along the curve of her cheek and down her neck. His hand continued down over her shoulder and pressed against the upper part of her breast.

He withdrew his hand quickly, as if he had been shocked.

He had been fighting to suppress the urges he'd felt since he had first brought her in. He remembered how it made him feel dirty as he had removed her clothing, his arousal growing as his hands brushed against her naked body.

The truth was that he had always *wanted* her. She had often been the object of his fantasies. Now, as she lay helpless before him, he felt disgusted by what he was feeling.

He turned and angrily walked toward the door. He knew what he needed to do, but he needed a clear head to do it. As he reached down to open it he paused and looked back at her one last time.

It wasn't like anyone would ever know, he reasoned to himself.

He chased the thought away before walking out and shutting the door behind him.

CHAPTER NINETEEN

Southampton, Suffolk County, N.Y.
Sunday, April 29th, 2012 – 8:14 a.m.

Melody laid back down in bed and stretched out beneath the sheets. Just hearing his voice had caused her heart to beat fast. She reached over, picking the cell phone up from where she had dropped it, and selected Genevieve's number. The phone rang several times before it connected.

"Please tell me that your head hurts as bad as mine," came Gen's groggy voice on the other end of the phone.

"You seriously might want to consider taming that piña colada recipe just a wee bit, chicky," Mel said back with a chuckle. "Either that or go and market it in Vegas."

"Ugh, what time is it?" Gen said, as she looked around her bedroom. "And how the heck did I get here?"

Melody thought about that for a moment and admitted to herself that she honestly had no idea. She didn't recall when the night had actually ended for them or how they had each gotten back to their respective beds.

"It's just after 8 o'clock."

"What day?" asked Genevieve.

Melody chuckled before realizing that she wasn't completely sure that Gen was joking.

"Sunday," she answered. "I think."

"Well at least we have a day to recuperate," Gen said.

"Not me, hon" Melody said. "That's why I called you. I've got a date to get ready for."

That got Genevieve's attention. She sat up and swung her feet over the side of the bed putting a little more effort into waking up.

"Shut up, when did you hear from him?"

"Right before I called you," Melody replied. "He's someplace in upstate New York. A place called Plattsburgh. I'm going to fly up tonight and meet him for dinner."

"Wait, you can't do this to me over the phone. I'm coming up."

"I'll be waiting, bring coffee," Melody said.

She hung up the phone and laid it on the night table.

Melody slid her legs over to the edge of the bed and sat there for a moment. She surveyed the surrounding area in an effort to locate her clothing, but failed. Somewhere in the deep recesses of her mind she vaguely remembered being in the hot tub which would account for her lack of attire.

She made a mental note to categorize Genevieve's piña colada mix as one of those dangerous things that needed to be kept under lock and key.

Melody got up slowly and made her way into the closet where she located a pair of gray sweat pants and an oversized matching gray hoodie which she put on before slipping into a pair of fur-lined slippers. She walked out of the closet and grabbed a pair of sunglasses from her desk, before heading out onto the patio.

The sun was shining brightly this morning and the reflection off the water made it seem as if the sea was made up of a billion shimmering diamonds. Despite the brightness, the sun's heat still hadn't managed to wrestle away the cold chill that hung in the morning air. There was a gentle breeze that continued to blow in off of the ocean and she sat down in one of the chairs and watched the waves break along the shore line.

She loved this view, loved the proximity to the water.

"Mel?" she heard Gen call from inside the house a short while later.

"Out here, hon," she replied.

Genevieve walked out onto the deck carrying a tray with a thermos and two cups of coffee, steam rising up from them before being dissipated by the wind. She set the tray down on the table between the two chairs and grabbed one of the mugs before sitting down. Melody reached over, taking the other mug, and clasped her hands tightly around it as she raised it to her lips and took a sip.

"Ok, so what did studly have to say?"

The comment caught Melody completely unprepared as she was taking a sip and she struggled not to spit out the hot liquid.

Genevieve laughed mischievously, as she watched her friend's discomfort.

"C'mon, missy, stop stalling and give me details," Gen said.

Melody wiped off some of the coffee on her sleeve.

"That's so not funny," Melody replied, as she regained her composure.

"No, actually it was pretty funny," said Gen.

"You are so incorrigible."

"Oh isn't that the pot calling the kettle black," Gen shot back. "Besides, you're still stalling."

"I'm not stalling," Melody replied, taking another sip from her coffee cup. "It's called a dramatic pause."

"Uh huh, whatever."

"Oh it's not that big of a deal. He called and said he got stuck on something upstate, something personal, and felt bad because he wanted to have dinner, but wasn't sure when he would be back," Mel explained.

"So, you're actually going to him?" Gen asked inquisitively. "Damn he must have been really good."

"Ha Ha," Melody said, as she turned away and looked out over the water.

Slowly, as her thoughts returned to their previous encounter, she began to smile; a devilish smile that confirmed the fact that Gen was actually right, he was that good.

Melody could almost feel the sensation of Gen staring at her. She raised her mug and slowly took a sip of coffee, savoring it, before she turned her face to meet Genevieve's stare. She lowered her chin slightly and peered dramatically over her glasses.

"What was it you asked, dear?" Melody said sweetly. "I seemed to have gotten lost in thought."

"I really need to meet Mr. Stud Muffin," Gen scoffed. "Anyway, what time do you plan on heading north to bring him his dessert?"

Melody laughed "I swear, sometimes it's like living with my mother."

"Yeah, if your mother happened to be extremely cool, wickedly funny and incredibly hot," said Gen. "Not to mention I make killer piña colada's."

"Ok, Mama," Melody said playfully. "I promise to bring James around so you can meet him. I'll even ask if he has any good looking friends for you."

"That's what I'm talking about, girlfriend," Gen laughed. "Anyway, where the hell are you going again? I'll call the aviation manager and have him make the flight preparations."

"It's a place called Plattsburgh. James said there is an airport up there. I said I would get back to him and let him know what time I was arriving," Melody explained. "Let's plan for a four-thirty arrival give or take."

"I'll let them know and I'll have the car waiting," Gen said. "You need reservations somewhere?"

"Nope," Melody replied. "I told him getting there was on me, but the food was on him."

"Oh, I bet you'd like to lick that plate, huh, Mel?"

Melody dropped her head low, in dramatic fashion, as Gen giggled and ticked off an imaginary box in front of her.

"I swear I can't win," Melody muttered.

"Ok, truce," Gen said. "So when do you think you will be back?"

"Not sure, probably around midnight I would assume," replied Melody.

Gen bit her tongue on the *assume* part.

"Ok, I'll tell them to plan for wheels down at around midnight at the Airport."

"That works, if there are any time changes I'll call the flight crew and let them know," Melody said. "You're still planning on heading to Montana tomorrow, right?"

"Yeah, unless you want me to stick around till you get back," Gen said.

"No, you go and do your thing I'll be fine," Melody replied. "Besides, I really need to be at that board meeting in the city tomorrow afternoon."

"I'll give you a call after I get settled in tomorrow night and fill you in on what I find out."

"I forgot to ask, where are you planning on staying while you are out there?" Mel asked.

"I spoke to Wilson Pope about that and he said that they actually have several executive residences on site," Genevieve said. "I just figured I'd hang out there. This way I'm not losing time traveling back and forth. Besides he said they are all fully outfitted and that he'd have the cafeteria bring food over and stock it."

Melody took a sip of her coffee. "What time are you planning on leaving?"

"Early," answered Gen. "As of right now I'm planning on leaving from here at about 5 a.m. I figured that would give Bob plenty of time to fly me down to the corporate office then come back and be ready to fly you into Manhattan for your meeting. I have a few paperwork issues I wanted to deal with there first. Besides, I figured it would be good to show the administrative people that we were getting involved right away."

"Sounds like a plan, I'm hoping to get in there one morning this week myself," Melody said. "How are you getting out to Montana?"

"Taking one of the GDL jets," answered Genevieve. "Wilson said he would have it waiting on standby for me. I figure if I can get out by around noon, I'll be wheels down early enough to get in a tour of the facility before dinner."

Melody took a sip of the coffee and looked out over the ocean. The glistening water seemed to mesmerize her. If she had her way she would have laid out here all day. That is until it was time to get on the plane to meet him.

She closed her eyes and began to mentally go through all the things she needed to do before she left. At the top of the list was a visit to the gym which she was dreading. With everything that had been going on recently, she had kept putting it off and she knew that she was going to suffer as a result.

"What are you thinking about?" Genevieve asked.

"How I need to get myself motivated," Melody replied. "That and wondering how my get up and go seems to have got up and went."

Genevieve laughed, but she felt it as well. The last few days had been a whirl wind. They had both needed a night to unwind. It had been fun, but it had been a long night and they were both feeling a bit worse for wear. To top it off it was already Sunday and tomorrow started another hectic week.

Oh well, success had its perks, but it came with a price as well.

"Come on," Gen said, as she got up from the deck chair and gathered up the tray. "We both have things to do and place's to go."

Melody sighed and surrendered to her friend's reason. In fact she was more than willing to get ready to go, but she wouldn't leave for at least another five hours. It was what she had to do in those five hours she dreaded.

She got up and followed Gen back into the bedroom.

"Care to meet me in the gym?" Melody asked, as she headed toward the closet.

Genevieve stopped in her tracks and turned to face her friend.

"Oh, wouldn't I love a really good workout," she replied with exaggerated exuberance. "But you know those pesky documents piling up on my desk just won't wait."

Melody stared at her friend who looked back at her with a feigned pouty face.

"That's what I figured," said Melody. "And that's the same face you're going to have when you look in the mirror and watch your hips grow wider."

"Ooh, so much hate," replied Gen, as she walked down the hall and out the bedroom door. "Ta-Ta and give my love to the leg press machine."

Melody walked into the closet and grudgingly changed into her workout clothes. She sat down in the chair and put on a pair of sneakers before making her way to the elevator for the short ride to the basement.

The home gym rivaled anything one would find in any of the high end fitness establishments. On one wall was a line of cardio machines that included treadmills, elliptical trainers, stationary bikes, and Stairmasters. On another wall were several racks featuring pairs of dumbbells ranging in weight from 5lbs to 120lbs, although the latter ones rarely got used. In the center of the room were a number of different Nautilus machines along with several different benches with Olympic bars and stands with assorted weight plates.

Melody groaned audibly as she walked in and made her way over to the opposite side of the room.

On top of a small table was an audio system whose speakers were inset in the ceiling throughout the gym. Melody scanned through several of the discs until she found the right one and put it into the tray. She jacked the sound up high and pushed the play button.

The first strains of a heavy metal song began to play over the system. She grabbed the worn leather gloves from the table and slipped them on her hands as she made her way to the other side of the gym, loosening up as she went. She could feel the manic pounding of the double bass drums reverberating inside the room, setting the tone for the workout that lay ahead.

Melody had long ago grown tired of the usual equipment. On the far end of the gym was what Genevieve had affectionately named *Hell's playground*. There was nothing nice here. It was like a garage gym where you made equipment out of what you had.

There were several heavy ropes lying on the ground,\ that would have been at home on the deck of a ship. A well-worn and patched heavy bag hung in the corner, along with several truck tires, heavy gauge chains and any number of barbaric pieces that Melody fondly referred to as *alternative* gym equipment.

She walked over to the chin up bar and reached up, grabbing the wide handles and lifted herself up and began knocking out reps.

Over the next ninety minutes she moved around the room with purpose, pushing herself harder and faster. By the end of the workout she found herself lying on the padded floor, covered in sweat and feeling her heart pounding in her chest.

Slowly she found the strength to get up. She grabbed the medicine ball she had been tossing into the air and returned it back to its place on the rack. Then she grabbed a towel and wiped the sweat from her eyes.

Melody walked back over to the table and turned off the audio system and grabbed a bottle of Gatorade. She took a long drink of the bright green fluid as she walked out the door.

She got back in the elevator and hit the button for the 2nd floor. When the doors open she walked down the hallway and into

Genevieve's office where she collapsed onto the couch opposite her friend's desk.

Genevieve looked up from the papers she had been going over; peering at Melody over the top of her reading glasses with a look of revulsion.

"*Eww*"

"I just thought I would show you what you missed out on," Melody said, as she ran the towel across the back of her neck.

"I hate to break the news to you, but you're not exactly the poster child for encouraging people to go to the gym right now," Gen replied.

"You say that now, but you'll be whining come June when you're trying to shimmy back into your bikini."

"That was hurtful," Gen replied.

"Life's tough, get over it," Melody said sarcastically.

"Aw, does someone need a hug?"

Melody laughed as she got up from the couch.

"What someone needs is a hot shower," she replied.

"Thanks for the de-motivation, coach, I'll wipe down the couch for you."

"Whatever, pudgie," Melody called out from the hallway.

"Love you to," Gen replied before turning her attention back to the paperwork.

CHAPTER TWENTY

Keenseville, New York State
Sunday, April 29th, 2012 – 10:41 a.m.

Maguire pulled the Mustang into the parking lot outside the New York State Police, Troop B substation. He got out of the car and walked through the front door. A uniformed state trooper sat behind a wide desk that divided the large room in two. He looked up as Maguire walked in.

"May I help you?" asked the trooper.

Maguire reached into his pocket and removed a small black leather case containing a gold NYPD detectives shield and ID card and held it up to the trooper.

"My name is James Maguire, I'm a retired New York City Police detective," he said by way of introduction. "I was hoping to speak with an investigator regarding the Browning accident."

"Hold on and let me check and see if anyone's back there," the trooper said, as he reached for the phone.

He lifted the handset and hit one of the extension buttons and waited. After a few rings someone on the other end picked up.

"Hey, Tom, I got a retired New York City detective out here asking to speak with someone about the Browning investigation, you got a minute? OK thanks I'll bring him back," The trooper replaced the handset back on the cradle. "Follow me, detective."

Maguire accompanied him down a long hallway to the back area of the building. The walls were lined with framed photographs chronicling the history of the New York State Police along with other significant events and incidents handled by the troopers assigned to Troop B.

The hallway ended at an office door with a frosted glass panel that had the word "Investigations" etched into the glass. The trooper opened the door and Maguire followed him inside.

An older man, in a rumpled suit, got up from a desk in the corner of the room and walked across to meet them.

"Tom Reynolds," he said and reached his hand out to Maguire.

"Nice to meet you, Tom," Maguire said, shaking the man's hand. "James Maguire."

"Grab a seat," he said, as he pointed to a chair next to his desk and sat back down. "So, what brings you so far up north?"

"Actually I used to live here years ago," Maguire said. "I heard about Tricia Browning going missing and thought I would come up and lend a hand if I could."

"Ah, Sheriff Browning's wife," Reynolds said.

Maguire noted that there was a slight edge to the statement.

"I'm guessing there isn't much love lost between the state police and the sheriff's office?" Maguire asked.

"That's one way to put it," Reynolds replied. "Actually we've always gotten along well with the road deputies, but when the sheriff got elected he came in with a huge chip on his shoulder. Unfortunately, it's only gotten bigger as time has gone on."

"Paul is certainly a polarizing figure," Maguire replied.

"You know the sheriff?" the investigator asked suspiciously.

"A lifetime ago," said Maguire. "We went to school together. From what I have been able to piece together since getting back in town I'd say he is just as big a douche bag as when I left."

Reynolds laughed at the reply and relaxed a bit. "Yeah, he certainly has made a name for himself, but he also has a lot of very well connected friends."

"Don't worry, Tom, we don't share the same Christmas card list," replied Maguire. "In fact, I have no use for him or his friends. My only concern is Tricia."

"I wish I could help you on that, but we were told to stand down before we even got started."

"How the hell does that work?" Maguire asked.

"Sheriff runs the county. By the time we showed up he had already had his people run a few laps around the accident scene and then told us we weren't needed," Reynolds answered. "Troop B covers five counties and around ten thousand square miles. I've got enough on my plate without having to make work. If the county sheriff wants to do it on his own, more power to him."

"I hear you," Maguire said.

He understood where the investigator was coming from. Criminal investigations never did seem to slow down. For each case you closed, your reward was generally another two. Still something bugged him about the crime scene.

"Did you get a chance to look around at all?" he asked.

"I did, but it was pointless," the man replied. "Browning seemed to have his deputies running around the woods like a pack of chimpanzees running amok."

"Yeah, I took a walk through the forest myself. Any potential tracks were completely obliterated."

"Between you and me, I don't see Browning putting much effort into finding her," Reynolds replied. "Rumor was that their marriage was shaky at best. He put just enough effort in at the scene to cover his ass and then pulled the deputies."

"Seeing as how it involved his *wife*, I wonder why he didn't just recuse himself and let you guys handle it outright?" Maguire questioned.

Reynolds noted the obvious inflection when Maguire had said the word wife, but let it pass, for now. Clearly there was something more to this story.

"Sheriff Paul step aside? Surely you jest," replied Reynolds. "He's got a stranglehold over that county. I'm surprised he hasn't pushed to change its name. Besides, his cousin is the District Attorney so nothing gets done unless Browning wants it done. We go in when we need to, but most of the troopers don't trust him as far as they could throw him. Majority are just happy they don't have to work for him."

"Yeah, I heard that he actually wrote one of his own deputies a traffic ticket."

"Oh yeah, that one got around pretty fast," Reynolds said with a sarcastic laugh. "For the most part the deputies have kept their mouths shut, but the general consensus is that they *might* go through a door for him, but no one would go through a door *with* him."

"I've heard as much," Maguire said. He recalled the early conversation he had with Keith Banning.

Maguire understood exactly what each man had inferred. Police work was an inherently dangerous job. Officers put their lives on the line each and every day for people they don't know, rushing through doors to help victims even when there might be some crazed gunman on the other side waiting to ambush them. They all do it because, at their very core, they trust the other cops, whom they are going through the door with, with their very lives.

Police work was a brotherhood, a fraternity forged in a crucible of adversity, hardship and danger. For those who are able to survive it, they are forever enjoined with one another. They may squabble over which is the best department or unit, but when danger confronts one of them; they will all drop what they are doing and rush to that person's aid without any concern for their own safety. They do so because in their heart they understand that every cop would do the very same thing for them.

George Orwell once wrote "People sleep peaceably in their beds at night only because rough men stand ready to do violence on their behalf."

They are the rough men, the last line of defense between the citizens and the wolves of society who seek to victimize them. Cops understand this and accept it, even when those they protect look down upon them and despise their very presence. They do it neither for glory or accolades, but because it is who they are. They will accept the enmity of the society they protect, without so much as blinking an eye, but to have one of their own cross that line is unspeakable.

Sheriff Paul Browning had engaged in an act of ego-boosting, chest thumping to prove who *he* was. In doing so he earned the worst aspersion that could be directed toward someone in law enforcement. He had been labeled by other cops as an *empty suit*; someone who only wore the uniform, but wasn't really a cop.

"Anyway," Reynolds continued. "He had the car towed away and then had his deputies resume patrol. He told us we could either stand around looking at the trees or go earn the paycheck the state was providing us."

"Sounds like Paul needs to work on polishing those *rough edges* a bit more," said Maguire sarcastically.

"I know more than a few road troopers who wouldn't mind catching him out on the thruway and returning the favor," Reynolds answered.

"So what was your initial take on the accident?" asked Maguire.

"At face value, classic car versus deer," replied Reynolds. "That's why everyone was so taken aback by his behavior."

"So do you think it just has more to do with him just being a pompous ass and not giving a damn about her well-being?"

"Listen, I'm paying alimony to two ex-wives," Reynolds replied. "I'd like to say that I'd care if one of them went missing, but honestly I'd be too busy fighting the hangover that would come from the party I'd throw to celebrate the pay raise I'd get."

Maguire laughed.

Cops and marriages never did seem to work out, which is one of the reasons he had worked so hard at being single.

"You on the other hand don't seem as convinced," Reynolds replied.

"I don't know," Maguire answered. "I just wasn't getting the warm fuzzies at the scene. Something just didn't feel right."

"I'd like to be able to help, but I don't have much of a leg to stand on here."

"No, I appreciate your position. I've been down that road before and still have the scars on my ass from the chewing out."

Reynolds laughed. Police work was the same where ever you went.

Maguire reached into his pocket and took out a business card which he handed to Reynolds.

"Tom, if anything does come up would you mind giving me a shout?"

"Not at all, James," Reynolds said, taking the card. "Hey if you don't mind me asking, how come you didn't just go to the sheriff with your concerns?"

"I think steering a wide berth around him is probably the best thing for me to do."

"Gotcha," said Reynolds tapping the business card against the desk. In that moment he knew that at some other time a triangle had existed. "Hopefully we will find her soon."

"Hopefully," Maguire replied as he got up.

Unfortunately, the reality was that neither man believed that it would happen anytime soon.

As James reached for the door handle he paused and turned back around.

"Tom, just one more question. Do you happen to know where the car was towed?"

"Let me check," Reynolds said and began flipping through a folder on his desk. "Looks like it got towed to Route 9 Customs."

"Is there any particular reason why they would have gotten the car?" Maguire asked.

"No, they just would have been the next one up on the tow list."

"Is it close by?" James asked.

"Just north of town," said Reynolds. "You know where the turnoff for the Port Kent Ferry is?"

"Sure do."

"It's about a quarter mile north of there on the right side of the road."

"You wouldn't happen to have a copy of the accident report would you?" Maguire asked.

"Yeah, I do," replied Reynolds. He got up and walked over to the copy machine and ran off a copy of the report and handed it to Maguire.

"Hey, do me a favor," Reynolds said. "Forget where you got this."

"Thanks, Tom, and I already did. You have a good one."

"You too, let me know if you come up with anything.

"Will do," said Maguire.

Reynolds walked back to his desk and sat down.

Yeah, it was probably wrong that he gave him that copy of the accident report, he thought, but the truth was he could care less if Maguire pissed in the sheriff's coffee. Reynolds knew he couldn't do it, so maybe deep down inside he hoped this outsider would.

Maguire waved to the trooper at the desk as he left the substation and got back in the car. He checked his watch; it was almost 11:30 a.m. as he pulled out of the parking lot and proceeded back toward Perrysville.

Twenty minutes later he arrived back at the house and drove up the driveway. Rather than heading directly in, he first went into the garage and proceeded to rummage through the cabinets and drawers of his father's work bench. He selected a hand full of tools and a tape measure, which he threw into an old beat up canvas work bag.

When he was done he walked backed to the car and tossed the bag into the passenger seat, before heading up the steps to the back door. He checked the monofilament line and found it still in place. He opened the door and went into the house. He was tempted to get something to drink out of the fridge and reminded himself that he had forgotten to make that trip to the supermarket so far today.

Maybe, instead of a mental note to pick up a few things at the store you should have written an actual note, he thought.

As he walked through the living room he checked the front door and found that it too was undisturbed.

Maguire went up to his room and grabbed one of the cameras from the shelf. An old Canon AE-1 body with a 35mm lens. He walked over to the desk and opened several of the drawers before finding an old aluminum clipboard to which he added several pieces of blank paper. He grabbed everything and headed back out of the house, resetting the tripwire on the back door as he left.

The Mustang roared back to life and he pulled out of the driveway and headed north toward Keenseville. When he reached the center of town he turned onto Route 9, heading in the direction of the *Ausable Chasm*. As he passed the turn-off for the Port Kent Ferry he began to look around for the towing company. A minute later he spotted the lot just off the roadway and pulled inside.

Maguire leaned over and grabbed the bag, clipboard and camera before getting out of the car.

"Sweet ride, mister," said the young kid in coveralls who approached him.

"Thanks," Maguire replied.

"You wouldn't be interested in selling it now would you?"

Maguire almost chuckled at that. It wasn't that he hadn't heard it a thousand times before, but somehow he guessed that the young grease monkey in training, who was now standing in front of him, had no clue as to the value of the vehicle, either sentimental or financial.

"Nah, I think I'm gonna hold onto it for a couple more years," Maguire replied.

"Damn," the kid said dejectedly. "What can I help you with?"

"You guys had a car come in from a wreck this morning," Maguire said, matter-of-factly. "Some sort of collision with an animal."

"Maybe," the kid replied, "who are you?"

"Oh, I'm sorry," Maguire replied "Patrick, Patrick Collins, I'm an adjustor for Lehigh and Montvale Insurance. Been a long weekend for me, I don't know if I'm coming or going."

"Oh, no, it's just that we don't get too many people out here on weekends," he replied. "Especially not insurance adjustors."

"Yeah, I was just doing one over in Peru and they figured since I was local they would ruin my weekend even more," said Maguire.

Maguire looked down at the accident report that he had secured to the clipboard. The young kid glanced down and saw the official report Maguire was reading.

"Says here, a 2012 Black BMW"

"Sure thing," the kid said. "That car is right over here."

He led Maguire toward the rear of the yard where they stored the towed vehicles. Maguire saw the mangled remains of the BMW.

Inside the shop a phone rang.

"I need to get that."

"No problem," said Maguire, "I just need to take a few photos and some notes and I'll be out of your hair."

The young man walked away as Maguire began to inspect the car.

It was clear the vehicle had struck an animal. There was enough blood, along with tissue and hair fibers, to show where the primary and secondary impact points were. Maguire wrote some stuff on the clipboard and took several photos of the car.

It was all of course for show in the event anyone had bothered to watch him. The camera contained no film in it and the only thing Maguire was interested in was what he could actually see.

He began a quick examination of the front of the vehicle. Locating the initial point of contact and followed its apparent trajectory as it careened up and over the front of vehicle. Maguire figured that it had to have been a small animal, most likely a young buck. He located an impact point where it appeared that one of the animal's antler tines had actually punctured the metal of the car's hood. He followed its path up into the windshield and noted where some coarse hair had wedged into the joint between the roof and the windshield. As Maguire made his way around to the back he observed a large smear of blood along the car's trunk.

He walked around to the driver's side of the vehicle and peered into the interior compartment. He noted the blood high up on the seatbelt. It was a decent enough indicator that she had been wearing it. He looked down at the seatbelt release button, but it was clean.

That immediately struck him as odd.

Blood on the seatbelt would most likely have indicated some type of facial or head laceration. Maguire pulled the seat belt over and snapped it in place. The staining on the seatbelt indicated that the injury would most likely have been on the right side. For most people who are injured it is human nature to check the injury for bleeding. If Tricia Browning was alert enough to get out of the vehicle on her own, she would have most likely felt her face for the injury.

Tricia was right handed, he thought. *So why was there no blood on the seatbelt release button*?

He looked around the interior of the car, but didn't see anything else that appeared out of the norm. He continued his examination of the car's exterior. As he walked toward the front of the vehicle something caught his eye. He looked over at the driver's side 'A' pillar, the vertical metal support of the windshield, and saw a gouge that went through the paint and into the bare metal itself. He examined the damage closer. It had all the appearances of being fresh.

Something had struck that portion of the car with considerable force, but all other indicators were that the animal had actually gone in the opposite direction. Whatever had caused the damage, it had nothing to do with the animal.

Maguire reached down into the bag and retrieved the tape measure. He quickly marked off the height and jotted down its location on the pillar and the angle. He quickly retrieved the cell phone from his pocket and covertly took several photos of the damage.

Another walk around failed to produce anything else of significance.

He turned around and made his way back toward the Mustang just as the young kid came out of the shop.

"Hey, mister, you all done?"

"Yeah, for now," Maguire replied. "I might be back later in the week or someone else from my office."

"Ok, well if you ever think about selling that car give me a call," the kid said.

"I'll do that," Maguire said, as he got back into the car and drove off the lot.

He headed back through the country; returning back to the scene of the accident. He pulled over to the side of the road and parked. He got out and began to walk along the roadway. Something just wasn't right. He just didn't seem to have all the pieces of the puzzle quite yet.

He walked along till he felt that he was in just about the right position. He stood in the middle of the road facing the direction that she had driven. He imagined the animal standing there, caught in the sudden blinding light of the vehicle's headlights coming toward him.

The curve of the road would have prevented her from seeing it until it was too late. It was the absolute worst possible place for it to happen.

Or was it? he wondered.

As he stood there he looked around, trying to figure out what it was that he was missing.

He reached his hand out, mimicking the approximate height of the damage he had noted on the cars pillar.

Right about there, he thought.

He turned slowly, 360 degrees, looking for any anomalies that he could see at around the height of his hand.

Then he spotted it; those strange gouges on the bark of the tree that he had noticed the previous day. He looked across the road and observed a matching one on another tree.

He walked over to the nearest one and examined it more closely. It was a circular pattern and appeared uniformed. Clearly they were not naturally occurring marks. The question now became what had caused them and more importantly why.

Judging from the depth of the marks in the tree trunk, whatever had been wrapped around them had been done so with extreme tension. You only do that when you need to secure something well or for something that had weight to it.

He looked over toward the other tree; clearly something had been stretched between the two. The only thing that made sense was some type of cable.

"So what would you need to hang above the roadway that would require a cable?" Maguire asked out loud.

His mind was racing furiously as he tried to figure out this mystery. To find those last few missing pieces.

He knelt down and took a deep breath, clearing his mind. This time he looked at the whole scene, the way a spectator would watch an event unfold from the sidelines.

In his mind's eye he saw the deer standing in the roadway, faintly lit by the glow of the moon above. Suddenly, the BMW came around the bend; the cars headlights filled the scene with bright light. For a brief moment he saw the limp body of the deer suspended over the road by a cable that ran between the two trees. He watched as the car struck the deer, the force snapping the cable that had held it up just seconds before. As the deer was forcibly wrenched from its tether he watched as one of the sheared ends of the cable snapped violently and struck the cars frame, slashing through the paint and into the metal. The lifeless body of the deer catapulted over the car before coming to a rest on the roadway, as the vehicle careened off the road and struck the tree.

Maguire got up and walked slowly over to where the imaginary carcass of the animal lay in the roadway and stared down at the pavement.

"You were already dead, weren't you?"

CHAPTER TWENTY-ONE

Southampton, Suffolk County, N.Y.
Sunday, April 29th, 2012 – 1:15 p.m.

Melody stood in the closet with a towel wrapped around her body going through her clothes. She came to the realization that she no idea what to wear.

"Whatcha doing?" Genevieve asked, as she walked into the closet.

"I'm getting ready to have a panic attack."

"What's wrong?"

"It's been so long since I have gone anywhere *normal* that I don't know what the hell to wear," came Melody's exasperated reply.

"Oh stop being so melodramatic."

"Ha! That's rich coming from you."

Genevieve crossed her arms and stared back at Melody with pursed lips.

"Do you want my help?"

"Please," Melody said, as she collapsed into the chair looking frustrated.

"The first thing you need to remember is he is going to be so happy to see you that he isn't going to care what you're wearing. Second, when he does finally see what you're wearing make it count."

Genevieve walked over and grabbed a pair of faded denim jeans and handed them to Melody. Next she pulled out a black, low cut cashmere top which she matched up with a tan wool sport coat. Next she scrounged around until she located a leopard print scarf.

"There, that should do it," she replied. "Just throw in those tan boots and *voilà*, you're fabulous."

"Thank you."

"What can I say, I have a gift," Genevieve said. "Oh, by the way the car will be here to pick you up in about an hour."

CHAPTER TWENTY-TWO

Keenseville, New York State
Sunday, April 29th, 2012 – 2:09 p.m.

The only problem with figuring out that things weren't exactly what they seemed to be was that you then had to figure out what the actual mystery was. Answers to such substantive questions as: why were you being misled and, more importantly, who was doing the misleading, seemed to grow more elusive with each passing minute.

Maguire made his way back to the house. He had a lot to think about and he needed to work on the answers to those questions as quickly as he could.

His cell phone beeped with an incoming text message: 'Arriving Plattsburgh Airport ETA 4:30.'

"Crap," he said out loud.

In all the running around he had actually forgotten to make the dinner reservations. He looked down at his watch and realized that he was quickly running out of time. He'd have to jump on that as soon as he got back to the house.

"Can this day possibly get any weirder?" he asked rhetorically.

As he turned onto the block he got his answer.

A big white Ford F-150 sat parked at the curb blocking the entrance to the driveway. It was a fully marked unit, replete with light bar, heavy duty push bumper and reflective graphics clearly identifying it as a county sheriff's auto. In the event that the casual observer was at all confused, the rear tailgate read in large block lettering: Sheriff Paul Browning. The very same Paul Browning who now sat behind the wheel of said pickup.

Maguire groaned and made a point never to ask himself another stupid question.

He pulled the Mustang up so that it was abreast of the pickup and watched as Browning lowered the driver side window.

"You didn't think you'd be able to come and go in my county without me finding out about it did you, Jimmy?" asked Browning.

"I didn't know I had to check in with local law enforcement when I wanted to come back home for a visit," Maguire replied.

Browning had certainly changed over the last two decades. He had a ruddy complexion and was overweight. In addition, he had lost most of his hair and what little did remain was relegated to the back and sides giving him the overall appearance of a modern day *Friar Tuck*. His white uniform shirt was opened at the collar and a clip on tie was hooked into the empty top button hole. Large, gold plated stars adorned the collar tabs.

"For someone who's supposedly just home for a visit, you sure seem to take in the strangest scenic attractions," replied Browning.

"Well you know that's the life of a photographer; you see the importance in the little things that no one else seems to notice."

"Does that include interfering with an official police investigation?"

"That's a pretty serious accusation there, Sheriff," Maguire replied. "I'm sure if you had more than just an accusation we would be having this conversation somewhere other than my driveway."

Browning clenched his jaw hard, pressing his lips tightly together. Clearly it had been a long time since someone had actually talked back to him. The fact that it was Maguire doing it just added more fuel to a fire that was already burning deep inside Browning.

It only lasted for a moment and Browning managed to regain his composure.

"Jimmy, is this any way for old friends to act?" he said. "I was just *sad* that you'd come back here and not look up your old buddy first."

"You know, Paul, I meant to, I really did, but every time I turn around things aren't exactly what they seem to be. I just wind up spending so much of my time trying to figure out what's going on that I completely forgot to allocate time to play catch-up with you."

Browning sat upright and leaned over in his seat, staring out the window.

"I'm not sure how things operate in whatever shithole you've been *hiding* in for the last twenty years," Browning snarled at Maguire. "But things haven't changed all that much here and you'd best remember your place, *Jimmy Boy*."

Maguire put the Mustang in park and jumped out, closing the distance between the two vehicles in an instant. He placed his hands on the door and stared intently at Browning who now recoiled backward at the sudden invasion of his personal space.

"Let me fill you in on a little something, *Paulie*," Maguire said sharply. "You might very well think that you're the big dog in this little watering hole, but just because all the people that you bullied twenty years ago still cower down to you when you walk by, don't you believe it for a moment. The world's a lot bigger place than this little spit of land and those people who are fortunate enough to make it out of here have the capacity to change beyond your wildest imagination."

Maguire pushed himself back away from the truck, crossing his arms in front of him and stood there staring at Browning.

"Of course, you don't have to believe all that happy bullshit," Maguire continued. "So if you'd like to test out that theory of yours, please, by all means, feel free to step outside and you and I can revisit our past relationship. Otherwise, *Paul*, you're blocking my damn driveway."

Browning swallowed hard and Maguire could see the deep red coloring beginning to distort his face.

"I'll be watching you, Jimmy," Browning managed to stammer, the words coming out in almost an apoplectic rage. "You can't move in this county without me knowing it. You so much as step on a crack in the sidewalk and I'll remind you who the alpha dog really is."

"You know, I really hate getting off to a bad start after all these years," Maguire said in a conciliatory tone that was completely contrived. "Where are my manners? I forgot to ask, how's the *wife* doing?"

Browning's eyes darkened dangerously.

"Fuck you, Maguire," he said.

Browning dropped the truck into drive and peeled away from the curb, his tires scarring the pavement with burnt rubber and leaving a trail of acrid smoke hanging in the air.

Maguire stepped out into the roadway and waved in the direction of the pickup.

"Good seeing you again, too, Sheriff," Maguire called out, as the pickup sped away from the scene.

James got back into the car and pulled into the driveway.

He sat there for moment thinking about what had just transpired. How exactly did Browning find out he was in town? The Mustang certainly stood out and it was conceivable that any of a number of people could have told him, including some of the neighbors.

He also thought about Browning's response to his comment asking about how his wife was. Clearly it had hit a nerve. Things just kept getting stranger.

Getting out of the car, he made his way to the back door. He scanned the door jamb, but didn't find what he was looking for. As he opened the door slowly he saw the monofilament lying on the sill and smiled.

Maguire examined the lock closer. The face of the lock itself was old and weathered. It made spotting the faint scratching on the tumbler face plate, where the tools had brushed against it, almost too easy. He was sure that if Browning could have physically reached around he would have most likely patted himself on the back for a job well done. The truth however was that the entry was an amateurish attempt. The key to successfully entering a locked location was to leave no signs that you had ever been there. In counter surveillance terms, the lock faceplate lit up like Las Vegas at midnight.

He opened the door and moved inside slowly.

The fortunate thing about not having anything inside the residence was that whatever was touched would immediately look out of place. He moved through the house looking to see if anything had been disturbed, but he imagined that Browning would most certainly have been stymied by the lack of anything important lying around. He made his way up to the bedrooms; but again, nothing had been disturbed, including the secret room in his bedroom closet. He wondered if Browning had even had the time to make it inside, let alone up to the 2nd floor.

Maguire took off his jacket, tossing it onto the bed, and unclipped the holstered pistol which he then placed on the night table. He sat down at the desk and rubbed his face. He suddenly felt as if he had hit the wall. There was so much to think about and he was running out of time. For a moment he almost regretted agreeing to meet with Melody tonight. It wasn't that he didn't want to see her, he did, but he didn't expect to find himself wrapped up in an ever deepening mystery. He should have postponed it till he got back to Long Island, but it was too late now and she was on her way.

He stared out the window.

That wasn't entirely right, he thought.

The truth was he needed some time away from here, something to distract his mind and give him a chance to pick-up tomorrow with a fresh outlook. He grabbed the cell phone and began searching the internet for restaurants in Burlington. It didn't take long to find a seafood place that came highly recommended and offered dining on the water's edge. He called the number listed.

"Savage Inn," said the woman who answered the phone. "How may I help you?"

"Hi, I'd like to make reservations for dinner tonight," Maguire replied.

"I'd be happy to help you," the woman said. "What time did you want to reserve your table?"

"6:30 if at all possible, we'll be coming over from Plattsburgh," James said.

"Very good, sir, and how many will be dining?" she asked.

"Two."

"That's fine and what name shall I list the reservation under?"

"Maguire," he said.

"Ok, and did you have any other questions?"

"No, that's all," he answered.

"We will see you then, sir," and she hung up the phone.

Maguire got up and went to the bathroom to freshen up. When he returned it was nearly quarter after three. She'd be landing in a little over an hour. He changed out of the polo, opting for the slightly dressier button down shirt. It wasn't exactly what he would have chosen to wear, but having dinner up here with Melody was something he hadn't anticipated and his clothing options were a bit limited.

He walked around the bedrooms, double checking the window locks. He felt uneasy with the second floor seemingly unmolested. When someone takes the steps to break into a location they don't want to leave without seeing everything. It's too inviting for someone to come back and finish the job. When he was sure that everything was secure he grabbed the pistol and attached it back on his belt and took his jacket.

He made it about halfway down the stairs before stopping abruptly and turned around and jogged back up the stairs. He went back into the closet and removed the rifle bag. The odds were no one would ever find the hidden room, but when you anticipate the crime being committed you don't risk leaving anything of value behind.

Maguire double checked the front door before he left and then reset the monofilament line in the back door. After he secured the bag in the trunk he got in, started the car up, and backed down the driveway slowly.

In true spring fashion it had begun to rain. He stopped at the edge of the driveway and reached into his pocket. He retrieved the cell phone and raised it to his ear. He sat there for about twenty seconds before making a show of tossing the phone onto the seat next to him and continued backing out of the driveway.

To the casual observer it would have seemed that he had simply stopped to take a call, but in the brief time that Maguire sat at the edge of the driveway he had seen much more than the casual observer ever would. Like the dark colored pickup parked just at the bend in the roadway, partially obscured by the hedges of a nearby house. As he had sat there on the phone he had watched out of his peripheral vision for any type of movement and caught the giveaway sign of the windshield wipers that had been set on intermittent.

Conducting covert observations was an inherently difficult business to begin with, inclement weather made it exponentially harder. Rain necessitated the use of windshield wipers, cold weather required heat, couple that with defrost and you got an exhaust plume which could be spotted even by the village idiot.

Surveillance professionals could mitigate many of these issues, but most of those conducting observations were not really true professionals of the craft. They refused to surrender creature comforts like smoking cigarettes, using the bathroom, along with staying warm and dry.

Truly effective surveillance required a multitude of people and diverse vehicles. If those tactics were employed the likelihood that you would see the team was remote.

As Maguire proceeded down the street, he scanned the rear view mirror waiting to see if the vehicle tried to close the gap too quickly and establish a tail. Under normal circumstances he would have headed out in the direction that the vehicle was sitting, but driving away afforded him the chance to stay on this particular road for a greater distance and confirm whether he was being followed. As he approached a T intersection at the end of the street he turned right, heading in the direction of the lake.

If he was being tailed the vehicle operator was doing a decent job as he had yet to catch a glimpse of the pickup in his rear view mirror. About a quarter of a mile down was the next street and he turned right again. This road ran parallel to the street his house sat on and was about a half mile longer. A third right brought him back to his street just to the rear of where he had originally spotted the pickup.

As Maguire drove past he noted that it was now gone and the road appeared reasonably dry where it had been sitting.

Perhaps it was just coincidence, he thought. Even though he knew he didn't believe in that sort of thing.

He pulled back into the driveway and ran into the garage for effect. He returned with an old tool box that he placed into the trunk. Had anyone actually been watching it would seem as if he had simply forgotten something and returned home to retrieve it. He pulled back out and resumed his trip.

Even though he felt secure in the fact he was not being followed, he still had a sense of uneasiness. It was an affliction that most special operators and police officers referred to as a *sixth sense*. It was never tangible, just a feeling. Like when you walk through a particularly bad neighborhood and you begin to see the potential threats even when things look *normal*. You just started to know when things were not right. It was one of the reasons he had racked up such an incredibly high number of gun arrests while working in the Street Crime Unit.

The further north Maguire got without spotting anything out of the ordinary, the more he allowed himself to relax a bit. His thoughts now turned back to the reason for this particular trip and he allowed himself to smile at the thought of seeing her again. It continued to amaze him that he had only met her less than forty-eight hours ago. He tried to chalk it up to being so new and yet deep inside he knew this was nothing like he had ever felt before. In a way, that scared him even more.

Maguire had made a habit of never getting too attached to anything, or anyone, he couldn't walk away from. Some would say that he was emotionally unavailable, but that wasn't exactly correct. It was true that he had spent the earlier part of his life behind a wall. The Navy wasn't exactly the best place to develop a relationship, especially when you get a zero-dark thirty phone call telling you to report back to command immediately and the next time you walk through your door a season or two has passed. Most women, even the understanding ones, don't handle playing second fiddle to the teams. Being a cop was nearly as bad. He had tried to overcome it before, but failed, so he figured that rather than fight it, he would simply embrace it. Now, with his career behind him, Maguire wondered if there could be something more, something that he had been missing out on.

The Mustang pulled up to the arrivals building at just after four and he walked inside. It was one of the quietest *international* airports he had ever been in. He looked around and located a lone ticket agent standing at a counter. As he approached her it was readily apparent that she was more engrossed in her texting than on watching out for any actual customers.

"Excuse me," he said.

The woman looked up, almost annoyed at the intrusion and then proceeded to drop her phone onto the counter as she struggled to find her voice.

"I'm so sorry," she finally blurted out. "What can I do to help you?"

Inside she cringed even as the words came out.

She sounded like such a dork, she thought.

Maguire smiled. "I'm just looking for some information. I'm meeting someone here at 4:30."

The young woman looked down at her terminal. It was a particularly slow day and she hadn't expected anyone this early in the night shift. She ran her finger down the monitor screen until she found it, a 4:30 private arrival from Long Island.

"That plane should be arriving shortly, sir. It will be going to hanger 17, which is just north of here," she replied. "If you go back out to Arizona Street, just make a left and go up to Tennessee and make another left. The gate for the hanger will be on your right hand side. I'll call over and let them know you're coming."

"Thank you so much, miss," Maguire said and headed back out the way he had come in.

The woman grabbed her phone from the counter and immediately began texting her girlfriend: *OMG, private flight, major hunk*!!!!!

CHAPTER TWENTY-THREE

Southampton, Suffolk County, N.Y.
Sunday, April 29th, 2012 – 2:15 p.m.

Melody stepped out of the house and walked toward the waiting car with Genevieve in tow. The driver held the rear passenger door of the Mercedes Benz sedan open and she got in. He waited to the side while the two women continued to speak.

"OK, so let me know when you get there will you?" Genevieve said. "And be sure and let me know that he picked you up."

"Yes, mom," Melody answered sarcastically. "And should I text you before or after we make out?"

"*Ha Ha*, very funny," said Gen. "But in all seriousness, let me know what's going on."

"I will, now let me go so I can have something to tell you."

Genevieve stepped back and the driver shut the door and reentered the car. She waved as the car started to pull away. Melody laughed and waved back at her.

She had never seen Genevieve so protective before. The reality was that Melody had never given her any reason to show this side of her before. Sure she had occasionally dated in the past, but they were never anything serious and they both knew it.

She reached into her bag and pulled out her iPad and began going through her emails as the car made its way toward Francis S. Gabreski Airport in Westhampton Beach.

Gabreski was a dual purpose airport that serviced predominantly corporate clients and air taxi services as well as being the home of the 106th Rescue Wing for the New York Air National Guard. The airport was named for Colonel Francis S. Gabreski of the United States Air Force who was a combat Ace in both World War II and Korea. Gabreski had also been the recipient of the Distinguished Service Cross, the Nation's second highest military combat decoration, awarded for *extreme gallantry and risk of life in actual combat with an armed enemy.*

A half hour later Melody turned off the tablet and slid it into her bag. The car turned right off of Riverhead Road and into the airport complex. It then made a left turn and headed toward the northern edge of the facility. This area was the section of the airport that housed the private aviation facilities, including that of her company. The Gulfstream G550 sat on the tarmac waiting for her arrival.

The plane was visually impressive from the exterior. The upper fuselage was painted white and the underbelly a royal blue. A broad gold stripe separated the two and ran from the nose to the tail.

Outside the plane stood Captain Katrina Mann who was just finishing her preflight visual inspection. As the car pulled up to the plane she began to walk over.

Melody already had the door open before the driver could come around. It was something that she actually did without thinking. It seemed so ridiculous to her to have someone open your door for you. The driver stood outside holding the door, as she slid out of the back seat.

"I know, George, I know, I'm supposed to let you open the door first," Melody said in a self-chiding manner. "I promise I'll do better next time. Just don't rat me out to Genevieve."

"I won't, Ms. Anderson," the man replied. "You have a good trip."

"I plan on it, George," she said with a smile and walked over to greet her pilot.

"Good afternoon, Kat," Melody said. "Hope I didn't ruin your weekend too much."

"No, ma'am," replied Kat. "You know me, if I'm not flying, I'm not happy."

"Well I'm certainly glad to make you happy today," Melody replied, as the two women headed up the planes stairs.

Katrina Mann, call sign 'Hurricane,' was a former United States Air Force A-10 Warthog pilot. The A-10 had gotten its nickname from its rather ugly appearance and Mann had gotten hers after someone commented how she rained ordinance down on the enemy like it was a hurricane. She had served several combat tours in Afghanistan and had earned a reputation as someone who had nerves of steel and an amazing battlefield presence.

In one particular mission she had been on station when an infantry unit came under a withering RPG and heavy machine gun attack from insurgents. The enemy had taken up position in a rocky outcropping that afforded them maximum protection as well as the high ground vantage point. As the infantry soldiers took cover they called in for air support, stressing the fact that it was *Danger Close*.

The insurgents had put a lot of thought into the position they had taken up. It was situated about half way up the mountainside that overlooked a narrow, winding ravine. It not only offered them the greatest protection from ground forces below, but from the air as well. That is unless the pilot happened to have ice water running through her veins.

Mann had taken her plane in at a pitch that closely resembled that of a lawn dart before unleashing her own version of hell with the Warthog's GAU-8 Avenger Gatling Gun. Over the course of the next few passes she delivered nearly a thousand rounds on target and completely decimated the enemy position.

A few days later, one of the infantry soldiers had showed up at the hanger looking for the pilot who had saved their collective asses. An Air Force airman thrust his thumb over to where Mann and a technical sergeant were inspecting one of the planes. The soldier approached her and blurted out, "You were beautiful out there the other day ma'am."

Before the sergeant even had a chance to react, Mann, shook the soldiers hand and said, in a slow southern drawl, "Aw, sugar, that's so sweet, but anything standing next to this ugly beast has to look beautiful."

As the soldier walked away, Mann turned to the sergeant and said "I do love those precious infantry boys."

When her commanding officer had read the after action reports concerning the incident he informed her that he intended to put her in for the Distinguished Flying Cross. Mann requested that he not submit it. When he questioned her as to why, her answer was that the Air Force had seen fit to supply her with a plane that carried one of the most powerful aircraft cannons ever flown. If she couldn't punish the enemy with the ordnance she carried then she needed more than a medal, she needed a *flying eye dog*. In the end politics prevailed and she was awarded the medal which she promptly shipped back home to her nephew.

As Melody got to the top of the stairs she peeked into the flight deck and said hello to the co-pilot, Rene Ashcroft, who was going through some preflight checks. Unlike Mann, Ashcroft had learned her trade in a more prosaic way, flying commercial routes before getting a job as a corporate pilot. Even though the two women were from completely different backgrounds they were both accomplished pilots and complimented each other quite well.

Melody turned and walked back into the cabin as Mann secured the plane's door. She sat down in her leather chair and took her iPad out of her bag. Since she had the time, there were a few projects she wanted to look over in the GDL files that Gen had downloaded to her.

Outside, the twin Rolls Royce turbofan engines came to life. Moments later the plane began to slowly roll forward as it made its way toward the runway.

"We are next in line for takeoff, Ms. Anderson," Kat said over the cabins speaker system.

Melody felt the plane turn and then come to a full stop. She loved this part of flying.

She closed her eyes as the engines throttled up and she the plane began moving forward, building speed as it raced down the runway. It reminded her of a rollercoaster ride as it raced along and just as smoothly she felt it leave the ground as it continued to gain altitude. Underneath the planes landing gear began to retract.

Melody enjoyed the moment and then turned back to the iPad. She began to scroll through until she found the report and began to read.

A short while later Melody heard Kat's voice again.

"We are at cruising altitude right now. Everything is clear ahead of us and we should begin to start our approach into Plattsburgh in about forty-five minutes. ETA for wheels down is 4:25 local time."

She looked out the plane's window and stared down at the mountains below. Melody had grown accustomed to the relative flatness of the Island, and the canyons she most often navigated where ones made of steel and concrete. But just beyond the urban jungle that was New York City was an amazing expanse of forests and mountains. It wasn't that she didn't know they were there; she just didn't have a reason to care before.

So this is where you are from, she thought.

She made a mental note to do a little more research on the area as she turned her attention back to the tablet. As she looked through the report she took notes on several of the projects in development and a few that were just in the concept phase. She sent an email off to Gen with several questions. A moment later she got a reply back saying that she would get back to her with the answers and reminding her to let her know as soon as *stud muffin* had picked her up.

Melody put the tablet down on the table and closed her eyes. She enjoyed the relative peace of the plane's cabin. It was one of the few times in recent days that she actually felt a sense of quiet. The oversized leather chair felt so comfortable, as if it were wrapping her up inside of it. She leaned back and reclined it, allowing herself a rare moment of relaxation.

"Beginning our approach now, Ms. Anderson, wheels down in five minutes."

Melody awoke with a start.

It took a moment for her to get acclimated to her surroundings and she realized that she had fallen asleep. The plane began to slow and she could feel it beginning its descent. As she looked out the window she saw a massive expanse of blue water off to the right and houses along the shore line began coming into view. She looked down at her watch; it was four twenty.

A wave of excitement washed over her at the thought of seeing him again. With each passing minute the plane dropped lower and then they were crossing over into a massive airport complex. Certainly larger than any she had seen before in this type of rural location.

Melody felt the rear wheels hit the tarmac followed a moment later by the front wheel and that familiar sudden deceleration, as Mann engaged the brakes, slowing the plane's forward momentum. A few moments later the plane pulled onto a taxiway and began heading in the direction of Hanger 17.

She got up, grabbing her bag, and walked back to the bathroom to make sure that her little nap hadn't made too much of a mess. Melody checked herself in the mirror and approved of what she saw. She reached into the bag and pulled out the lipstick which she applied, smiling as she recalled the *note* she had written with it the day before.

The plane came to a stop and she heard the engines begin to power down. When she was done, she walked back to her seat and collected the iPad, returning it to the bag.

Melody paused for a moment and peered out one of the windows trying to see if he was there. She spotted him immediately, leaning back against the big red car, one leg crossed in front of the other and his hands in his pockets.

Rene had come out and opened the cabin door which in turn lowered the staircase.

"I'll call you guys if anything changes," Melody said, as she walked down the stairs.

Maguire came walking up to meet her.

"Hey there, welcome to *Shangri-La*," he said. "I hope you like it."

"I like it so far," Melody replied with a smile.

"Well, I have to admit," James replied. "This place just became a whole lot prettier when you stepped off that plane."

Maguire took her in his arms, kissing her passionately, as he felt her wrap her arms tightly around him. The reunited lovers allowed their kiss to linger just a moment longer before pulling back, each staring into the other's eyes.

"I missed you too, cowboy," Melody said with a mischievous grin.

He took her by the hand and led her over to the waiting car.

Kat had now joined Rene in the plane's doorway and watched their boss walk off with this mystery man.

Rene turned to face Kat. "She'll call us if anything changes."

Kat looked back at her and said "Honey, I don't know about you, but judging from that kiss, I'd expect to still be here in the morning."

Both women laughed knowingly and got back to work.

CHAPTER TWENTY-FOUR

Upstate New York
Sunday, April 29th, 2012 – 3:13 p.m.

The man paced the floor nervously as he came to terms with his decision. It had to be done, he knew that. He just couldn't understand why it had become so difficult all of a sudden. He had meticulously planned this through. He had considered every minor detail. Yet now he found himself struggling.

There was, after all, nothing that he could do now, right? he wondered. *Wasn't it all just a fait accompli, as they say.*

He put on a pair of black, heavy weight latex gloves and opened the large canvas carrier. He began to remove the tools from the bag and set them out on the table in front of him. They were crude for what he intended to use them for, but they would certainly accomplish the task at hand. There were a variety of different saws and knives. He had originally thought about using a chainsaw for some of the larger pieces, but decided against it at the last minute. The risk of someone hearing it and, more importantly, remembering that they heard it, was just not worth taking the chance. He opted for a reciprocating saw with a number of oversized wood and metal blades. When he was sure that he had everything he needed, he replaced them back in the bag.

He then reached into his jacket pocket and removed a county plat map, several local topographical maps, and a nautical chart showing water depths of the lake. These he spread out on the table. He sat down and began to go over the maps, marking off certain areas in deserted sections of land that had either limited or no nearby residences. The lake would be a little trickier as most of the decent areas were also well known fishing spots. It was fortunate for him that he was an avid angler so his presence in any of those areas was not likely to generate any suspicion.

Still, he wanted to make sure that the areas he had selected were as far off the beaten path as they could be to minimize the chance that they would be found by anyone out hiking, sightseeing, or fishing.

He leaned back in his chair and rubbed his eyes. He reached into his pocket, pulling out the pack of cigarettes and lit one. He inhaled deeply and let out a long slow stream of smoke. He stared out the window watching as the sun began to descend into the forest on the far edge of the property.

He loved the peace and tranquility of this place, it was the one respite he had in his otherwise tumultuous world. Yet that peace had been interrupted since he had put his plan into motion. He no longer found comfort here, as if his sanctuary from the world had forever been tainted by the presence of the woman that lay in the room one floor below him.

When he had first begun his planning he had actually anticipated this moment with a sense of euphoria. He knew that reaching this point would signal the next stage of his plan, but now, at the very moment that he was poised to move forward, he began to fall victim to his own thoughts.

It seemed like such a waste to him, but he had known that this day would come. However, now that it was upon him he felt a sense of great sadness.

He thought about the moment at the accident scene when his hand had brushed against her face. How he had felt when he brought her back here and undressed her. It was as if he was seeing her in a whole new light. He felt an ache deep within him that begged to be released. Each passing moment it grew stronger threatening to overwhelm him.

He felt his face flush and a flood of anger washed over him.

He couldn't believe how stupid he was.

How could he even entertain the thought, when doing so could mean risking losing everything at this defining moment? he wondered.

His mind was racing. He wanted to scream.

He crushed the cigarette out in the ash tray and got up from the desk. He grabbed the canvas bag and walked over to the door that led to the basement. He paused for a moment at the door and brought his emotions back under control.

Recklessness was what destroyed great plans, he chided himself.

He had gone to extensive lengths to ensure that he had been as careful as one could possibly be. The average criminal failed simply because they couldn't think beyond the moment. They lacked clarity of thought and sound judgment. They had no vision.

He felt the calmness return, felt the anger begin to dissipate from his body.

No, he wasn't like those fools, he thought. *He had a plan, a purpose*.

He took a deep breath and opened the door and began his descent into the basement. And yet, with each step that he took, the hunger within him grew stronger and he knew he was losing the battle with himself.

CHAPTER TWENTY-FIVE

Keenseville, New York State
Sunday, April 29th, 2012 – 3:35 p.m.

The F150 pickup pulled into the parking lot of the Sheriff's Office spitting gravel as it came to a stop. Paul Browning got out and slammed the door shut before storming off toward the front door. Deputy Tommy Ward was just leaving and held the door open for him.

"Good afternoon, Sheriff," Ward said, as Browning brushed past him.

"Get your ass on the road, Ward," Browning bellowed. "I don't pay you to be a goddamn door opener."

The deputy let the door slip from his hand as he walked toward his patrol car shaking his head.

"Next election," he mumbled to himself. "I just have to make it 'til the next election."

Browning made his way to his office and shut the door hard enough to rattle the photos hanging on the wall, startling the other deputies who had been working in the large open squad room. Moments later they heard the unmistakable muffled sounds of a rather loud telephone conversation from the office. In turn each man made an excuse to the others and left before the sheriff had a chance to come out of his office and find an unwitting recipient to vent his fury upon.

Inside the office, Browning sat in an oversized brown leather office chair, gripping the desk with one hand while the other pressed the cell phone hard against his ear.

His encounter with Maguire had not improved his overall disposition; if anything it had made his mood even fouler and was causing him to question everything else. More than anything he was angry at himself. It had been stupid to confront him like that.

"Don't tell me not to worry," he screamed into the phone. "The last thing I need now is some little prick showing up here and sticking his nose where it doesn't belong."

Browning listened.

"Calm?" Browning exploded. "You're telling me to stay fucking calm? Let me explain something to you my friend, I did not get to where I am today by letting some two-bit Raggedy Ann, candy assed, sonofabitch tell me what to do. Do I make myself absofuckinglutely clear?"

Browning continued to listen to the person on the other end, but it did nothing to improve his present mood.

"No, I haven't had a chance yet, but I'm working on it."

He reached into his shirt pocket and pulled out a pack of cigarettes and lit one, taking a long drag before exhaling.

"Yeah, yeah, I heard you," he replied dismissively. "No, I'm not going to do anything stupid, but let me remind you that I'm not the only one who has his ass in a sling should the situation deteriorate. So when you say you're going to take care of it, take care of it goddamnit."

Browning ended the call before angrily throwing the phone onto the desk. He sat fuming in the chair. His mood was dark and his thoughts were growing even darker by the minute. He reflected back on high school. Life would have been so much easier if he had just been able to get rid of that little piece of shit back then.

That thought made him smile.

The back door had been so easy for him to get into; he just wished he could have found something to hang the little prick by. Everyone had dirt, secrets and ghosts. He'd just have to find a time to revisit the house and look a little harder. Hell maybe he'd wait in the shadows and just snap his neck. That would have ended this once and for all.

Browning sat there for a moment contemplating it all and realized that he was actually starting to feel better. Yet something about the incident with Maguire had unsettled him. Try as he might, he couldn't recall a time when Maguire had actually stood his ground before.

Does it really matter? he thought.

He pushed the thought away.

He began to look over some of the reports and other paperwork on his desk. He picked the cigarette up from the ashtray and took another drag. He remembered the day the union representative had come in and threatened to file a complaint about his smoking in the office. The rep said it created an unsafe work environment for everyone else.

He knew which little prick had set him up. It was the middle of January and he had that *sonofabitch* standing on the banks of the lake watching for illegal ice fishing. The deputy had rightfully tried to claim retaliation until he was asked how his father's loan application was progressing. That bullshit about no smoking ended soon enough.

Browning longed for the old days when people, like that deputy and the Maguire's of the world, were smart enough to just accept their place in the overall hierarchy. Maybe he just needed to put boot to ass more often. Then he remembered seeing a bunch of *doe dicks* hanging around the office when he had first come in.

He got up from the desk, crushed the cigarette out in the ash tray and opened the door intent on ruining someone's day. To his surprise the squad room was completely empty, only the sound of a portable radio receiver broke the silence.

Browning looked around feeling rather pleased with himself.

Hell, maybe you could actually teach these morons something, he thought, as he made his way toward the kitchen to get some coffee.

CHAPTER TWENTY-SIX

Plattsburgh, New York State
Sunday, April 29th, 2012 – 4:37 p.m.

Maguire navigated the Mustang east, making his way through the maze of streets that at one time had made up the former residential section of the Air Force base.

"So, where are you taking me for dinner?" Melody asked.

"Well, I thought we would head on over to Vermont," Maguire replied. "I made reservations at a seafood place over there on the water. It's supposed to be really good."

"Sounds wonderful to me," Melody answered. "By the way, I hope you weren't too mad at me for cutting out early yesterday. I really did have a plane to catch."

"No, not at all," he said. "Everything happens for a reason. So how was your trip? Business or pleasure?"

"Business," she replied. "But since I love my work I still think of it as part pleasure."

Maguire looked over at her with a smile. "Someone once said if you love what you do, you never work a day in your life."

"I agree," she replied. "Hey, how'd things go with the search for your friend?"

She saw a physical change in his face, a pained look chasing away the smile.

"Not good," he answered. "Nothing has turned up so far."

"I'm so sorry, James, maybe I shouldn't have come up. I don't want to be a distraction to you."

"No, Melody," Maguire replied. "To be honest, I'm glad you came up. I can't think of any place I'd rather be than here with you right now."

Melody leaned over and kissed him on the cheek. "Well you've got me now, cowboy."

As he turned north onto Route 9, Melody noticed the massive B-47 Stratofortress bomber sitting majestically on the side of the road.

"What's that over there?" she asked.

Maguire glanced over quickly, as he made the left turn.

"That's the *Pride of the Adirondacks*," he replied matter-of-factly. "You just landed at what used to be an Strategic Air Command Base."

"I was wondering why it was so large and yet it seemed so quiet."

"Yeah, this place was pretty busy when the Air Force was here," Maguire replied. "It was like having a city within a city."

Melody took in the surroundings, as they made their way through the city itself. It was an eclectic mix of both new and old buildings. She reached into her jacket pocket and pulled out her cell phone and sent a quick text message.

"Checking in?" he asked.

"My best friend, Gen," she replied. "She was worried I'd get up here and you wouldn't show."

"The *Four Horsemen of the Apocalypse* couldn't have kept me away from you."

"So where exactly is this place you're taking me?" She asked with an impish smile.

"It's in Burlington, on the Vermont side of the lake. I figured it would be nice to go someplace quiet and have dinner."

"It looks pretty damn quite here," she replied, "but I'm all yours."

Melody began looking around the interior of the car.

"I've never been in a Mustang before," she said. "Did you restore it?"

“No, this is all original,” Maguire answered. “It was a gift from a very special person.”

“I’d say. I can’t remember ever seeing any vintage car in this nice of a condition.”

They made their way along Cumberland Head, eventually pulling in to the Grand Isle ferry dock.

“Wow,” she replied, as she gazed around. “You want to know something; I don’t think I have ever been on a ferry before.”

Maguire stared at her. She had the most amazing look on her face and it caught him by complete surprise. He looked around at what she was seeing and realized that he had sadly become immune to it all, like the residents of big cities who laugh at the gawking tourists. At that moment he envied her. She was seeing the same thing he was and yet she appreciated the beauty that he no longer saw.

That wasn’t entirely true, he thought, as he looked over at Melody. He did see something beautiful that was just as captivating to him as the scenery was to her.

She leaned on the dock railing with her arms crossed and stared out across the lake. Maguire watched as wisps of her blonde hair would rise up when caught by the breeze and flutter in the air. He took in every feature of her face, from her warm brown eyes to the gentle curve of her lips. The moment seemed so fragile to him, like catching a fleeting glimpse of an angel. He stood transfixed by her, not wanting to breathe, lest anything disturb this moment. He remembered feeling the same sensation the first time he saw her.

In the distance the ferry was drawing closer.

He watched as her lips scrunched together, a smile slowly creeping across her face.

“Didn’t your momma teach you not to stare?” she said before turning around to confront him.

"My mother tried to teach me a lot of things," he replied in an attempt to deflect attention anyway, "but I guess I wasn't a very good student."

"Oh," she said, "so you were a bad boy, huh?"

"More like *misguided*," he replied with a laugh.

"I preferred to call it being *adventurous*," Melody replied and he saw that little mischievous sparkle in her eye.

As the two looked into each other's eyes, caught in the moment, the ferry's air horn broke the silence with a deafening blast.

Melody's eyes went wide and she jumped back with a start. Once she had gained her composure she laughed at her reaction. She reached over and grabbed his hand, pulling him in the direction of the car.

"Come on, James, this is going to be so fun."

He felt his body being dragged playfully along as he surrendered to her will.

There were very few cars making the crossing at this time of the day and he pulled up to the front of the ship. The two of them got out and walked to the front of the Mustang and leaned back against the hood.

"So, you've been on this before?" she asked.

"Once or twice," he replied. "There are actually a couple of different crossings. Most close for the winter months, but this one stays open year round."

"It's so beautiful," Melody said. "Is it a long ride?"

"Not really," Maguire answered. "You see that land over there?"

He took her hand in his and raised it up in the direction of Grand Isle.

"We're going to dock on that Island over there. From there we'll go over a bridge into Vermont."

"How long before we get to the restaurant?" Melody asked.

"About an hour," he replied.

"Good, I'm not ready to eat just yet."

They felt the sudden surge of the ship as it pulled away from the dock and began the trip toward the terminal on the other side of the lake.

She leaned in close against him and he put his arm around her, pulling her body close against him. He could smell the scent of her perfume.

The trip across to Grand Isle didn't take that long, certainly shorter than either of them would have liked. Grand Isle was the last, and largest, of the big islands that stretched north into Canada from Lake Champlain. It was connected to mainland Vermont via the Roosevelt Highway.

After the ship docked, they got back in the car and began their trek across the heavily wooded island. Once they had crossed over into Vermont they headed south on Interstate 89 until they got to Burlington. Maguire then made his way west through the city, toward the water front area.

As luck would have It, he found a spot about two blocks from the restaurant and parked the car. He walked around and opened the door for her. Melody stepped out, thinking to herself how *natural* it felt letting him open the door for her, as he took her hand in his and they began walking down the street. It seemed as if she felt so at ease with everything he did.

For the better part of half her life Melody Anderson had been in charge of everything. She enjoyed that power; the inherent responsibility of being in control of one's own destiny. Yet when she was with him there was a willingness on her part to surrender that control.

Was this the way it was supposed to be? she wondered. *Where these the life lessons she had missed out on by having a mother who was more focused on herself then in teaching her children*?

Melody chased away the thoughts. There was no reason to ruin this moment with painful memories that could never be changed anyway. She looked at him as they walked hand in hand.

There was something about him, something so radically different from anyone she had ever known before. Right now, at this very moment, she felt safer then she had ever felt before in her life. Yet there was also something that she couldn't quite put her finger on.

As they continued to make small talk she allowed her gaze to linger on him a bit longer. His eyes were so beautiful, so alive, but as she watched she caught them darting back and forth, taking in everything in front of them.

It was something that was so subtle that it could almost be overlooked. He seemed so at ease and yet she realized that what she was really watching were the mannerisms of a predator. Like one of those majestic big cats that prowled the plains of the Serengeti. They moved about so naturally that you could easily find yourself mesmerized by their beauty and ignorant of the danger that crept ever so closer. Each and every step they took was calculated, ready to pounce, in the blink of an eye, on unsuspecting prey.

No, Melody corrected herself, the reason why she felt so safe with him was not because of how caring and attentive he was, but because of how dangerous he was. She realized that there was still so much she didn't know about him and yet the one thing she did know was that the danger that emanated from him was nothing that she needed to fear.

"Now you're the one who's staring," she heard him say.

"You are so different," she blurted out in response without even thinking.

"Is that a good thing?" he asked, as he led her up the stairs of the restaurant.

"It's a unique thing," she replied.

"Well, I've been called a lot of things before, but unique is one of the *kinder* ones," he said, as he opened the front door.

"I actual believe that, James," she said.

"After you, *M'lady*," Maguire replied with a slight bow and flourish of his hand.

Melody stepped through the door of the restaurant and into a dimly lit waiting area where a young woman stood behind a large mahogany hostess station directly in front of them.

"Good evening," the woman said. "How can I help you?"

"I have reservations," James replied. "They should be under Maguire."

The woman glanced down at the reservation book and found the name.

"Would you like a table indoors or out on the deck?" she asked.

Maguire looked over at Melody.

"Outside," she whispered.

"On the deck please," he told the hostess.

"Good choice," the woman said with a smile. "Follow me please."

She led them through the interior of the nautical themed restaurant and out a back door to a deck that overlooked the lake, selecting a table closest to the water and laid the menus down.

"Your server will be with you shortly," she replied. As she headed back inside she turned on two of the outdoor patio heaters.

Maguire pulled the chair out for Melody, sliding it under her as she sat down, before taking his own seat directly across from her.

"Good choice," Melody said approvingly, as she glanced around at the scenery.

A moment later their server approached.

"Hi," the woman said. "My name is Lacy and I'll be your server this evening. Can I get you drinks?"

Melody smiled at Maguire, deferring to him.

"Any local Sauvignon Blanc that you would recommend?" he asked.

"I like the Monkey Bay," the woman replied. "It has a light citrus taste."

"Perfect," Maguire said. "We should be ready to order when you get back."

"So, what are you going to get?" James asked.

"Oh no," Melody replied mischievously. "My job was to get here; you're in charge of everything else."

"Oh really?" he said with a laugh. "Are you testing me?"

"Uh huh, so you'd better choose wisely."

"Ok, I think I can handle that."

The server re-appeared a short while later with a bottle of wine that she opened and poured into the two glasses.

"So have you had a chance to decide?" she asked.

"I think we will start with the Cajun Walleye Rollup appetizer," Maguire replied. "For the *entrée* I think we will both have the Citrus Herb Baked Bass."

"Excellent choice," the server replied. "I'll get your order in."

"How'd I do?" Maguire asked.

"You're doing good so far," Melody said with a smile, "but you'd better not screw-up the dessert."

"Perish the thought."

She stared out over the lake, watching as the sun began to set behind the mountains on the New York side.

"It's so beautiful here, James," she said. "Why would you ever leave?"

Maguire looked out over the water, listening to the waves lapping gently against the rocks below, as he contemplated his reply.

"I guess for the same reason every young man does," he replied. "Deep down inside he's searching for some noble adventure."

"Huh," Melody said, more than a little shocked. "A *noble adventure*?"

"Yeah," James said, turning back to look at her. "Deep down inside every young man longs for the same thing. It's encoded in our DNA, we need it and it's how we become who we are supposed to be."

"You've lost me," she replied.

"It's who we are," Maguire said looking back over the water. "God designed us this way. Look at the dreams of every young boy. We yearn to be a hero, to be a warrior, to live a life full of adventure and risk. It's only when reality crashes in that we surrender our dreams and we succumb to the expectancies of life."

"So, what noble adventure did you undertake?" she asked inquisitively.

She wanted to know everything about him, what made him tick and she was thankful for this opening.

Maguire stared across the lake, toward the area that he once knew as home.

She had played it perfectly, he thought.

Here he was, at the crossroads so to speak, where he had to make the decision. Did he let her in or did he just continue to play the game?

He picked up the wine glass, swirling the liquid around slightly before taking a sip and made his choice.

"I left here back in 1989 and joined the Navy," he began. "I spent the next six years traveling around the world on Uncle Sam's dime and doing a little growing up I guess."

"What did you do?" Melody asked.

"Don't ask, don't tell," he said with a laugh. "Eh, mostly I painted ships, washed decks and spent way too much money in ports of call, all while trying to keep my chief's boondocker boots out of my ass."

"Sounds like *fun*," she replied.

"Yeah, that's what I thought at the time," he explained. "Then I got to a point where I had to decide whether that was what I wanted to do for the rest of my life or if I wanted to settle down. So I made the choice to retire from the Navy and I joined the NYPD."

Melody sat there listening intently to him all the while struggling to keep the shock from showing on her face. Deep down she hadn't actually known what to expect.

She knew that he was different; that he didn't fit in the world that she had met him. He *played* the part well enough, but inside she still knew he had been playing. He had learned the mannerisms, but they didn't fit him. He wore the suit well, but it didn't actually suit him. The people in the circles she frequented liked to pretend that they were tough, but she instinctively knew that he was and yet he didn't talk about it.

"So are you still with the NYPD?" she asked.

"No," he replied, as he took another sip of wine. "I left in 2010 on a medical disability."

"Medical disability?" Melody said questioningly. "I didn't seem to notice any *issues* the other night."

Maguire laughed. She seemed to have a way of effortlessly deflecting even the most serious of topics.

"No," he said. "It was their decision, not mine."

The waitress reappeared with the appetizer and set the plate down on the table between them. She took the bottle of wine and topped off each of their drinks.

"Can I get you anything else?" she asked.

"No thank you," Maguire replied. "We're fine."

"So, if you don't mind me asking, were you working that day?" Melody asked, when the waitress had stepped away.

"Yeah, I was."

Instinctively he knew *that day* referred to September 11th, 2001. It had always struck him as odd when people learned that he was a retired cop that the first questioned they broached was whether or not he was there.

In the beginning it bothered him to talk about it, but then he came to terms with the fact that they all seemed to want to know more. It was as if they were able to connect to that event through someone who had been there.

Melody, like most everyone else, remembered exactly where she had been on that day. She had flown into Reagan National Airport the day before and had spent the night at the Willard Intercontinental Hotel. She had just been getting ready to head over to the Rayburn Office Building to meet with several members of Congress when American Airlines Flight 11 struck the North Tower of the World Trade Center in lower Manhattan.

Like most others, her plans had immediately changed. She recalled the horror of watching as United Airlines Flight 175 struck the South Tower on live television. Thirty-three minutes later Melody herself had become a witness to history. From her room on the upper floor of the hotel she looked out toward Virginia and watched as black smoked billowed from where American Airlines Flight 77 had hit the Pentagon.

She recalled how she suddenly felt trapped and terribly alone. Sitting at the foot of the bed, curled up with a pillow in her lap, and remained glued to the network coverage for the next few days, as she remained grounded in Washington.

Now she found herself thinking back on that horrific day and wondered how it must have been for him, someone who had actually been in the middle of all of it.

"I understand if it is something you don't want to talk about," she said apologetically.

"No, it's ok," he replied. "I admit that in the beginning it was tough to talk about, but as time went by I began to realize that people were only asking because they really felt a need to connect on a more meaningful level. I imagine it must have been the same thing for those guys back during Pearl Harbor. When something of such magnitude happens, people can't fully comprehend it. So they try to understand it better through someone who was there."

"I never thought about it that way," Melody said. "That makes sense. Did you know anyone who died?"

"I knew a couple of the guys in Emergency Service," he replied, "and several of my friends have come down with cancer through the years and have died."

"Yeah, I knew some people too. I just could never make any sense of it. They were just business people. I went to a couple of the funerals and then I couldn't do it anymore. I couldn't stand to go anywhere because it just seemed as if everywhere I went there was another funeral. At some point I just stopped going outside and worked from home. I guess I just locked myself away from all the tragedy."

As Maguire watched her, he could see tears welling up in her eyes as she recalled the painful memories.

"I only made it to one funeral myself," he said. "The weeks and months afterward they just had us working six, seven days a week. Then they moved some of us from the *pile* in Manhattan to the landfill in Staten Island. That was the hardest part for me. At least on the pile you held onto the fact that, as slim as it was, you were searching for someone. Getting shipped over to the landfill was defeating. You had to accept that you were just looking for something to give the families back to bury.

"That most have been horrible," Melody said.

Maguire picked up his wine glass and finished the drink off.

"Made me long to be back in the Navy," he replied.

She reached out and took his hand in hers. "Well, I'm just glad you're here now."

Maguire looked over at her. He could see she was being honest.

"Me too," he replied. "So tell me, how'd you get that big jet, little lady?"

"Twelve the hard way at the Bellagio," she said with a straight face.

"Must have been a helluva pot," he replied sarcastically.

He reached down and stabbed his fork into one of the appetizers. He felt the slight burn of the spices.

"How are they?" Melody asked.

"Overall, pretty good, but New Orleans isn't exactly facing serious competition."

She reached down and took one. *He was right*, she thought, *they were good.*

"So what does someone who survived both the Navy and the NYPD to do for fun now?" she asked.

"Besides stalking incredibly hot, blonde venture capitalists?"

"So you think I'm hot, huh?"

"And you just completely ignored the part about stalking?"

"Some risks are worth taking," Melody chuckled and took a sip of wine.

"Well, you'd be surprised how many people love to pay me for my opinion," he replied. "Basically I do security consulting work now. You know, lock your doors and windows, don't go out in the rain without an umbrella, etc."

"Hmmmm maybe I should have you come over to my place and check out my physical well-being," she said playfully.

"We could arrange that," he replied.

Just then the waitress returned with the entrees and they spent the remainder of dinner engaging in small talk that was interlaced with a mix of humor and double *entendre* that left no mistaking that each of their thoughts was still rooted in the night spent on the boat. When dinner was finished Maguire paid the bill and the two of them walked outside. Melody took his hand as they started off toward the promenade which ran along the water's edge.

"So what time does that jet of yours turn into a pumpkin?" he asked.

Melody looked down at her watch. It was just past 8 p.m.

"Eleven," she said with a tinge of melancholy. "I have a board meeting in Manhattan that I have to go to tomorrow afternoon."

He thought for a moment, doing the calculations in his head, and figured they'd have to leave in about an hour to make it back.

"It's okay, we still have plenty of time," he replied.

The two of them continued walking along, sharing more about themselves to one another. As they made their way along the promenade Maguire kept a watchful eye on three young men about twenty yards ahead of them. One was sitting on the rail smoking while the other two were speaking in an animated conversation, gesturing wildly with their hands.

He felt that nagging *sixth sense* creeping up inside him.

"….in those early days we didn't have much going for us. The big boys in the industry really had no use for two women who were dead set on disrupting their apple cart," Melody was saying.

She looked up at Maguire and saw the change in his face. Felt his hand tug her gently and redirect her back in the direction that they had just come.

"What is it, James?" she asked.

"Nothing, we just probably need to start heading back now," he said coolly.

But something had happened. Melody could sense the change in him, felt it transfer from his hand into hers, as if a switch had been flipped and he was no longer the same person she had just been talking with.

They turned around and headed back in the direction of the restaurant. Their conversation had ended abruptly and he walked with a sense of purpose, holding her right hand firmly in his. Suddenly, she heard the sound of running feet coming up from behind them.

The kid who had been sitting on the railing shot past them, stopping a couple of feet in front of them before being joined a moment later by his two friends.

Maguire mentally ticked off the positions of each of the kids. Besides the *Smoking Kid,* who now stood in front of them, one of them was standing slightly behind Melody while the other one was in front and off to the left of her.

Maguire guessed that they were all in their late teens. They were what the Street Crime guys used to call *wiggers*. That is white kids, most often born and raised in suburbia, who liked to pretend they were thugs and rap hip hop songs about how bad-ass they were. The only ones who laughed harder at these idiots than the cops were the actual hard core thugs who felt that the only reason for not *bustin' a cap* in their sorry lily white asses was the fact that the bullet was actually worth more to them.

They all bore the tell-tale signs of perps, police vernacular for perpetrators. The Smoking Kid held his cigarette with one hand while the other played the role of a belt, holding up his saggy pants. He wore a ball cap on his head with a subdued sports team logo on it, tilted to the side, and the latest style of Nike sneaker. He finished the ensemble off with a tee shirt, which had Bob Marley's face superimposed over a Jamaican flag, and a heavy plated gold chain dangling from around his neck to which a big medallion of Jesus' face was attached.

The image was so comical that Maguire almost laughed in the kid's face. There was nothing like bringing the good Lord along with you when you're committing a crime.

Perp number two looked like a clone of the Smoking Kid, just with less courage. He couldn't get a good look of perp number three, who was behind Melody, but he really didn't hold out much hope for an overall improvement.

"Hey, mister, what time is it?" the Smoking Kid asked.

"Just about eight thirty," Maguire replied.

"Yo, how do you know, chief?" Smoking Kid asked. "You ain't never even looked at your watch."

"It sounds about right," he said.

"Well why don't you just give me your watch and then I'll know for myself," the kid replied.

Maguire slowly pulled Melody's hand toward him. It was about then that perp number two seemed to have found his courage.

"Look, the bitch is scared," he said with a laugh.

"Should be scared," Smoking Kid replied, as he reached into his pocket and pulled out a switchblade that he held up high, directly in front of Melody, and opened with an exaggerated flick of his wrist.

What happened next occurred far too quickly for any of them to actually process.

Maguire had intentionally pulled Melody's hand close enough so that he could now grab it with his right hand. He then yanked her body to his right, out of harm's way, while at the same time his left hand had come up and grabbed the hand of the Smoking Kid, which held the knife. Maguire began to twist the kids hand while pulling him closer, knocking him off balance. A second later the knife fell from his hand, as the wrist was dislocated, and Maguire delivered a punishing blow to the kid's left jaw that dropped him immediately onto the wooden planks of the promenade. The only consolation was that the blow rendered him unconscious long before he hit the ground.

Perp number two made the mistake of thinking that Maguire was now exposed since his back was turned slightly away from him. He lunged forward and was immediately rewarded with an elbow to the face for his effort. The kid reached up in pain, clutching his now broken nose, even as his knees buckled and he dropped to the ground.

Up until this moment, perp number three had remained frozen in shock. He couldn't fathom how something they had done dozens of times before had gone so horribly wrong, so fast. Shocked back into reality, he fumbled in his pocket until he found the butterfly knife he carried and withdrew it, snapping it open.

At that moment his eyes came up to confront Maguire, but all he actually saw was the cavernous opening of the Sig's barrel that was pointed directly at him.

"It's time to go home now," Maguire said calmly to the kid who was now lined up in his sights.

The kid dropped the knife and began to back away slowly.

"Th-th-this is-is-isn't over," he said with a false sense of bravado that was betrayed by the uncontrolled stammering in his voice.

"Yes it is," Maguire replied. "There's nothing here worth dying over, son."

He watched cautiously as perp's two and three gathered up the limp body of the Smoking Kid and took off.

When he was sure they weren't going to come back he re-holstered the gun and turned toward Melody.

"What the hell just happened?" she said.

"Dumb kids," was all he replied, as he took Melody's hand in his and led her back toward where the car was parked

Melody sat in the car, looking out the window, as Maguire headed north, away from Burlington and back toward the ferry. They rode in silence.

She replayed what had happened in her mind over and over again. She wasn't sure if she had even seen it at all. All she remembered was the kid in front of her holding a knife. At that moment her mind reverted back to the Israeli tactical martial arts course, *Krav Maga,* which she had taken. But before she had even had a chance to react to the threat, she felt her body being jerked away so fast, so powerfully, that she thought something had exploded. By the time she regained her senses two of those little shits were on the ground and James now had a gun in his hand pointed at the third kid, whom she was reasonably sure had pissed his pants.

It was all so unreal.

Who the hell moves that quickly? she wondered.

It was Maguire that finally broke the ice.

"I'll take you back to the airport," he said.

"No, don't," she said, reaching into her pocket for her cell phone.

"I thought you had to leave tonight?" Maguire asked. "What about the meeting?"

"I'll leave in the morning," Melody replied. "It's only an hour flight."

"Are you sure?" James asked.

"Positive," she answered.

She scrolled through the address book and selected the number to call.

"Kat? Change of plans. I'm staying over. Can you file a new flight plan for the morning?"

"Can you get me to the airport tomorrow by seven?" she asked, looking over at Maguire.

"Sure," he replied.

"Yeah, I'll be there. Thanks, Kat," she said and disconnected the call.

The next call she decided needed to be a text: *Gen, there's been a change of plans. Too much to explain, but I'm flying out in the morning. Can you reschedule the car to get me at eight*?

She sat the phone in her lap and waited. Thirty seconds later she got her answer: *Here's my shocked face :-O*

Followed a few seconds later by another text that read: *Will do, you go, girl*!

"Done," Melody said. "I don't know about you, cowboy, but I seriously need a drink."

"I can do that."

The weather had cooled down considerably and they spent the ferry ride back to Cumberland Head inside the car. As they drove back Maguire remembered to stop at the local market where he grabbed some coffee before heading back to Perrysville. A short time later he pulled the car into the garage. He decided to leave the gun bag in the trunk. She'd already been through enough and he didn't want to have to explain that to her as well. He made a point to lock everything up.

He and Melody walked up to the back door. At the top of the step Maguire fumbled with the keys, dropping them on the stair. He stooped down to pick them up and felt for the strand of fishing line which was still where he had left it. Internally he breathed a sigh of relief when he found it in place. He wasn't sure just how much more Melody could take this evening. However, he would not feel one hundred percent ok until he had the chance to check the front door.

He opened the door and let her walk inside. He locked the screen door and the interior one, then set the coffee on the counter.

"Come on," he said. "I'll get you that drink."

He led Melody into the living room and poured them both a glass of whiskey. He handed one to her and raised his up toward her.

"*Sláinte*," Maguire said in a traditional Irish toast.

They both took a drink. Melody felt the warmth of the whiskey as it went down her throat. She needed it.

"So, tell me about this place," she said.

"Welcome to the home I grew up in," he replied.

"Seriously?"

"Yep, this is Casa Maguire in all its rural glory."

Melody cradled the whiskey glass in her hand as she looked around. It was so small, so quaint. In her mind she pictured James as a boy running through the house.

Maguire casually moved over in the direction of the front door and checked the filament. It too hung in place where he had left it and he felt a bit more relaxed now.

He walked over to the fireplace and began working on starting the fire. There was still some charred wood remaining from the night before and it didn't take long before the flames took hold. In a few minutes he had a respectable fire going and he sat down in his father's chair.

Melody walked back toward where James sat and looked at the rows of books on the shelves behind the two chairs.

"Someone loved to read," she said.

"Both my parents, actually," Maguire replied, glancing back at the book cases. "I can't remember too many nights when the two of them didn't read."

Melody looked at one of the shelves in astonishment. She put the whiskey glass down onto the table that sat next to the chair and reached over and picked up a wooden Irish whistle off the shelf, wiping it off reverently. It was a beautifully constructed, hand carved piece made from blackwood.

"Who's was this?" she asked.

"It was my mother's," James replied. "She loved to play it. It used to annoy me to be honest. I'd be sitting up in my room and I would hear this God awful sound carrying through the house. It always sounded like she was in mourning. I remember she used to say 'For the great Gaels of Ireland are the men that God made mad; for all their wars are merry and all their songs are sad."'

Maguire took a drink and looked back down at the glass.

"Then again, my dad used to say God made alcohol so the Irish wouldn't rule the world."

Melody laughed. "They sound like they were a cute couple, James."

"For a time I thought they were the biggest pain in the asses in the world."

"Would she mind?" Melody asked, as she held up the whistle.

"No, I don't think she would," he answered.

Maguire sat back in the chair and took another sip. He watched the fire burning brightly, casting its warm orange glow against the stone. He closed his eyes.

What wouldn't I give for one more minute with them? he thought.

Softly the first strains began to rise up from the wooden instrument, filling the room with an enchanted melody whose tones ranged from unspeakable happiness to low plaintive wails. Maguire sat enrapt as he watched her play the instrument in the same way his mother had done so many years ago.

When she was finished she laid it back on the shelf gently.

"Melody, that was absolutely beautiful," James said.

"Thank you," Melody replied, feeling a slight bit embarrassed. She sat down in the chair opposite him. "It's been quite a number of years since I played last. It was an escape from my world at the time."

"My mother used to say no one understood suffering like the Irish."

"I bet you made a cute family," she said.

"Actually, we hadn't spoken in years," Maguire said.

"Why was that?" she asked.

He finished his drink and got up, pouring himself a refill. He looked over at Melody, who held out her glass, and topped off her drink.

"They weren't particularly happy with my joining the Navy," he explained. "My mom and dad were both educators and they saw things a bit differently. To make things worse they had come over here from Northern Ireland in 1968 to escape the Troubles and had an inherent distrust of both the police and military."

"The *Troubles*?" Melody asked quizzically.

"It was a violent period of time in Northern Ireland that the *experts* will tell you ran from the late 1960's until 1998; when they signed the Good Friday accords," Maguire answered. "The bumper sticker version is that it stems from nationalists and unionists who are at odds over a divided Ireland. The sectarian violence still continues today, although it isn't as rampant as it was back in the day. My uncle Jimmy was killed in August '69. That's who I'm named after."

"Oh my God," Melody said. "That's horrible. How did he die?"

"There was a huge protest in County Derry, in a place called the Bogside, and the whole thing went to shit real quickly. My family lived in Belfast and a call had gone out to tie up the local police, so that they couldn't be deployed to Derry. So my parents and uncle went out, joining up with the local protestors, but just like in Derry things got out of control. That was when my uncle was shot and killed. By the time my parents made their way back home, they'd found that the unionists had burned down all the homes belonging to nationalists on their street. My parents had lost everything. So, they left and made their way south to Dublin where my mom had some family. Then they made their way to America by the end of the year."

"I have to admit that I honestly have no clue about the politics in Ireland" Melody admitted.

Maguire laughed. "It's been my experience, Melody, that anyone who tells you that they understand the politics of Ireland has no clue about the politics of Ireland."

Melody stared at the fire, watching the flames dance along the logs, as she held on tightly to the emotional rollercoaster she was on. A part of her felt scared; which she attributed to hearing the story along with what had happened earlier on the promenade. All she knew was that she wanted that safety back.

Melody took a drink and got up, walking over to where he was sitting, and sat down in his lap. She curled up, feeling his arms wrapping around her. As she gazed at the fire flickering in the fireplace she felt him kiss her head gently. The two of them sat there without speaking, mesmerized by the flames and lost in their own thoughts. The events of the night drifted away in the security of his embrace. There was no place else that she wanted to be. Well, that wasn't necessarily true. After a while Melody turned to face him.

"James," she said. "Take me to bed.

CHAPTER TWENTY-SEVEN

Perrysville, New York State
Sunday, April 29th, 2012 – 11:32 p.m.

The orange glow, from the cigarette's ember, lit up the interior of the pickup truck, as he watched the shadows of the figures moving inside. He had just gotten back when he had decided to take a ride by the house and see if there was anything going on. As he turned the bend in the road he saw the Mustang pull into the driveway. He had quickly killed the lights and pulled over just far enough to make out the side door. He caught a glimpse of Maguire, as he walked up the back stairs, and watched as the klutz dropped something and bent over to retrieve it.

He was still the same old pathetic jerk, he thought.

But then he watched as Maguire stood aside and he caught just a fleeting glimpse of another figure, with long blonde hair, step inside.

This was not something he had anticipated. He watched the shadows appear in the living room and he waited. He had things to do, but he couldn't leave, not now. Minutes slowly ticked away as the discarded cigarette butts began to build up on the sidewalk outside the pickup; as he subconsciously began to chain smoke. The shadows had stopped moving around and he wondered if he had missed something. Finally he watched as the light in the living room turned off followed a few seconds later by one turning on upstairs and then quickly turning off.

He could feel his heart pounding in his chest, could almost hear the rush of the blood coursing through his body. He felt so amazingly alive. He had always planned to look him in the eye at the exact moment he took his life. He wanted to see the fear, the terror, in his eyes as he ended his life. He was caught between his desire to carry out the plan as he had created it and the desire to free himself of the bonds that restrained him; to finally unleash his pent up fury on his prey. It took every ounce of control to maintain his calm.

He thought for a moment about the cargo he now carried in the bed of the truck. He realized just what a risk he had taken by coming here instead of going directly back home. He took another drag on the cigarette and dropped the truck into drive; pulling slowly away from the curb before turning his headlights on.

As he passed by the house he noticed that the car was not parked in the driveway. *That was odd*, he thought. *He must have parked it in the garage*. He would have liked to investigate it further, maybe make some mechanical *adjustments*, but the night was growing old and he still had a lot more work ahead of him.

He realized that he was tired and relished the moment when all this would be behind him so that he could finally rest for a while.

How long had it been since he had really rested? he wondered. *Days? Weeks?*

Try as he might, he couldn't remember.

Not that it mattered, he counseled himself. *It would all be over soon and then nothing would deny him the rest he so justly deserved.*

CHAPTER TWENTY-EIGHT

Perrysville, New York State
Monday, April 30th, 2012 – 4:55 a.m.

The cell phone on the night table began to beep incessantly; the alarm shattering the silence in the bedroom and waking up the two lovers who had not been quite ready to surrender the night.

"No," he heard her moan, as she pulled the pillow over her head. He reached over her body, grabbing the phone, and turned off the alarm.

"You're the one who has a board meeting to go to, angel," Maguire said, as he laid back down on the bed.

"Come with me," she said from beneath the pillow.

Maybe I should go with her, he thought.

It was already past the forty-eight hour mark and the odds of this turning out good were extremely slim at this point. Besides there seemed to be little interest of looking into this at any level and maybe he just needed to let it go. He knew from personal experience that bad things happened to good people every day.

Melody rolled over, onto her stomach, lifting herself up on her elbows, and stared at him.

"No, James, don't even think about it," she began. "As much as I would love for you to come with me, I'd hate myself if you did. I know you have things to do here and I would never put you in the position of having to choose. I want you to take me back to the plane and then go and do what you are good at. I'll be waiting for you when you're done."

Maguire leaned over and kissed her.

"You know you're kind of *bossy*," he said with a laugh.

She grabbed the sheet, wrapping it around her, before swinging her legs over the side of the bed. As Maguire watched she stood up and made her way to the doorway where she looked back over her shoulder coyly.

"Finally, a man who understands me," she replied and walked out.

He laid there for a moment, staring at the spot that she had just vacated, until he saw her hand reappear. As he watched, she pointed a finger at him. Then she turned her wrist over, flicking her finger back and forth, beckoning him to join her.

Maguire got up and walked toward the doorway. When he arrived, the hallway was empty, save for the sheet that lay discarded on the floor.

What the hell, he thought.

He was accustomed to following orders and she was, by far, the best looking boss that he had ever had.

CHAPTER TWENTY-NINE

Perrysville, New York State
Monday, April 30th, 2012 – 5:23 a.m.

Deputy Keith Banning banged on the front door again; a bit harder this time. The Mustang was parked in the garage so he knew that Maguire was still inside.

He was just about to knock again when a light finally went on inside the house. He heard the lock snap and the door opened slightly. Maguire stood off to the side partially obscured by the door. Banning could see that his hair was wet.

"It's too early for coffee and playing catch-up, Keith," Maguire said. "What the hell's going on?"

"I don't know how to say this, Jim," Banning said.

Maguire leaned over, sitting the pistol on the small table behind the door, and opened it a bit wider.

"Spit it out, Keith," he said, understanding what was about to come next.

"A couple of fisherman found some *remains* down along the shoreline, over by Willsboro Bay," Banning explained. "It's nothing official, but it doesn't look good. I just figured you'd want to know."

"Let me just finish getting dressed and I'll come over," Maguire said.

"Not a good idea, Jim," Banning said, almost apologetically. "Not sure what happened between you and the sheriff yesterday, but he was ranting and raving like a lunatic. I'd consider myself *persona non grata* for the foreseeable future."

Maguire considered that for a moment. He had no fear of Browning, but he also didn't need that piece of shit hampering his movements while he was here, especially since he knew the accident was in fact not an *accident*.

“Ok, Keith,” James said. “Can you keep me updated without too much trouble?”

“Sure,” Banning replied. “I owe you that. Give me your cell number.”

Melody had walked down the stairs and now stood off to the side by the fireplace.

“Everything alright,” she asked, seeing the deputy at the door.

Banning looked over at the blonde haired woman.

“No,” Maguire replied, as he walked over to the end table where he removed a pen and a piece of paper.

“Morning, ma’am,” Banning said.

James wrote down the number and handed it to Banning.

“I’m sorry to have to wake you up with this,” Banning said.

“No, Keith, I appreciate you taking the time to let me know,” Maguire replied.

“Ok, if anything changes or updates I’ll keep you posted” he said.

“Thanks,” James said.

“Sorry for the intrusion, ma’am,” Banning said, tipping his hat to her, before turning and stepping off the porch.

Maguire watched as the man made his way back toward the patrol car parked in the driveway, then closed the door and walked over to sit in the chair.

“What was that about?” Melody asked.

“They found some remains down by the lake,” Maguire answered. “Nothing confirmed yet, but the area is in the same general vicinity as the accident.”

Melody walked over and sat down next to him.

“Do you think it’s her?” she asked.

“It fits,” he replied. “It’s not too far from where the accident occurred and the road does run parallel to Willsboro Bay at one point. She could have made it there.”

He sat in the chair, the fingers of his left hand rubbing his temple as he thought about everything.

"You don't sound overly convinced," Melody replied.

James looked over at her and the two of them just stared at one another.

How did this woman, whom he had only known for less than three days, manage to connect with him on such a level that simultaneously excited him and yet scared the heck out of him? He had lived by a simple code that dictated that trust was something that was not easily earned and yet everything inside of him told him she could be trusted.

"No, I'm not," he answered.

"Then do what you need to," she replied. "You need to find the truth. More importantly she deserves it. I told you, I will be waiting for you when you're done."

He leaned over to kiss her and she met him in the middle.

"You are one helluva lady, Melody Anderson," he replied.

"You bet your ass I am, cowboy," she said with a smile. "And you better not forget it."

"I won't, I promise."

"Good," she replied. "Now get me to my damn plane so that you can do whatever it is you need to do here and get back to me."

"Sounds like a plan," Maguire said, as he got up. "You want some coffee?"

"Oh God yes," Melody replied. "I need to finish getting ready"

"Go get ready," he replied. "I'll bring it up when it's done."

Melody went upstairs while Maguire headed into the kitchen. He opened the coffee and brought down the old percolator coffee pot from the cabinet above the sink. It was a relic from a bygone time and yet it always seemed to brew the best cup of coffee. At least he thought so.

When it was done he poured two cups and brought them upstairs. As he got to the top of the stairs he paused for a moment and stared down the hallway, into the bathroom at the far end, where Melody now stood doing her hair.

At that moment he realized the irony in what he was seeing. Here was this incredibly beautiful woman, who in less than an hour would be back on her plane, heading into the city for a corporate board meeting, and yet she looked perfectly at home in this old, two bedroom house up in the Adirondack mountains.

For the briefest of moments he actually wondered if he could come back to this world before chasing the thoughts away.

You can never go back, only go forward, he thought, as he walked toward the bathroom to deliver the hot cup of coffee.

"Thanks," she replied and took a sip. "Mmmmm, I really needed that."

Maguire checked his watch it was 5:55 a.m. "Better get a move on, angel, or you'll be flapping your wings back to the city."

She dropped the brush back into her bag.

"*Voilà*," she declared triumphantly, as she turned back toward him, her arms outstretched dramatically, palms held upward.

Maguire examined her closely, taking in every detail.

"I guess it will have to do in a pinch."

"Oh you'll pay for that later, mister," she replied.

"Promises, promises," he said with a wink.

They walked back to the bedroom and each of them grabbed their jackets before heading downstairs. As they made their way through the living room she paused to look around and wondered if she would ever see the little house again. Melody stared at the two chairs they had sat in the night before and the whistle on the shelf. It was as if she was taking a photograph in her mind, just in case.

Maguire walked into the kitchen and took another drink from his coffee cup before setting it down in the sink. She followed a moment later and put her cup in there as well. They headed out the back door and made their way toward the garage. Maguire pulled the Mustang out, stopping half way down the driveway.

"What's wrong?" she asked.

"Forgot my wallet," he said. "I'll be right back."

He went back into the house, resetting the tripwire in the backdoor from the interior this time and then moved to repeat the process on the front door, through which he then left. He made his way around the front of the house and came up to the vehicle from behind and jumped in.

Melody had been staring at the back door, daydreaming, and was caught off-guard by his sudden reappearance. She let out a scream and then, realizing it was him, punched him in the shoulder hard enough to sting.

"Oww," he said feigning mock pain.

"Jeez, are you trying to give me a heart attack," she asked.

"What did I do?" he asked innocently.

"You went in that door, why didn't you come out that way?"

"Remember to always check your six, baby girl," Maguire replied, as he dropped the car into reverse and pulled out of the driveway.

"I thought that's what I had you for," she laughed.

As they made their way up the road he felt the lingering burn of the punch.

Maybe he had underestimated her, he thought. *She wasn't all girly-girl that's for sure.*

They headed west on County 22 toward the thruway. As they drove along the winding road Maguire spotted the unmistakable vehicle coming toward them. As their paths converged he looked up and into the passenger compartment of the Ford Pickup. Paul Browning was staring back down at him, eyes set and an angry scowl fixed upon his face. Maguire watched as the vehicle faded away in the rear view mirror. He assumed he would be heading to Willsboro.

"Friend of yours?" Melody asked.

"Not in this lifetime," James replied tersely, as he pulled the car onto the thruway and headed north toward Plattsburgh.

It was a short trip back to the airport and Melody remained quiet for most of the ride. As they exited the highway and began to make their way back through the roads of the old air base, she turned slightly in the seat to look out the passenger window. Maguire didn't have to see the tears to know that they were there. He let her have her moment without saying anything, just reached down and put his hand gently on her thigh. He felt her left hand grab it tightly.

He turned right at Arizona and made his way through the gate. The big plane was already on the tarmac with the stairs down awaiting her arrival. Outside, a woman in uniform talked to one of the ground crew personnel. Maguire pulled the Mustang off to the side and turned the car off.

She sniffed slightly and James reached into the glove box, pulling out a tissue that he then handed her.

"Springtime in the Adirondacks," he said. "It can be really bad on your allergies."

She took the tissue and dabbed her eye before looking at him. They both knew it was a lie.

"Thank you," she said.

"No need to thank me, Melody," he replied, taking her hand. "In ten or fifteen minutes it could very easily be me."

She smiled at that and understood what he was saying to her.

"Find your answers, James," she said. "And then come find me."

He leaned over as she drew closer to him and the two lovers embraced in a passionate kiss.

Outside Kat peered over at the car and saw the two of them locked in their embrace.

"Way to go, girl" she whispered to herself and smiled.

A few moments later Maguire got out and walked around to open the passenger door. Melody slid out of the seat, kissing him again, before turning and making her way toward the waiting plane. Maguire shut the car door and leaned back against it.

As Melody climbed up the stair case she stopped to look back at him and blew him a kiss. After she had stepped inside he watched as the stairs rose up and the door closed. Inside the cockpit he could make out the pilot and co-pilot working in tandem inside, checking gauges and flipping switches. A moment later the engines came online and roared to life.

Outside, a grounds crew member stood in front of the plane using his directional wands to give marshalling instructions to the pilot. When the checks were done he gave them a thumb's up and jogged out of the way of the aircraft. As the plane turned in front of him he saw Melody starring out the window. She waved at him and he raised his hand to his head, giving her an off-handed salute. He could make out her smile just as the plane finished its turn and headed toward the runway.

Maguire waited until the plane passed the hanger and disappeared from view before he got back into the Mustang. It was time to go shake some trees and get some answers.

CHAPTER THIRTY

Willsboro Bay, New York State
Monday, April 30th, 2012 – 6:23 a.m.

Paul Browning made his way down the narrow dirt path, that led from the roadway to the shoreline, and headed over to where his deputies were talking to some fisherman.

"What do you have, McDermott?" he asked in an irritated tone, as he led one of the men away from the others.

"Those two fisherman over there came out this morning and found it," he replied nervously.

"McDermott, you're a goddamn deputy sheriff. Stop talking in circles. What the hell is *it*?"

"It's over here, Sheriff," McDermott said.

The two men walked over to where an old massive cedar tree lay fallen over into the Lake. Its dead branches extending out into the water like the lifeless fingers of some colossal grim reaper. Caught among the twisting limbs was a mangled hunk of what appeared to be pale colored flesh, a section of denuded bone protruding out from it, was partially wrapped in a torn piece of black material.

Browning knelt down to take a closer look.

"Is it human?" McDermott asked.

"How the hell am I supposed to know, McDermott? I'm the sheriff not the goddamn medical examiner."

"I just thought with Mrs. Browning missing….."

Browning stood up and glared at the deputy.

"I don't recall too many walleye getting *dressed up* to go for a swim," he replied. "But this lake is nearly five hundred square miles and borders two states and another damn country. So until we know something factual let's not assume anything. Speaking of the M.E. have you managed to ruin her morning yet?"

"Dispatch is still trying to reach her."

"Well I'll tell you what, you just stay here and wait for her and you let me know what she tells you."

"Yes, sir."

Browning walked back to where the fishermen were standing with the other deputy.

"I think McDermott has this covered," he told the other deputy dismissively. "You can resume patrol."

As the deputy made his way back up to the roadway, Browning turned back toward the fisherman and turned on his politician's charm.

"I just wanted to thank you men for alerting us to what you found. You know law enforcement is a partnership with the residents of the area they serve. My men couldn't be as effective as they are without the help of the good people of this community."

"Well, we just heard about what happened to Mrs. Browning and we were concerned when we saw this," said one of the men.

"Well I appreciate your concern very much. It's a difficult thing to have to deal with personal issues, but I think my wife understands that I am the sheriff of the county and I have to also be there for all the people who put their trust in me. I'm hoping for the best possible outcome."

"We'll be praying for you, Sheriff."

"Well thank you so much. It's my privilege to serve such wonderful folks like you. You have a great day."

Browning walked back up the trail and made his way back to his truck. It was physically draining to have to constantly cater to these damn idiots sticking their noses into places it didn't belong. As if having to attend all those early morning coffee get-togethers with these yahoo's wasn't bad enough for him.

“Why the hell couldn’t they just come down and fish for crying out loud,” he muttered.

He sat in the truck and stared out over the water; anger and frustration etched into his face.

“You just couldn’t stay gone could you?”

CHAPTER THIRTY-ONE

Plattsburgh, New York State
Monday, April 30th, 2012 – 7:17 a.m.

Melody sat looking out the window of the plane and watched as the buildings of the airport streaked by. The excitement she had felt during takeoff the previous day had now been replaced with a sense of melancholy. She understood that each passing moment now took her farther away from him.

She reached down, removing the cell phone from her purse, and sent Genevieve a text: *On my way back.*

Melody looked down at the lake and tried to see across to the Vermont side, imagining where they had eaten the night before. She had so much still to process.

The cell phone buzzed on the table top. She reached down and opened the reply from Gen.

In Maryland, wish I was there with you :-(I'll call you tonight.

Melody smiled.

She wished Gen was going to be back at the house too, but she knew that she had to get her act together. It had been a whirlwind weekend, but she also had responsibilities that needed to be taken care of. If her life was going to involve him, then she would need to find a way to accomplish that and it couldn't be to the exclusion of everything else.

CHAPTER THIRTY-TWO

Keenseville, New York State
Monday, April 30th, 2012 – 8:03 a.m.

Maguire pulled into the parking lot adjacent to the art gallery and walked around to the front door. There were no lights on inside so he made his way around back; to the side door that he had seen Lena come out of the day before. He knocked several times on the door and waited.

There was a camera positioned just above the doorway so he knew she could tell who it was. A moment later he heard the door unlock and she opened it.

"Have you heard something," she asked, the question coming out almost frantically.

Maguire stared down at her, she looked terrible. The waiting game had begun to take a physical toll on her. She had a robe wrapped around her and looked as though she had not gotten any sleep. At that moment James felt a bit ashamed that he had taken the previous night for himself.

No, he chided himself. There was nothing for him to be ashamed of. He was doing more than anyone else around here and feeling bad about needing a break was wrong.

"Yes and no," he replied. "We need to talk."

Lena stepped back and let him come inside, locking the door behind him. He followed her up to the apartment on the second floor.

The apartment was an open style floor plan. The brick walls had been stripped down to their natural red coloring. The exposed ceiling beams had been sanded down to their original wood grain and then sealed with a high gloss finish. The old tin plate ceiling and duct work that ran above were painted with a flat white that gave the room the impression of being higher than it actually was.

It reminded Maguire of the loft apartments in some of the trendier parts of lower Manhattan. The only thing missing was the view.

Lena collapsed on the couch and picked up her cigarette and took a drag. She was trying to steel herself for what was to come.

"There's coffee in the kitchen."

"Thanks," he said and walked over to the coffee pot, pouring himself a cup.

"Refill?" he asked.

"I switched to something heavier already," she replied. "So what's going on?"

"A couple of things," Maguire said, as he sat down on the couch opposite her.

"This isn't sounding good."

"I don't think it was an accident."

Lena took another drag on the cigarette.

"Neither do I," she replied, "but I only have a hunch, what do you have?"

"I've gone out to the scene of the accident several times, each time I just left with a nagging feeling and more questions than answers. I spoke to someone in the state police who told me where the car was towed to. I inspected it and found some damage that wasn't consistent with the accident."

"Go on."

"I think it was staged to look like an accident, but I think it was planned."

Lena perked up.

"You think Tricia is alive?"

"I think she was alive after the accident and that someone took her from the scene."

"That doesn't tell me how you feel right now."

Maguire stared back at her. She was fragile, he could see that. The last fifty plus hours had clearly taken its toll on her. He needed to tread carefully, but he also knew she deserved the truth.

"Honestly, Lena, I don't know. I got a knock on the door this morning by someone who told me that some fisherman may have found something down by the lake; not too far from the accident scene."

Lena crushed out the cigarette that was in the ash tray and lit another.

"So what do you think?"

"I think it's amazingly convenient," he replied.

"How so?"

"If the accident was staged, as I believe it was, and Tricia was taken from the scene, why does evidence show up in the immediate area to make it look as if she is dead?"

"You think someone doesn't want her to be found?"

"Yeah, I think it's a false flag."

"What's a *false flag*?"

"It's an old naval term," he replied. "Basically an enemy ship would run up the flag of his opponent to trick him into letting his guard down and allowing him to get close enough before attacking.

"So you think Tricia is alive and we are being made to think she is dead?"

"I think I still have enough questions to make it plausible."

"What do we do?" Lena asked.

"Play the game and try to figure out why we are being misled," Maguire replied. "For the time being act as if everything you are being told is the truth. Remember, this is still just a hunch and I could very well be wrong."

"I trust you more than anyone else in this county," she replied.

“Do you remember what Tricia was wearing that night?”

“I do,” she answered. “Actually I can do you one better, I have a photograph.”

Lena got up and walked over to the laptop computer that was sitting on a desk across the room. She went through a few files until she pulled up the one from the opening. She selected a photo and printed it out. When she was done she got up and walked back over to Maguire, handing him the photo.

James stared down at the image. The photo showed Tricia standing with Lena and a male. She was wearing a fashionable pinstriped dark gray suit with a black blouse underneath. The three were holding up fluted champagne glasses and were all flashing huge smiles. She looked filled with life and energy.

“Do you mind if I keep this?” he asked.

“No, I’d like you to keep it.”

Maguire stood up.

“I’ll let you know if I find out anything, but for the time being keep a low profile and make sure the door is locked.”

“I will,” she replied.

He followed her back down the stairs. When they got to the door, Lena turned around and threw her arms around his neck and held him tightly. Maguire put his arms around her and hugged her back.

“Thank you, James,” Lena said. “Not just for me, but for Tricia as well. You’re all either one of us has left.”

CHAPTER THIRTY-THREE

Willsboro Pointe, New York State
Monday, April 30th, 2012 – 9:01 a.m.

"I don't know," Paul Browning said into the cell phone. "It looked like a hunk of meat wrapped up in some black material."

He was in his den pacing back and forth in front of the bay window that overlooked the lake.

"How the hell do I know what she was wearing?" he said angrily in response to the question. "She was a big girl. She came and went as she pleased."

"Fine," he said and hung up the phone.

He stared out the window. That was all he needed, some candy ass medical examiner asking questions. The worst thing was that she wasn't even from the same party and there was not much pressure he could put on her. The fortunate thing was that she really didn't strike him as being all that competent. Hopefully there wasn't enough for her to make a major issue out of it.

Browning took out a cigarette and lit it up.

Things were beginning to unravel a bit. He needed some time and space to regroup.

CHAPTER THIRTY-FOUR

Keenseville, New York State
Monday, April 30th, 2012 – 9:13 a.m.

Maguire sat in the car and picked up his cell phone. He selected a number and hit the call button. The phone rang a few times before he heard it connect.

"How much is bail?" asked Rich Stargold on the other end.

"Wow, you know that never gets old," replied Maguire sarcastically.

"I thought so."

"Besides, if I was in that much trouble I'd call Mary first."

"That hurts."

"I need a favor," Maguire said. "I need you to look up an address for me for a Paul Browning. Should be somewhere in the area around Keenseville or Perrysville. Date of birth would be around 1970, give or take. This is all strictly under the table."

"Ok, you're not doing anything dumb now are you?"

"No, at least not at this moment," he replied. "Just looking to rattle a tree and see what falls from it. I could find out locally, but I'm trying to keep it low key and time isn't exactly my friend."

"Let me pull it up and I'll get back to you in a little bit."

"Ok, thanks," Maguire replied before ending the call.

He made his way across town and back up to the highway. He needed time to think and something to eat, but he didn't want to chance running into anyone he knew. He got off at the Peru exit and headed into town, stopping at a local Dunkin' Donuts. He had heard all the jokes before about cops and donuts, but the truth was he just had a thing for their coffee. However, if pressed, he would have to admit that he did have a special fondness for their toasted coconut donut. He justified it all because he had read an Esquire magazine article that once called it 'the greatest donut of them all' and it really was.

This time however he would forego the donut and just settled on an extra-large coffee along with a ham and cheese sandwich. He knew he would have a lot of making up to do, as far as working out, when he got back. He was grateful to the folks over at the Shinnecock Coast Guard Station who let him use their gym. They were a great bunch of guys and when they worked out as a group he tried to go easy on them.

Maguire ate in the car as he went over all the things he knew up until this point. It was clear to him that someone was directing things, he just wasn't sure who.

At that moment the phone rang. He looked down and saw that it was Rich.

"What do you got for me?"

"Ok, according to New York State DMV records he lives over at 37 High Pointe Road in a place called Willsboro Pointe."

"He's moved up in the world"

"You know this guy?"

"Yeah, we grew up in the same town."

"Then you know he's the local sheriff right?" Rich asked.

"Oh yeah," Maguire replied. "We already had that little class reunion."

"Anything I need to know?"

"The long version is too much to get into right now; I'll fill you in when I have more time. Bumper sticker version is his wife went missing from a car accident that, at least from what I can piece together, looks like it might be staged."

"You can never get involved in easy stuff can you?"

"I'd be boring then and you wouldn't take my calls," James said.

"Not to change the subject, but I need to get together with you and go over something important. What are you doing this weekend?"

"I hadn't planned that far in advance to be honest with you. I only packed for three days, but I'm hitting a ton of brick walls up here."

"Well keep me posted will you. If you're back in town by then plan on coming out to the house. I'll barbecue," Stargold replied.

"I will, I have something I need to talk to you about as well."

"Ok, listen I have to go get ready. Guys from PPD are coming in for a meeting. POTUS needs an influx of cash from the faithful and the kids want to go see the *Lion King*."

"Hey, if you expect any sympathy from me you're sadly mistaken. I believe I was the voice in the wilderness telling you to run like a girl when they offered you the Special Agent in Charge slot. So you just go do that *bossy thing* you do so well."

"You're just jealous because I make an honest living."

"Receptions bad, Rich, I can't hear you. It's gonna sound like I hung up, but you just keep talking," Maguire said and disconnected the call.

It was their typical banter.

Deep down inside Maguire couldn't have been happier for his friend. After the shooting, Rich had been transferred to headquarters in Washington, D.C. for a brief time during a review. The reality was the head of the field office in New York City was retiring and he was being vetted for the top slot. Six months later he was transferred back and named Acting Special Agent in Charge. After cutting his teeth for three months he was officially named as the head of the New York field office.

Maguire was glad that they kept him local. He couldn't imagine not having him and Mary around, let alone the girls. They were the only real family he had left; which was precisely the reason why he wanted to talk to them about Melody.

He finished off the sandwich and took a sip of coffee. He reached down, grabbing the phone from the seat next to him, and sent off a quick text: *Thinking of you.*

Maguire started the car up and pulled up next to the trash can, tossing the garbage into it. He then made his way back out to the highway. Armed with the address, he headed to his destination.

CHAPTER THIRTY-FIVE

Midtown Manhattan, N.Y.
Monday, April 30th, 2012 – 11:53 a.m.

Melody sat in the meeting, feeling terminally bored, and wishing that she had canceled her trip back. If she had expected a quick arrival and departure she was sadly mistaken. Inside her pocket she felt the phone vibrate. She reached in discreetly and removed it, looking down at the message and smiled.

I wish you were here, she texted back to him.

CHAPTER THIRTY-SIX

Willsboro Pointe, New York State
Monday, April 30th, 2012 – 12:01 p.m.

Maguire made his way out to Willsboro Pointe, an area in which he was only vaguely familiar. It was a secluded, residential area which jutted out from the mainland. On the west side was Willsboro Bay and on the east side was Lake Champlain proper. The real money, in terms of real estate, was on the east side where the houses had an amazing scenic view.

After a brief search Maguire located the house or, more accurately, the driveway that led to the house. In fact, he could just make out the actual home through the trees. It was set back about two hundred feet from the road and, from what he could see, it was pretty impressive. He would have liked to have taken a better look around, but it just didn't make much sense in the daylight with so many potential witnesses. Besides, there was only one person he actually wanted to be seen by.

He pulled the car to the side of the road, facing the driveway, and put it in park. It didn't take long for his wish to be fulfilled. As he peered down the long driveway he watched as the big pickup truck came roaring toward him.

Browning's thoughts must have been focused on something else, because they surely weren't on his immediate surroundings. The truck rocketed past the Mustang and drove off down the street. The memory lapse lasted for only a few seconds longer.

As Maguire watched in the rearview mirror the red lights came on at the same time he heard the brakes lockup on the truck. A second later he heard the gears grind as Browning threw it into reverse and accelerated backward toward Maguire's car.

James casually took a drink from the coffee cup as Browning pulled up alongside the car.

"What the hell do you think you're doing outside my house?"

Maguire returned the coffee container to the dashboard and looked out the window at Browning.

"Oh, do you live here, Paul?" Maguire asked with feigned innocence. "It's a beautiful neighborhood. I didn't know the county paid their employees so well?"

"You're crossing a line here, boy, that's not going to end well for you," he replied.

Browning was enraged by the clear invasion of his personal space. No one had ever dared come out to his house. If they had ever thought about it, they surely had come to their right minds and abandoned the idea. Yet here was this little insolent prick thinking he had somehow left his past behind.

"I don't know what you mean, Paul. I was just out taking a drive and thought I might look at some real estate in the area. You know being back here has made me sort of homesick and I thought it might be time for me to put roots back down in the community."

"We consider this to be a private community. The folks out here don't take well to strangers showing up and snooping around."

"I'm sure a friendly word from the sheriff would put their minds at ease."

Browning was struggling to control himself and Maguire could see that he was just at the edge.

"We have never been friends, Maguire," Browning said in a low dangerous tone. "I've taken everything you ever wanted and all you could do was turn tail and run away. You're nothing to me, just a waste of my time and energy, just like all those other pathetic losers you hung around with. Hell I even have a few of them working for me now."

Browning regained his composure and leaned back in the seat, an arrogant smile formed on his face.

"Is that what you want, Jimmy? Do you want to come and work for me like your other loser friends? It'll be just like old times."

James looked up at Browning who sat there looking smug. It was an old trick. Find a way to deflect things away from you by getting your antagonist to respond to your questions. Browning had always played the *bully game* well. He had years of experience torturing those that were weak willed. Physically breaking an opponent was an easy thing, but in the end very counterproductive. Mentally breaking an opponent, where the real enemy becomes that persons own thoughts and ideas, is an art form.

It was time to turn the heat up and see how long it would take to break him.

"I think the more important question is who would want to come and work for *you,* Paul?" Maguire asked. "I honestly can't imagine any of your people showing up for work simply because they think you are a better cop or even a better leader for that matter. In my personal opinion I think it would be a fascinating experience for someone to just see how things work in your narrow little world. However, I have to admit that, from what I have seen so far, I'm not overly impressed by the caliber of your investigatory skills. I mean let's be honest, Paul, you don't even have the rudimentary ability to answer the nagging question of '*what happened to my wife and where is she now?*'"

Browning's eyes narrowed.

"Sadly, Paul," Maguire continued. "I'd be willing to bet that your capabilities could easily be trumped by a minimum wage nerd who got his criminal justice degree from an online course, advertised in the back of a comic book, but that's just my personal opinion."

Silence hung in the air between the two men for a moment. Maguire held his stare and waited patiently for the man to kick start his brain back into gear.

When Browning did get control of himself, his words came out in a stutter.

"If-if-if y-you th-think..."

"Come on, Paul, that's it, you can *do-do-do it...*," Maguire goaded the man, before casually taking another sip of his coffee.

Browning blew up, his face dark with anger, and this time the words came out like a torrent.

"If you think you're going to just waltz back in here and play some half-assed game of *King of the Hill* with me, you're sadly mistaken. I broke you before, Maguire, and I wasn't even trying. I'll break you again and this time I'm going to make you disappear for good."

"Wow, now you're threatening me, Sheriff?"

"That's not a threat, you little prick, it's a promise. You just keep playing whatever little game you think you've got going and we'll see how well it plays out for you."

"Me play games?" Maguire asked. "No, I don't play games, Paul, but I do have a riddle for you. When is an accident *not an accident*?"

The color completely drained from Browning's face. Without saying a word, he dropped the truck into gear and sped off.

Maguire watched as it disappeared from his view before starting the car.

Well, that went remarkably easy, he thought.

CHAPTER THIRTY-SEVEN

Keenseville, New York State
Monday, April 30th, 2012 – 2:41 p.m.

Maguire pulled the Mustang into the parking lot of the Troop B substation and made his way into the lobby. The trooper from the previous day was sitting behind the desk.

"Hey, detective, how can I help you?" he asked.

"I need to speak with Tom Reynolds right away," Maguire said.

"He's not in the office right now, can I take a message?" the trooper asked.

"No, this is time sensitive. Is he on the road right now?"

"Yes, but I think he was heading over to Franklin County."

"Can you raise him on the radio and see if he can call in?"

"I'll try," the trooper replied and walked over to the base radio that sat on the desk.

"5B75 on the air?"

A few seconds later the radio crackled with a response. "5B75 on the air."

"5B75 can you 10-21 base."

"5B75 10-4."

Less than a minute later the phone rang.

"State Police Troop B, Trooper Willets how can I help you?"

The Trooper listened for a moment.

"Yeah, that NYPD detective is here asking to speak to you, said it was important," The trooper said into the phone.

"Ok, let me switch you to the admin desk."

The trooper placed the call on hold and pointed to a desk across from his. Maguire walked over and sat down, waiting for the call to come through. When the phone rang he picked it up.

"Tom?"

"Yeah, what can I do for you?" came Reynolds reply.

"You asked me to get back to you if I found anything. Well, I went out and took a look at the car yesterday. I found some strange marks on it that don't match up with an accident."

"What kind of marks?"

"Gouges on the 'A' Pillar, inconsistent with any of the other damage," Maguire replied. "So I went back out to the accident scene and poked around. I found marks on two trees, directly across from one another, that matched the height of the marks on the car. I think whatever she original struck was intentionally placed there. This was no accident, Tom."

"I'm going to need you to walk me through this, James," Reynolds replied. "I'm heading back now. Can you meet me over at the lot where the car was towed in about forty-five minutes?"

"Sure thing," Maguire replied.

"But wait for me to get there before you talk to anyone."

"Will do, it's your show now," Maguire said and hung the phone up.

"Thanks, trooper," he said to Willets before leaving the station.

CHAPTER THIRTY-EIGHT

New York State Thruway, East of Perrysville
Monday, April 30th, 2012 – 2:55 p.m.

Paul Browning sat inside the truck which was parked in a rest stop on the thruway. He had to get away and he needed a quiet place where he could think.

Everything seemed to be unraveling for him.

He picked the cell phone up off the center console and called a number. He listened to it ring several times and was just about to hang up when he heard the call connect.

"Where are you at?" said the voice on the other end.

"I left town for a bit, I needed to clear my head."

"You think that was wise?"

"I don't know what to think anymore," Browning replied, reaching down to retrieve a cigarette from the pack sitting in the cup holder and lit it.

"Did you do everything I told you to do?"

"Not yet goddamnit," Browning yelled out.

"Calm down, we went over all of this already. You have a solid plan you just need to stick with it."

Browning leaned back against the seat and closed his eyes. He felt incredibly tired.

"He was just at my house."

"That's unfortunate, but not entirely unexpected. Seems like you both share an affinity for showing up at each other's doorstep. If you stick to the plan you have nothing to worry about. What is there left to do?"

Browning leaned on the door's armrest and gazed out the window lost in his thoughts.

“Not much,” he said wearily.

“Good, then go and finish up whatever is left. Then take a moment and just relax.”

Browning ended the call and stared back out the window at the cars whizzing by on the thruway. He took a long drag from the cigarette and blew the smoke out the open window. He wished that he could just *relax*, but that little prick showing up at his house had never been part of the plan.

CHAPTER THIRTY-NINE

Ausable, New York State
Monday, April 30th, 2012 – 3:29 p.m.

Maguire watched as the unmarked, black Dodge Charger pulled off the main road and onto the gravel driveway of Route 9 Customs. He dropped the Mustang into drive and followed Reynolds onto the lot.

The two men were just getting out of their cars when a large, heavyset man, in grimy overalls, walked out of the office. Maguire judged that the man was in his late fifties with a very ruddy complexion. He held an automotive part in one hand that was covered in grease, wiping it down with a faded red, garage rag.

"What can I help the state police with today?" he said, directing his question toward Reynolds.

"You had that BMW come in from a wreck on Saturday, Troy," Reynolds replied. "We need to take a look at."

"I'd like to help you out, but that car was released already."

"Who did you release it to?" Reynolds asked.

"To Sheriff Browning," the man replied. "He said he wasn't going to deal with insurance people."

"Do you know where it is now?"

"He had us drop it off to his place over in Willsboro last night," the man said. "Why? Is there a problem?"

"No," Reynolds replied. "Thanks for your help."

Reynolds turned around and he and Maguire began walking back to their cars.

"Well this little journey keeps taking the most interesting twists," Reynolds said. "I'm going to head out to Browning's place, you want to tag along?"

"Absolutely" said Maguire.

CHAPTER FORTY

Southampton, Long Island, N.Y.
Monday, April 30th, 2012 – 4:15 p.m.

Melody sat in bed reading through some briefing papers. She had long ago surrendered her business attire for a comfy oversized navy blue sweat shirt and matching pants. Her hair was pulled back in a ponytail and she wore a pair of old reading glasses. It was hardly the look of a feared corporate juggernaut and more like the look of a nerdy librarian.

She laid the papers down on the bed and removed the glasses, rubbing her tired eyes. For the first time she actually felt lonely in the house. In the past when Gen was gone she would always have her work to delve into, but now she just couldn't seem to find the same relief.

Melody got up, slipping her feet into the slippers at the edge of the bed, and made her way down to the kitchen. When she had gotten home she had told the staff not to prepare dinner and to just take the evening off. She wasn't hungry and didn't relish the idea of sitting at the large dining room table all alone. Walking into the kitchen she began rummaging through the refrigerator.

"Can I help you, Ms. Anderson?"

Melody looked up and saw one of the cooks come out of the back room.

"Oh, no thank you, Maria," she replied. "I'm not even sure what I want. Actually, I thought everyone had left for the night."

"Most did, I just wanted to be around in case you had a change of heart. You haven't been yourself lately."

"I know," she replied. "I feel a bit out of sorts."

"What you need is some comfort food. Sit down and let me make you something."

Melody sat down on one of the stools as instructed; at the prep island positioned in the middle of the kitchen.

Maria walked over and began removing food from the refrigerator, setting the various items she had taken out on the counter.

"How long have you worked here, Maria?"

The woman looked over at Melody. "Four years in June, ma'am."

"Do you like working here? I mean do you like your job?"

"Yes, ma'am, I do," she replied.

"Why?"

"Because I like working for you," she said, as she continued to prepare dinner for Melody.

"I'm glad you do, but do you actually enjoy the work?"

"It's all I have ever known, Ms. Anderson."

Maria Gonzales was an attractive, thirty-one year old woman who had come to this country with her parents at the age of seven. The family had settled in the Washington Heights section of Manhattan, where her father had found work in a restaurant. Her mother worked as a housekeeper for a Broadway director's family who lived just south of them in Morningside Heights. Maria had grown up loving to cook and had always dreamt of going to culinary school, but the high cost of tuitions had always kept those dreams at a distance.

After high school she had gotten a job, working in a trendy restaurant in midtown Manhattan, as a kitchen assistant. Despite her lack of formal training, she exhibited a natural aptitude in food preparation. The *sous-chef* who she worked under recognized that she was a diamond in the rough and took her under his wing. He was so impressed with her that he had highly recommended her to his friend, who also happened to be the head of Melody Anderson's staff.

"I guess what I'm asking is whether you still love what you do or has it just become a job that you do?"

The way Maria looked at her, Melody understood she was trying to construct a diplomatic response.

"You don't have to worry, Maria," Melody said. "This conversation is what you would call *completely off the record*."

The woman laughed as she slid the turkey club sandwich across the island. Melody got up and walked over to the refrigerator and removed a bottle of water. She looked over at Maria and held the bottle up. "You want one?"

"Sure," Maria replied.

Melody grabbed a second bottle and handed it to her before she sat back down. She took a bite out of the sandwich.

"Oh wow, this is amazing."

"Thanks, I've been working on something a little bit different. I created my own sauce," Maria replied.

"It's really good," Melody said, taking another bite. "So tell me how you really feel about working here."

"To be honest, I'm torn. Cooking has always been my passion and I do enjoy preparing meals for you and Ms. Gordon, but lately it seems that the only time I get challenged is when we have a party."

"I do understand that," Melody said thoughtfully. "Like you, I'm extremely passionate about what I do, but lately the fire seems to be fading."

"Like you have no new challenges?"

"That's exactly it. I was at a meeting in Manhattan today and I was sitting there, wishing I could be anywhere else other than there. Yet I also remember my very first one and how I had felt as if I had finally made it big. The meetings haven't changed, but my feelings have."

"But how do you find that fire again?"

"I guess you need to find a *noble adventure* for yourself."

"Huh?"

"A friend of mine told me recently that God designed us to live a life full of adventure and risk, but that we surrender those dreams when we submit to the daily grind of life."

"It certainly feels that way doesn't it?"

"What was your dream, Maria?"

"To go to culinary school," she replied.

Melody saw the sadness behind the smile. It was something she had seen a number of times in her life. The cruel reality was that money didn't matter so long as you had it. For those that didn't, those same dreams usually remained as elusive as shooting stars.

"So what's stopping you now?"

"I'm thirty-one; my school days are long behind me."

"I hate to break the news to you, but Julia Child was almost forty when she started at *Le Cordon Bleu*."

"If only it were that easy," Maria said, taking a sip of water.

"What's keeping you from your dreams?"

"What you said before about life," she explained. "My father got hurt and my parents have no medical insurance. We were just making ends meet until I got this job. By living here I have been able to send most of my paycheck home. Because of that my mom was able to stop working and stay home with my dad. They gave so much to me that it's the least I can do for them. Like your friend said, sometimes we have to surrender those dreams for reality."

"Do you get to see your parents?"

"Not as much as I would like to. They live in Washington Heights so getting there is tough. One of the gardeners has some family in the Bronx, over by Yankee Stadium. So when he goes to see them he drops me off and I take the train over to Manhattan."

Melody let that sink in.

The two women were close enough in age that Melody related to her and they both understood growing up poor. Melody remembered back to her childhood in Richmond Hill. She wondered what might have happened if she had stayed in touch with her family and then dismissed the thought. The unfortunate thing was that, when it would have mattered, it didn't exist.

You can't build a strong house without a foundation, she mused.

However, she had been able to stay in touch with the one person who mattered to her, who truly believed in her. At least long enough to influence her and give her the safety net to take the big risks.

Was that what this was all about? she wondered. *Was this what you had been trying to teach me?*

"Ms. Anderson?" Maria interrupted, drawing Melody back from her thoughts.

"So you wouldn't risk leaving here because of them?"

It came out as a question, but was actually just Melody thinking out loud.

"Yes, ma'am," Maria answered.

"You know something, Maria, you and I are not all that much different," Melody said. "In fact, the only thing that truly separates us is having that one person in our life with the capability of giving us a chance at catching our shooting star."

"I'm not sure that I understand?"

"Tell me, Maria, have you ever heard of Professor William Oswald Thomas?"

"No, ma'am, was he a cook?"

Melody almost choked on her water, as she tried to suppress the laugh.

"No, actually he was a horrible cook," she replied. "In fact he used the smoke detector as a kitchen timer."

"I don't get it?"

"You will," she replied. "Pack your bags, Maria; you're the first recipient of the *William Oswald Thomas Continuing Education Scholarship*."

"But, Ms. Anderson, I can't leave, what about my family?"

"Maria, your family will be fine. If they want to stay in Washington Heights they can or I will move them closer to where you will be going to school. You will continue to draw your normal salary and your education will be completely paid for."

Maria stood there in a state of shock.

"What school?" she asked.

"It's up to you, but personally I'd recommend the Culinary Institute of America."

CIA was a world renowned private culinary college with campuses in New York, California, Texas and Singapore. It counted among its alumni two *Iron Chefs* and at least a half dozen hosts of nationally syndicated cooking shows.

"Ms. Anderson, I appreciate the very kind gesture, but I can't get into CIA," Maria answered. "I'm just a girl from Washington Heights who likes to cook."

"Sure you can," Melody replied. "I was just a girl from Queens who liked math until someone gave me a break. Now the President of the United States calls me for business advice. Besides, I sit on the same charity board as the school's president."

Maria ran around the island and nearly launched herself into Melody's arms.

"Oh my God, Ms. Anderson," she said, as she hugged her tightly. "I don't know what to say."

Melody thought back to that day in her senior year when Professor Thomas had made her a similar offer. It seemed like only yesterday and she wondered if he had felt the same way as she did at this very moment.

"Shall I take that as a yes?" she asked.

CHAPTER FORTY-ONE

Willsboro Pointe, New York State
Monday, April 30th, 2012 – 4:17 p.m.

A plume of heavy black smoke rose high above Willsboro Point, contrasting sharply against the clear blue sky. Maguire watched as the unmarked car in front of him accelerated suddenly, its emergency lights activating, flashing alternating blue and red strobe lights, as it raced ahead.

Maguire hit the gas and caught up to the car as the two vehicles made their way north along High Pointe Road. They arrived at the site of the fire within minutes. The Charger pulled into the driveway of Paul Browning's residence, while Maguire pulled the Mustang just beyond the entrance to the driveway, parking the car on the street outside the property so as not to impede responding emergency vehicles. He got out and ran back to meet up with Reynolds.

"5B75, 10-70 vehicle fire at 37 High Pointe Road, fully engulfed. Start FD and a marked unit."

"Copy 5B75, vehicle fire, 37 High Pointe Road, dispatching fire and a marked unit."

Reynolds exited the car after he heard the dispatcher's confirmation. Maguire was coming up from behind and both men made their way toward the burning vehicle. Despite being fully engulfed by the flames, Maguire could clearly see that the car was the BMW he had previously examined.

"Tom, that's Tricia's car," he said.

"Yeah, now the question is who wanted to burn it and why?"

The two men made their way toward the house, drawing their firearms as they approached the door. Reynolds banged his fist on the door.

"State Police," he called out.

No one answered the door. Maguire moved toward the large bay window that looked out over the front of the property.

"Tom, you might want to take a look."

Maguire holstered his pistol as Reynolds walked over and looked inside the residence.

The interior was in shambles. Papers were strewn across the floor along with books and other items. It was a good indicator that the occupant of the home had left in a hurry.

Maguire made his way toward the back of the house and climbed the stairs that led to the back deck. He stood in front of the sliding glass doors and was greeted with a similar view in the kitchen. He walked back down and met Reynolds in the driveway.

"More of the same, Tom," Maguire said

"I'm not getting the warm fuzzies from all of this," Reynolds replied, as he reached into his pocket for his cell phone. He scrolled through the numbers and selected one.

"Hey, boss, this is Tom Reynolds. Sorry to bother you, but we may have a situation developing over here in Keenseville. You think you can send me over another investigator and also reach out to the arson guys? Let them know that I have a suspicious fire involving a car that was previously involved in an accident with a missing person."

Reynolds listened for a moment.

"Yeah it's the car from the Browning accident. This case has all the makings of going bad really quick. I appreciate the help." Reynolds ended the call and began going through his phone book again. He selected another number from the directory and called it.

In the distance they heard the wail of sirens as responding fire trucks descended upon the scene.

"Mike, Tom Reynolds, over at Troop B. Listen we have an issue that's developing and I need your help."

Over the next few minutes Reynolds explained the situation to Assistant District Attorney Mike Shaw. Shaw was the ADA assigned to felony cases for the county.

"I know you guys work closely with the Sheriff's Office, so I'm not sure how far you want to go with this. Right now I need a search warrant to take a look inside. After that I can give you a better idea of what we may be dealing with."

Mike Shaw sat on the other end of the phone rubbing his forehead. He had just been about to leave the office when the phone rang. It had been a tough Monday to start with and now it looked like it was going to take a turn for the worse.

"Give me five minutes to reach a judge and I'll get back to you," Shaw replied.

"Thanks, Mike."

By the time Reynolds had gotten off the phone the responding firefighters had managed to get the burning vehicle under control. Minutes later all that remained of the former luxury car was a smoldering burned out hulk with steam rising up off the superheated metal.

"First thoughts," Reynolds asked Maguire.

"Someone's trying to keep us from looking further into the accident," James replied. "The only question is why?"

"Well, you need to stay close to me because right now you're the only witness I have that has actually examined the car."

Reynolds phone began to ring.

"Hello?"

"Tom, Mike Shaw, I spoke to Judge Olsen and I explained the situation. He just gave the green light to enter and look around, but just *look*. This is the sheriff's house after all, so unless you find something in plain sight, he wants a call back and a justification for a deeper search."

"Understood, Mike, I will keep you posted."

"What did they say?" Maguire asked.

"We are a go, but just to look around."

A uniformed trooper arrived and approached Reynolds.

"Ryan, no one comes down that driveway except state police personnel, understood?" Reynolds said.

"Yes, sir."

Reynolds and Maguire made their way toward the back of the house. As they climbed the stairs leading to the back deck the man turned around and looked at Maguire.

"James, just for the record I want to congratulate you on being selected as winner of the 'trooper for a day' contest that Troop B Investigations held. So just follow me around and I'll show you how we conduct potential crime scene searches."

Maguire laughed. "I appreciate that. Please, lead the way."

Reynolds removed the lock pick kit from his jacket pocket and began to work on the back door deadbolt. He slid a tension wrench into the key slot first, adjusting it till it was off set enough to create a slight ledge. He then slid a pick inside and began to lift the internal pins. After a few minutes he had managed to set each of the pins on the ledge and the tension wrench turned over, opening the lock.

Reynolds stood up and turned to look at Maguire.

"Not bad, huh?" he said with a smile, as he put the pick set back in his pocket.

"I didn't know the state police offered a remedial lock picking course," Maguire replied with a laugh.

"Remedial my ass," Reynolds replied. "That takes finesse."

"A couple more minutes and I thought I was going to have to order dinner to be delivered."

"Everyone's a comedian," Reynolds said.

He reached into his jacket and pulled out some latex gloves, handing a pair to Maguire.

"It's probing time," Reynolds said, twirling his gloved index finger in the air with a laugh.

As he stepped inside the house he located a switch and turned the lights on.

The two men made their way through the house. It was in a state of total disarray. In the living room was a large book case that stood from the floor to ceiling. Some books were still on the shelf while others were tossed haphazardly on the floor.

"Looks like they were trying to find something," Maguire said.

"Yeah, but the question is what?"

The men continued searching the first floor of the house. At the far end they located a room that was clearly Paul Browning's office. The desk drawers were all open and had been rummaged through. A painting was tossed on the floor and the wall safe it had previously hidden was open and bare. Maguire walked over to a large wooden gun cabinet that sat in the corner next to the fireplace. The door was open and the cable lock that secured the weapons was removed and discarded on the floor.

"Looks like we have some missing guns," Maguire said.

Reynolds walked over and frowned.

"That's just great," he said sarcastically.

He reached into his jacket and pulled out his phone. He selected a number from the call list.

"Hi, this is Tom Reynolds, from Troop B. I need you to locate a record for me. Name is going to be Paul Browning and the address is 37 High Pointe Rd, Willsboro."

Reynolds pulled out a note pad and began writing.

"Ok thanks," he said and ended the call. He turned back and looked at the gun cabinet.

"Looks like we are missing two twelve gauge shotguns, a .308 caliber rifle and a .223 Caliber rifle; along with any *company* guns he might have had on hand."

The men moved up to the second floor of the house and into the master bedroom. It was a repeat of what they had found on the first floor. The night table and dresser drawers were pulled out, their contents dumped on the floor.

Maguire peered into the massive walk in closet; it looked like a bomb had gone off. Clothing lay strewn about. They checked the *en suite* bathroom, but it appeared to have been undisturbed. As they made their way out of the room Reynolds stopped.

"James, wait a minute"

Reynolds turned and made his way into the master bedroom and began looking around.

"What is it?" James asked.

"Doesn't it strike you as odd that the only clothes here look to be Paul's? Where are Tricia's? I mean there isn't one dress, one pair of shoes, nothing."

"From what I heard they were having serious problems. I don't think they shared the bedroom."

The men headed down the hallway to continue searching the two remaining rooms. The first was an unremarkable guest room that appeared untouched. The second was clearly her room. A few of the dresser drawers were open and empty, but nothing seemed to have been discarded. It was completely different from the scene in the master bedroom.

"None of this makes any sense," Reynolds said.

"No, it doesn't," replied Maguire. "Browning's room looks like it was searched, this room looks like things were just taken."

They made their way back downstairs and located a door which led into the garage. A beat up old red Chevy pickup truck sat in one of the three bays. Maguire walked around the vehicle inspecting it as Reynolds walked over to the work bench.

The truck was otherwise unremarkable except for some damage to the front right fender.

A work bench sat on the back wall with tools scattered across the top of it. On the wall above the bench were a row of cabinets with the doors wide open.

"That's funny, Browning never struck me as being the mechanical type," Reynolds said.

He looked under the bench where there were a number of tool boxes. Adjacent to one was a canvas tool bag. Reynolds pulled it out and peered inside.

"Fuck me," Reynolds said out loud.

"What's that?"

"Take a look at this, James."

Maguire walked over and peered into the bag. The inside of the bag held a number of tools and both the bag itself and the tools appeared to be stained in what looked like dried blood. In addition there were a number of papers inside. Maguire began to reach inside, Reynolds grabbed his hand.

"We can't touch."

"You want to call a judge and ask him for a warrant to search a bag only to come up with some tools dowsed in power steering fluid and some old brochures for *Frontier Town*?"

Reynolds thought about that for a moment. Technically it was wrong, but Maguire was right. Wasting a judge's time for something that didn't pan out was something that could potentially factor into a decision the next time he needed to apply for a search warrant with that judge.

"Ok, we peek and put it back."

Maguire pulled the papers out. They were several local area maps that had markings on them. One was a nautical map Maguire noted. He saw that an area over in Willsboro Bay, near the accident scene, had been circled.

"What do you make of it?" Reynolds asked.

"I think you better call that judge now."

The two men walked out of the garage and headed toward the back door.

"Might as well check out the basement first, no sense in making multiple calls when I can just do one," Reynolds said.

He opened the door and flipped the switch, but the light remained off.

"It figures," Reynolds moaned.

"You got a flashlight?" Maguire asked.

"No."

Maguire recalled that he had left his gun bag in the trunk.

"I have one out in my car," he replied. "Let me go grab it."

He went outside and made his way down the driveway past the burnt out shell of the car. One fire truck still remained on the scene and it appeared that a senior firefighter was giving instruction to a couple of newbie's on how to properly put hoses away.

The trooper was talking to a sheriff's deputy next to Reynolds car in the driveway.

"Everything ok in there?" the trooper asked.

"Yeah," Maguire replied. "Just need a flashlight."

"Any idea how much longer it might be?" the trooper asked.

"Well, Reynolds is getting older, so the stairs are slowing him down a bit," Maguire said.

All three men laughed. He didn't want to say anything specific with the deputy standing there.

When he got back to the Mustang he opened the trunk and pulled the gun bag toward him. He reached inside and removed the flashlight, then zipped it back up. When he was done, he shut the trunk and turned to walk back to the house.

He saw the explosion first, an intense flash that overloaded his senses, followed immediately by a concussive blast that hurled him backward into the roadway just before everything went black.

CHAPTER FORTY-TWO

Willsboro Pointe, New York State
Monday, April 30th, 2012 – 6:37 p.m.

When Maguire came to he found himself sprawled in a small ditch on the opposite side of the road. He struggled to get back up on his feet. In the background he could hear the muffled screams of someone who'd been injured.

He crawled up the embankment and crossed the road to the back of the car. Using the bumper as support he managed to get back up on his feet and made his way back toward the scene.

As Maguire turned the corner the sight that greeted him was reminiscent of *Dante's Inferno.* The house was gone, all of it, and what remained was a massive pit engulfed in flames. The fire truck that had been parked in the driveway was flipped on its side, like a child's discarded toy, and burning. As he made his way down the driveway he came across the deputy lying on the gravel road unconscious. He checked for a pulse and found one, but it was weak.

In the distance he heard sirens as emergency vehicles were responding back to the scene.

He left the deputy and made his way toward the trooper. Upon reaching him he found that he hadn't fared as well. The trooper was lying next to the remnants of Reynolds car and he had significant burns over most of his body. Maguire grabbed him to pull him to safety, but as his body turned he saw the true extent of the damage. Most of the left side of his head was gone, sheared off by an errant projectile launched by the explosion.

James left him and made his way forward. He couldn't find any sign of the three firemen that had been standing near the BMW when he had come out. He looked around, but there was nothing left, everything was on fire, including the trees that surrounded the property.

"Jim..... Jim!"

He turned around to see Keith Banning rushing toward him. In the background he could see firefighters dismounting from their trucks.

"What the fuck happened?"

"I don't know, I was getting a flashlight out of my car and the whole place just went up."

"Who else was here?"

"Tom Reynolds was inside, a trooper over there and a deputy. I think there were still several firefighters as well, I saw at least three."

"Ok, you need to get checked out by EMS."

"No, I'm fine."

"Not until the professionals say you are," Banning said. "You're a witness now and you're going to listen to me."

As the firefighters rushed past them Banning walked him back out to the street. They passed the deputy who was now being put on a stretcher.

A second ambulance was just pulling up as the two men made it to the roadway.

"Over here," Banning cried out. One of the EMT's ran over.

"What do we have?"

"I'm fine," Maguire said. "I was out here when the blast went off."

"Ok, we'll just check you out and make sure."

"Go, Keith, I'll find you when they're done," Maguire said, as he climbed up into the ambulance.

James sat on a stretcher in the back as the two EMT's went over him. They checked him for injuries along with his vital signs. Considering what he had just gone through they were quite taken aback at the normalcy of all the readings. Aside from a minor scratch on his forehead, there was no indication that he'd gone through something as traumatic as what he just had.

As he was being medically cleared, the doors of the ambulance flew open.

Maguire immediately made the man out to be a cop. He estimated that he was in his late fifties, with a stocky build and a presence about him that immediately caused Maguire to think of a bulldog. He was wearing a suit and his hand held the remnant of a cigar.

"Are you Maguire?" he asked.

"I am."

"Are you going to live?"

Maguire looked at the techs who both sort of shrugged.

"It looks that way."

"Then let's get your ass out of here so you can tell me what in God's name just happened."

Maguire grabbed his jacket and climbed out of the back of the ambulance.

"I'm Lieutenant Dennis Monahan, I'm the head of State Police Investigations for this region," the man said by way of introduction.

"Maguire, James Maguire. I'm a retired NYPD detective."

"Tom called me and said that you had reached out to him about some strange markings on the Browning car," the man said. "You're my new best friend, Maguire, walk me through this cluster fuck and tell me what happened to my people."

Before Maguire could begin Banning caught up with them.

"Excuse me," Keith interrupted. "This is my witness."

"Who the hell are you?" Monahan asked gruffly.

"Deputy Keith Banning, sheriff's office," Keith replied. "Who the hell are you?"

"Lieutenant Monahan, state police. Now do me a favor, deputy, and gather up your people. I need you to secure the perimeter of my crime scene."

"*Your* crime scene?" Banning asked incredulously. "Let me remind you that you're in *my county,* lieutenant."

The man glared at Banning menacingly.

"Morgan, Peters," Monahan called out.

Maguire looked over as two of the biggest troopers he had ever seen approached the lieutenant and took up a position on either side.

"Let me remind you that you're in *my state,* deputy. I've got two dead troopers and a crime scene that used to be the home of *your* sheriff. Get your people out of here now or I'll have these two troopers escort you off the scene."

Banning looked at the man, then at the troopers and finally at Maguire, who just shrugged his shoulders. He realized the futility of the situation. He turned around angrily and made his way toward the roadway.

The men watched as Banning stopped and exchanged words with another deputy. He pointed back toward Monahan and then the two men left.

Monahan turned back toward the troopers.

"Until you hear directly from me, our people are the only ones allowed on scene."

"Yes, sir," both men replied in unison and moved to take up positions to keep watch.

Monahan turned back toward Maguire.

"Ok, so tell me why my men are dead and you're still alive."

Over the next half hour Maguire filled him in on what had happened when he and Reynolds had shown up at the house. He then explained to him what he had found at the initial accident scene and what he had observed when he inspected the car at the tow shop.

"You need to come back with me to the substation and make a statement," Monahan said. "I'm sure the DA's going to want to talk to you as well."

"No problem," Maguire said. "My cars out on the roadway, I'll follow you back."

As Maguire walked back toward the Mustang, he took out his phone and sent Melody a text: *There was an incident up here. I wanted you to know that I am okay. I'll call you when I can.*

Monahan got into his car and picked up the radio.

"5L3 to dispatch."

"5L3 go with message."

"5L3 requesting a statewide *BOLO* for Browning, Paul; date of birth 12-8-70. Subject should be considered armed and dangerous. He's wanted for questioning in connection with the disappearance of Patricia Browning and the deaths of two New York State Troopers."

CHAPTER FORTY-THREE

Keenseville, New York State
Monday, April 30th, 2012 – 11:41 PM

Maguire sat in the hard industrial office chair in the Troop B investigations office. He looked over at the desk that Reynolds had sat in just the day before. Maguire rubbed his eyes wearily. The days were now beginning to run into each other. He looked down at his watch.

How long had it actually been, he wondered?

The interviews had been going on for hours; first with state police investigators and again later with the assistant district attorney present. They had also brought Lena in as well. He had a brief opportunity to see her, and then she was whisked away. The ADA had made the decision to put her into protective custody until the killer was caught.

Initial indications were that the explosion was caused by a mixture of ammonium nitrate and fuel oil. It consisted of porous prilled ammonium nitrate (AN), that acted as the oxidizing agent and absorbent for the R2 fuel oil (FO).

AN/FO had long been a favorite explosive for a wide variety of terrorists, both foreign and domestic. It was used by the Irish Republican Army in the early 1970's in the detonation of car bombs and in 1993 Ramzi Yousef used it during the first attack on the World Trade Center. A more sophisticated variant, ammonium nitrate with nitromethane, or AN/NM, had been used in the 1995 Oklahoma City bombing.

Paul Browning owned a thousand acres of farmland so obtaining the basic components was something that would have been completely unremarkable for him, especially considering that he was also the county sheriff.

"Good news is you're done," said Monahan, handing Maguire a cup of coffee.

"Thanks," said Maguire, as he accepted the cup and took a drink. "So what's the bad news?"

"Assistant District Attorney thinks you need to be in protective custody."

"That's never going to happen," Maguire replied with a laugh.

"That's what I told him, but he is still not happy."

"Oh well, it's not like he's the first ADA that I have upset."

"I would however suggest keeping a low profile until we locate Browning. It's clear that he has no qualms about taking out anyone who gets in his way."

"Any ideas on where he might have gone?"

"He's a typical good old boy, knows his way around the mountains and the lake. Honestly he could be anywhere. Family owns a good amount of land; it's going to be a tough slog. Their bringing up a bunch of helicopters with FLIR so we can start looking for heat signatures. For once the weather might actually help us."

Maguire was well acquainted with FLIR technology. He had used it routinely while he was in the teams. The acronym stood for *Forward Looking Infrared.* Infrared radiation is emitted by all objects, above absolute zero. Since the amount of radiation emitted by an object increases with temperature; thermal imagery allows the viewer to *see* by variations in temperature. When viewed through a thermal imaging camera, warm objects stand out against cooler backgrounds. As a result, humans and other warm-blooded animals easily become visible against their environment, day or night.

"Are you going to be staying local?" Monahan asked.

"For tonight," he said. "There's no point in trying to make it back to the city now. I could use some shut eye."

"If it's any consolation I had a team sweep your house. They didn't find anything."

"I appreciate that," Maguire said and stood up. "If you need me, you know how to get in touch."

“Will do,” Monahan replied, “and if I hear anything I’ll let you know.”

“I’d appreciate that.”

Maguire walked out into the cold night air and zipped his jacket up.

The empty parking lot he had pulled into earlier today was gone. Rows of marked and unmarked patrol cars filled the lot to the point of overflowing. Along the side of the building sat several mobile command post vehicles and crime scene trailers. All resources were being deployed now because of the deaths of Tom Reynolds and the other trooper.

For a moment Maguire wondered what would have happened if it had been him. It struck him as odd that he worried more about how she would find out. He’d been through too much in his life to be fazed by a brush with death, no matter how close. It wasn’t that he was dismissive of his mortality, but he had long ago come to terms with the fact that no one makes it out alive. The more you worried, the less focused you were and that’s when you got hurt. If Reynolds had waited for him to get back with the flashlight the outcome most likely would have been completely different.

He got in the car and started the engine up. He took a look around the parking lot one more time. He didn’t like having to step away from the case, but he was after all just another civilian and it would overly complicate matters if he tried to stay involved. Tricia became just one more piece of the puzzle, one more victim on the list. The focus was on capturing Browning and no one would tolerate anyone meddling in that investigation, even if that person was a retired cop.

His phone had died during the interviews and now was the first chance he had to plug it in. He powered it up and before long he was hit with nearly a dozen text messages and missed calls. He began to scroll through them. The first text was from Melody which just said: *ok*. The second and third were from Bill Malloy and Peter Bart. Neither was unexpected. Malloy would have known almost immediately when the reports came over the wire and Peter was a news junkie. The fourth was from Melody and read: *I know you're okay, but worried. Saw TV reports so call when you can, anytime*.

He called her number and put the phone on speaker. It rang once and she picked up.

"Are you Okay?"

"I'm fine, Mel."

"What happened?"

"It's a long story, but they went to the sheriff's house to question him and the house was rigged with explosives. Two troopers were killed."

"Oh my God," she gasped. "Are you sure you're ok?"

"I am, Mel, I wasn't near the blast."

He'd been on the roadway and not on the property, so technically he hadn't been *near* it. It was a white lie that he didn't mind telling her.

"When are you coming home?"

"Not tonight," he replied. "I need a shower and some sleep, I'll be back tomorrow, probably in the evening."

"Please be careful."

"I will, and please don't worry I am fine. I'll call you in the morning, ok?"

"Ok, James, I…" she paused. "Goodnight."

"Nite, Mel."

Maguire ended the call and replayed what it was that she *hadn't* said over in his mind.

CHAPTER FORTY-FOUR

Southampton, Suffolk County, N.Y.
Tuesday, May 1st, 2012 – 12:17 a.m.

Melody sat on the bed feeling the stress that had gripped her for the last few hours beginning to dissipate. She picked the cell phone off the bed and sent a text to Genevieve: *I just heard from him, he's ok.*

Melody laid the phone back down and replayed the events of the evening in her mind. She had been having a great evening, especially after the earlier talk she had with Maria. After dinner she had grabbed a bottle of wine and gone upstairs. She fired off an email to the president of the Culinary Institute of America informing him that she needed a spot in the upcoming class for one of her staff. Afterward, she decided that she was going to spend the rest of the night enjoying some much needed rest and relaxation. She undressed, grabbing a robe before heading outside, and got into the hot tub.

Melody was enjoying the breeze and the wine when she had gotten that mysterious first text from James. The hot water and the wine had just about chased it from her mind when her cell phone had gone off. It was Peter Bart asking her if she had heard from James. He then went on to explain what the news was reporting. She'd rushed inside and turned the TV on, but they just kept repeating the same generic information. Finally she turned it off and sat on the bed waiting; working hard at trying to keep herself from panicking.

She fired off a text to him and then called Gen to tell her what she knew. Genevieve did her best to reassure her and offered to come back right away. Melody had told her no. She knew he was okay and was just going to have to wait until she heard back from him. To get her mind off things, Gen gave her an indepth rundown of her day. She said the operation in Montana was massive and she had only a brief time to look at things. They were picking her up at 6:00 a.m. to begin the full walk through. Melody knew what her friend was trying to do and told her that she needed to get some rest. When she knew something else she would text her.

When the phone had gone off she had nearly jumped out of the bed. Hearing his voice had helped calm her, but it had also driven home the extent of the feelings she had for him, something that had nearly slipped out at the end of the call. She wondered how she could feel this way about him so soon, and then, in the same thought, wondered how she had lived before knowing him.

Melody got up from the bed and poured herself another glass of wine. She walked back outside, leaning on the top rail of the deck.

It was late, but she wasn't tired. She had nothing going on tomorrow and didn't have to worry about getting up. Emotionally, her mind was all over the place and she seriously doubted that she would be able to sleep anyway.

The moon hung suspended in the air above the ocean, lighting the waves as they rolled toward the shore line. Like silver streaks cutting though the massive expanse of blackness. Melody closed her eyes and wished that he was there with her, wanting to feel his arms wrapped tightly around her.

She needed to come to terms with what she was feeling, but she found herself afraid to face it. It wasn't that she was afraid of him, but of how her life would change when she opened that door. Subconsciously she knew that she had always kept that part of her life closed for a reason.

There had never been any regrets about her choice, but then again there had never really been any worthy rival for her affection. That was until now. She felt the internal tug-of-war going on, felt her mind pulling her in one direction while her heart pulled in another. The dispassionate, analytical business side of her ticked off all of the appropriate reasons as to why it was a bad idea, yet deep down inside she knew she could no longer fight her heart.

The question then became how could she reconcile the two and if she couldn't which one would win out?

As she stared out into the vastness of the ocean she once again heard the voice of William Thomas in her ear.

"Do not make the same mistake as I did. When the opportunity presents itself, allow yourself to live, love and laugh."

Melody smiled as she recalled the words he had written to her so many years before.

In the end it was the easiest decision she had ever reached.

CHAPTER FORTY-FIVE

Perrysville, New York State
Tuesday, May 1st, 2012 – 5:17 a.m.

Maguire sat up in bed with a start, remnants of the nightmare replaying itself over again in his mind.

It was as if he were a ghost in the house.

He saw himself walk out the back door while Reynolds stood at the entrance to the basement. He watched as the man flicked the light switch a few more times before deciding to walk down the unlit staircase. He made it all the way down to the floor and had just started to turn when his foot caught the tripwire that ran several inches above the concrete floor.

The switch at the top of the stairs had been a dummy, the wires intentionally disconnected.

As his foot dragged against the tripwire, it pulled a wooden shim free from the firing device that had been connected to the electrical line in the basement that controlled the lights. This allowed the pin to strike against the metal tab and complete the circuit. At that same instant the light flickered on, as electricity flowed through the now connected circuit.

It lasted only a fraction of a millisecond.

The lighting fixture on the far end of the room had been removed. This exposed the electric wiring which in turn was connected to two wires that ran to a succession of blasting caps. These had been inserted into sticks of dynamite which were then inserted into the barrels of AN/FO stored in the basement. The resulting massive explosion vaporized Tom Reynolds instantly as it ripped through the house, reducing it to rubble.

The entire process was literally over in the blink of an eye.

Maguire rubbed his eyes as he chased the images away.

He got up and headed down to the kitchen and started the coffee before going into the shower. He physically ached and the hot water felt good on his sore muscles. When he was done he went back to the bedroom and got changed before heading back down to get his caffeine fix.

Maguire took a sip of the dark coffee. It was strong and it tasted good. He walked into the living room and sat down, looking around. So much had happened in such a short period of time. As much as he didn't want to leave, there was nothing to keep him here anymore. In some ways he had missed the house, missed the memories, but it was no longer his home and the memories were always with him.

He enjoyed a second cup before making the decision to head out. He washed the cup and the pot and dried them before putting them away in the cupboard. He then went back upstairs and retrieved his bags. He made his way through the house, ensuring that everything was secure and in its proper place, just as he had found it.

As he walked back through the living room he stopped one last time to take a look around. He had no idea when he would be back again.

As he was walking out of the room he spotted the whistle on the shelf behind his mother's chair. Hearing Melody play it the other night had reminded him of how much he had missed hearing it. He reached up and took it, placing it in his travel bag.

He walked out the back door, locking it behind him. He opened the trunk and placed the bags inside before closing it back up. Maguire heard a car pull into the driveway behind him and turned around to see who it was.

Keith Banning stepped out of the patrol car and walked toward him.

"You leaving already?" Banning asked.

"Didn't see any point in hanging around now that the state cops are taking over."

"Yeah, it's become one helluva mess. I guess I'll have to take a rain check on that beer."

"Sorry about that, I was looking forward to playing catch-up."

"Eh, it happens. You want to grab a cup of coffee on the way out? I thought we might be able to go over some stuff."

"Sure, I was going to hit Margie's for breakfast anyway. I'll follow you over."

"Sounds like a plan," said Banning, who headed back to the car.

Maguire followed the patrol car to the diner. The two men got out and made their way inside, choosing a booth at the far end.

"So what's the scuttlebutt around the office?" Maguire asked.

"Odds are the sheriff's pretty much fucked," said Banning. "Deputies from the Essex County Sheriff's Office found his truck abandoned last night in Thrall Dam Park."

Just then a waitress showed up with a pot of coffee.

"Can I offer you boys some coffee?"

Both men nodded yes, as they turned their cups over and proceeded to place their orders. They waited for her to leave before restarting their conversation.

"State investigators came in last night and raided the office, didn't leave till about four this morning. They are keeping a tight lid on things, but word is that they found evidence that the sheriff was apparently shaking down out of state motorists."

"Who have they got running things now?"

"Chief Deputy took over, at least for the moment. No one's really sure what to do next. Sheriff hasn't been officially charged with anything so the whole place is in limbo."

"What a mess," James replied.

"That's not what we're calling it, but close enough. For now we're just going to have to learn to live with a whole bunch of state guys working out of our office."

"They have any ideas about what happened?"

"If they do, they're not saying too much," Banning replied. "Speaking of which, what the hell happened over at the sheriff's house yesterday?"

"It's a long story, but the short version is I had talked to Reynolds about seeing some strange marks on Tricia's car. He asked me to show him and when we went out to the tow facility they told him they had brought it out to Paul's place. When we got there, Reynolds found the car on fire. Next thing I knew he was getting a search warrant for the house and then it blew up."

"Strange markings? Like what?" asked Banning.

"Just some scratches on the door posts," Maguire said. "It was probably nothing, just my overactive imagination."

"This whole investigation gets weirder by the day."

"Any word back from the medical examiner yet?"

"Nothing conclusive," replied Banning. "Whoever did this went through a lot of trouble to degrade the DNA. The M.E. thinks they soaked the body in sodium hypochlorite."

"Bleach?" asked Maguire.

"Yeah, but I guess a more jacked up solution."

Just then the waitress returned with two plates, setting them down in front of the two men. She returned a moment later and refilled their coffee cups.

"Can I get you anything else?" she asked.

"No, we're good," Banning replied.

Maguire thought for a moment about what he had seen in the house. He didn't want to think about it, didn't want to imagine what Browning might have done to Tricia, but the pieces of the puzzle were beginning to fit together.

"I guess they showed the material that they had found to that woman that managed the art gallery and she said it looked like Tricia's," said Banning, breaking the silence. "They've started to send out search teams around the area looking to see if they can find anything else and they've also got scuba teams in the water around Willsboro Bay."

"Any guesses on where Paul might have gone?"

"No one really knows. They already checked the known places, parent's home, hunting cabin, but nothing turned up. Hell it's all speculation. With any planning he could have taken the ferry over to Grand Isle and made his way north through Alburgh and slid over the border into Canada undetected if he wanted to."

Maguire knew he was right. The United States – Canadian border, officially known as the International Boundary, is the longest border in the world shared between two countries. Despite all the talk in Washington about border security, the northern border with Canada was wide open. In fact, much of the border crosses through dense forests and mountains. While there are hidden sensors in these areas, the reality was that neither side had the resources to prevent a well-planned illicit crossing. Unlike the heavy military and law enforcement presence seen in some places on the border with Mexico, the border with Canada has been termed the world's longest *undefended border*.

"I guess he'll turn up eventually," Maguire said. "The state police won't let this one go cold."

"I hope you're right, Jim, but if I've learned anything over the years it is that Paul Browning is a pretty resourceful man. I wouldn't bet on it happening any time soon."

"Well, you have my number," Maguire replied. "If anything changes I'd appreciate an update."

"Will do."

The two men spent the remainder of the breakfast talking about other things, mostly centered on school and their classmates.

When they were done Banning picked up the check and they left the restaurant.

"Hey," Banning said, as they walked toward the cars. "Who was the hot blonde the other morning? She certainly wasn't a local."

"Nah, she's a friend of mine from the city. She flew back yesterday."

Banning shook his head ruefully, "I really need to get out of this town more often."

Maguire smiled and shook his hand "Call me if you hear anything. When things quiet down I'll come back up and we'll go have that beer."

"That's a deal," Banning replied. "Hey, I might even let you beat me in a chess game."

Maguire laughed as he got into the Mustang. "It's good to have dreams, Keith."

Banning waved good-bye and walked toward the patrol car as Maguire pulled out of the parking lot.

Mentally the ride back south was quicker than the one that brought him north. Before he knew it he was already passing through Albany. He had accepted that he had done everything he could to advance the investigation. Now he would have to trust those who had picked it up to figure out what had happened to Tricia. In some ways investigations were like sorting out puzzles based on Jackson Pollock art, even when you had all the pieces you still had to figure out the right order to put them in and then you had to figure out what the hell it all meant. In fact the list of questions that remained unanswered was growing longer by the day.

Why was the accident staged to make it look like Tricia had wandered off?

Why was there what appeared to be blood on the tools in the bag?

What had been in the basement that Browning didn't want anyone to find?

Had Browning used the explosion to get rid of the evidence?

No matter how Maguire looked at it, this was now a homicide investigation and Paul Browning was the prime suspect. The question was did that investigation include Tricia Browning?

Everything seemed to be going perfectly well. No one was looking into the accident, nor did anyone seem overly interested. That was until he had shown up. Maguire didn't want to think about that part, but he had to. Had his appearance caused Tricia's death? *No*, he chased the thought away. It may have pushed the timetable up, but he believed that her death was most likely inevitable.

The most logical reason is that it was a red herring. If you make everyone believe that she is alive, then they wouldn't be looking for a body. This gave you ample time to dispose of it. Is that where the tools had come in? Why soak the body in bleach? Was he trying to prevent a DNA match should anyone stumble upon any of the pieces? So what was in the basement? If he had dismembered her, then the only thing that made any sense was that the murder had been done there and that he had rigged it to explode to prevent anyone from finding the evidence.

Now, the biggest question of them all was: *Where was Paul Browning*?

Too many questions and not enough answers, he thought.

Maguire rubbed his eyes. He needed to let go, to let the locals deal with it. After all, he was retired and it wasn't his case. He reached into his pocket, withdrew the cell phone and selected her number.

"Hey there, cowboy," said the cheerful voice on the other end of the phone.

"How are you doing, Mel?"

"I'm doing great. I was just going through some emails and thinking of you."

"Be careful of what you write in those emails if you're thinking about me."

"Yeah," Melody said with a laugh. "That could be a little *awkward*."

"Ya think?"

"So what are you doing?"

"Driving south on the thruway right now."

"I was hoping you were going to tell me that. When are you going to be back?"

Maguire looked down at his watch. It was just past noon.

"Probably not till at least five, depending on how bad traffic is."

"Are you going to stop off somewhere and eat?"

"No, I'll probably just go straight to the boat."

"Why don't you give me a call when you're about an hour away and I'll have dinner delivered?"

"You sure you don't mind?"

"I think you know me better than that. I wouldn't have asked if I didn't want to."

"*Touché*," Maguire said. "I'll call you when I get into Queens and let you know how the traffic is."

"Sounds good, drive careful, cowboy."

"I will, I'll talk to you later, Mel."

He disconnected the call and scrolled through the contact list again before selecting a number. The phone rang a couple of times before it connected.

"You're scaring me now."

"Has anyone told you that you're becoming more melodramatic in your old age?" Maguire asked. "I'm going to tell Mary to make you quit watching those touchy-feely chick shows on cable."

"That's funny. So what do you need now, a weekend stay in the Lincoln bedroom?" Stargold asked.

Maguire laughed. “Nah, that room has gotten more action over the last few administrations than a cheap bordello in a red light district. The Queen’s bedroom would be my first choice. Actually I need another favor.”

Stargold groaned. “You know, I’d like to keep my job, Mary and the kids have gotten used to eating regularly.”

“Where is your sense of adventure? Besides this is boring request. I just need a DMV history for Paul Browning, same guy you checked on before.”

“How far back?”

“The beginning.”

“Ok, let me go pull it up. If you don’t mind me asking what the hell is going on?”

“Besides almost getting blown up? Not much.”

“What the hell are you talking about? I thought you said you weren’t doing anything dumb.”

“No, not me,” Maguire protested. “I was just along for the ride.”

“How the hell do you *almost* get blown up?”

Maguire spent the next fifteen minutes bringing Stargold up to speed.

“Jeezus, James, you don’t do anything little do you?”

“Hey, I can’t help it. I’m like a shit magnet.”

Stargold laughed. “Well I’m certainly not going to argue that point. Let me run your check and I will call you back.”

“Hey, before I go, I was wondering if you guys wanted to get together Friday night?”

“Yeah, that will work.”

“I’m bringing a friend.”

“You’re what?”

“I’m going to bring a friend with me.”

A silence hung over the phone line.

"Hello?" Maguire said.

"When the hell did you find the time to find a *friend*? Was it before or after almost getting blown up?"

"You know, I do get out from time to time."

"Well I for one can't wait to meet this mystery woman who is able to put up with you."

"No stories, I mean it."

"*Moi*?"

"*Oui*, *vous*."

"I'll be on my best behavior."

"That's what I'm afraid of. Call me back when you have my DMV history."

CHAPTER FORTY-SIX

Brooklyn, New York City
Tuesday, May 1st, 2012 – 12:22 p.m.

Rich Stargold laid the phone on the desk and sat looking out his office window. To be honest, he was more than a little bit shocked.

In almost the decade that the two men had known each other he had never known Maguire to have a *friend* before. In fact, it had been a running joke between the two men. Stargold had told him that he didn't want to know anything about anyone that Maguire had known for less than forty-eight hours. As a result, he couldn't recall the last time the two men had a discussion about a woman. The fact that he was actually going to bring someone out to the house to meet him and Mary was huge.

Stargold picked up the phone on his desk and hit one of the buttons.

"Tom, I need you to run a DMV history for the guy I spoke to you about yesterday. Do you still have the info?"

Stargold listened to the man on the other end.

"Great, bring it up to my office when you get it printed out."

Rich hung up the desk phone, than he reached over and picked up his cell phone. He called his wife, Mary, to tell her about the conversation he had just had with James.

"What did he mean a *friend*?" asked Mary Stargold.

"Your guess is as good as mine. All he said was that he was bringing her out on Friday."

"For someone who interrogates people for a living you did a crappy job. I swear it's amazing you men are able to capture anyone."

Stargold laughed, even though he knew she was right. Had it been Mary on the phone with James she would have known not only her name, but where they had first met, where she lived, how old she was, what she did for a living and what her favorite dessert was.

"I'm sorry I failed you, you'll just have to wait till Friday like me."

"Men," said Mary with a loud, dramatic sigh.

Just then his phone buzzed and he heard his secretaries' voice.

"Sir, Tom Jennings is here to see you"

"Get back to work, I'll talk to you later," Mary said.

"Love you, dear."

"Love you too."

Stargold hung up the phone as he hit the intercom button on the desk phone.

"Send him in, Stacy."

Special Agent Tom Jennings walked into the office carrying the computer printout.

"Not much here, boss," he said and handed the paper to Rich.

"Thanks, Tom."

"One other thing, the state police have him flagged as a *BOLO*."

"Yeah, I kind of figured they would. He's apparently wanted for questioning in the deaths of two of their people in upstate New York."

"Are we doing anything with it?"

"No," Stargold replied, "but go ahead and send the state police information out as an inter-office email just in case."

"Will do, boss," said Jennings who walked out of the office.

Stargold looked over the printout. It was sparse. He picked up the cell phone and called Maguire.

"Whatcha got?"

"Not much to be honest," said Rich. "It looks like he has only had four different vehicles registered to him since 1988."

"Current ones?"

"Looks like a 2012 BMW M6 and a 2010 Dodge 2500 pickup."

"You got a Chevy Pickup on that list?"

"Nope, the only others are a 1994 Ford Bronco and a 2000 Chevy, but that's a suburban."

"What color is the Dodge?"

Rich checked the list. "Blue."

"How about the Chevy?"

"Gold" said Rich. "What's the problem?"

"Not sure, when we were checking out the garage there was an old red Chevy pickup sitting in there."

"You want me to dig a little deeper?"

"No, I told the state police investigators what I had seen, I'm sure they'll look into it. Besides, at this point I don't have anything else to narrow it down."

"Ok, well let me know if you need anything else, otherwise I'll see you Friday."

"Thanks, Rich, talk to you later."

Maguire ended the call and tossed the phone onto the passenger seat.

He could see the red Chevy in his head. It didn't make sense to him. Why would Browning choose to leave behind a vehicle that no one knew about and instead leave in a marked unit? And for that matter where was the Dodge?

James reached over and picked up the phone again and dialed the number he had for the investigations unit in Troop B. The phone rang a half dozen times before Maguire hung up. He made a mental note to follow-up with him about the mysterious Chevy when he got back to Long Island.

CHAPTER FORTY-SEVEN

Southampton, Suffolk County, N.Y.
Tuesday, May 1st, 2012 – 4:23 p.m.

Melody sat in the black leather chair pouring over the data on the two computer monitors. She was still wrapped up in the heavy Turkish bathrobe after her post workout shower, one of the perks of working from home. The cell phone on her desk began to buzz softly. She grabbed the phone and answered it.

"How close are you?"

"I just crossed over into Nassau, traffics *normal*. I'm thinking I won't be there till at least six."

"Ok, that's not a problem. I'll plan on getting there around six thirty; give you a chance to get settled in. If it looks like it's going to be later just let me know."

"Thanks, Mel, I really appreciate this."

"No problem. I'll see you soon."

Melody hung up her cell phone and picked up the desk phone to call the kitchen.

"Hi, Maria, I'll need those dinners for six."

When she was done Melody grabbed the cell phone and called Genevieve.

"Hey, chicky, how are things out in God's country?"

"Awesome, I can't wait to sit down and go over everything with you."

"Are you still planning on coming back tomorrow?"

"Yeah, the IT guys set things up so we can have secure access from the house. Now we can follow any of the projects in real time."

"Sounds interesting can't wait to go over it all with you. When do you think you're going to get in?"

"I should be back at the house around four*ish*. I figured we could go over everything during dinner."

"That works for me. I'll clear everything off the schedule and we can have the evening to ourselves."

"Ok, hon, I'll see you tomorrow."

Melody got up and headed off to the bathroom to get ready.

CHAPTER FORTY-EIGHT

Upstate New York
Tuesday, May 1st, 2012 – 5:23 p.m.

The man sat in the dark room and took a long slow drag on the cigarette, exhaling deeply. He liked the darkness; it was cool and quiet and afforded him the opportunity to think clearly.

It had been a long, tiresome process. He was actually surprised that the mental fatigue seemed to be so much stronger than the physical. Much to his surprise, everything had gone off almost exactly as planned. He wasn't sure whether he was as much a maestro as he was a magician. In the end he fancied himself a little of both.

The hardest part sometimes was just playing the role he had created. In some ways it annoyed him to be viewed that way, but it had served its purpose. In the end he always knew who he was and that was all he needed.

He picked up thc drink from the table, it was the first one he had in quite a while. He had abstained from drinking because he didn't want to risk any slip ups. Now he allowed himself this small luxury during what he considered to be the *intermission* of his grand play.

Tomorrow everything would change.

CHAPTER FORTY-NINE

Ponquoque Beach, Suffolk County, N.Y.
Tuesday, May 1st, 2012 – 6:26 p.m.

Melody pulled into the parking lot of the marina and parked next to the Mustang. She got out of the Mercedes and walked over to the passenger side. She opened the door and removed the bags containing the food. With her hands full she walked around and *hip checked* the car door shut before heading down the ramp.

Maguire opened the back door just as she stepped onto the rear deck.

"Hey, beautiful," he said and kissed her.

"Mmmm I've missed those lips."

"Let me take those from you," he said, as he took the bags and held the door open for her.

Melody made her way down the small hallway and couldn't help but smile as she passed the bedroom doorway. She made her way into the kitchen and sat down on one of the bar stools at the small counter. Maguire followed behind her and sat the bags down on the counter.

"Want some wine?" he asked.

"Sure," she replied. "By the way that's Chicken Marsala, so choose accordingly."

"Gotcha."

Maguire opened the wine refrigerator under the counter and selected a local pinot noir from the Peconic Bay area of Long Island. He opened the bottle and poured two drinks.

When he was done he opened one of the cabinets, removing two plates and began to serve the food.

Dinner was spent with the two of them catching up with what had taken place over the last thirty something hours.

After dinner they took their drinks and moved up to the top deck. They sat down on one of couches that looked out over the Shinnecock Bay.

"I wanted to ask you if you had any plans for Friday night?"

"Not that I know of, why?"

"My buddy Rich invited me out for a barbecue. He and his wife Mary are like my only family. I was wondering if you'd like to take a ride out with me?"

"I'd love to, what time?"

"They have a place over in Hoboken, I figured we could leave here around one-thirty, two at latest, that way we'll beat most of the traffic."

"That sounds fine to me. Do I need to bring anything?"

"Nah, if I know Mary she'll have enough food to feed a small village. I use to go out to their place for dinner and I wouldn't have to food shop for a month."

Melody laughed at the mental image of the Mustang overflowing with food containers.

James put his arm around her and she moved closer to him, pressing herself against his chest. She felt so small next to him. He kissed her head softly.

"What time is your curfew?"

"Well that all depends on what you're cooking me for breakfast," she said, with an impish grin.

CHAPTER FIFTY

Southampton, Suffolk County, N.Y.
Wednesday, May 2nd, 2012 – 7:41 a.m.

Melody awoke from the most amazing dream, but as her eyes slowly became acclimated to her current surroundings she realized that it hadn't been a dream. She found herself alone in bed and, after a few minutes, she grudgingly got up. She thought about looking for her clothes, but opted to steal one of the long sleeve shirts out of the closet. She then made her way into the bathroom where she attempted to fix the tangle mess that was her hair this morning. After a few minutes she gave up, he'd simply have to find a way to love her for who she was, especially in the mornings.

She walked out and headed toward the kitchen.

"Good morning, sleepyhead," Maguire said, as he flipped the eggs that where cooking in the pan.

"Yes it is," she replied.

Melody sat down on the barstool as James poured her a cup of coffee.

"You know, you have some unresolved issues when it comes to stealing my clothes.

"I know, better learn to deal with it now, cowboy," she said with an evil laugh, as she cupped the warm mug in her hand. "You know, I used to love getting up in the morning and getting right to work, but now you have ruined that."

"Hey, I've been up for two hours already."

Melody yawned and took a drink of the black coffee.

"I blame you," she said. "You're a bad influence on me."

"Whatever makes you feel better, baby."

Melody peered over the counter at the stove.

"You can really cook?"

"Yeah, being single it was either I learn to cook or starve. As a rule I don't do fast food."

Maguire plated the western omelet and served it to her.

"*Bon appetite, mademoiselle.*"

"*Merci beaucoup, monsieur.*"

When they finished breakfast they grabbed their coffee and made their way to the upper deck where they sat down on the couch. The sun was shining brightly and Melody could smell the saltiness in the breeze blowing off the water. A seagull perched on one of the pylons squawked loudly at the intrusion of his privacy before taking flight.

"So what's on your schedule today?"

"Besides going back to bed?" she said with a laugh. "No, I have to head back. I've got a ton of work to do. Besides Genevieve is coming home tonight and if it looks like I have been goofing off she is gonna ride my ass."

"Hey, that's my ass."

Melody looked up and smiled at him without saying a word.

"I do know what you mean though. I don't even want to think about turning on my computer. I'll be stuck there for days."

"Why don't you come out to the house for dinner tomorrow? You can meet Gen and then she can stop worrying that you are some deranged ax murderer."

"Glad to see you speak so highly of me," he said with a laugh.

"Oh she is just incorrigible."

"Well, she does have her hands full with you."

Melody looked up from her coffee cup with an impish smirk.

"You just worry about what's filling *your* hands, mister."

"Hey, if having dinner with Gen gets you in my hands more often, than just name the time and place."

“That’s my cowboy. Tomorrow night, say six o’clock, at my place.”

Maguire looked out over the water, a frown growing on his face. Melody, sensing something was wrong, sat up and looked at him.

“What is it, James?”

“I just realized I have no idea where your place is, Mel.”

Melody broke out in a laugh.

“I can fix that for you.”

She took his hand in hers and raised it up, pointing it across the bay in the direction of the house on the other side. James looked over at Melody with a mix of shock and amusement.

“Seriously?”

“Uh huh, what do you think?”

“I think I better start keeping my blinds closed.”

Melody slapped him playfully, as he wrapped her up in his arms and kissed her.”

“Oh no,” she said pulling herself away. “Don’t think you’re getting off that easy, mister.”

“If you buy the land on the other side of the road I could moor the boat closer.”

Melody shifted her body a few inches away from him and crossed her arms in front of her.

“Who says I want you closer?”

Maguire moved closer, brushing the hair off the back of her neck and began kissing her softly.

“Then again it might not be a bad real estate investment,” she said as she tilted her head slightly exposing more of her neck to him.

“Uh huh, investments are good.”

She closed her eyes as she felt his hands exploring her body.

"Really good," she said, as she lay back on the couch, pulling him down on top of her. "I changed my mind; you are getting off that easily."

CHAPTER FIFTY-ONE

Keenseville, New York State
Wednesday, May 2nd, 2012 – 8:12 a.m.

Monahan continued to sort through the pile of documents that had been amassing on his desk. He knew that there was a needle somewhere in this haystack; the only question was how long it was going to take him to locate it.

He removed the glasses from his face, laying them on the desk, and massaged his temples. He looked at his watch and wondered how long it had been since he slept last. He got up from the desk and walked out of the investigation's office, making his way down the hall to the small kitchen. He picked the coffee pot up and swirled it around a bit. It didn't smell too old and at this point beggars couldn't be choosers. He poured a cup and took a sip of the strong, hot liquid.

"Morning, sir."

Monahan turned around as a young trooper made his way into the kitchen.

"Good morning," Monahan replied. "The media still camped out on our front lawn?""

"Last count I think there were nine of those mobile news trucks with their dishes out."

"I don't even want to go out to my car at this point."

"Well, you could always climb into the bed of my pickup and we could pull a tarp over you."

Monahan looked out the window into the back parking lot. It looked like a small city. Certainly more traffic than this substation had seen in quite a while, if ever.

"What did you say?"

"Just that we could smuggle you out of here in the back of my pickup."

It was as if he had been hit by a bolt of lightning.

"Son of a bitch," Monahan said and bolted from the room back toward the investigation's office.

He began going through the files. He couldn't believe how he had missed it earlier. Clearly the lack of sleep was clouding his ability to decipher the material in front of him. When he found the report from the explosion at the Browning residence he began to go through the property inventory. And there it was: a red Chevy pickup truck. He grabbed the phone and called the front desk.

"Yes, sir," came the reply from the trooper.

"Tucker, I need you to run a VIN for me," Monahan said, reading off the vehicle identification number from the inventory sheet.

CHAPTER FIFTY-TWO

Ponquogue Beach, Suffolk County, N.Y.
Wednesday, May 2nd, 2012 – 10:51 a.m.

After Melody had left, Maguire had sat down at his desk and faced the daunting task of getting caught up. It wasn't an easy thing to do. In addition to dealing with the normal everyday stuff, he had to get back to his regular clients along with a litany of other people who had tried to contact him over the last several days. Being away for four days meant at least a week to ten days of playing catch-up.

At any given time, there was always someone who felt the need to have a professional evaluate their personal security concerns. The ironic thing was that, more often than not, those that didn't need security wanted it, while those that actually did often rejected it. The real job for him was weeding out the two. To those that lived and breathed security, life was one continuous head scratching session.

Unfortunately, his mind still wasn't back in the present time. He kept replaying things over in his mind. He recalled the conversation he had with Rich and reached down for the cell phone on the desk. He dialed the number for the investigations unit and listened as it rang several times. He ended the call and typed in a search on the laptop for the main number of the substation. When he located it he called the number.

"New York State Police, Troop B Substation, Trooper Tucker, may I help you?"

"Lieutenant Monahan, please."

"I'm sorry, but he's out of the office right now can I leave a message?"

"Yeah, this is James Maguire. I need him to call me back as soon as he gets in."

“He has your number?”

“Yes he does, tell him it’s urgent.”

“I will let him know as soon as he gets in.”

“Thanks,” James said and disconnected the call.

He sat there and decided that there wasn’t much more that he could do and he certainly had enough work on his plate to keep him busy.

On top of all the emails and phone calls he had to respond to, he also had to finish working on a threat assessment report for a client in Colorado. He pulled up the file and reread his notes, then began to draft his recommendations.

The cell phone began to ring. He reached over and picked it up, looking at the name displayed on the screen.

“Yes, Peter, what do you need?”

“You back in town yet?”

“Yeah, I got back last night. Just playing catch-up, what’s going on?”

“I’m heading overseas for the week, I was wondering if you wanted to tag along?”

“You know, I’d seriously consider it, but this is one of those times where I literally am swamped. Besides with everything going on with the upstate thing I figure I should stay local.”

“I was going to ask what happened, but I figured if you were back it wasn’t good.”

“No, not really.”

Maguire spent the next few minutes explaining what had transpired.

“I’m so sorry, James. If you want I will let my flight people know to keep the helicopter on standby if you need it.”

“I appreciate that, Peter, I really do. But one of the things I have learned is that sometimes you have to take a step back and let the locals handle it. If they need me I will do whatever I can, but it's their can of worms for lack of a better word."

"Well, I'll be out of town until the 15th. Most of the boys will be with me, except for Gregor. He volunteered to stay behind to mind the house."

"I'll be sure to harass him while you're gone."

"Ok, well have fun and let me know if you need anything."

"I will, stay out of jail."

Maguire ended the call and laid the phone on the desk.

Bart was the kind of boss everyone should have. Twice a year he hauled his entire security team, all expenses paid, over to Europe to allow them to visit their families. Gregor was the perennial hold out, but that was only because he had an ill-tempered ex-wife whose father was a presiding judge in the *Bundesgerichtshof*, the German equivalent of the U.S. Supreme Court, in Karlsruhe. It wasn't that Gregor was paranoid, but why tempt fate either.

Maguire stood up and went into the kitchen to refill his coffee mug. He looked back in the direction of the office. For a moment he questioned whether he wanted to return to the room, but then responsibility kicked in and he made his way back to the administrative morass that beckoned to him like a Greek siren luring an ill-fated sailor to his demise.

CHAPTER FIFTY-THREE

Keenseville, New York State
Wednesday, May 2nd, 2012 – 10:59 a.m.

Monahan watched as a member of the Special Operations and Response Team made their way toward the small house at the base of the mountain. SORT was the state police tactical team and each member was all too familiar as to what had happened the previous day at the Browning residence.

The six man team moved painstakingly slow through the heavy underbrush. The point man was rotated out every fifteen minutes to keep fresh eyes moving forward. So far they had managed to clear a safe path of just over a hundred yards. In that time they had already deactivated four IED's.

It had taken them nearly two hours to make their way to this point and they still had about a hundred feet more to traverse until they got to the house itself. They were all too aware of the fact that, if there was someone in the house, they were completely exposed. The other side of that coin however was that there simply was no easy way to deactivate bombs *quickly*.

Monahan had already requested two additional teams be dispatched from the Capital and Central regions, anticipating that the current team would be spent after clearing the way to the house.

He was just about to call for an update when he watched the point man raise his clenched fist. A fifth tripwire had been uncovered. The man leaned down and planted a small bright orange flag near the wire.

As he watched, the point man signaled one of the team members forward to speak with him. While he wasn't one hundred percent positive Monahan assumed they were screwed royally when he saw the man move forward, in the direction of the device, then hurriedly move back from where he had been, making a slashing motion across his throat as he directed the others to retreat.

Monahan moved forward to meet the returning team members.

"How bad?" he asked, as the SORT trooper who had ordered the retreat came forward.

"Oh we've gone all the way to *FUBAR,* sir," said Trooper Ramon Otero.

Otero was a former sergeant in the U.S. Army and had served with Explosive Ordnance Disposal in Afghanistan.

"The first four were simple, stuff they teach the kindergarten kids in Kabul. This last one looks like a Russian PMN-3, sir."

"Talk to me like I'm an idiot, who has to explain this to a bunch of other idiots in Albany, Otero."

"The device has an anti-disarming mechanism, sir. Bottom line is it's designed to kill or wound anyone trying to disarm it. This one is going to have to be blown in place. We're gonna be here for a while."

"*Outfuckingstanding*," replied Monahan before turning around and making his way back down the hill to the command post vehicle parked in the roadway.

CHAPTER FIFTY-FOUR

Southampton, Suffolk County, N.Y.
Wednesday, May 2nd, 2012 – 4:21 p.m.

Melody sat inside the car and watched as the helicopter came to a rest on the helipad. As the blur of the rotor blades slowly began to subside she watched as the aircraft's door opened and the stairs came down. Genevieve exited the helicopter and handed her bags to the driver.

Melody stepped out of the car and walked around to greet her friend with a hug.

"Hey, chicky, how was your trip?"

"Hectic, tiring, fun," she exclaimed. "I need a drink, food and a long soak in the hot tub."

"We can do that, come on get in."

She opened the passenger door and watched as Gen collapsed into the seat.

A few minutes later they were inside the living room catching each other up on the latest events.

"I did bring you something back."

"I love presents. Whatcha got?"

Genevieve got up and walked over to where the garment bag was draped over the back of the couch and unzipped it. She pulled out a black waist length leather jacket and handed it to Melody.

"Tada," she exclaimed with extravagant fanfare.

Melody examined the jacket. It appeared to be a high end, military style, pilot's jacket, although it was a bit heavier than it looked.

"Go ahead, try it on."

Melody slipped into the coat. The sleeves extended a bit beyond her hands giving her the appearance that she was wearing her big brothers coat.

"Can we exchange it for a smaller size?"

"Seeing as it's in the prototype phase, no. But it's not all about fit; it's about how you think it feels?"

"I like it. Maybe a bit heavier than I would have guessed, but you could wear it three of the four seasons I would think."

"Considering that it will defeat an AK-47 round I think it's a good trade off."

"Are you serious?"

"Uh huh, I watched the testing. They unloaded an entire magazine and the best part was there was no blunt force trauma. Over 95% of the kinetic energy is dissipated before contacting the body."

"How?"

"I don't know the exact science, but it involves nanotechnology. Honestly it's freaky. They've come up with this reactive liquid that is sandwiched between the layers. It's supple until something hits it. Then it hardens for a fraction of a second, while it displaces the energy, and then reverts back to liquid. I just started calling it *flubber*."

Melody took the jacket off and laid it on the couch and sat back down.

"Do we need to send it back?"

"Nope, just another of the perks of owning the company."

Genevieve then went over everything she had learned during the last couple of days, explaining the status on several of the projects and the capabilities of the facility in Montana.

"So what have you been doing while I was gone?"

"Not much, just been working around here. I did have dinner with James last night and he's coming out for dinner tomorrow."

"Really?" Genevieve said with a mischievous smile. "That should be fun."

Melody watch as Gen slowly curled her hand, mimicking a cat's claws.

"You will be on your best behavior."

"Oh, if you insist."

"You know how I feel about him, but you also know how I feel about your judgment."

"I'm only giving you a hard time love, you know I will behave and tell you exactly what I think"

"Thank you."

"Now can we go eat and catch-up on our hot tubbing?"

"If you make the piña coladas."

"Deal."

CHAPTER FIFTY-FIVE

Ponquogue Beach, Suffolk County, N.Y.
Wednesday, May 2nd, 2012 – 10:25 p.m.

We're sorry the person you are trying to reach is unavailable or has traveled outside the service area. Please try your call again later.

Maguire hung up the cell phone. He looked down at his watch, it was twenty after ten. He'd done all he could for the moment. He scribbled a note on the desk calendar to try again tomorrow.

He got up from the chair and turned off the light before making his way out of the office. He had made a lot of progress today, but it would still take most of tomorrow to really feel that he had gotten caught up.

He walked into the kitchen and grabbed a beer from the fridge. It was time to relax. Maguire made his way to the upper deck and sat down on the couch. He stared out over the water and soon found his attention drawn to the house across the bay.

He wondered what she was doing this evening.

CHAPTER FIFTY-SIX

Keenseville, New York State
Wednesday, May 2nd, 2012 – 11:37 p.m.

The whole scene was now lit up with portable lighting towers, the kind used at night-time construction sites. Brilliant white light flooded the scene while the sound of diesel motors filled the air with a constant droning noise.

Daytime operations had come to a grinding halt while they had waited for an expert to be flown in.

Two bomb squad technicians were helping remove the heavy ballistic helmet and jacket from a third technician who had just spent the last thirty minutes evaluating the device. The bomb disposal suit weighed in at around eighty-five pounds and, despite the built in fan, the tech was drenched in sweat.

Sergeant Robert *'Pappy'* Moore was a twenty-three year veteran of the state police and had spent the last eighteen with the Bomb Squad, hence the nickname.

"How bad is it, Pappy?" asked Monahan.

"Worst I have ever seen," replied Moore. "This guy is either a friggin' genius or certifiably insane, most likely a little of both."

"Can you blow it?"

"Hell, Dennis, I don't even know if that's the beginning or the end."

"What do you mean?"

"I've counted at least eight separate wires running either into or out of it. I have no idea what they are connected to, but they all appear to be under tension. If we blow the device I have no idea what else it will trip."

Moore sat down on the edge of the Bomb Squad truck tailgate and lit up a cigarette. Monahan watched as the man took a long drag, his mind trying to process everything he had just seen.

"We're gonna have to figure out where those lines run to before we can decide what to do."

"How long will that take?" Monahan asked.

"It'll take as long as it takes, my friend. I try not to rush things that can permanently ruin my day."

"I really need to get into that house, Pappy."

"I know you do, Dennis, but my job is to make sure there's still a house left for you to get into."

CHAPTER FIFTY-SEVEN

Ponquoque Beach, Suffolk County, N.Y.
Thursday, May 3rd, 2012 – 3:07 a.m.

It was lighter outside than he would have liked, but sometimes you just had to adapt your plans to fit the circumstances. The moonlight lit up the surrounding sand dunes that he was nestled between.

He checked his watch; it was just after three in the morning as he continued to watch the marina through the night vision goggles. It had taken him awhile to make his way here on foot. He hadn't wanted to take the chance of his vehicle being seen so he had parked his car in one of the empty parking lots along Dune Rd and made his way back along the beach. When he spotted the Mustang he back tracked and found a good vantage point in the tall grass to scan the scene.

It was an odd place for someone to live, but he had always thought of Maguire as being a bit odd.

His original plan had simply called for him to locate, draw out and kill Maguire. But he had already seen fit to alter his plan once before, so he decided to see just how much more pain and suffering he could cause him before he dealt the final blow.

When he was sure that there was no identifiable risk to his being seen, he began to move as stealthily as possible toward the car. He positioned himself behind the rear driver's side quarter panel and slid a GPS tracking device underneath it.

It was a risky move, but the location was much too sparse to allow him to effectively surveil the car without standing out like a sore thumb. He'd almost gotten burned once before and he was not going to take any further chances this late in the game.

After affixing the device, he left and made his way back to his car. He opened the laptop and started the program. Within a few seconds a map appeared on the screen along with an icon that indicated the position of the car.

Now the waiting game began.

CHAPTER FIFTY-EIGHT

Ponquogue Beach, Suffolk County, N.Y.
Thursday, May 3rd, 2012 – 4:51 p.m.

Maguire shut down the laptop. It had been a long slog, but he had finally gotten caught up with the lion's share of work.

He stood up and made his way to the bedroom, removing the t-shirt he had on and tossing it into the corner. In the bathroom he splashed some cold water on his face and dried off. When he was done he put on some cologne and walked back into the bedroom. He opened the closet and thought about what to wear. In the end he selected a long sleeve denim shirt to go with the jeans he was wearing and slipped on a black leather jacket. Before he left he went back to the kitchen and grabbed two bottles of wine out of the fridge.

As he passed Peter's house he slowed down, cruising slowly along Meadow Lane. It helped that he had the visual reference in his mind, but Melody had said to come up a private drive and he didn't want to overshoot it.

When he located the right driveway he pulled up slowly and pressed the number sequence she had given him into the keypad. When the gates had opened fully he proceeded up the driveway and through the arched entryway. As he pulled into the courtyard he took a moment to assess his present location, wondering where he should park. As if on cue, a garage door opened on his left and he pulled the Mustang into the open bay.

As Maguire exited the car, the garage door closed behind him. He looked to his right and saw the Mercedes Melody had been driving the day they had met. On his left he saw that he was parked next to a Lamborghini Aventador. Beyond that was an Aston Martin *Virage Volante,* an Audi R8 Spyder and further down he could see the curved lines of a Rolls-Royce. The lady obviously had an affinity for high end cars.

Maguire walked past the Mercedes and headed up the stairs, reaching for the door knob. Before he could take it in his hand the door swung open and he found himself standing in front of Genevieve Gordon, who let out an audible gasp.

Maguire smiled, "You must be Genevieve?"

Genevieve nodded, motioning him through the doorway, as she tried to find her voice.

"I'm sorry," she blurted out. "I don't know what I was expecting."

"Not at all," he said. "The way I'm dressed I should consider myself lucky you didn't call 911 or at the very least point me to where the garden tools are kept."

Gen laughed.

Melody certainly hadn't exaggerated about his looks, she thought.

Maguire held up the wine bottles, "I wasn't sure what we were having so I brought choices."

"Choices are always good," she replied, taking the two bottles from him. "Melody is waiting inside, just follow me."

Genevieve led him into the salon where Melody was sitting on one of the couches working on her laptop.

Melody looked up as they walked into the room, watching as Genevieve silently mouthed the words: *Oh My God.*

She did her best to suppress the laugh that desperately wanted to come out. She put the laptop down on the table in front of her and got up to meet him.

"Hey, cowboy, you made it."

"Well I would have been here sooner, but I got lost coming up the driveway."

"That's funny," she said, as she kissed him. "I'll get you a tour guide if you need to use the bathroom."

"I'm going to take these to the kitchen," Gen said holding up the bottles. "Anyone want a drink?"

"Don't ask for a piña colada," Melody whispered conspiratorially.

"Wine is fine for me."

Melody took him by the hand and led him out onto the back deck.

"Wow, beautiful view."

"Yeah, it's beats the heck out of the one I had growing up."

"Well you've certainly done well for yourself."

"Oh I've had a lot of help along the way. In fact, I'd probably be working in some midtown Manhattan cubicle of hell with fluorescent lighting if it wasn't for Genevieve."

"I seriously doubt that, Ms. Anderson. Not to diminish Gen, but from what I have seen you're one pretty tenacious lady."

She leaned in closer, playing with the collar of Maguire's jacket and looked up into his eyes. "Only when I want something really bad," she said with a sultry smile.

"Ahem," said Genevieve, as she brought out the drinks out. "Dessert isn't served here until *after* dinner people."

They both laughed sheepishly and turned to face Genevieve who handed each of them a glass.

"It's like living with my very own hall monitor."

"I thought you said *not* to have the piña colada," Maguire said pointing to the drink in Melody's hand.

"Oh, I'm a professional, so trust me; you'll thank me in the morning."

"So, James, how is it that a good looking guy like you has managed to stay single so long or have you?"

"Gen!" Melody exclaimed.

"What?" said Genevieve. "I thought this was about me getting to know James better?"

Maguire laughed. "No it's okay. I actually like getting the tough questions out of the way first and yes, I have managed to stay single, but it wasn't anything I had intentionally set out to do. My career choices took up most of my time and I didn't think it was fair to get into a relationship with someone that I couldn't devote one hundred percent of my time to."

"Good answer," said Gen, as she turned toward Melody and stuck her tongue out at her.

"How did you make it to New York City? Mel said you were from upstate."

"I was," he replied. "After high school I left and joined the Navy. It was fun, but the traveling started to get old after a while. I heard the NYPD was hiring and the rest, as they say, is history."

"So now you have your own business? How's that working out?"

"Good actually, seems like the crazier the world gets the busier I get."

"You ever shoot anyone?"

"Alright, that's enough with the interrogation," Melody said, as she got up and grabbed Genevieve's hand, pulling her up from the couch. "I think we should go check on dinner, don't you, Gen?"

Gen looked back at Maguire, as Melody pulled her along in the direction of the kitchen. "S'okay, you can tell me later."

James smiled and gave her a thumbs-up.

When they left the room he got up and walked over toward one end of the room where an audio system sat. It was surrounded by a collection of CD's that equaled anything he had ever seen before. He looked through the rows of discs until he found one that surprised him. He withdrew it and slid the CD into the player; listening intently as the first strains of *Stardust* filtered through the room.

"Don't tell me you like John Coltrane too?" Melody asked, as she walked back into the room.

"I grew up with him. My father loved jazz music. Unfortunately I didn't learn to appreciate it till I was working in Manhattan. We were out on a protection gig and went to this old jazz bar on the upper west side. There was a guy doing a bunch of Coltrane's stuff and I realized I knew most of the songs."

"Dinners ready," called out Genevieve from the edge of the room.

"After you, my dear," said Maguire.

The three of them sat around the table talking and laughing. All in all Genevieve was completely taken with him. He was at the complete opposite end of the spectrum from anyone else that Melody had dated in the past. For starters, he was ungodly handsome, but, looks aside, he was also very funny and completely down to earth.

Gen really hadn't been sure what to expect. In a way she had been worried that he might be one of those Southampton *hanger-on's* she had come to know and loathe. They made friends with someone just in order to be a part of the *in*-crowd. Then they would hop and skip from one person to another in an attempt to elevate themselves to ever more popular groups. Gen was terrified that he was going to try to use Melody and break her heart. She had to admit that he was nothing like that. In fact she had never even heard him drop any names, something as rare in Southampton as a blue moon.

Now, as she watched the two of them talking and laughing, she could see how connected he was to her. More importantly she could see that Melody had fallen head over heels for him.

When he had excused himself to use the bathroom, Melody leaned over and asked her what she thought of him.

"If I were you I'd lock him up in the basement and never let him leave this house again."

"Oh God I was hoping you'd like him."

"Like him? I think we need to buy ourselves a genetic research firm and figure out how to clone him."

Melody laughed. She could always count on Genevieve to think outside the box.

CHAPTER FIFTY-NINE

Hampton Bays, Suffolk County, N.Y.
Thursday, May 3rd, 2012 – 5:53 p.m.

The room at the Water's Edge Motel and Marina was exactly what you'd expect for the price. He had selected it solely for its proximity to Maguire and he didn't plan on staying very long. The *décor* had lost its luster sometime between the moon landing and Nixon's resignation, not that he thought any of the usual occupants would have noticed anyway.

He had been watching the news when he heard the audible alert sound on the laptop; indicating that the vehicle was in motion. He lit up a cigarette and watched in real time as the icon moved slowly north along the roadway before heading east.

Technology had really made this all too easy.

He tracked the car for about a half hour, watching as it turned south and then began heading back west. As he watched, the icon track made an almost complete oval and started heading back toward the water. He was growing concerned that something had malfunctioned with the system. Just before it ran out of road it came to a stop and he breathed a sigh of relief.

All things considered, he felt very lucky that the car had stopped where it had. The device was accurate within a fifty yard radius. The sparseness of homes in this particular area made it easy for him to specifically identify which house Maguire had went to.

He opened a window in the internet browser and brought up the general area in Google maps. Unlike many rural areas in the fly-over states, which provided only grainy images, this location was highly detailed. The satellite imagery was clear enough to allow him to see the entire house, including the lounge chairs on the back deck. He even noticed a person walking their dog on the beach. In fact, the only thing it didn't provide was real time updates, but he figured it wouldn't be long before that capability existed.

Once he had narrowed down the house number it was just a matter of researching the online tax records to find the owner. It was of course a corporation, but those are headed by real people who had easily searchable names. In all it took him just about a half hour to find his next target along with a photo courtesy of the corporations website.

For a moment he wondered when exactly privacy had died to technology.

By the end of his search he knew how many bedrooms and baths the house had, the number of floors, the square footage, the size of the land plot, when the house had been built, as well as the demographic makeup of the area.

Unfortunately, he would have the same issues he had with Maguire's place. Judging from the aerial shots it would be highly difficult place to do any actual extended surveillance. It was just too isolated and he certainly couldn't drive into the area and just park. It was clearly obvious that it was in a very affluent area which meant security and home owners who probably had the local cops on their speed dial. More importantly, those cops would respond very quickly to any call. It was something that he didn't like, but sometimes your options were limited and he would just have to figure something out.

He took a drag on the cigarette and leaned back in the chair staring at the computer screen. He pulled back on the map a bit and took in the lay of the land. The house itself was located on the western edge of a long spit of land. There were no houses to the left and the nearest one on the right was over two hundred feet away.

On the western side was the Shinnecock inlet. There a breaker wall, constructed out of massive boulders, extended about a thousand feet from the bay, all the way around to the ocean, where it jutted out about a hundred feet or so into the water.

He got up and walked over to the night table and pulled out the phone directory. He thumbed through the pages until he found what he was looking for. Reaching into a bag that sat on the bed he pulled out a prepaid cell phone, which he had purchased in Albany a day earlier, and dialed the number.

"Moriches Bay Marina, how can I help you?"

"Yes, I was wondering if you rented jet skis and if you do what are the rates?"

"Yes we do, we offer one and two hour rentals for ninety bucks and a hundred and fifty or full day for four seventy-five."

"Great, thank you so much."

He disconnected the call, setting the phone on the desk and stared at the map.

The ocean side of the breaker wall was nearly three quarters of a mile from the house. It was conceivable that, under the cover of darkness, he could slip in undetected and make his way on foot through the high grass. Once he got to the property edge it appeared that there was an abundance of foliage that would help conceal his presence. In addition, there appeared to be a guest house off to the side with a rather large deck. Those could be a blessing when you needed to disappear quickly.

All in all it had the workings of a doable plan. He would however have to gauge the security on the fly.

Oh well, what was life without a little bit of adventure? he thought.

CHAPTER SIXTY

Southampton, Suffolk County, N.Y.
Thursday, May 3rd, 2012 – 10:23 p.m.

"It really was great meeting you, Gen," Maguire said and kissed her on the cheek.

"Same here, next time we'll talk about Melody's college days."

"Sounds like a plan."

"Not in this lifetime people," replied Melody. "Now say Goodnight, Gen."

"Goodnight, James."

"Goodnight, Gen."

Melody opened the door and she and Maguire stepped out into the garage.

"So, what do you think of Genevieve?"

"I think she's a blast. I had a really great time."

"I'm so happy. I was worried she might be a little too much for you."

"Oh heck no, I thought she was funny as hell."

Melody paused and hopped up on the long work bench that ran the entire length of the garage wall. James stepped in front of her and she wrapped her arms around his neck.

Maguire looked into her warm, sultry eyes.

"I don't want you to go."

"I know," he said kissing her lips.

"Is that wrong?"

"No, there's nothing more I'd rather do then go back inside with you, but I think Gen is probably ready to bust down the door for some girl talk. Besides, we have a date tomorrow that you need to get ready for."

Melody pouted her lower lip.

"That's a look."

"Is it working?"

"Yes."

"Really?"

"No."

Melody playfully socked him in the arm. "In that case be gone with you."

Maguire grabbed her in his arms and lifted her up off the bench. As she wrapped her legs around his waist, the two lovers kissed each other passionately.

After a moment Melody pulled back and looked at him. "I'm falling James and I'm really scared."

He stared back at her, she could feel the penetrating gaze of those blue eyes and she physically shuddered.

"I know," he said. "Don't be scared, Mel, I won't let go."

She buried her head into his shoulder and wrapped her arms tightly around him. She had already surrendered her body to him and now she was going to give him her heart.

Inside the house Genevieve sat in her office staring at the computer screen watching them in the garage.

"Please don't hurt her, James," she said softly and closed the cover of the laptop.

CHAPTER SIXTY-ONE

Hadley Cove, New York State
Thursday, May 3rd, 2012 – 11:01 p.m.

"Fire in the Hole, Fire in the Hole, Fire in the Hole."

Monahan covered his ears and looked away, as Pappy Moore depressed the fire button on the remote detonation switch. A split second later the ground ahead of them erupted, sending dirt rocketing up toward the heavens before it eventually fell back to earth as a rain of debris.

It had taken nearly a day and a half to reach this point. Along with the combined efforts of both the New York State Police Bomb Squad as well as soldiers from the New York Army National Guard's, 501st Ordnance Battalion. In all, seventeen devices were either disarmed or detonated on the property surrounding the house.

The final entry was made by the SORT with a bomb tech in tow. Ironically, while the exterior had been a labyrinth of IED's and anti-personnel mines, interconnected by a spider web of tripwires, the interior of the small house was completely clear.

Well, clear of any explosive device that was.

When they had finished the search one of the team members came out and signaled for Monahan.

"What do you have?" he asked, as he slipped on a pair of shoe covers and donned a pair of latex gloves.

"Well, we found the sheriff," the man replied. "It looks like a friggin' butcher shop in there, LT."

Monahan walked into the house which reeked with the smell of decaying flesh.

Sergeant Tim Scott was just walking out of one of the back rooms.

"Did you guys find Browning?" Monahan asked.

"What's left of him, boss," Scott said. "Body is tied up in a chair back there. Whoever did this is a friggin' psychopath."

"What makes you say that?"

"You got to see it for yourself."

Monahan walked into the back room and began examining the scene. A chair sat in the middle of the room, bolted to the floor beneath it. The victim's back was turned toward the doorway and the arms and legs were securely tied down to the frame of the chair with thick rope. The floor underneath was stained a dark red from the pool of blood that had coagulated beneath the chair. He walked around to the front and fought the sudden urge to retch. The face of Paul Browning stared back at him; two black holes were all that remained where his eyes had been gouged out from the sockets.

Monahan walked out of the room slowly, feeling the unsteadiness in his legs. It wasn't so much the death as it was the macabre scene. It was clear to him that Browning was most likely alive when his eyes had been removed.

What sick bastard gouges out another human being's eyes, he wondered?

"Are there any other bodies?" he asked.

"Hard to tell," replied Scott. "We found a table in the basement covered in blood. Looks like whoever did this to Browning had some experience. There are several fifty-five gallon drums downstairs with some type of caustic *soup* cooking in them. I'd say whoever did it was trying to get rid of the evidence. Could be one, two, who knows. I'm thinking he got rushed and never finished disposing of Browning."

"Anything else?"

"Oh yeah, something really odd actually."

"What's that?"

"There's a hospital room set-up downstairs."

"A what?"

"You heard me right. There's a hospital bed, medical equipment, bandages, the whole works. This is some really sick shit."

"LT!"

Monahan turned in the direction of the door.

"We found Browning's pickup in the garage."

"Anything else?"

"Yeah, it's got a bunch of things, books, papers and some women's clothes in the back."

Monahan shook his head and headed toward the front door. As he stepped outside he grabbed one of the investigators who were heading up the stairs.

"Get on the horn and put out a *BOLO* on Keith Banning and cancel the one for Browning."

"You think he's involved in this?" asked the investigator.

"Hell, your guess is as good as mine," Monahan said. "For all I know he could be in one of those drums downstairs, but since this is his damn house, and until we know one way or the other, I want to make sure we cover all our bases."

CHAPTER SIXTY-TWO

Moriches Bay, Suffolk County, N.Y.
Friday, May 4th, 2012 – 9:31 a.m.

The man walked into the Moriches Bay Marina and up to the counter behind which a young man sat working on a large, deep sea reel.

“Hi there,” he said. “I’d like to rent a jet ski for the day.”

Without looking up, the man laid the reel on the desk then reached over and grabbed a form from the rack on the wall behind him.

“I need you to fill this out and I need a valid driver’s license along with a major credit card.”

The man reached into his back pócket and withdrew his wallet. He removed the license and credit card, laying them on the counter and began to fill out the form.

The man behind the counter examined the license and confirmed that it was valid. “You want it for the day?” he asked.

“Yes I do.”

“That’ll be four hundred and seventy-five dollars. You need to have it back by eight o’clock. It has a full tank and you are responsible for putting any additional gas in it throughout the day. If you refill here you’ll get a discount.”

“Great, thanks.”

The man swiped the card and waited a few seconds until he got an approval and printed out the receipt. “Please sign here.”

He scrawled his signature on the paper and slid it back.

“You ever ride before?”

“Yes I have.”

"Ok, here is the key, it's in slip five."

"Thanks and you have a great day."

CHAPTER SIXTY-THREE

Southampton, Suffolk County, N.Y.
Friday, May 4th, 2012 – 1:52 p.m.

Melody walked out of the house looking like the epitome of the country girl next door. She wore a red flannel shirt and pair of faded jeans which she had tucked into a pair of tan boots. Draped over her left arm was a tan leather jacket and in her right she carried another bag.

Maguire got out of the car and walked around to open the door for her.

"How do I look?"

"Like an angel," he replied.

"Be serious, James. I didn't know what to wear."

"I was being serious Melody, you do look like an angel."

"Thank you," she said and kissed him. "Oh, I've got something for you."

She handed him her coat.

"It's nice, but I doubt it is going to fit me," he said with a laugh.

"No butthead, this is for you."

Melody opened the bag and reached in to remove the jacket she had gotten from Genevieve.

"What's this?"

"You are going to be my guinea pig," she replied. "One of my companies just designed that and I felt that you would be the perfect person to give me an honest assessment about what you thought."

"Ok, I don't mind being your test subject," Maguire replied and slipped the jacket on.

Overall it was a pretty good fit. Maybe a little stiff, but he chalked that up to being new.

"Well, I have to admit that it does look really good on you."

"You know what looks even better on me?" he asked with a smile.

Melody raised her finger to his lips. "Easy there, cowboy, just get in the car."

They made the trip to Hoboken, New Jersey in just a little over two and a half hours. Overall not a bad time considering it was a Friday.

Maguire pulled into the driveway and put the car in park.

"You know, you can back out now and we can go get a pizza or something?"

"Stop it," Melody said. "I'm looking forward to meeting your friends."

"Well Mary and the girls are fine; I'll let you make your own judgments on Rich."

Maguire had just closed the door to the car when he got hit like a ton of bricks by the eight-year-old rocket with pig tails that was his goddaughter, Emily Stargold.

"Uncle James," Emily cried out, as she wrapped her arms around him. "I've missed you."

Maguire picked her up in his arms and twirled her around in the air.

"Well I've missed you too, pumpkin."

"Who is she?" Emily asked pointing to Melody.

"This is Melody, she's my friend," Maguire said, as he set her back down on the ground. "Melody, this is the world's greatest goddaughter, Emily."

"Hi, Emily," Melody said.

"Hi," Emily replied before turning back to Maguire. "Did you bring me anything?"

"Did I bring you anything?"

Maguire leaned through the open window and grabbed a stuffed animal from the back seat. It was a large frog who wore a sailor's *Dixie Cup* hat on his head and clenched a cigar in his mouth. In one hand he held a trident spear and in the other a stick of dynamite.

"This is Freddie," Maguire said. "He needs a good home, Em. A home far, far away so that mommy doesn't see him."

"Ok," Emily said, as she turned and ran back into the house clutching the frog. James took Melody's hand and the two of them headed up the walkway to the front door.

Melody looked over at Maguire, a frown on her face. "We really need to work on your gift giving skills."

"Hey, Sophie," Maguire said, as they entered the house.

Sophie Stargold sat on the couch doing what most fifteen year old girls do best, texting. She looked up from her screen briefly to acknowledge his presence. "Hey," she said before returning her gaze to the screen.

"This is Melody," he continued.

"Hey," she repeated without looking up.

"Hi," Melody replied.

Maguire looked at Melody. "That's about all you're going to get."

He led her into the kitchen just as Mary was coming in through the back door.

"James, when did you get here?"

"Just a minute ago," Maguire replied, giving her a hug and kiss on the cheek. "Melody, this is Mary, Rich's much better half."

Mary Stargold had long ago given up her day job as a lobbyist for the role of stay at home mom, but that didn't mean she was your typical suburban housewife. In between shuffling the girls to and from school she still managed to hit the gym four to five times a week and had just started her own consulting business, just to get back into the swing of things now that the kids didn't need her as much.

Melody extended her hand, "Hi, I'm so glad to meet you, Mary. James has spoken so much about you."

"It's nice to meet you to, Melody. Can I get you something to drink?"

"No I'm fine, thank you."

"Rich is outside putting the food on the grill," Mary said to James. "Can you make sure he doesn't overcook the steaks again?"

"Sure thing," Maguire replied. "Come on, Mel, I'll introduce you to the high priest of burnt offerings."

Maguire opened the sliding glass door and led her out onto the back deck where Rich was in the process of grilling dinner.

"Hey, Rich," Maguire called out. "The fire department just pulled up outside, I think the food's done."

"Like that would ever stop you from eating," Stargold replied and laid the tongs on the small shelf adjacent to the grill.

"Rich, this is Melody Anderson. Melody, this is Rich Stargold, I taught him everything he knows."

"Hi, Melody, it's so nice to meet you," Rich replied, as he shook hands with her.

"It's very nice to meet you too, Rich."

"If you're able to put up with him in the beginning, he does eventually grow on you after a while. Sort of like a fungus."

"Don't mind him," Maguire said. "He's just grumpy because he works for the government."

"I'll let you boys have your fun," Melody said and kissed Maguire on the cheek. "I'm going to see if Mary needs help in the kitchen."

The two men watched as Melody walked back inside the house. When the sliding door was closed Stargold looked back over at Maguire. "Where the hell did you meet her?"

"A charity event."

"Charity event? What did she do, take you up as her personal cause?"

"Jealous much?"

"Shocked is more like it, she doesn't seem like your usual type."

"I'm maturing," Maguire replied, cutting him off before Stargold could respond. "You said you wanted to talk to me about something."

"Yeah, I do. What do you know about Alan McMasters?"

"As in State Senator Alan McMasters?"

"That would be the one."

"I assume you mean beyond the fact that he is running for New York City Mayor."

"Correct," said Rich, as he turned back to the grill and flipped the steaks.

"Decorated Marine combat veteran," Maguire replied. "He cut his teeth as a 2nd Lieutenant back in the first Gulf War and finished his military service after the battle of Fallujah in '04. Guess he wanted to go out on a high note. Parlayed his service into a campaign and got elected to the state senate. Only grumblings I hear is that he's fair, but tenacious; which sounds about the norm for most of *Uncle Sam's Misguided Children*.

"Well, I got a call from his camp about two weeks ago indicating he wanted to speak with me. I just assumed it was about an upcoming POTUS visit or something," Rich explained. "So I met with him at the beginning of the week. Kind of an odd meeting at first, until he turns around and says that, should he get elected, he would like me to consider becoming his police commissioner."

"Are you friggin' kidding me?"

"That was my first thought as well, but apparently he wasn't."

"What did you tell him?"

"You know the usual answer. I'm honored, I have to talk to my wife, blah, blah, blah."

"This isn't a 'hey I just want to make you feel good' offer," said Maguire. "He's clobbering Jesse Walters in the polls. Short of them finding photos involving whips and a cigar, he's pretty much a lock."

"I know. That's why I wanted to ask you what you thought about all of it."

"Rich, it's a no brainer. I know that you love what you do, but it is police commissioner of the biggest department in the United States. Hell, the NYPD is larger than the standing armies of some countries."

"I know, but I'm an outsider. I have no idea about running something as massive as the NYPD."

"Here's a newsflash, it hasn't stopped any of the other PC's before and some of them were outright lunatics."

"In my heart I know it's the right choice, but that fear of screwing things up is gnawing at me."

"Rich, you've been in this game how long now?"

"Twenty-one years."

"You know what to do. More importantly there are still a lot of good men and women left in the department to help you. You just have to elevate the right ones to the right spots."

"So are you going to help me pick them?"

"No," Maguire answered, "but I'll help you find the ones with the right qualifications; picking them is entirely up to you."

"Ok, I can deal with that."

"Great, now can you get the steaks off the grill before you set fire to the backyard?"

CHAPTER SIXTY-FOUR

Keenseville, New York State
Friday, May 4th, 2012 – 2:00 PM

Monahan walked back into the Troop B substation looking the worse for wear. He desperately needed coffee, a shower and a bed. At this stage of the game he would be happy to get even one of them.

"Evening, sir," the trooper behind the desk said.

Monahan mumbled a greeting before heading down the hall.

"Oh hey, LT, you had a call."

Monahan stopped and walked back. The trooper had gotten up and was walking toward him with a piece of paper in his hands.

"Thanks," Monahan replied, as he took the paper and looked down at it. "Damn, I forgot about him."

Walking past the kitchen he peeked inside, a full pot of coffee sat on the burner. He quickly poured himself a cup and continued on back to the office. He took a sip of the coffee and laid the cup on the desk. Reaching into his coat pocket he removed the piece of paper that he had written Maguire's number on previously. He then took off his jacket and laid it over the back of the chair. Monahan sat down and rubbed his eyes, he felt so incredibly tired. This was a young man's game and with each passing day he began to feel more and more like a dinosaur. He pulled out his cell phone and dialed the number that was written on the paper. The phone rang a few times and went to voicemail.

"Yeah, this is Dennis Monahan. I just got your message. Call me back when you get this and I'll give you an update on what's going on. Just for the record we are looking for your buddy Keith Banning. It was his pickup you saw in the garage. We hit his house earlier today and it looks like a butcher shop. There were bodies all over the place, including Paul Browning."

Monahan ended the call and leaned back in the chair, staring at the growing pile of reports. At this point he was running on adrenaline and that tank was just about empty.

CHAPTER SIXTY-FIVE

Southampton, Suffolk County, N.Y.
Friday, May 4th, 2012 – 11:43 p.m.

James pulled the Mustang up to the front door and turned the engine off. Melody shifted slightly in the seat so that she could face him.

"I really had a great time tonight, James. I wanted to thank you for taking me and sharing that part of your life with me. I know they are very dear to you."

"Well, I figured if you could put up with Rich and Mary you're tough enough to handle me."

"Oh I can handle you, trust me."

"I have to be honest with you, Mel, this is all really new to me."

"What do you mean?"

"I mean that I have shared more with you in this one week then I have ever shared with anyone else before. This is all uncharted water for me."

"How do you think I feel?" she asked. "I've spent my whole life focused on business. I've never had the time or need for anyone, until you. "

"I just don't want to screw this up, Melody."

"Just be you, James, and you won't."

"How can you be so sure?"

Melody leaned over and kissed him softly. "Cause you had me at *hello*."

She opened the car door and stepped out, closing it behind her. She looked back through the open window. "You want to come in for a drink?" she asked.

“Can I take a rain check till tomorrow night? I have to be up on the north fork in the morning to do a walk through on a new security installation. Celebrities’ apparently don’t understand the concept of weekends off.”

“It’s a date,” Melody said. “Call me when you get back in town.”

“I will,” he said and watched her walk into the house. For a moment he thought about following her in, but fought the urge, at least for tonight.

On the ride home he went over the events of the day. He was really happy that the dinner had gone so well. It might have seemed strange, but knowing that Rich and Mary both liked Melody was a great reassurance to him. Rich’s news about McMasters offering him the job as PC was a shock, although he knew Rich could handle it.

Truth was that the Department really needed an outsider. It had become like a house that had been shuttered too long and was in desperate need of fresh air. The current police commissioner was merely a political puppet, parroting the whims of his boss over in City Hall. He was more at home as a micromanager than as an actual leader. From the beginning he had put people into high ranking positions who were more accustomed to saying ‘yes’ than they were at being effective. Unfortunately, people like that had a habit of staying in those spots and in this case it was going on twelve years now. As a result of this institutional stagnation, a lot of highly qualified people were simply packing their bags rather than suffer under the whims of the egotistical police commissioner and his sycophants.

He was just heading over the Ponquoque Bridge when he felt his phone vibrate. He pulled it out of the jacket pocket and saw that he had missed a call. He hit the voicemail button and listened to the message.

“Son of a bitch,” he said out loud.

He pulled the car into the marina parking lot and killed the lights. He looked around at all the empty slips, it wouldn't be too long before all the boats came back and then the parking lot would be filled to capacity. Oh well, it was only for a few months out of the year.

He got out of the car and made his way down the pier and onto the back deck. He opened the door slightly and peered down at the jamb and froze.

The wire had been tripped.

Maguire reacted immediately, reaching back with his right hand and drawing the pistol from its holster.

"The only easy day was yesterday," Maguire mumbled to himself before breaching the door.

Room clearing is hard. Often your quarry knows that you are coming and they have taken the best possible tactical position they can. You can offset that a bit if you are equipped with flash bangs or concussion grenade, and you can certainly improve the odds by bringing along a half dozen or more of your closest friends armed with automatic weapons. Unfortunately, for Maguire, he had none of those luxuries at the present moment.

He did however have one thing going for him, it was his boat and he knew his way around it like the back of his hand.

As he entered he moved to his left, slipping into the bedroom and scanned it quickly for threats before moving into the bathroom. He repeated the actions as he went through the remainder of the boat, hugging the wall as he cleared each room.

When he was certain that there was no one onboard he turned the lights on and began doing a closer search to locate any evidence that might help identify who had been on the boat. It didn't take him long. As he re-entered the office he saw the chess pieces on his desk.

There were three pieces on a crudely hand drawn chessboard pattern, the white king and queen along with a black pawn. The king and pawn faced each other while the queen was lying on its side. Maguire picked up the queen and examined it. Inscribed on the bottom of the piece were the initials SM.

Anger welled up inside him, as he held the fragile wooden piece in his hand. He looked back down at the *chess board* and he realized that there was printing on the other side of the paper. He picked it up and turned it over to see an aerial shot of Melody's house.

Maguire bolted from the office.

As he made his way down the hall, he stopped for a moment, grabbing the rifle bag from the bedroom closet. He ran out the back door, sprinting up the dock, and jumped into the Mustang. The engine roared to life and he raced out of the parking lot, heading back to Melody's.

Maguire reached into the pocket of his coat and pulled out the phone. He hit the speed dial for her, but the call immediately went to voicemail.

"Fuck," he exclaimed, as he ended the call and hit the number for Gregor, listening to it ring.

"Answer the damn phone, Gregor," he screamed.

"*Ja*, Ritter here," he heard Gregor's drowsy voice say.

"Gregor, it's Maguire. I need you to get over to Melody Anderson's house and I mean now. I think there's a shooter in the house."

"What are you talking about?"

"Someone broke into my boat; they left a map with Melody's house circled. I'm on my way, but you're closer. I need you to get over there now. The access code for the gate is *2416*"

"I'm on my way."

Maguire hung up the phone and gunned the engine. He covered the fourteen miles in just less than eight minutes. There was no doubt in his mind that there were probably at least half a dozen calls placed to the county police already. The only consolation was no one would have been able to read the license plate at the speed he was going anyway. As he pulled up to the gate he locked the breaks up. He pressed the code into the keypad and watched as the gates opened agonizingly slow.

“C’mon, c’mon,” he said impatiently.

As he waited he reached into the bag and withdrew the M-4, slamming a magazine into it and chambering a round. When the gates had opened far enough he gunned it and sent the car rocketing up the driveway.

When he pulled in through the archway he saw Ritter’s Humvee parked diagonally to the front door which was wide open. He killed the engine and made his way silently up the steps, pausing just inside the entryway to acclimate his eyes to the darkness. He brought the rifle up and began scanning. What he wouldn’t have given at this moment for a pair of night vision goggles.

“Gregor, *wo bist du*?” Maguire said, choosing to ask where he was in German in hopes that anyone else wouldn’t understand.

“Here,” Ritter replied. “Come quick,”

Maguire moved forward, silently into the salon until he found Gregor who was kneeling over Genevieve. She was propped up against a wall and had a laceration on her scalp. Gregor had come prepared with both his MP-5 and a trauma bag. He was in the process of applying a bandage to the wound.

“When I found her she was unconscious, but I think she is going to be fine,” Ritter said. “No other injuries and her vitals are good.”

“Gen, where’s Melody?”

“Upstairs in her bedroom, I think,” Genevieve replied. “Go through my office, it’s on the 2nd floor. There’s a hidden door behind my desk that will bring you into her bedroom without being seen. Bottom shelf of the bookcase has a button to open it.”

“You’re going to be okay,” Maguire said. “Take care of her, Gregor. I’m going to find Melody.”

"I'll move her out of the house as soon as I can."

Maguire made his way back to the entryway and climbed the staircase slowly, scanning for movement as he went along. He could see up to the 3rd floor landing which appeared to be clear. When he reached the 2nd floor landing he made his way down the hallway until he located the office. He felt along the bookshelf till he found the button and pushed it. The wall behind the desk popped open and he drew it back revealing the small staircase.

He stepped inside and began to move slowly up the cramped stairway. When he reached the top he paused to listen. He couldn't be sure whether the insulation was just that good, but he heard no noise coming from inside the room. He located the release latch that allowed the door to open. Before he pressed it he reached up and unscrewed the light bulb above the door.

Maguire was grateful when the door opened without a sound. He peered into the room, but had a limited field of view. Slowly he opened the door, enough so that he could slide through, and then closed it as much as he could without shutting it. Maguire didn't know if it would make an audible noise when it locked and he didn't want to take the chance.

He quickly scanned the room and realized that he was in an office. He moved behind the large partition wall and took up a position near the rear edge that afforded him the best view. It was an open floor plan overall, but there were still some areas he couldn't make out clearly.

He moved up toward the forward edge of the wall where he could make out the side of the room that faced the exterior. He could make out a deck and, as he peered further around the edge of the wall, he could see Melody sitting in a straight back chair, her back toward him. A closer examination determined that she was tied to the chair.

Maguire could make out the rope that wrapped round the back of the chair and around her torso. Other ropes held her wrists to the sides of the chair while her ankles were tied to the front.

He moved back to the rear edge of the wall and got down on his stomach crawling his way toward the privacy wall behind the bed. He drew himself up until he had a better view of the exterior. As he watched, Melody's head moved slightly.

At least she's alive, he thought.

On the far side he could just barely make out the edge of a person's body leaning against the railing. He needed to get a better view. He rolled around and made his way to the other side of the wall. This time he drew the weapon up, peering down the scope, and put the red, holographic sight reticle on the head of the man responsible for all the recent death and carnage: Keith Banning.

He lined up the sights; aiming for the bridge of the man's nose. As his finger began to slowly draw the trigger back he stopped.

Something felt wrong.

He lowered the gun and began taking in the entire picture.

Banning was leaning casually against the railing facing Melody. *He knows I'm coming*, Maguire thought. *He's waiting for me before he does anything.*

He immediately went back to the chess pieces. *Of course, it's my move, but why stand out in the open and expose himself?*

As Maguire watched, Banning stood up and stretched. It was barely perceptible, but it was there. He saw something clasped in the man's right hand.

Maguire slipped back behind the wall. *This is so not good*, he thought.

Without knowing what was in his hand he was risking Melody's life and that was a risk he would not take. He needed to get a closer look at whatever it was.

He cautiously made his way back to her office. He had seen a patio door that led out onto the deck. It was clear that Banning was expecting him to do something, Maguire just decided to do the unexpected. He placed the M-4 behind a large flower pot that sat next to the door. Next he withdrew the folding knife from his pocket and opened it; using his hand to ease the spring loaded blade into the locked position without making its tell-tale noise. He grabbed the tape dispenser off the desk taking several small strands and affixed the knife to the inside of his left leg.

When he was done he walked back over to the door and slammed it open before stepping out onto the deck.

Banning was startled by the sound of the door opening suddenly behind him. He spun around quickly to confront this unexpected event and came face to face with Maguire.

"Whoa, Jimmy, how the hell did you get here?" Banning said with a mix of shock and confusion.

Clearly he had expected Maguire to come straight into the room. That was why he had positioned Melody where she could easily be seen. He had counted on James rushing in and it had been a big miscalculation on his part.

"It's a big house, Keith, must have gotten lost, took a wrong turn," Maguire said, his voice devoid of emotion.

He glanced over at Melody. She was gagged and sat there with a look of fear on her face. Immediately he realized that she had a good reason to. Strapped to her chest was what appeared to be some type of explosive device.

So that's what he has in his hand, Maguire thought. He needed to get a better look at it.

By this point Banning had managed to regain his composure and with it his bravado.

"I was wondering when you would get here, Jimmy, I was beginning to think you'd turn tail and run away again."

"Why would I run away, Keith?" Maguire asked, as he moved slowly in the direction of the railing which afforded him the best view he could get of the device on Melody's chest.

“That’s what you’re good at, isn’t it? Banning asked. “That’s what you did last time around.”

“What the hell are you talking about?”

“Oh, Jimmy, don’t be so fucking stupid. Think back, you’ll figure it out.”

“If this is about you and me, then let her go. You have me here now. Let’s take our walk down memory lane in private.”

“Oh I would love to,” Banning said. “But you brought her into the mix, so now she gets a front row seat to watch this epic game finally come to an end.”

“This isn’t a game, Keith.”

“Sure it is, Jimmy. Isn’t that what life is, one big game?”

“People’s lives are not games, Keith.”

“You’re right, people are fools. The vast majority of them are ignorant and inconsequently. They live their lives like a pathetic game of checkers. Then there are those of us in the minority who are smart, cunning, and ruthless. For us, we live our lives as it should be, like a game of chess. Strategy, complex moves, guile.”

“So what was Tricia?”

“She was just an expendable piece to draw you out of hiding,” said Banning. “Nothing more, really.”

“I wasn’t hiding, Keith.”

“Really? You could have fooled me,” Banning said with a contemptuous tone. “I expected you to show back up when your folks bought the farm. You have any idea how much trouble I went through to arrange that and you just blew it off. I realized then that I’d have to jack things up a bit more to get you interested.”

Maguire’s jaw clenched tightly. All he wanted to do was close the dozen or so feet that separated the two of them and choke the life out of this low life piece of shit. Unfortunately, he was reasonably sure he wouldn’t make it before Banning had a chance to activate the device in his hand.

"Looks like I hit a nerve, huh, Jimmy?"

He had to slow things down, to keep Banning talking, while he figured out how to get closer to him.

"What about Paul?"

"Browning was a pompous ass who just needed to die. In fact you should be thanking me for that one. The fact that I even let him live as long as I did was magnanimous on my part."

"I'll make sure they engrave that on your tombstone."

"That's good, Jimmy, glad to see you are keeping your sense of humor," Banning said with a laugh. "You know it was actually quite sad. For all his blustering the man was actually a complete idiot. I hooked him so easily. He couldn't get past his ego or, more importantly, his greed. When he got the *anonymous* tip from the poor out of state citizen that a certain deputy, *yours truly*, was shaking down motorists all he wanted to know was where his cut was. Once he got a taste of the money I was his new best friend. That is right up until I killed the obnoxious fucking prick. I did however give him one last happy mental image to send him off to the afterlife with. Maybe I'll give you one too."

"Why?"

"Why what?"

"All of this. I mean what's the fucking point, Keith?" Maguire said, as he moved slowly forward. Banning had already moved away from the railing and took several steps toward Melody, effectively putting her between him and Maguire.

James was only about two yards from her now. From what he could see the device was like the vests worn by suicide bombers in the Middle East. There was a small electronic device affixed to the center. It appeared crude, but it was deadly none the less.

"Why does there have to be a point?"

"So you killed them for no reason?"

"Oh no, I had a reason," Banning said. "I fucking hated all of them, how is that for a reason? Is that good enough for you? But you know what the funny thing is, Jimmy, I didn't hate them as much as I utterly despise you."

"Really? I'm flattered. I might even feel bad for a moment after I kill you."

"So the picture taking pussy has found his backbone. I'm gonna have to mark it on my calendar."

"You won't live long enough to do that."

"Oh, Jimmy, give it up will you. You don't exactly have the *Billy Badass* reputation," Banning said. "You know what the funny thing is; this would have all been a moot point if you had just shown up graduation day, but you even fucked that up."

"Why do you say that?"

"You'd be surprised how much shit you can hide under those fucking graduation gowns. It was a lot more impressive than your girlfriends little package here, but no, you had to go and screw everything up by being a no show."

"Sorry to have disappointed you."

"Eh, you're here now, its water under the bridge. In a way I owe all of this to you. I guess it is sort of that whole *circle of life* bullshit."

"What the hell did I do?"

"It was you who set this game in motion the day you gave everything up to be with that little slut."

What the fuck is he talking about? Maguire thought. He started going through his memories of Tricia and high school. *No, this can't be about that. Could it?*

"Keith, this is all about fucking chess club? It was just a goddamn game!"

"Maybe it was just a game to you, but for some of us it was all we had," said Banning coldly. "The only escape we had from an otherwise cruel world."

Maguire noticed the change immediately, as if somewhere deep inside Banning's mind a switch had been flipped. What appeared before him now was much different. Even the humor was gone, replaced by something much darker.

"I thought the day you dropped out was the end. It certainly was for the others in the club. What was it that Nietzsche said? '*That which does not kill us makes us stronger.*' In time I realized that the rest of them were just weak. However, it turns out that it was only the beginning for me."

"I admit that I was angry at first," Banning continued. "I sought only comfort in the distraction that the game provided me, but I soon learned that the game is like a beautiful, but demanding, mistress. I locked myself away and learned every nuance, every reaction. I devoted every waking moment to studying her, the way one does the body of their lover."

Banning reached down and ran his fingers slowly along Melody's cheek and up through her hair, letting the strands slip through his fingers. He raised his hand to his face as if taking in her scent. Maguire stood still maintaining a stoic façade, while inside his body was struggling to control the seething rage building within him.

"Then one day I came to the realization that she is not only beautiful, but she is deadly as well. To truly master her, you need to be able to kill with precision and ruthlessness. She demands it, expects nothing less, a complete submission to her."

"I had planned for the perfect endgame at our graduation, what I perceived to be the ultimate checkmate. When you ran away you stole my rightful victory by resigning our game. I learned from that mistake, Jimmy, and I went back to the drawing board to find the moves that would commit you to play the game to its rightful conclusion."

"I thought killing your parents was an entertaining move, but you passed on them. That was an interesting play to say the least. So I took a step back and re-examined things. I counted on your chivalry and knew you would rush back up to save your precious little Tricia. Imagine my surprise when I realized that you had found yourself a new queen," Banning said, grabbing Melody's face roughly in his hand.

Melody cried out in pain, but the sound only came through as a muffled yelp.

"You're a goddamn fucking lunatic you know that, Keith?"

"No, Jimmy, right now I *AM* God," Banning said, his tone low and menacing. "I alone have the power to decide who shall live and who shall die."

"Where are you going with this, Keith?"

"The question isn't where I'm going, but what are you willing to do to stop me?" said Banning. "Let me break it down for you. I'm nothing but a lowly pawn and you are the mighty king, Jimmy, but you arrogantly played your way right into check. One of you has to fall, so, are you willing to sacrifice your queen so that you can live another day?"

"You're a sick fuck."

"True, but we all have decisions in life to make. Sadly, there really is only one choice for you. The real struggle is whether or not you can live with yourself afterward."

"I won't decide."

"Sure you will, Jimmy," Banning said. "I learned from my mistakes. In this game there is no luxury of resignation. If you refuse I simply kill you and take your queen for my own. As delightful as I am sure she would be, I can't help but think that I would eventually grow tired of her one day. Once she outlived her usefulness to me I'd have to dispose of her. Trust me; it's not a really good image. You could ask Paul, if he were still alive. So the only real choice is whether you can sacrifice her today and live to fight another day."

"You could have killed her before."

"Are you that stupid, Jimmy? This isn't about me killing her or you for that matter. I could have done that when you were in Perrysville. No, this is about whether or not you are strong enough to play this game. I want to know if you can make the hard choices. Can you live with her blood on your hands if it means you get to win and kill me?"

The enormity of the situation struck him hard. Banning had played his game perfectly. If he refused, Banning would simply kill the two of them and continue to live out the twisted life he had created. How many more would suffer under his warped reality? If Maguire chose, he would end it once and for all, but could he live with the ramifications of that choice?

Maguire knelt down in front of Melody. He reached up with his left hand and gently brushed away the hair from her face.

"Oh, Melody, I am so sorry," James said looking into her eyes. "I never meant for anything to happen to you. I never got a chance to say it before, but I just wanted you to know that I love you."

Melody looked back at him; tears streaming down her face.

Banning watched the scene play out. It was truly touching given the finality of the situation. It was a moment that he was sure would be forever etched into Maguire's mind.

Maybe it was what he needed, Banning thought. *A person needed to experience true pain and hardship first hand in order to become stronger.*

"Ok, Jimmy," Banning said, reaching down and grabbing Maguire by the back of the jacket. "It's time to go."

Magicians call it sleight of hand, the simple redirection of a person's focus from where they should be looking to where you want them to look.

Banning had gotten so caught up in the tender display of affection, watching intently as James gently caressed her face, that he had never seen his right hand remove the knife.

Maguire plunged it deep into Banning's thigh, stopping only when he had driven it in to the hilt. The man let out a horrific scream, as the nerves in his leg exploded in sensory overload. In that moment his hand involuntarily spasmed and the detonator dropped out and fell to the floor. Maguire seized the moment and swatted the device away, sending it clattering along the deck and out of reach.

At that moment Banning had more pressing issues to worry about than the detonator. He reached down, frantically grabbing at his leg, just as Maguire's body exploded upward, slamming into him and driving the two of them backward toward the railing. The force of the collision took his breath away and he found himself gasping for air, as the pain in his leg began to radiate throughout his body.

Banning regained his senses, quickly realizing that he had severely underestimated his opponent. Instinctively he began trying to pummel Maguire, but the majority of the blows were ineffectual, falling on the man's upper back. Maguire had him on his back now and had managed to get his left hand on the knife, twisting it for effect, which elicited another loud howl of pain from Banning.

"How's that God thing working out for you now, you *sonofabitch*," Maguire growled, before driving his right forearm into the man's jaw.

Banning's head snapped back, striking the hard wood deck. Maguire was on top of him now and landing blow after blow on Banning's face and upper body. Banning felt himself beginning to drift in and out of consciousness.

How had things gone so horribly wrong? he wondered.

He was in the fight of his life now, adrenaline coursing through his body. The knife in his leg seemed to be the least of his problems. He slipped his right hand into the small of his back desperately trying to reach the handgun.

His fingers wrapped around the polymer frame and he felt the stippled grip against his palm. With every ounce of energy he could muster he drew the gun out and thrust it up at Maguire.

Maguire saw the gun coming up out of the corner of his eye and grabbed Banning's wrist with both hands. The two men struggled over the weapon. Maguire pressed the man's arm down and away, moving the gun farther away from himself. Then suddenly he realized that Banning was no longer trying to direct the gun at him, but *behind* him.

Melody! was all he had to time to think before he heard a shot ring out.

He glanced back toward Melody, but the bullet had missed its intended mark, striking the exterior wall of the house just above her. Maguire erupted in rage, as he jerked Banning's arm upward and redirected the gun away from Melody. However, the move overextended Maguire, leaving him in an awkward, and indefensible, position. Banning seized that exact moment to drive several punches into his ribs.

Maguire drove his knee up into Banning's groin, stunning him momentarily. He then slammed the hand holding the gun repeatedly into one of the deck posts until he jarred it free, sending the small semi-automatic hurling down to the sandy beach below.

James got up, physically dragging Banning's limp body from the deck. He drew his right arm back and delivered a punishing blow to the man's jaw that sent him tumbling backward and rendering him unconscious.

"Checkmate, bitch."

He scanned the area looking for the detonator, but came up empty.

It must have gone over the edge, he thought, as he made his way back over to Melody.

"It's okay, angel, I'm going to get you out of here," he said, as he removed the gag from her mouth.

"What the fuck was that all about?" Melody screamed.

"Nothing, don't worry about him. Just calm down and I'm going to get you out of here."

Maguire crouched down and began examining the device. There were about a half dozen sticks of explosive on each side of the vest. Each was connected to one another by a series of wires that ran into the electronic device in the center. He followed each wire, watching the circuit that it created.

One cut, he thought.

His examination was cut short when Melody let out a scream.

He spun around, instinctively drawing the Sig from its holster and pointing it at Banning, who now stood across from him, the detonator back in his hand and his finger on the button.

Maguire hadn't found the device because when Banning had tumbled backward his body had landed on top of it. It was a mistake he would pay dearly for.

"Drop the gun, Jimmy," Banning said matter-of-factly, blood running down his battered face.

Maguire stared down the barrel, the three tritium dots forming a perfect sight picture across the man's forehead. The shot would have to be perfect. If it wasn't, they would all be dead.

Maguire lowered the gun to deck. He needed to buy more time.

"Now step back."

James took several steps back, watching as Banning limped forward and retrieved the gun from the deck.

"I have to admit, Jimmy, you played that rather well, but you still can't avoid making your choice. So what will it be, you or her?"

"Fuck you, Keith."

Banning fired three shots. The first hit Maguire in the left chest, spinning him around, while the other two struck him in the back, driving his body forward before it collapsed, his head striking hard against the deck.

"Sorry, wrong choice, Jimmy," Banning replied.

He looked over at Melody. Her eyes were wide in terror and her mouth hung open, as if she was caught in mid scream.

"I'd love to spend more time getting to know you better, my dear, I'm sure I would enjoy the opportunity to break both your mind and your *body*. So maybe it's better this way."

Browning depressed the button on the detonator which started the three minute countdown on the vest's timer.

"If it's any consolation, neither of you were ever going to leave this place alive."

Banning made his way to the railing. It was a painful way to make his escape, but he didn't dare try to navigate the interior of the house. He had no idea who might have been waiting for him and he was no condition to fight further. He chose to stick with the most direct route. When he had scaled his way down the two decks, he took off his belt and made a makeshift tourniquet for his leg. He needed to get to the Jet Ski and make his way back to the car where he had medical supplies.

"James!.......... James!" Melody screamed.

Maguire started to move, his head throbbing from where it had hit the deck. In the distance he could hear Melody's voice.

"James, get up, please."

He struggled onto his knees, hands grasping the railing tightly, trying to shake away the cobwebs. His head hurt, but his body really didn't, not the way it had when he'd been shot before. He opened the jacket up and did a self-check, but couldn't find any entry or exit wounds.

What the hell had just happened? he thought.

Maguire looked around. "Where is he?"

"He left. James, he did something, this thing is counting down."

James looked at the device. There were red numerals in the display now, 2:27, and they were ticking off second by second.

He came over and squatted down in front of her, again taking a hard look at the device. Something just felt wrong about it and he was having a difficult time figuring it out.

"James, leave.... Please."

He reached up and pressed his finger to her lips. "Not now."

2:07

One wire out, feeds the explosives, returns back. *One cut and done, right*?

1:58

"Please go, I don't want you to die. I love you, James."

Maguire looked up at her. She wasn't crying anymore, but her eyes were pleading with him. All he wanted to do was hold her for the remaining seconds they both had.

1:34

Why did they still have seconds? Maguire wondered. *Why hadn't Banning just detonated it? Why put a timer on it?* Maguire's head was going a hundred miles an hour.

1:12

He looked at Melody, her upper and lower torso, arms and legs were all tied securely in place, she couldn't move at all. He put his hand under the vest and began to slide it up slowly.

"James!" Melody screamed.

"Melody, remember at dinner, you asked me what I did in the Navy? I lied, I didn't paint ships. Just be quiet and trust me."

Maguire jumped up and ran back into the office. He opened the center desk draw and rummaged through it. He grabbed a letter opener, scissor and a small eyeglass screwdriver and ran back to Melody.

0:36

Maguire felt along the box itself. There was a small lip near the back. He took the screwdriver and ran it along the lip until he found a place to slip it inside. He began to leverage it until he had opened it enough to where he could slide the letter opener in and heard the top pop off the rails. Despite the relative coolness of the evening, sweat poured off his brow.

0:14

He pulled the case off and stared at the interior of the device. Sitting in the middle was a clear glass tube with two exposed metal contacts and a small shiny silver liquid ball. A mercury switch.

The timers a ruse, he thought. *It's a game, it's his failsafe. The choice wasn't between me and her; it was between her and him. He knew I'd get caught up in the timer and he could get away.*

0:04

Maguire took a deep breath, picked up the scissors and snipped the two wires leading out of the switch.

0:00

He closed his eyes and exhaled.

"James, what just happened?" Melody asked.

Maguire stood up and removed the vest, setting it off to the side, and then began to untie the ropes binding Melody to the chair.

"The vest was constructed so that someone seeing the timer would try to just take it off. All the detonator did was to activate the actual power source," James explained. "Cutting the wires wouldn't have done anything. The visible ones are all fake; it was actually wired from the back. Trying to remove the vest would have tripped the mercury switch and detonated it."

When he finished untying her ankles she leapt up from the chair and wrapped her arms around him tightly.

"It's okay," he said. "I told you I'd never let anything happen to you, angel."

"I know."

"By the way," said Maguire. "You and I need to talk about this jacket."

In the distance they heard the roar of the jet ski come to life.

CHAPTER SIXTY-SIX

Southampton, Suffolk County, N.Y.
Saturday, May 5th, 2012 – 2:32 p.m.

Maguire sat at the side of the bed and looked over at Melody. With each breath her chest slowly rose and fell underneath the sheet. *She was finally sleeping soundly*, he thought. He reached over and gently pulled up the blanket.

He leaned back in the chair and rubbed at his face, feeling the stubble on his jaw line. It had been a very long night and an even longer day. Outside the sky was filled with ominous dark gray clouds and the driving wind pelted rain against the windows. Off in the distance he could see lightening flashing violently across the horizon. The weather had changed drastically, as if to mirror his mood.

The events of the previous evening continued to play out in his mind. Overall it had taken nearly nine hours for the Suffolk County Police Department to wrap up their preliminary investigation. This included the removal of the explosive vest by the Bomb Squad, followed by interviews of Melody, Genevieve, Gregor and himself, as well as a thorough going over of the house and property by the Crime Scene Unit. His interview had taken the lion's share of the interview time. In addition to tonight's escapades, they wanted to know everything about what had occurred upstate.

Prior to their arrival, James and Gregor had sanitized the place a bit, making sure that the weapons were all put away and Maguire had taken the vest out of the house and moved it out near the helipad. This had caused a bit of brouhaha with the Bomb Squad technicians because of the whole 'moving the explosive device' issue. James feigned ignorance, explaining he just wanted to get it as far away as possible and hadn't been thinking clearly. Whether they believed him or not was irrelevant, he took the admonishment with indifference. They had a job to do and so did he.

His reason for getting the vest off the deck was fairly straightforward; he wanted to get things back to some semblance of normal for Melody as soon as he could. Having the device on the 3rd floor balcony would have proven fits for the local bomb guys to remove, especially given the recent events upstate. Trying to get the technicians and their equipment up to the third floor would have been tough enough, not to mention the robot they were prone to deploy. Trying to remove the device from the beach side would have been next to impossible. In the end it would have dragged things on even later and he just wanted to give her bedroom back to her as quickly as possible.

The EMT's had checked Genevieve over and given her a thumbs up to remain at the scene, with all the legal stipulations of following up with her own physician and going to the emergency room should she experience any dizziness, etc. Gregor's initial treatment of her had caused some raised eyebrows at the degree of skill, but Gregor had just brushed it off saying he had been a Boy Scout in Germany. Maguire made a mental note to use that particular little line against him at the first available opportunity.

After the interviews were done Maguire had reached out to Monahan and brought him up to speed on what had happened. Monahan had briefed him on what had taken place at Banning's house and what they had discovered once they had gotten inside.

"So who the hell is Keith Banning?" Maguire asked.

"That my friend is the million dollar question that everyone seems to be asking. I can tell you who he is not and that is Keith Banning. Records indicate that the real Keith Banning died a few days after his birth in a hospital in Oswego, New York. It still amazes me that shit like this keeps happening."

"Yeah, I hear you."

"Unfortunately, with each new clue just comes more questions. No one seems to really know anything about him or the family. When we've talked to any of the locals, they seem to have a vague idea about who they were, but no one seems to have any specifics and they certainly didn't socialize. We brought in cadaver dogs and went over the area around the house. Got a bunch of hits, so it looks like whoever Banning is, he certainly isn't new to this game. It's going to take forever to figure out how big of a cluster-fuck we have on our hands."

"Well, it looks like he is out of your neck of the woods for the time being. I'd like to think I took the fight out of him for good, but unless I see a body I won't believe it. The question is where is he going to hole up?"

"Honestly, I think there is more about him that we don't know than what we actually do," Monahan replied. "He could have any number of aliases and any number of places to hole up."

"You have any luck with school records."

"No, he started high school in his sophomore year. He was enrolled by someone named Lois Banning and then she went off the radar. He never had any issues at school so no one thought it was odd that a parent never showed up. No problems, no phone calls. The house was set so far back on the property that no one would have been able to see if there was ever anyone else around."

"It sounds like you've got a ghost on your hands."

"More importantly it looks like you have a target on your back."

"It's not my first rodeo," Maguire said with a laugh.

Something was bugging Maguire, something Banning had said to him. "Tell me, Dennis, what was the story with Browning?"

"What do you mean? What he was up to or what happened to him?"

"How'd he die?"

"It was freakiest thing I ever saw. He was tied up in a chair that was bolted to the floor in the middle of the room. Poor bastard had his eyes gouged out. Why do you ask?"

"Something Banning said to me when everything was going on last night. He said that he had given Browning a happy mental image to send him to the afterlife with."

"How'd he do that with no eyes?"

"Maybe it was what happened right before. You said the chair was bolted to the floor?"

"Yeah, big heavy lag bolts."

"What else was in the room?"

"Nothing," Monahan said. "Well, except for a table. It was across the room, opposite the chair."

"*No man should be considered fortunate until he is dead.*"

"What the hell is that supposed to mean?"

"It's a line from *Oedipus Rex*," Maguire replied. "It's a Greek tragedy. The bumper sticker version is Oedipus unknowingly kills his father and marries his mother. In the end he gouges his eyes out to live with his guilt."

"What does this have to do with Banning?"

"I think he may be rewriting the story. I'd have the forensic guys check the table and see what they come up with."

"What do you think they are going to find."

"When we were on the deck Banning said he'd give me the same mental image as he gave to Browning. No one else was there, but Melody. It serves to reason that there would have to have been someone else there with Browning."

"You think Tricia's alive?"

"I have a hunch she may have been at the time."

"Ok, the Crime Scene people are still out at the scene. I'll have them take a closer look at the table."

"Let me know what they find."

"I will. Hey, until we figure out who the hell Banning really is, you watch your back. I'll let you know if I come up with anything else."

"Thanks and if I hear anything more I'll do the same," Maguire said and ended the call.

James shook the thoughts away. He got up and walked over to the window, staring out into the cold gray seascape. The waters of the ocean roiled below and massive whitecaps filled the horizon for as far as the eye could see. Wave after wave pounded the coast, surging forward at breakneck speeds until they crashed violently on the shore line.

This is not over, he thought. *Not as long as he is still out there.*

He glanced back over his shoulder at Melody. As long as Banning was alive she would never be safe.

He had seen something in Banning's eyes last night. Something had gone horribly wrong with him.

During Maguire's life he had found himself in the position of having to take another's life. It was something he had done, not with fanfare, but merely because it was his job and it needed to be done. Like they said, it was business, it wasn't personal. He may not have mourned their loss, but he had recognized that they were living, breathing human beings. They were however the enemy and he chose not to lose any sleep over it.

What he had seen in Banning's eyes was pure blood lust. He actually enjoyed it. People had ceased to exist to him. Life had simply become a game for him to play and humans were relegated to nothing more than the pieces. He had gone over the edge, detached himself from reality and replaced it with one of his own creation.

The only way to protect her would be to track him down and put an end to this once and for all. It was also something that he knew would have to be done outside of the law. Putting Banning in a jail would only be delaying the inevitable. It would be nothing more than a *time out* for him, an opportunity for him to plan his next move. There was no comfort in a life sentence if you had no faith that a prison cell would hold him.

He heard the click of the door lock behind him and he instinctively reached for his gun, releasing it only when he saw Genevieve walk in.

She paused briefly to check on Melody and then continued toward him. In her hands she held two cups of coffee, one of which she offered to him.

"Thank you," Maguire said, as he took a sip of the hot coffee.

He had desperately needed the caffeine, but he wasn't ready to leave Melody's side.

"You're welcome. How's Mel doing?"

"She's been sleeping for a while now."

"I wanted to thank you for what you did last night."

"Don't," Maguire replied. "He got away, I really don't consider that a win."

"I do. You saved her life."

"She was only in danger because of me."

"James, the tragedies of life don't occur by appointment. Bad things happen to good people every day. It's what we do when those events occur that define who we are. You improvise, adapt and overcome."

Maguire looked at Genevieve and smiled. "Well, I know you didn't pull that saying out of a fortune cookie, little lady."

"Nope, daddy was a career Marine. Did tours in Vietnam and Beirut. Needless to say excuses didn't go over well in the Gordon household."

"I imagine not. So is this your way of a pep talk?"

"That's right," she said with a grin. "Suck it up, Popeye."

"Melody's lucky to have you."

"It's a two way street, James," she replied. "She would do anything for me too."

Maguire looked at the bandage on Genevieve's head. *She had held up remarkably well*, he thought. After he had brought Melody down to the living room Gen had taken up post at her side and never left, except during the interview and then only grudgingly.

What was even more interesting to him was that Gregor had become Genevieve's shadow, never more than a few feet from her side. He was actually surprised he hadn't followed her in here.

"The two of you won't be safe until this is over."

"So what are you going to do?"

"I'm going hunting."

EPILOGUE

Northern Maine
Monday, May 7th, 2012 – 11:15 a.m.

It had taken longer for him to make his way back to the cabin than he had expected. It was situated in an extremely desolate region of the Longfellow Mountains region of northwest Maine.

After fleeing the scene he had returned back to the car and tended to the leg wound. He'd managed to stop the bleeding by wrapping the wound with gauze wrap impregnated with a clotting agent. After he had cleaned himself up he immediately headed out of the area, locating a cheap motel near John F. Kennedy International Airport in Queens. Once he'd gotten checked in he dealt with the wound in earnest. He'd injected the area with lidocaine and then cleaned it out and sutured it up. It would not kill him, but it was going to slow him down for the foreseeable future.

He had spent the remainder of the day resting and monitoring the cable news networks which had picked up the coverage of the incident in Southampton. The reports were sketchy, but he could tell from the beginning that something had gone wrong. The reporters were quite a distance from the house and local cops maintained a cordon around the perimeter.

As Banning watched, a news camera had zoomed in and he caught a brief glimpse of Maguire talking to another man. The shock lasted only a moment or so as he came to terms with the fact that his nemesis still lived. In a way he found it odd that he was not angered by the sudden turn of events, in fact it actually pleased him. Now he had something to look forward to; their game was still in play.

A day later he gathered up his belongings and drove the car over to the long term parking lot at the airport and abandoned it. From there he took the airport's rail link system to the local bus station. After a short ride he got off in front of the Hilton Garden Inn. It took less than fifteen minutes before someone pulled up and ran into the hotel leaving their running car unattended. He simply got in and drove away. Before the police even had a chance to respond he was heading north on the Van Wyck Expressway. By the time they had taken the report he was already in the Bronx and making his way north. A quick pit stop at a local Walmart got him a new license plate and then he simply vanished.

More than two decades ago, Banning had purchased a fifty acre plot of land, using a fictitious name, and had paid for it in cash. The cabin that sat on it was perfectly suited for life in these rugged conditions. He walked into the house and dropped his bags down. As much as he disliked the idea, he knew he would need to rest up. He was happy that he had been stocking the place up on a regular basis. He could easily sustain himself for the next twelve months without ever leaving.

He went into the kitchen and grabbed a beer from the refrigerator, then walked back outside and took a seat on the porch. He retrieved a cigarette from the pack and lit it up.

It was time to get back to work, he thought. *He had a new game to prepare for.*

He had been positive that he had planned everything to perfection and yet he had been proven wrong. Maguire was clearly not the dimwitted opponent he had known in high school. Something had changed in him and he would need to figure out what that was before their next encounter. He was determined to come out victorious the next time they met up.

In the distance he could see the majestic peaks of the mountains. He could hear the sound of the wind as it passed through the branches of the pine trees. Everything smelled fresh and alive. Just being here did wonders in improving his overall outlook.

For a moment he had gotten so caught up in the sights and sounds of this mountain oasis that he had forgotten that he still had things to do. Reluctantly, he crushed the cigarette out in the ash tray, as he got up from the chair and went back inside the house.

It had taken him awhile, but he had made one alteration that was invisible to the naked eye. He walked to the back bedroom and opened the closet door, lifting up the rug to reveal a trap door beneath it. He opened it up and walked down the metal stairs that led into the bunker.

The underground bunker was constructed out of three large forty by eight foot Conex shipping containers that he had buried into the ground nearly a decade ago. He'd welded them together to provide a secure living and storage space. Over the years he had added plumbing, electricity, running water and an air filtration system. The space now featured a living room, kitchen, full bath, bedroom and a large storage room for provisions.

Banning turned the lights on and walked through, making his way to the very back of the complex. This part, comprised of about twenty feet of one of the containers, was partitioned off from the rest of the bunker. It had a steel wall with a door in the center of it. When he designed it he had intended it to be the final fallback position. He'd taken his time constructing this part. It was completely self-contained and had its own bathroom and sink.

He walked over and opened the door.

At the far end of the room, curled up in the corner, was Tricia Browning.

"Hello, my love, did you miss me?"

ABOUT THE AUTHOR

Andrew Nelson spent twenty-two years in law enforcement, including twenty years with the New York City Police Department. During his tenure with the NYPD he served as a detective in the elite Intelligence Division, conducting investigations and providing dignitary protection to numerous world leaders. He achieved the rank of sergeant before retiring in 2005. He is also a graduate of the State University of New York. He and his wife have four children and reside in central Illinois with their Irish Wolfhound.

He is the author of both the James Maguire and Alex Taylor mystery series, as well as the NYPD Cold Case novella series. He has also written two non-fiction books which chronicle the insignia of the New York City Police Department's Emergency Service Unit.

For more information please visit us at:

www.andrewgnelson.org

Made in the USA
Middletown, DE
09 September 2019